VENGEFUL *GODS*

ELLIOTT ROSE

by Elliott Rose

VENGEFUL GODS

THIS BOOK IS INTENDED FOR MATURE AUDIENCES 18+

Published by: Cosmic Imprint Publishing

Cover Design: Maldo Designs

Copy Editor: CreedReads Author Services

1st Edition - 22 March 2024

Kindle: 978-1-991281-01-2

E Pub: 978-1-991281-02-9

Paperback: 978-1-991281-03-6

Alternate Paperback: 978-1-991281-04-3

Hardcover: 978-1-991281-05-0

Created with Vellum

For those of us
who fell in love with
the Beast
and wanted him
to stay exactly
as he was.

CONTENTS

INTRODUCTION

Hello dear reader,

Welcome to Port Macabre... where you'll be presented with a bouquet of bright red flags upon arrival, and the rules of everyday society are sneered at. There are three male main characters in this story who you'll likely want to slap, punch, kiss, and/or straddle...perhaps all of those things, all at the same time. Don't worry, they tend to enjoy that.

For those of you who wish to go in to this book blind, please keep in mind this dark romance is a work of FICTION, and ripe with morally gray men whose actions are certainly not condoned in real life.

This is a dark, polyamorous romance, where the villains get the girl.

What you'll find on these pages are flawed characters living with trauma. Safe words and open communication with sexual partner(s) are merely a concept to these men, and certainly not something that features in their vocabulary during the events of this book. This is not to be taken seriously, and is purely a work of smut-loving pleasure.

Please be aware that if you have triggers commonly found within dark romance, this story may contain topics or subject matter that you may want to consider before proceeding.

CONTENT NOTES:

This book includes the following, but not limited to:

Death of parents/siblings (*off page*); death (*on page non graphic*); blood; kidnapping; torture/ interrogation/ mutilation (*non graphic/ both on and off page*); suicide (*off page*); child abuse/ paedophilia/ trafficking/ sexual assault (*occurs off page - mentioned and referred to throughout*); guns; FMC being drugged (*on page*); FMC being tracked/ monitored without consent; and explicit sex (*including DP/ DVP/ somnophilia/ non consent/ dubious consent/ consensual non-consent/ period play/ forced orgasms/ handcuffing/ spanking/ impact play / breath play / edging/ emotional bullying/ degradation/ voyeurism/ sharing/ chasing/ masks/ spit play/ snowballing / toy usage*)

Please note, you can visit my website for more information on CWs.

Playlist

Lullaby - The Cure
6 Figures - Kings
You Don't Own Me - SAYGRACE, G-Eazy
I Don't Even Care About You - MISSIO
Monsters - Ruelle
Venom - Little Simz
Tennis Court - Lorde
Chokehold - Sleep Token
Play with Fire - Sam Tinnesz, Yacht Money
she calls me daddy - KiNG MALA
Scratch - HINA
Closer - Nine Inch Nails
Devil's Playground - The Rigs
Gasoline - Halsey
Guest Room - Echos
all the good girls go to hell - Billie Eilish
Such a Whore (Baddest Remix) - JVLA
I Feel Like A God - DeathbyTomy
Aqua Regia - Sleep Token
Talk - Hozier
Dirty Mind - Boy Epic
Sex And Candy - Small Town Titans
Pretty - The Weekend
Slow Down - Chase Atlantic
Black Mirror - Sophie Simmons
Eat Your Young - Hozier
Heathens - Twenty One Pilots
Beautiful Crime - Tamer
Man or a Monster - Sam Tinnesz, Zayde Wølf
Start a War - Klergy, Valerie Broussard
THE DEATH OF PEACE OF MIND - Bad Omens
Miss YOU! - CORPSE
Break Your Heart Worse - Crimson Apple
Victim - memyself&vi
Beyond Today - James Gillespie
Beautiful Things - Benson Boone
Lose Control - Teddy Swims
Skin and Bones - David Kushner
FOR YOUR LOVE - Måneskin

The anguis

The Households

Noire House

Lilith House

Elysium House

Coronis House

Aeterna House

THE ANGUIS

To serve as a member of the Anguis, a person must forever commit to one of the five Households of power:

Noire, Lilith, Elysium, Coronis, or Aeterna House.

One must be prepared to enter the eternal cycle, knowing that the path does not come without sacrifice.

As a Household member, one must exhibit complete devotion. In doing so, endless power is given in exchange.

Orders are to be followed without question.
The Council has complete authority over the lives of individual Household members, each of whom dedicates themselves to no singular person over and above the Anguis.
In failing to uphold this commitment, there will be no mercy shown.

None are above recrimination or recourse.

None may put anything or anyone above their loyalty to the Anguis.

None may be excused from the Anguis once a declaration of allegiance and service has been presented before the Council.

None may be relinquished, regardless of whether they are born into the fold, brought in by an existing Household member, or initiated.

A Household member promises to commit to nothing greater than one's dedication to the Anguis. In exchange, one will receive unlimited power and wealth and the legacy of the Households behind one's name.

Those who betray the Anguis will pay their debt in blood, and through the sacrifice of their tongue.

CHAPTER 1
Foxglove

"Darling, just because you get to ogle hotties all day long and get *paid* for it does not exempt you from actually having to engage in human-to-human interactions." Emerald does her best to give me one of her stern looks. Those gorgeous hazel eyes of hers glow in the light of the screen.

When I chew the inside of my cheek, she raises one manicured eyebrow at me in silent questioning.

"I know. I know." Muttering more to myself than anything, I readjust my hair in the video chat image.

"And don't think for one second that you can replace actual human beings with that giant squid dildo monstrosity you've got lurking in your bedside drawer." She waves an almond at me before popping it into her plump mouth.

This woman knows nearly all my secrets. I'm sure she could successfully discover the answers to all of the world's greatest mysteries from the comfort of her couch. She'd do it all without chipping a single one of her perfectly lacquered fingernails, too.

"I promise I've been good. I replied to like three of those weirdos in my inbox the other day." What I don't tell my best friend is that by *reply* I mean I actually deleted their messages without even opening them.

Life's too short to waste time on idiots with stomach ulcer-inducing pickup lines. The kind of frat boys who have no interest in anything except for finding a warm hole at two in the morning after they've manwhored their way around town.

"You know I can see right through your bullshit, don't you?" Her eyeball is so close to the screen I can't help but snort with laughter. She looks like a creature from the deep. "Have you got any more clients booked in for the evening? Or can I finally convince you to come and have dinner with me tonight like a fully functioning human being?"

Emerald is the definition of relentless. I guess it comes with the territory of being in the online space and representing anything from lifestyle to clothing brands. She oozes class, sophistication, and style in a way that I've always hoped would rub off on me. But I've yet to see any results of my hoped-for style by osmosis.

"There's a nibbles and mingling event at eight down on the waterfront, and it will be full of people who only drink kale smoothies and think that athleisure is a valid vocabulary term."

I prop my phone up on the bench in front of me and flip open my trusty planner. While I love technology for some things, nothing beats my foolproof system of writing things down in a calendar in ballpoint pen.

Shaking my head, I glance back up at her. "Nope, I'm free and all yours for the rest of the evening...although I'm not entirely certain that you could call me a willing participant in whatever this is."

Em grins at me with perfectly whitened teeth. Mine will never come close to dazzling as brightly as this girl's smile.

She was born to be looked at. Em is the kind of natural beauty inside and out who deserves to be worshiped and appreciated everywhere she goes. Which is why I'm the first one to cheer her on every time she scores a new contract or a new opportunity to represent a brand. My best friend is paving the way for women who are beautiful and who just so happen to be curvy and luscious and decidedly not twig-thin.

And she unapologetically owns every single one of those curves on her frame. Since we first met years ago—randomly in a coffee shop on a rainy Tuesday, and she complimented my hair—I've been blessed to be in this girl's orbit. Safe to say, I inserted myself in her world and now refuse to leave.

"Wait, did you say eight? As in *p.m.*?" I grimace and scrunch up my nose.

Em scowls at me. "Bitch, your pussy is going to close up for good if you keep acting like a grandma and complaining that anything after seven is too late at night."

"Oh, I'm sorry, I didn't realize you were a vampire." I tease. "But for you, my queen, I shall make an appearance...even though I'd much rather be wearing my slippers and doing my knitting."

"More like spread out on your couch with your vibrator, moaning your way through an orgasm."

I produce an ungodly noise. This girl definitely knows far too many of my secrets.

"Let's meet up earlier, and we can grab something that actually resembles real human food." Em is busy tapping at the screen while she's still on video with me. No doubt she's already searching for whichever place is closest, where we can enjoy a meal and chat without being overwhelmed.

She also knows me so well that the thought of being in an overly crowded place gives me hives.

There are some shadows of my past that I simply can't shake.

My best friend might not know the true reasons why I prefer to keep a low profile, but she supports me anyway, and I can't help but love her endlessly for it.

She's humming away to herself as her eyes flicker over whatever is showing on the screen in front of her.

"Okay, I think I've found us a..."

The door to my studio clicks shut, stealing my attention away from what she's saying. As I look up, a presence fills the air. I'm not expecting anyone, and to be honest, I had no intention of taking any walk-ins this evening. Especially not now; I've just committed to plans with my best friend.

Whoever this is, they're going to have to learn how to book an appointment or come back at another time.

"Hang on a moment, Em. Someone's here." I pick up my phone, keeping her on video chat as I walk around the corner of the partition and nearly forget my own name.

There's a man—no, a finely carved specimen of artwork—standing in the waiting area of my cute little tattoo parlor peering at the set of latest flash designs I have on the wall.

Holy fucking shit, he's like a god stepped straight off the pages of a men's health magazine. I must make a strangled noise because Em is suddenly chattering away to me and calling my name with a little tinge of concern in her voice. My thumb immediately stabs the mute button, and I manage to plaster on a smile.

But my mouth and my brain and my body are going in about ten different directions at once. Meanwhile, I am convinced that every inch of my skin must be looking like a neon pink sign right now. Surely, I resemble a flamingo with the flush racing from my forehead to my toes.

Somewhere from the recesses of my hindbrain, I dredge up some words.

"Umm. Hi. Can I help you?"

His head swivels slowly to look in my direction, and fucking hell, he's got a jaw cut from granite, covered in dark stubble. Combine that with his mussed, dark brown hair falling at just the right length, and my ovaries start dancing with joy.

Everything about this man screams wealth and power and magnetism. He's a little older, too, which is like pussy-nip to me. *Damnit.*

I don't know what the fuck he's doing standing in my pint-sized bohemian tattoo studio in a part of town I'm almost certain he has never stepped foot in before. But whatever weird alternate universe this is that I've stumbled into, I'm certainly not mad about it.

Out of all people, I, for one, know you cannot judge a book by its cover. But there's something that just doesn't add up about the man standing before me and this oddly jarring set of circumstances.

That's when I suddenly feel a flopping sensation in my stomach. Not the good kind that you'd associate with swoony moments in movies, but the kind that tells you when something is wrong. The logical part of my brain begins to function. What if he's here because I missed a payment on something? Or I owe the bank some money, or...

I'm spiraling, fast. And as if he can sense that I'm not processing things in a rational way, he straightens up to his full height—which towers over mine—and hitches his shoulders inside his designer suit.

"Are you available for a small tattoo? I know it's late, and I haven't made an appointment..." His hands are strong, with veins popping in all the right places; I can't help but notice as he casually unbuttons the front of his jacket to reveal a crisp white dress shirt. "But I was in the neighborhood."

Mystery hottie stops a little abruptly. He doesn't give any more of an explanation, and I don't think I'm buying for one second that he was just in the neighborhood, so I immediately start coming up with reasons why I'm going to politely decline this incredibly gorgeous man's request.

All the while, my pussy is screeching at me in protest.

When I glance down at my phone still clutched in my hand,

Em's face fills the screen, and she gesticulates wildly at the camera with a finger twirling in the air, demanding I turn her around. Discreetly tapping my thumb on the icon, I flip the camera lens.

At the same time, I open my mouth to respond to the man waiting silently. Only, he beats me to it, and with a voice like velvet, his words rumble across the space between us.

"I'm more than happy to pay any kind of additional fee you might like to charge. Business is business, and I appreciate that I would be putting you out not only by walking in here like a prick without a booking, but also doing so at this time of day."

The promise of being able to charge this guy probably twenty times my normal rate stirs up something inside me. I'm sure his suit costs more than a month of my rent. So I jump in with both feet.

"I have a standard fee for late-notice booking requests." *No, I don't.* "But I'd be more than happy to fit you in for a special appointment this evening." *Oh, god.* Will I even be able to tattoo this man without drooling all over him?

He regards me with sapphire blue eyes that seem to bore straight through me, and simply nods. His scent is winding its way around me. Citrus and fresh sheets and heavy wood tones that call to me on a cellular level.

I dart a glance back at my phone screen and see that Em has since ended our call. Instead, my screen is blowing up with her texts.

OMG.

WTF?

Is he real?

Did I have an aneurysm?

I take it all back.

Ogle Daddy alllll you like.

Make this the longest tattoo you've ever done, bitch.

Take your sweet time.

And then promise to have his babies.

PS. Please tell me he has a lonely brother.

Inhale. Exhale. I count to four each time and pause for the same count in between breaths.

I've tattooed my fair share of gorgeous men and women. But none have left me in quite this kind of visceral mess. My palms are clammy as all hell as I set my phone aside and snap on my black latex gloves.

"Have you decided which one you'd like?" I nod toward the range of designs. Keeping my hands busy, I gather up my inks and cups on my workstation beside the tattoo chair and get my stencil paper ready.

"Yes." That deep timbre to his voice makes my skin flicker a little.

God, Em was so right. Maybe I *do* need to go out and engage in some kind of action because the way I'm all bubbly and gooey over this complete stranger is messed up.

He shows me which one he'd like: a simple fine-line rose with thorned tendrils intertwining with a serpent. I get the stencil prepared.

While I do so, I take another chance to sneak a look at this man I'm about to ink a piece of my own artwork into. Objectively, he is handsome as sin. A little on the silent and broody side, but he exudes a dominant kind of energy that makes my pussy sit up and take notice.

And then this fucking asshole takes off his shirt.

CHAPTER 2
FOX

There's a half-naked man lying on the chair beneath me, and I'm biting my lip so hard there will absolutely be a bruise there in the morning.

Stranger-with-abs-for-days has got the kind of naturally even tan to his skin that conjures up images of long afternoons in an olive grove surrounded by the chirp of cicadas while he hand feeds you grapes. It's the kind of warm, honeyed coloring people pay good money to try and achieve.

I could only ever hope for skin that looks as smooth and gorgeous as this.

Another unavoidable fact is that he's all muscle in a way that I'm certain only comes from a diet of boiled chicken and leafy greens matched with forty hours a week spent in the gym.

My gloved fingers press against the skin covering his ribs, holding it taught as the needles fly. The only sound filling the studio is the monotonous, quiet buzzing of my machine. Some clients like to listen to music or bring their own headphones, but the two of us are sitting here, with only the night and ink for company.

Oh, and not to mention that ribs *hurt*. Like a motherfucker.

Yet, this guy is a stoic man-mountain. Not giving one ounce of a hint that this might be painful for him. I've even checked in multiple times to assess his comfort level, but all he does is grunt something that sounds like *fine.*

So now, I'm doing exactly as Emerald said. Straight up ogling the man.

He has other tattoos. A couple of other similar style designs wrapping his ribs on the opposite side. Plus a hawk with outstretched wings and talons across his pectoral.

Not that I should be looking at that part of him.

Nope. This is one hundred percent me, professionally focused on the side of his ribcage where I'm currently inking and wiping away the excess. Ink. Wipe. Repeat.

The longer the silence stretches on between us, the less I remember what it feels like to have a regular conversation. There's so much testosterone coming off this man I want to melt into a puddle on the floor. Jesus Christ, I bet he has a big dick.

Foxglove Marlina Noire. Pull it the fuck together. Right. Now.

Back to lip biting and fragile attempts to stop imagining his cock, is where I go for the next hour.

I've been tattooing for five years now, with my little studio apartment being my safe haven and place of refuge for the past three of those years. Em was the one who started to help me find clients when I was still in the early days of finding my feet in the city. Between her PR clients, social media gigs, and photoshoots, there are always creative souls ready to drop wads of cash on fresh ink.

When I was finally able to put my deposit down on this cute little space, I sobbed all over her shoulder. Then we stuffed ourselves full of sushi and made a makeshift nest in the middle of the floor together, talking half the night, planning our dream futures.

A far-removed vision of what life might be, compared to the

bleak reality I escaped from as a teenager. Some days, I feel the long shadow of my father creeping around corners, ready to snatch me back into his clutches. But I try to only look forward.

I can't spend my life terrified that my past will drag me back down into the darkest depths.

He knows exactly where I am.

The fact he's allowed me to remain free for this long is nothing short of a miracle.

All I can do is live every day as if it might be the last breath of freedom I'm ever permitted to take.

Putting the final touches of the shading on the underbelly of the serpent, I can feel the weight of the man's stare. He hasn't volunteered his name, and something tells me that is one hundred percent intentional.

Then I'm wiping the last of the inky residue off to clean the artwork, and I'm pleased to see it's not very red at all. He's going to heal beautifully. The fine black lines and shading look gorgeous against his skin tone, and even if I never see his face again, he'll forever carry some little part of me imprinted onto him.

Maybe a lover of his will caress those lines each morning when they wake up beside him.

Perhaps she'll run her tongue over them as she moves down his body before taking his cock into her mouth and sucking him down.

Oh, fuck. Now I'm flustered and speechless and imagining the velvety feel of this man's dick on my tongue.

My eyes snap up to meet his, and his piercing blue stare is right fucking there. Looking down his strong nose at me with cool indifference.

That's when my brain decides to wake the fuck up, and from this angle, he seems somehow familiar. But for the life of me, I can't pick why. Maybe I've seen him in the news, or in an article online somewhere? He's obviously powerful and wealthy...

He clears his throat, and that jolts me out of my haze.

"Let's get you wrapped up." I nearly fucking bite my own tongue as I stumble over the simplest of words. You always think they're joking when people say you can get tongue-tied around someone, but here I am with my tongue forming the shape of a pretzel inside my mouth.

Applying the clear adhesive square to cover his new artwork requires more touching of his obscenely sculpted torso, with the outside edge of the plastic covering extending onto the side of his abs. Christ, they're rock hard and indented beneath my fingers as I smooth the adhesive bandage against his warm skin, and my greedy eyes drop straight to the v pointing at his pants.

I'm being the world's least professional tattooist in the history of forever.

So I do a very inelegant maneuver to slide off my stool and yank the disposable gloves off with a loud snap. Tossing them in the trash, I quickly wash off my hands in the corner sink and dry them on a paper towel. All the while giving myself a strict lecture.

When I turn back around, the ab-show has been put away, and he's doing up the last of his shirt buttons. This time, he leaves the top two undone, and I notice his navy blue tie is tucked inside the matching suit jacket he's got folded on the chair beside him.

He must be fucking with me because he then proceeds to roll his white shirt sleeves up his forearms. Slowly and excruciatingly, he tucks the material in on itself, giving me the most pornographic show of my twenty-eight years.

This entire fucking situation calls for an immediate date with my vibrator once he leaves and I can lock the door.

My phone chimes over on the counter, and that snaps me out of whatever trance I'd fallen into. He's busy collecting his jacket and pulling out his own phone from the inside pocket, so

I take the opportunity to flee and put a large slab of wood between my body and his.

It might be pathetic, but girl's gotta have something to defend herself in the face of such potent masculinity.

As he strolls over toward me, I'm babbling about details like not getting the tattoo wet and how to rebook in case he needs any touch-ups done once everything has healed. It's my standard spiel and I don't really hear the words I'm saying. My mouth is moving and apparently there are sounds coming out.

I give him a little tub of aftercare ointment to put on and ring up the total—adding a generous surcharge because fuck it; I'm not going to pass up the opportunity to cushion my bank balance a little above the red line this week. This enigmatic man can front Em and me our favorite sushi dinner, followed by gelato on the riverbank.

"Is that all?" His icy tone cuts across my chatter. He's thumbing the screen of his phone and ignoring me completely now.

Okay. That was definitely rude.

My mouth forms a firm line. Turns out all rich dicks are the same. Entitled assholes who think they can buy their way out of any situation and that money solves everything. Including having a shitty personality.

"Yes." My eyes do their best impression of shooting daggers, while my face does the smiling thing.

With his other hand, and without taking his eyes off his phone, he tosses a black, elite-looking credit card onto the counter. It's one of those ones with an all matte finish, without any details on it. The kind that only the *filthy-richy-rich* have.

A credit card that comes with no limitations, I suspect.

The allure of how attractive he was all of a few minutes ago shrivels up. He's got the personality of a doorknob, it would seem, not to mention the manners of a knife. So I reach out and slap the credit card against the screen and rue not adding a few more zeros onto the final total.

He wouldn't even have noticed.

But that isn't my style. And besides, I don't even know if I like the idea of taking this man's money now anyway. He probably kicks puppies to earn his squillions.

I hand him back his card, and he finally looks up from the phone in his large hand.

"See you." Never. Asshole.

He grunts something that resembles a caveman version of a goodbye and heads toward the door. I'm about two seconds away from rushing over there to lock and bolt it behind him, but first, I grab my phone.

Opening up my chat with Em, I start furiously typing. The dick with lots of money and who has succeeded in making me horny as fuck, but then ragey as all hell, is getting roasted in my half-drafted text message when a shadow looms over me.

"It's Foxglove, isn't it?"

My body clenches at the sound of my name coming out of his mouth in that sonorous voice.

"That's what it says on the door." I'm still pissed at him, but I can't help the way my body is still catching up with the memo that we *don't* like said gorgeous man.

"I feel the need to apologize." Citrus and woodsy scents wind around me like a cat rubbing up against my legs.

"Why?" My eyes dart over him. Bouncing between the exposed stubble covering his throat, his broad shoulders inside his shirt, and back up to his heavy gaze.

His throat works a swallow.

My knees go a little weak.

No. Remember. *Asshole.*

One of his hands rubs over the back of his neck, and he genuinely seems to falter for a splinter of a moment.

"I'm not the most comfortable with people I don't know."

He levels me with a look that could melt panties and hearts. "My line of work is very...difficult. Sometimes I come across as a dickhead when I don't intend to."

Right now, I'm really hoping he can't hear how hard my heart is hammering in my chest.

I lick my lips. There's something in his honest confession that undoes me just a little and diffuses the simmering need to punch him in his junk from a second ago. "It's ok. I get it. I'm used to being on my own a lot."

Fucking hell. This night has been a roller coaster of sensations.

There'd better not be another swing of the pendulum, or I might topple off my perch.

"What are you doing tomorrow evening?"

My brain stalls like one of those spinning wheels of death on a laptop screen.

Is he...is he asking me out?

Before I can do anything to stop it, a maniacal sounding laugh falls out of my mouth.

"Is this some kind of a joke to you?"

He looks a little taken aback; that stern, dominant energy in him clearly isn't used to anything but fawning over his handsomeness.

"No." His brows furrow slightly. "I'd like to know if you're free tomorrow evening."

"You're serious?" There must be a hidden camera here somewhere. I'm incredulous. In no possible universe is *Mr. Perfectly Toned Stomach and Angular Cheekbones* asking me if I'm available tomorrow.

"Very much so."

"Why?"

"Why not?"

"Uhhh...because look at me...and look at you..." I flutter my hands in his general direction.

"I'm looking at you."

Oh, I'm in so much trouble here. The way he says that makes my stomach do backflips and my thighs squeeze together.

"You have a nondescript, matte-black credit card." Somehow, this seems like an important detail he appears to have overlooked.

"And?" He cocks his head to one side, studying me with an unreadable expression.

"I have an overdrawn bank account and a stack of unpaid bills." The fact my voice has gone up an octave will forever haunt my dreams. When I lie awake at three in the morning replaying this conversation word-for-word, I will officially combust in a fiery inferno of embarrassment.

"I'm sure neither of those facts prevent you from eating, do they?" If he didn't have such a stern look on his face, I'd almost be convinced that he was teasing me. But there's nothing in this man's aura that tells me he's the teasing type.

Maybe in the bedroom...

Fuck. For the love of god, concentrate, Fox.

"Well, no."

"Then, please, would you agree to spend tomorrow evening with me?"

There's a puddle on the floor where my brain has dribbled out my ear.

This man just said *please.*

He carries on, entirely ignorant of my plight. "I have a black tie event I need to attend for work, and I am required to bring a plus-one with me."

My mouth opens and closes, but I've been rendered unable to form words.

"So that's a yes?" He fishes out a business card-sized piece of thick paper stock from his jacket pocket and presses it into my hands. There's handwritten contact information and some other items written on it with black ink. “All the details you need are on there.”

He pushes off the counter before pausing. Those blue eyes of his glitter in the soft light of the lamp on the counter.

“I’ll pick you up tomorrow night at six, Foxglove.”

CHAPTER 3
FOX

I finger the buttery, soft fabric, and it's only the fact I have a full face of makeup on that prevents me from rubbing it against my cheek.

This dress even *feels* expensive. It glides over my palms like a tropical breeze might caress your skin on a warm night aboard a luxury yacht.

Expensive, it absolutely is. It costs more than two weeks rent and utilities combined. Oh, don't I know how the other half live.

A shiver runs through me, remembering how long I was trapped in my father's gilded prison for.

There's no way I could afford something as luxurious as this with my current circumstances, but it seems my mystery man, and date for this evening, took care of everything.

Only, he's a mystery no longer. He has a name, as was printed on the back of the card he gave me. Thorne Calliano.

My neck and chest flush. It's a seriously sexy name; I'll give him that.

I can imagine myself moaning it, and the wanton image

that conjures up leaves me in complete certainty that I'm already way out of my depth with this man.

The card he gave me last night listed out details on which boutique to shop at, along with instructions to put whatever purchases I required onto his spending account. Also, very specifically, that I didn't need to concern myself with a budget limit.

Holy fuck.

My feminism flew giddily out the window as I tried on one gorgeous dress after another under Em's scrutiny.

Once she had stopped screeching like a parakeet at me down the phone, we met up with coffee in hand outside the high-end boutique. There was no fucking way I'd trust myself to pick something appropriate for the kind of black-tie event I'm evidently attending tonight.

She's the one with a wardrobe to die for and professional modeling credits to her name. Girl knows how to dress, and I need every scrap of her superpowers to get me through this in one piece.

A text pops up from the woman in question. It reads like a drill sergeant putting me through beauty school boot camp.

> Remember the earrings and wear your hair up, but loose. You want your sexy lil collarbone to pop and wear the bra I gave you for your birthday. For the love of god, match it with your cute peep toe wedges, and don't forget to shave your legs.

More dots start bouncing as she continues to type.

> Have you trimmed up down below lately?

> I should have booked you a wax.

> Why couldn't he give me more time to get you ready???

The urge to roll my eyes at her through my phone screen is overwhelming. But I know she only means well.

Yes, mother.

I shoot back my reply.

Then, I shimmy into the midnight blue gown, which hugs my curves perfectly, and with thick enough fabric that it doesn't feel clingy. The straps are delicate and show off my tattoo sleeve to its fullest extent.

We went back and forth, trying to choose between this dress and one with long sleeves that would have concealed my tattoos. But I didn't want to hide; if these rich assholes can't handle some artwork on the skin, then Mr. Thorne Calliano had better think twice before inviting me to another event with him.

The deep blue compliments my skin tone and sets off my lilac curls perfectly. I do as my drill sergeant says, sweeping my hair into a simple updo with loose strands framing my face. I add the gold drop earrings and triple check I haven't missed any stubble on my shins as I slip into my wedge heels.

Approved?

I snap a photo in my mirror and receive a flurry of heart-eye reactions immediately.

If he doesn't bang your brains out tonight, he's an idiot.

Anyone who can resist you does not deserve to breathe the same air as you.

I'd do you. *wink face*

Don't know how I'd ever manage without you.

I know, right?

She sends me a meme of a troll.

Bitch.

Another image comes through, this time it's a devil wearing a halo.

My alarm goes off, which means shit is about to get real. In five minutes, my ridiculously suave date will be picking me up, if he isn't already waiting outside.

Quickly scooping up my phone, wallet, and keys, I stuff them all in the matching clutch I got today to go with the dress. Honestly, I tried to refuse, but it was easier to agree to add the clutch to the eye-watering bill than the sheer lingerie Em was trying to force me into getting.

I point-blank refused to have a total stranger buy me a pair of designer panties and matching see-through bra. It felt way too *Pretty Woman* for my liking, and I'd rather crawl in a hole than have him think I bought lingerie specifically for him.

The irony being that I would very much like him to peel me out of this dress at the end of the night, so maybe I should have just embraced my inner slut and gone all out with the high-end lacy lingerie after all.

It's Saturday night, and there's a handsome devil standing outside my front door.

He's wrapped in an immaculate midnight blue suit; collar propped open to reveal that alluring stubble-coated throat of his. With a soul-eating stare in his eyes, he takes in my appearance in one long glide from head to toe.

I'm not entirely convinced I don't look like a hot mess. But the way this fabric falls over my skin makes my tits look amazing, with a sultry neckline that scoops down, not to mention the cut does wonderful things for my ass.

Now that I see what Thorne is wearing, I'm glad this one was my eventual choice. We're obviously not going anywhere near the parts of the city I'm used to frequenting on my shoestring budget.

"You look beautiful, Foxglove." He has both hands tucked loosely in his pockets, and my body purrs to life at the way my name sounds on his lips.

I thought I'd hate someone using my full name like that, but he makes it work, goddamn him.

"Thank you...I hope you realize you wear the hell out of a suit." I wave my hands in an appreciative arc, my lips curving into a tiny, awfully nervous smile. "Mere mortals could only dream of making bespoke tailoring look so good."

He's a stone wall, but there's a flex in his jaw that tells me Thorne Calliano is, in fact, *not* frozen solid—even though he seems immune to my compliment. Turning on his heel, he gestures with a dip of his chin for me to follow him. Lengthy strides carry him quickly to the curb, and I'm not sure how long it's going to take this man to thaw this evening.

I guess he's still in the 'uncomfortable around strangers' zone.

As I stuff my keys in my clutch, I look up and nearly forget how to walk.

"My security." He offers no further explanation, as the sight waiting to greet us throws me completely off guard.

Flanking my handsome devil are two men in black shirts, dress slacks, and earpieces. These must surely be his henchmen.

Or pussy slayers. Jesus, these three could all cut glass with their cheekbones and muscled jaws.

If this is what security looks like, sign me up for twenty-four-seven surveillance.

One of them has unruly-looking black hair, a boxer's nose, and a deep tan. He's also littered with tattoos crawling up from below his shirt collar, and my pussy squeals with delight at the sight of his ink. The other is a straight-up Viking descendant who chose to live on the beach, I'm sure of it. He looks like a Norse god and a mermaid had a baby, with long sun-bleached hair tied up in a bun and the kind of lean, muscled frame that yearns to be floating in the ocean.

Each of the men seem to be the same height as one another, except the broody, tattooed one is slightly bulkier than the other two. He's stupidly cut, with a look about him that screams, 'I scrap in the back alley for fun.' Those muscles of his are displayed wonderfully by the way his black shirt is snug around his shoulders and chest. The other man is leaner but pure muscle. He looks like the kind of person who lifts weights like it's his only job.

They're so insanely good-looking, my knees give out a little as I try to gracefully move closer to the ink-black armored tank they've turned up in.

These men couldn't travel in a normal vehicle? It's big enough to seat seven and looks like it would survive a nuclear fallout.

"Well, if you aren't just a stunning jewel." Nordic surfer-boy takes my hand and stoops to kiss the back of it. His short beard lightly scratches me, while his mouth is plump and warm. There's the tiniest hint of wetness as he brushes those lips over my skin.

I fight back a shudder of pleasure.

"I'm Kyron, over there is Raven." His chin gestures in the direction of the tattooed man, who seems intent on ignoring the rest of us. "What's your name, then?" Still holding my hand, his eyes drop to meet mine. They're a mossy green with gold flecks, and for a moment, I wonder if Thorne minds that his excessively hot bodyguard is locking eyes with me while rubbing the pad of his thumb over the palm of my hand.

"I'm Fox," I murmur. More than a little entranced.

"Pretty name for a pretty girl. You can call me Ky."

Lord, he's smooth. I'll give him that. My guess is that this man only has to crook a finger, and bras spontaneously pop open everywhere he goes.

If Thorne has any thoughts about this interaction, he's keeping them to himself.

"I'm surprised this old grump got you to agree to go with him this evening." Another slow glide of his thumb sends my pulse racing. "Did he kidnap you? Force you into it?"

There's a cheeky glint in his eye, and goddamnit, a dimple pops below his facial hair as he flicks his eyes across to Thorne, then back down to me.

I shake my head with a twist of my lips. "No, he was a complete gentleman."

That very kissable-looking mouth twitches. "Blink twice if you need to be rescued."

Oh, fuck me. He's funny, too. I'm not equipped to be surrounded by such a buffet of man-sized delicacies.

Do not, under any circumstances, flirt with your date's bodyguard.

Rolling my lips together to hide the laugh that threatens to bubble up, I gently extract my hand and use it to tuck a curl behind my ear.

"No force, no coercion. I'm here of my own free will."

I'm still struck by the incandescent green of his eyes. *Shit.*

The other man on Thorne's security detail—the living statue—moves now for the first time. He has a predatorial air about him. A big fuck off sign stamped across his forehead: *Do not approach.*

But, he opens the door to the backseat for me all the same, ever the gentleman-predator.

I can't help but notice he still hasn't looked my way. Instead, his eyes are busy, scanning the quiet street with cold, calculating intent.

While I suppose it's his job, there's something about it that makes me a little uneasy. Who is Thorne that he needs not one, but two, bodyguards with him to attend a simple party?

Whatever, that's the least of my concerns right now.

I'm going to need a damn step stool in order to get in and out of this tank; it's so high off the ground.

"Allow me." Thorne sweeps in front of the open door and offers a hand to help me step up into the monstrous vehicle.

I gingerly rest my fingers on top of his offered palm, and there's a jolt of electricity that flashes between us upon contact. So much so that I can't help but gasp and steal a glance at his face.

His expression is a guarded fortress. I'm reminded for a brief second of my initial hesitation to even agree to go out with him tonight, but swallow that instinctive fear down.

I've been safely away from that world long enough. My father has always known where I am. If he wanted to take me by force, he could have done so years ago.

Move forward. Live a full life. I toss one of the little mantras I've clung to for years around my mind.

As I settle into my luxury, caramel-leather seat, my door is slammed shut and the men all move around the outside of the vehicle with choreographed precision.

My date slides into the back to join me from the other side of the vehicle; meanwhile, the two most gorgeous security operatives the world has ever seen clamber into the front.

The engine rumbles to life.

My door locks automatically with a menacing thunk.

Out of nowhere, and before I can react or cry out or punch the fucking devil himself in the throat, a flash of metal catches the corner of my eye.

A syringe is jabbed into the back of my neck.

I futilely try to slap or grab at it, but the man beside me is a viper. Pinning my wrists together while heartless eyes watch me succumb to his poison.

I'm nothing more than a foolish, stupid girl.

One who has fallen head-first into their trap.

The luxury leather interior, the locked door, and the evening sky outside slip sideways as I'm tugged under. The effect of whatever he just shot me up with takes hold almost immediately.

A powerful wave consumes everything.

Drowning me in darkness.

CHAPTER 4
Kyron

There could be much worse ways to spend an evening than with a beautiful stranger drugged and comatose in the backseat of your car.

It sure beats spending my night knee-deep in blood.

Although there's still plenty of time left for that if duty, or the Anguis, calls.

I steal another glance in the rearview mirror at our lilac-haired captive.

Her face is slack, body lying twisted against the door at an awkward angle—slumped, pale-faced, and pressed into the window—from when the drugs kicked in and her muscles went limp.

This was all Thorne's plan. He found a way for us to collect our vengeance owed, and who would have thought it would come in the form of Andreas Noire's only daughter.

She's ours now, set to serve in the stead of the asshole who, by all rights, should be hanging from a meat hook in our warehouse, bleeding out, while we slowly extract every pound of flesh we're owed.

Only, that plan got fucked over a week ago when someone

made a move and murdered the leader of Noire House in his own bed. Chopped that motherfucker's tongue out and dismembered him, leaving no clues or calling cards.

He deserved a longer and more creative punishment than that. A lingering, torturous death should have been his final sentence.

"The audio is confirmed?" Thorne snaps from his spot in the backseat. He's glued to his phone, brows knitted together in that way he does. As always, he's scheming on multiple levels.

"Yes," Ven grunts back from the front passenger seat, not taking his eyes off the display of footage in front of him. He's got a laptop balanced on his knees as he transfers the dash cam recordings and audio files.

These two could win awards for least words spoken; both are verbally constipated at the best of times.

My eyes drift to the rearview mirror. Again.

For a long moment, I let myself really look at her. She's got amazing fucking tits, curves that beg to be gripped hard, and a pouty little mouth painted the perfect shade of red to leave a ring around my cock.

Don't even get me started on her tattoo sleeve. It's a cute mix of flowers and skulls and little memento kinds of designs. Books and the moon and shit that girls like her go nuts for.

Too bad she's a pretty toy about to be broken.

Being the heir to Noire House is about to cost this girl her life.

"Copies are securely stored." Ven is still talking at the screen, his tattooed fingers jabbing aggressively at the keyboard.

Thorne makes a noise of approval.

I flex my fingers around the steering wheel. Being in the city —any city—makes my skin crawl. But we had to collect our payment and do so while also obtaining the evidence Ven is currently backing up on secure servers and our encrypted drives.

We aren't taking any chances.

Once a snake, always a fucking snake.

"Got it." From the back seat, Thorne confirms the data is loaded. Our insurance policy for when this girl wakes up and will probably try to tear our faces off.

Oh, she might look like a pretty fucking package, but she grew up in the heart of the snake pit itself. Girls in this world don't survive, let alone escape unless they're capable of getting their hands dirty.

"Ten minutes until we're boarded." I glance at the timer counting down on my phone. We need this extraction to go smoothly, with our jet already running and prepared to return us to Port Macabre with our pretty little revenge package in tow.

Good thing she doesn't have anyone who will notice she's gone. Ven has already hacked into her bookings while we've been on the move, alerting her clients that she's had a bereavement in the family, so will be closing her studio for the time being. They don't need to know that means permanently.

The friend—seemingly her only one—has also been dealt with. We've got some of our best operatives tailing her and running interference.

By the time she suspects anything is amiss, we'll be nothing more than ghosts. The way we've always worked best.

And now the Noire House lineage is about to be ours to destroy.

But not before we take the power this girl is going to give us—whether she does so willingly or not, is irrelevant—and use it to blow everything to fucking pieces. Including her.

"You drive like a bitch. I could have had us there already." Ven is scowling at his laptop, still messing around with her accounts and private data, but as always, thinks he can do everything better.

"And you'd have drawn too much unnecessary attention while you were at it. You drive like you've got a fucking death wish." Thorne is all business tonight. Something has him unusually dialed in. He's a grouchy prick at the best of times, but every so often, he allows that ice-cold facade to drop.

I secretly live for those moments.

Not that I'd ever tell him that; there's some kind of unspoken bro code that goes on between us. To all intents and purposes, I'm a younger brother. Even if there's no blood between us, the Calliano brothers took me under their wing as a kid. They saved my life, and I'd follow them into the fiery pits of hell without question.

"Her digital footprint has been scrubbed." Ven ignores him. "No tracing her location."

"Accounts, too?"

"Emptied."

Removing any evidence of this girl from the outside world is one part of this plan. We need to make sure she doesn't have anything or anyone to turn to. Her life belongs to us, and seeing the faces of all the other House members when we parade her in front of them as *ours* is going to be the sweetest kind of revenge for what her father did.

Thorne Calliano.

Raven Flannaghty.

Kyron Harris.

Three names that the unconscious girl with pastel purple hair and tattoos is going to have nightmares about for the rest of her life.

Reaching up, I adjust the rearview mirror slightly to look at Thorne. His dark brows are drawn tightly together, and his jaw is working as he glares at his phone.

Something happened with this girl. I can't pick what it was, but he's on edge in a way I haven't seen before. It's like he's one second away from flinging himself out the door while we're moving.

Which is precisely what he does before we've even come to a complete stop on the tarmac at the private airstrip. Both he and Ven are on the move, and I quickly insert myself into the role of handling the girl. I unbuckle her and toss her limp form over my shoulder before boarding the jet. Behind us, the others move with the fluidity of having worked alongside one another in times of urgency—times just like this—for years. It takes us a matter of seconds, rather than minutes, to be securely onboard and ready to depart.

Over my shoulder, as I enter the darkly furnished cabin, I can hear Thorne confirming details with our pilot, and Ven is securing the door. We don't have crew; we don't need shit like that. In our world, the less people who know our movements and catch a glimpse of our secrets, the better.

The girl's breathing is shallow, and she doesn't stir, even as I buckle her into the large leather chair. Her lilac hair stands out vividly against the charcoal interior. Black on black to match our souls.

This creature has got me lingering—hovering as I catalog as many tiny details as possible—using the excuse of securing her lap belt as my reason to stay here, taking a deep lungful of the coconutty scent of her shampoo and the wisp of jasmine fragrance she's applied to her collarbone. Things I only caught a brief glimpse at earlier peek out at me, like the fact she has a delicate silver ring in her left nostril.

I'd have to be dead not to notice how fucking stunning this girl is.

Wrapping one hand around her ankle, I use the other to flick her heels off. Less chance of her using them as a weapon in the unlikely event she wakes up early. Considering the dosage

Ven cooked up for her, she's going to be in dreamland for a long time.

But I can't stay here like this. Not with her.

"Ky." Thorne barks my name. As if that fucker always seems to have a sixth sense for when my dick is thinking for me.

The salacious grin I throw over my shoulder is my best effort at telling him to relax. Something that comes about as naturally to the Calliano brothers as shoving your hand in a viper's nest.

"Just checking her...you know...in case she's packing any concealed weapons or devices we should be concerned about." I tease.

What I want to do while she's unconscious and what I *should* do are two very different things. So, instead, I straighten up and toss her clutch at Ven while I move around to take my place in the seat beside him. Across the table from us, Thorne has already shed his suit jacket, piling it onto the empty chair beside him in a crumpled heap. His top collar buttons have been loosened a little further, and his shirt sleeves rolled to his elbows in record time.

Ven, of course, is as dark and brooding and hot as ever.

Whatever it is that we are to one another...we've been that way for years now.

He's morphed from being a stray wolf, all snarls and razor-sharp teeth, to now being more of a feral creature. But I still lose him regularly to the night and his demons.

We fuck. We stick by one another. In Ven's world, that's about as intimate as he gets.

I'm not one for putting labels on things, and neither is he.

He's a tightly bound tomb of mysteries, this man. I haven't seen him look at the girl once, but that doesn't mean shit. We've shared plenty of pussy between the two of us when the mood strikes at Noire House, and I know underneath his indifferent-asshole exterior, he loves a luscious pair of tits and a rounded ass like she's got going on.

He'd rather stab me than admit that out loud, but I probably know him better than he's willing to know himself.

Pain wears a thousand different masks, and Ven conceals his with deadly precision. The kind that he keeps hidden while in the ring, coated in blood and bruises.

I swirl my skull signet ring around my middle finger and allow my gaze to linger on Thorne. "I still think you didn't need to go to the lengths of getting a fucking tattoo." He's been cagey as fuck about that part of his plan.

Safeguarding his secrets as always.

"It had to be done."

"You could have drugged her right from the start." I'm pushing, waiting for the inevitable moment he'll give me a withering look and rise to my challenge. I'm eager, as always, for the moments he fights back.

Right on cue, Thorne pinches his brow and fixes me with steely eyes. "She had to trust me enough to walk out and get into that car voluntarily. You know we needed the dash-cam evidence to prove that she willingly did so. If we ever need to use it as collateral against the bitch, we've got it." He's bristling beneath that perfectly starched collar of his. Leveling me with the kind of look I've worn countless times from both him and his brother since our lives first collided.

I run my tongue over my teeth and stare right back. These assholes taught me everything I know about not flinching.

"Well, I'm just saying, I wouldn't have minded having her lean that soft little body all over me for a few hours."

Thorne hits me with an arch of his eyebrow that makes my stomach swoop a little. I hate that after all this time, he still affects me like this, but I can't seem to ever damn well turn it off. He's always exuded that stern, in-control kind of vibe, and it's fucking hot. But I keep that information locked away behind a bolted door.

"You would have tried to fuck her, and Ven would have tried to strangle her." He taps a forefinger on the leather armrest of his chair. "It had to be me."

I don't buy it. There's more to it than the line he's feeding me.

"I'll happily dispose of the bitch. She'd better keep her door locked at night if she wants to see the next morning," Ven says through gritted teeth.

Thorne makes a disapproving sound.

"I might still try to fuck her. A hate fuck is fine by me." A smirk plays on my lips as the jet gathers speed. That's not a lie. She's just my type, and my dick is more than interested.

Especially since this girl is ours to control and own and command like a good little piece of ass from now on.

A shame such a pretty thing has to be locked away. But what would vengeance be without a sacrifice, after all?

CHAPTER 5
FOX

My fucking head.

Everything aches like I've been mowed down by a bus. Then, reversed over for good measure.

What hell-hole kind of party did I go to last night? I try to swallow, but my tongue feels glued to the roof of my mouth. Water has never been higher on my list of priorities than at this moment.

If only I could open my eyes to make it to my kitchenette. Each eyelash feels glued shut and weighed down by elephants.

That's when it hits me. Maybe my temporary lack of vision has heightened my other senses, but the glide of these sheets against my skin is different from my own linens. There's a scent clinging to my nose that I can't pinpoint. And it's as if my body can tell there's an entirely different space surrounding where I'm lying.

The effort it takes to blink my eyes open is extraordinary, and I'm instantly thrown into a stomach-falling-through-the-floor type zone at the sight hazily coming into focus before me. Although it's darkened in here by the heavy curtains, this is not my place.

This is not my bed.

This is a nightmare resurfacing in my mind's eye like one of those reverse video clips. One where a glass vase shatters against the floor in slow motion. Only all the scattered shards are knitting themselves back together as the video plays through.

The last thing I remember comes into sight as those thousands of deadly sharp points of glass rearrange themselves into a single object within my mind's eye.

That asshole drugged me.

Now, I'm wide awake, albeit woozy as all hell.

Every single one of my childhood horrors comes thundering in. Muscle memory of how often I woke up terrified, fearing the worst might happen at any moment, delivered at the foul hands of one of my father's *many* friends lurking around Noire House.

I managed to escape before anything as horrific as that ever did happen. But now...

Using my elbows, I propel myself sideways out of the bed and crumple on shaky legs. Everything in my body feels as though it's made of heavy rubber, and there's an acidic taste rising in my throat.

My stomach flops in a sickening fashion, and I run my hands over my body. I'm still fully clothed...but that doesn't necessarily mean anything. As much as it sends a wave of anxiety through me, I have to check.

An open doorway stands off to the side of where the bed is oriented, and I stumble my way there. Panic drives me forward without taking a second look at my surroundings. When I reach the relative safety of a bathroom—one that comes with a lock on the inside of the door—I seal myself in.

The sight that greets me is even more terrifying than I imagined. My makeup has been removed, but I'm still wearing the exact outfit I had on when I left my place. My dress looks rumpled. Is that from sleep, or because of another reason?

God, I have no idea how many days ago I was taken. How long have I been out for?

My hands tremble as I grip the black marble counter beside the sink. One hand holds me partially upright; the other seeks out the hem of my dress.

Wincing, I gingerly brush up the length of my inner thighs. Running my shaking fingers across the surface of my skin to check for bruising. My underwear is still in place, but that doesn't guarantee nothing happened to me in the hours I've been knocked out. I take my time lowering the fabric to around knee height and begin slowly testing around my core. With two fingers, I press at my entrance while dread lurks within my mind at what I might discover there.

I gently, and carefully, examine myself.

All the while focusing on drawing in long, deep inhales through my nose.

That's about all I can do, considering the circumstances.

My skin feels smooth. There's no foreign residue left on my flesh that would send me into an immediate anxiety attack. No bruises that make me wince. No swelling or other indication that *something* happened to me while I was drugged.

Relief pours through my veins like a monsoon. Followed by violent nausea, which rushes at me like a wailing banshee, roaring in my ears and tearing me apart with teeth and claws.

The next thing I know I'm clutching the rim of the toilet. Hurling up nothing but bile. My stomach empties itself, convulsing while my body spasms with each disgusting, retching noise.

As the urge passes, I slump to one side and rest my clammy forehead on the cool floor tiles. It's hard to know if my being sick is purely from relief, or the after-effects of whatever drugs they shot me up with. Maybe both.

Eventually, the foul taste in my mouth gets the better of me. While my hands are nothing but a jittering mess, I manage to drag myself upright and hang over the sink. *Focus on the small steps.* Which means scooping some mouthfuls of water from the tap to my lips. Eyeing up the expensive-looking black marble and modern copper fixtures of the hand basin as I swish and spit out several times, before ravenously gulping down a few handfuls.

There's nothing in here to use as a makeshift weapon. I'm certain that is entirely intentional on the part of the fuck-faces who took me. Or, the more likely explanation, based on orders given by my father.

My feet are bare. Not having footwear makes the prospect of escaping more challenging—although not impossible—without something to protect my soles from getting cut to shreds.

But there's no time like the present to assess my options. I'm not going to sit here waiting til someone comes and either takes advantage, forcing themselves on me, or finishes off what these men have started.

On rubbery legs, I move over to the door and twist the lock open as quietly as possible, taking a second to confirm the bedroom is still empty before leaving my place of safety. Being forced into captivity or stolen like this was always a risk, especially if my past was going to one day catch up with me.

The Anguis do not tolerate anyone—no matter what your family lineage might be—leaving their clutches.

I know what I'm looking for, and every suspicion is confirmed when my eyes fall on the symbol that has haunted me for decades. On the sleek, black bedside table lies a small card. Cut from a heavy-weight black textured card stock, on the back a gold embossed ouroboros serpent reveals itself. Curled around in that familiar circular shape, swallowing its own tail with bared fangs and wild eyes.

The eternal cycle.

Every Household within the Anguis has its symbol. This one belongs to Noire House.

My father's legacy, that I have done everything in my power to escape from.

Wrapping both hands around the back of my neck, I exhale a shaky breath. Seeing that symbol tells me all that I need to know. While my imprisonment might not come with handcuffs and torture, yet, there's no doubting that I'm here as a captive.

For how long, or to what end? Well, I can only imagine that is going to be up to my father.

I refuse to fucking cry.

That man deserves nothing but a slit throat and to have his insides strewn for the crows to feast upon, like in some medieval torture scene.

He doesn't get my tears.

Crossing to the offending tarot card, I flip it over. As I suspected, the symbol of Death stares vacantly back. A gold skull surrounded by a snake that winds through the toothy mouth and reappears with a forked tongue protruding through the right eye. On the other side of the skull's face, a moth hovers over the empty left eye socket.

My heart is thrumming a steady rhythm that keeps me alert to every possible nightmarish reality coming for me. Or, more to the point, *whoever* might turn up at any moment is the sickening reality now facing me.

I was never anything more than a piece of flesh for my father to bargain and trade with—a jewel in his crown of bloodied bones. There's every possibility he's made his deals, sold my body, and now I'm the prized lamb being readied for slaughter.

To be forced into a fucked up arrangement, all in the name of greasy, syphilitic, old men making grabs for power.

He'd threatened me with that future enough times before I'd even turned sixteen.

Those men would arrive day and night, and he insisted on parading me in front of them. Aged men who examined me with sick hunger in their eyes and only saw the keys to the Noire House empire.

My throat tightens, and chilled fingers wind a long trail up the length of my spine. Suddenly, I'm transported back to the very moment I realized who my father was and what his line of *business* entailed. A trade in underage flesh and selling the rights to own minors for whatever these twisted fucks desired.

That was the night I started to form my plan of escape—once I had finally woken up to the reality of the hellish world around me.

Adrenaline begins to make its presence known. My body is operating on muscle memory and fight or flight, and there's only one thing I'm intent on doing right now. That's getting as far from here as possible. Even if it means having to run barefoot through fields of broken glass wearing a couture evening gown.

Casting my eye around the room, it has an unbelievably high ceiling. The interior is dark and foreboding, all charcoal colorings, with heavy velvety drapes of forest green. Other than the bed on a modern-looking wooden platform and some expensive-looking linen sheets in matching shades of deep emerald, the room hasn't got anything in it to indicate who the monsters might be who have taken me hostage.

If I'm going to escape this ordeal intact, or most likely bloodied and bruised, I need to gather some information. Determining where I have been taken is my best bet, or at the very least, trying to establish what time of day it might be. My stomach feels hollow enough that I can tell I've been knocked out for a relatively long time. Maybe a whole day? Possibly more?

As I cross to the imposing length of curtain, I tug on the center parting and can't help the gasp that rushes past my lips.

I'm left standing in place with my mouth hanging open, and not in a good way. The sight that greets me is heavy forest rolling in every direction, shrouded in a thick bank of mist. Pointed tips of tall pines and firs extend above the swirling gray that billows toward the windows. This entire wall is made of glass, and each massive pane has been encased in black joinery. Somehow, the entire scene is vast and ominous and delicate all at once.

There isn't a single road or house or evidence of life beyond the forest scene that sprawls before me. From what I can see, the building must be elevated, as I'm looking out over treetops rather than being immersed in the dense woodiness of a forest floor. If it wasn't terrifyingly isolated, it might even be awe-inspiring.

From the gray pall of the sky, it's hard to tell what time of day it might be. I can only guess it might be morning from the way dew clings to the branches of the trees closest to the windows.

But I could be wrong.

Fuck. This gives me no clues to go on. And even if I did manage to escape this building, there's no telling how far I might have to try and make it on foot wearing next to nothing. Unless I can find some clothes to steal, of course, but I don't know what these hills might be hiding. Would becoming the next meal for a wild creature really be any worse than the psychopaths waiting to consume their pound of my flesh?

I decide I'm willing to risk it. Being savaged by wolves or wild pigs can only be a kinder fate than the thought of one of those sweaty old men drugging me and having their way with me against my will over and over.

Even just the thought of it has me dry-retching again. My hand clutching the heavy curtain drops to hug my stomach.

How could my life have flipped so fast and so brutally since setting foot outside my front door for a date of all fucking things.

Oh, Jesus. *Emerald.* I can only imagine the hell she's going through trying to contact me. The girl has probably got half the city out searching for my body since I've long missed our compulsory *check-in after a date* deadline. But then, in a small way, I'm relieved she's safely far away from this world and the sickness that infects every corner of Noire House.

There's no reason for anyone to come after my friend.

I hope.

Steeling my spine, I decide there's no sense in wondering about whatever awaits me outside this pretty little prison any longer. Short of hurling my body against this glass wall to see if it'll break—which I doubt, considering it seems to be triple-glazed and probably bulletproof—I'm going to have to find another route out of here.

Testing the door is like willingly putting my hand on a flaming hot grill. I know it's going to burn me; the consequences of turning this handle might be fatal, but I'm willing to take the risk.

It turns in my hand, and my heart pounds in my throat when I inch the wooden door open. Cracking it just far enough to see what lies beyond the threshold. I fully expect to be greeted by the muzzle of a gun or a beefy security guard with missing teeth and a facial scar, but there's only silence outside the room.

The corridor is light, thanks to more floor-to-ceiling glass. As I slide through the doorway and inch my way into the hall outside, my eyes bounce around my surroundings. Marble tile floors in glittering black, dark walls, and an enclosed courtyard lie beyond the glassed-in corridor. A space that comes complete with tropical potted plants and the shimmering indigo water of a tiled swimming pool.

This place is masculine as all hell. All angular, charcoal

lines, and heavy textures. I'm walking through the pages of an architectural magazine, but the only thing missing is the requisite blood this place has obviously been built on.

Noire House is drenched in rivers of crimson. The only currency my father and his associates trade in, and this place is no different from all the others in the ranks of the Anguis.

From what I can make out as I creep along this glass box of a hallway, the building forms a square around the central courtyard. Each side must house a different wing, and I'm yet to find another door that could possibly give me a means of escape.

My footsteps slow when I reach the point where the hallway emerges into the next wing. There are low voices, too deep and distant for me to make out what is being said, but at the realization they're right in front of me, I frantically look around for a place to hide.

Only, there's nothing. This entire place is like a glass cage, and it's too late by the time I see that three sets of eyes have already locked onto my presence. They all watch me from behind several layers of glass walls where they're located diagonally across the courtyard.

Three dangerous men. The ones who took me.

My rage and defiance and pure determination to go down swinging with every ounce of savagery I can muster kicks in. So I continue around the corner to where they are gathered as if I always intended to do so.

They didn't lock me up or restrain me, so they must know it would only be a matter of time before I emerged.

Unfortunately, I'm yet to find anything that could be used as a way to slash their fucking throats, but my eyes keep scanning for something that I might be able to defend myself with.

As I draw closer, my mind takes note of as many details as possible. Maybe I'll get the chance to have my revenge on them one day. These are the type of powerful and well-connected men who don't go to jail or serve consequences like normal society.

Each of these pricks are House members.

Untouchable. Living and existing in a secret world only a few know about.

They're all various glimpses of strong features, powerful muscles, and sun-kissed skin. One looks like he's been forcibly dragged from the depths of the forest to be here. The other two look like they'd be equally as at home in a boardroom as a graveyard. Lethal with their words and their weapons. Meanwhile, wolf boy seems like he'd prefer teeth...or claws...or perhaps knives judging by the way his fingers flex around an imaginary handle.

The one who held my hand and hit me with the charm offensive is dressed in workout gear, while the other two are in matching black shirts and dress slacks.

But I see them for what they truly are.

Grim Reapers, ready to claim their next soul.

CHAPTER 6
Thorne

Her baby-blue eyes glisten with the fake tears I'd bet my hard-earned fortune she thinks will save her life. A pretty little performance.

Not a single one of us is buying her crap.

Does she think we have any care for the likes of her?

We've seen what the women of Noire House are capable of a thousand times before. They beg. They plead. Anything to save their own skin. They'll even offer to suck your cock, before turning around and putting a bullet in your skull without a second's hesitation.

Those cunts are as foul as the man who ran that Household.

"How long have I been here?" Her demand echoes around the open-plan kitchen. Her arms are crossed, and she's still wearing the dress from when we took her, long purple hair piled in a wild heap on top of her head. It might be the mist billowing gray sheets against the windows, but her skin has a definite paleness to it this morning; she's a sickly chalk color.

The after-effects of the drugs in combination with an empty stomach will be stringing her out.

Perfect.

"A day, give or take." I narrow my gaze on her, daring this girl to try anything. We'll gladly dispose of her in an equally as bloodstained fashion as whoever dealt to her father.

"Are you working for him?"

Swirling my coffee around, I take a long sip. Carefully weighing how to answer that question.

Ven ignores her presence, keeping his back to her while seated on one of the stools at the granite-topped island. There's no missing that Ky's eyes are hungry, raking over her tits, and that's a fucking problem. But I don't have time for his shit right now; I'm already on a tight schedule, and dealing with our new captive's tantrums isn't high on my priority list. Leaving her to Ven's style of hospitality will be more than enough to have her falling into line. One glimpse at his demons and she'll behave exactly as we need.

"I asked a question, asshole." She's shifted her arms down to wrap her stomach, but lobs hand grenades in my direction with her eyes.

"I would have thought you'd know the answer to that. Being the Noire House heir and all." Placing my mug on the counter, I cross my arms and give her nothing.

Ky will be dying to interject and run his mouth like always, but even he knows now isn't the time. Fortunately for my sanity, he keeps his lips sealed and quietly drinks his coffee.

"That world was never my choice. My father can go fuck himself if he thinks hiring you dickwads will bring me back in." Her anger is a palpable thing.

She thinks her father is still alive. *Interesting*. Either that, or there's some gambit she's trying to play here, but I suspect even a girl like her isn't smart enough for those kinds of schemes.

I run a thumb over my mouth as I consider exactly how dangerous the cunt standing in my kitchen is going to be. How much is it going to take to break her, mold her, and have her dutifully doing our bidding while we tear apart the House she represents.

"Your father is dead." My harsh words don't even cause a flinch. In fact, her small frame straightens and she sets her shoulders.

"Good. Now let me go, you sick fucks."

"Not happening."

This brings a flush to the paleness of her face. A tiny spot of color graces each cheek.

"Jesus, you brainwashed idiots are all the same. I have a life. My business. My work. My art. You can't just drug someone—"

"Enough." I cut off her little rant, striding around toward her. I'm already sick of the sound of her voice, and she needs to be under no illusions as to how this is going to play out.

She holds her ground, even as I loom large, forcing her chin to jut out and her head to crane back to face me.

"So, if he's gone, what is this about? If you're not working for my father, then you can fuck right off." Her eyes spark with azure fire.

"We are owed vengeance." My voice is low and calm as I stare down my nose at her. "And since your father isn't here, the stench of his blood flowing through your veins will have to serve in his place."

Her mouth opens, but I don't let her toss out whatever poison she intends to spew.

"We're going to parade you around like a bitch on a leash for the rest of your pathetic life." My sneer grows wider as I eat up every hateful look crossing her features. "Your life belongs to us now. You're going to do exactly as we say, if you want your friend to keep breathing and if you want your mother's memory to be preserved."

For the first time, I see the flicker of something resembling panic cross her features.

"Leave them out of this." Her teeth clench around her words.

"Do everything we say, and we won't have to take any further measures. I assure you our methods of ensuring your cooperation are very effective." I take the opportunity to tap the video clip already loaded on my phone screen, pressing play and spinning it in the girl's direction so she can see herself on screen.

It shows a view from the dash-cam footage, with Ky holding her hand like a goddamn imitation Prince Charming, and her sooty eyelashes fluttering at him.

"No force, no coercion. I'm here of my own free will." The evidence of her own compliance echoes off the glass wall beside the kitchen.

Her big eyes bounce between the phone screen and up to look at me, before staring down at the recording once more. There's every chance the girl has drawn blood with how hard she's bitten her tongue.

"What do you want?"

"You'll cede us control of Noire House."

"Have it. Take it. I don't want anything to do with that shit-hole—the filthy money and perversions are all yours. Put any papers you want in front of me, and I'll sign them in my own damn blood if that's what you need."

Shaking my head, I allow a curl to form at the corner of my lips. This is the best part of all.

"No, you aren't going anywhere, Foxglove. Like an obedient little toy, you're going to step in to take your father's place and run Noire House while under our control. You're going to tell everyone how enthusiastic you are to take his seat." Her breathing grows more rapid, and her nostrils flare as I lean closer and hiss in her ear. "And you're never going to fucking escape us. We own every inch of your life, and exacting revenge for what your father did...well, let's just say he left behind an extremely long list of debts owed."

She balls her fists and swallows heavily. But doesn't flinch as I deliver the news of her fate.

"Understood?"

Her head nods ever so slightly, but her body vibrates with fury.

I step back a little and incline my head to the direction she came from. "Good. Now get the fuck out of my sight."

KY STEERS us down the access road of the peninsula, heading away from where our compound is situated.

We're due at a gathering of council members, so while the two of us make our way into the city, I text instructions to Ven.

Make sure she eats.

She needs to look healthy when they see her.

I don't care what you need to do; force her if you have to, but no visible cuts or bruises.

The fucker reads the texts but doesn't reply, as usual. Leaving me on read is that man's default setting.

My thumb hovers over the keyboard on-screen for a moment.

I want to tell him I know how hard this must be, that I understand exactly how much pain he's in. How I wish exacting vengeance on this girl would absolve some part of the responsibility he shoulders like a chain around his neck. But instead of typing out another message, I shove my phone back inside the pocket of my suit jacket.

The world outside flits past in shades of deep, woody green, and the shrouds of gray mist cling to everything.

I can't stand leaving this place. It aches in every corner of my soul as we begin to depart the sanctuary of forest and isolation, making our way from gravel onto tar-sealed roads before finally emerging into the outskirts of civilization.

I detest where we're going even more.

But this is my reality. The fate my brother and I have been cursed with simply by being born into something that exists outside of the bounds of reality for the vast majority of people. I'm as much of a product of this system as I am a part of it. I hate that I don't want to leave and go live in normal society with their white picket fences, forty-hour cubicle work weeks, and once-a-month missionary position. Nothing about me will ever be able to conform, and for all the faults of the Anguis, I want a life that means something.

If there's only one thing I do with however much time I have left, it's to rid this underworld of the evil it breeds. Sex and pleasure and allowing people to feel comfortable as themselves is honorable work. It's all the other twisted, grotesque shit that the likes of the Noire lineage has perpetuated over the years. Neither Hawke nor I will stop until it's been dismantled.

In this world, you can be born in, initiated, or bought. No matter which way it occurs, once you are deemed to be part of the Anguis, you do not get to leave.

The men and women of the council have been called to meet, and as the heads of security for the Households, both Ky and I have to be there. When a room full of the world's most elite and powerful assemble, there can be no risks taken.

All of them have their own security teams who travel with them, of course. Each has been trained and assigned by us. That's our role that we uphold within the clandestine group we are part of.

It's no accident that I worked my way up to this position.

Eating shit and pushing down my monsters, and having to spill blood over and over to gain the level of trust required, but it has given me everything I needed to be able to dismantle the infected parts of the Houses from the inside. To tear them apart piece by fleshy piece.

For the most part, the Anguis are thirsty for power and control. However, there is a hidden subset that feast on the lives of those who are most vulnerable and innocent.

They are the ones who you might have the misfortune to be *bought* into this rotten world by.

Today shouldn't be anything out of the ordinary, but the murder of one of their own has every single member of the Gathered on edge. I've been fielding increased requests for security left, right, and fucking center as they all arrive in the city tonight, and there are only so many times I can smile through my teeth and grant their wishes.

When all I want to do is line the rot hiding amongst them up and ensure they meet a shallow grave.

These are the council members, leaders who come together and meet like this in clandestine operations, deciding the fate of the world through heavily planned and choreographed moves.

The Gathered are the nameless and faceless entities behind everything that happens, and if there is a whiff of power to be had, you can guarantee they've already sold their soul in exchange for it.

A world that the vast majority of people have no idea exists.

In order to dismantle Andreas Noire's operations hidden within the underbelly of the Anguis, we have to play a part. My brother and I, we have to stay inside the walls, no matter how much it slowly kills us to do so.

Our moves are made from the shadows, too.

We swing into a back street behind a warehouse-style block of high-rise buildings. One that is about as unmemorable as it gets. No signage. Nothing but glass frontages and steel beams.

Ky steers us into a parking garage on the left, following the curve downward as we leave street level and head for the basement. To get down here, you need double security clearance, and Ky stops at the barrier to supply both his thumbprint against the small monitor and his swipe card.

My fingers drum impatiently on my thigh, and my knee bounces.

As we pull into the darkened lower level, there's only a faint glow in a handful of spots coming from a broken light here and there. The empty level is gloomy and oppressive. It always feels like the air down here is filled with sulfur instead of oxygen.

I can't stop my mind from drifting back to the moment in the kitchen earlier before we left. Thoughts of Foxglove Noire and the plan we are so close to executing.

What I don't need is for the handsome asshole sitting beside me to go getting any ideas. The car has barely been put in park before we're moving, as if it's embedded in every fiber of our muscles after so many years. I climb out my door and glare at him as he gets out on the other side.

We haven't said a word to each other since leaving the compound, but that's nothing out of the ordinary. Besides, he has spent long enough around my brother and me to know by now that we won't waste time on small talk if it isn't necessary.

I grunt in his direction. "Keep your hands off the girl. Keep your cock in your pants."

He gives me a shit-eating grin over the roof of the vehicle, blowing out a low whistle.

"That's what you've been stewing over for that whole drive? Thinking about my dick?" Ky shakes his head and touches his tongue against his front teeth. His eyes glint brighter green with mischief.

Christ. I pinch my brow.

His charm works on just about everyone except Ven and me, which is undoubtedly why he's managed to keep his head for this long. That boy would have gotten himself into God knows what trouble if it weren't for his ability to flash a devilish smile and turn on the charisma.

"You know what I mean." I shove my earpiece in.

"And what if I do...or don't...listen to either one of your rules?" He checks his piece, adjusting the holster at his side, before slamming the driver's door shut.

My patience is thin at the best of times, and right now, Ky is prancing all over fragile ice with reckless abandon, and he knows it.

"Don't touch her." My jaw is tight, and I button my jacket as we round the front of the car.

Ky huffs out something between a scoff and a laugh. "Threaten me with anything you like from your kinky little bag of tricks, Calliano. But all I'm saying is, if that girl touches *me*... then all bets are off. I'm not going to be held responsible for what happens next."

I don't have time to rebuke him or shove him up against the wall with the threat of a bullet to his ribs in order to emphasize my point. There isn't time for any of that. Besides, you never know who is watching or listening in this cesspit.

So we wait in silence for the elevator to arrive, standing in the nondescript foyer just off the parking bay beneath flickering fluorescent bulbs, and when the doors open, we step inside one after the other.

Ky swipes his access card—still grinning to himself like a smug prick—followed by a press of his thumb against the biometric scanner. Once the system registers him, a green light illuminates on the panel, and the elevator whirs to life. As the doors silently close, we start to move.

Descending straight into the pits of hell itself.

CHAPTER 7
FOX

I'm suffocating. Slowly but surely, this glass box is closing in on me, and I can't suck enough air into my lungs. Slumping forward, my spinning head drops between my knees, and I try to slow down my frantic, shallow breaths. Black spots crowd the edges of my vision, and the tingling sensation in my fingers only spreads further and faster with each passing minute.

Of all the horrific scenarios that ever crossed my mind—wondering what might come clamoring for me from out of the shadows, I somehow missed this one. In my imaginings, I always thought things might end with torture or being sold to someone as their slave to do as they wished, or simply being murdered in my own bed.

But I never imagined I would be *forced* to fill the shoes of my father.

That shit burns my lungs, leaving me struggling for air.

I can't.

I won't.

He was a terrible man, intent on perpetuating a trade built on trafficking and warm bodies. They could never get me to even pretend for one second to continue his evil ways. I'll find a way to either escape, or end my own life, before these twisted fucks ever put me in that position.

Everything I've worked for...the life I had built for myself... has all been wrenched away from me with cruel precision. Taking a scalpel to my world and slicing away anything I held dear.

My mother gave her life rather than see me abused. Yet, even in death, there are awful people intent on tarnishing her memory.

She protected me as much as she could and for as long as she could, even though we spent more time apart than together. In the world of the Anguis, children—if any are ever conceived—are notoriously seen as a liability. Having an heir is a carefully curated practice. Especially for the elite families of the Households, children are raised by nannies and tutors and boarding schools.

The woman who was determined to protect me flitted in and out of my life to the best of her ability, as much as the Anguis would allow her to, always being glamorous and kind, if only ever in a distant sort of manner.

But I understood why. Amongst the skull-masked security operatives always stationed outside my rooms within Noire House, to the constant presence of being watched while at boarding school—being the offspring of Andreas and Giana Noire was as dangerous for me, as it was for them. She had no choice but to concede to their customs; I don't blame her for being absent.

I knew how much she cared for me.

Little did I know it was my father who posed the greatest threat of all. He had nearly nothing to do with my life, until around the time of my fourteenth birthday. That was when I first met the man who proceeded to flaunt me like a bauble, entertaining offer after offer for the key to his bloodline. Manipulating me with threatening precision every step of the way.

Just as these men intend to do, also.

Rage burns a bitter path up the back of my throat as I replay Thorne Calliano's toxic words.

Do exactly as we say if you want your friend to keep breathing and if you want your mother's memory to be preserved.

They might be powerful men with unchecked egos and a god complex, but I won't let any of these men harm the two most important people in my life, even if one of them is long dead.

Right before her funeral was the moment I escaped. There was nothing but chaos inside the mansion in the wake of her body being discovered, and I didn't dare wait around to say my farewells. I knew she'd done it for me. Given me the only opportunity I would ever get to run, and she gave her life in exchange for my freedom.

I still haven't been to her grave. I don't even know the details of how she died. Giana Noire's body is buried in the plot on the Noire Estate reserved for Anguis elite, and knowing that I'm trapped right back where I started feels like I'm pissing all over her memory. Somehow, I wasn't careful enough or didn't run far enough.

Let my tombstone read: tricked by a handsome asshole.

I hate myself for thinking Thorne Calliano was anything decent while burning up on the inside with bitter shame, knowing that my own artwork is inked on his skin. He probably looks at it every morning and laughs at the reminder of how stupid and naive I was.

Screaming into a pillow until my lungs explode sounds like a fantastic idea.

There is absolutely no telling how long I have been their captive. Nor how long I've been back in this architecturally designed jail cell masquerading as a bedroom. He said a day, but I don't trust anything from that man's mouth.

After the altercation in the kitchen, wolf boy followed behind me every step of the way to make sure I returned to this room. As he closed the door this time, a distinct thud of a lock turning echoed after me.

His energy is terrifying in a hypnotic kind of way. Like I imagine a flame must appear to a moth floating through the night air on fragile wings. There's no evading the knowledge that even just a fraction of a moment spent in his presence could incinerate me.

As I sit here in a crumpled heap on the floor beside the bed, I swallow the bitter pill of knowing I really am their captive. A stupid girl who allowed her pussy to make a decision that ruined everything.

But then again, even if Thorne hadn't gone to the lengths of betraying my trust as he did, these are the type of men who take what they want and never ask for permission. Nor do they seek forgiveness, for that matter. There wasn't anything I could have done to prevent the inevitable.

Thanks to the cocktail of drugs—which are probably still swimming in my bloodstream—I have no idea where I am. My only clue is that the weather here feels similar to Noire House, and I would put money on the fact that this location is within driving distance since they are involved with the Anguis.

The den housing my father's shameful empire, hidden within their secretive ranks.

I don't know how they fit into it all, but the reality is I am far, far from my apartment and my tattoo studio. Heat pricks behind my eyes at the intrusive thought, and I rapidly blink away the sensation.

There is no point wasting tears.

I got out once; I'll do it again. Even if it kills me, like it did my mother.

THE DAYS RUN TOGETHER in a blur.

After the first night, Raven stood over me in all his predatory glory until I showered, threatening to strip me naked and hose me down outside if I refused to comply with his orders.

Clothes? Well, I've been given an assortment of what must be their belongings to wear. Everything is huge on me and smells like them, which I hate.

I still have no footwear. Not even socks.

Despite the gray, cold gloom outside, the house is permanently warm. I'm comfortable walking around in bare feet and an oversized t-shirt the majority of the time. They've given me some pairs of boxers to wear, but no underwear. I'm also not sure where I'm at in my cycle, but I'd finished my period a day or so before Thorne walked into my tattoo studio. They'd better be prepared to get me some supplies when it comes time, or else they're not going to like the mess I leave all over their multimillion-dollar interior decor.

There's nothing to do here except watch the forest outside. I lose hours lying on the floor, watching the morning slip silently into twilight through the enormous floor-to-ceiling windows. Birds flit around, and deer occasionally creep past with cautious eyes and twitchy ears.

I don't see another soul.

The other two men haven't reappeared in however many days it has been since I made it as far as the kitchen.

Only my murderous jailor has interacted with me ever since.

As if I've summoned his black presence, the lock on my door clicks, and he enters the room. No knocking, no formalities. Just lets himself in as and when he pleases. Dressed in what must be his requisite wardrobe of black on black—the optimal color for hiding blood.

I refuse to acknowledge the fact he's got a freshly purpled bruise beneath one eye and a cut on the bridge of his already slightly crooked nose. By any luck, it's been broken again and hurts like a bitch.

He pauses inside the doorway, taking in the sight of the untouched trays of food I've stacked over there. At least my captors have been humane enough to provide me with water, even if I can't eat anything they offer as part of my daily rations of bread and pasta dishes.

By this stage, I'm more than a little woozy with hunger. My stomach has been gnawing at itself, not having eaten anything since I was taken. Not that I'm intentionally on a hunger strike; I just can't eat any of what they've given me.

On top of being drugged and kidnapped, the last thing I need is to be weakening myself further. I'll have no fucking way of escaping if I'm poisoning myself with every bite.

Even the coffee is off-limits, since I'm certain it will be regular milk they've used to give it that creamy color. Who would have thought having food allergies would add to the likelihood of my imminent death at the hands of these monsters.

His heavy footsteps cross the room to where I'm lying cocooned in my blanket in front of the window. "I don't give a fuck if you die a skeleton in here, but orders are that you eat. So fucking eat." Tattooed fingers cross my vision, and he shoves a new plate with a buttered bread roll in front of my face.

The smell is incredible. Warm and rich and fresh from an oven.

But that innocent-looking plate is toxic to my body.

So I turn my head away and do my best to ignore the riot going on in my stomach.

The noise he makes sounds like a thunderstorm. Ominous

and maliciously lurking on a distant horizon. "You're nothing but a spoiled cunt. A precious little Noire House princess, aren't you? Fucking pathetic."

His boots with laces up the front of his shins fill my field of vision, even though everything in the background is a little blurry.

"I can't," I murmur.

"Don't test my patience, or you'll live to regret it." With one of those boots I'm sure have stomped on countless windpipes, he pushes the plate even closer to me. If I wasn't feeling so utterly defeated right now, I'd take the thing and smash it. A shard of porcelain to jab into his thigh might come in useful.

Maybe I'll do that later after he leaves me alone again.

"Please don't make me eat this." Keeping my face tucked into the blanket, I curl away from him.

This man already believes I'm weak and disgusting. They're all convinced I'm no different from my father, and maybe I should be fighting back against his bullying behavior, or standing up for myself, but something breaks inside me. Being considered pathetic like *them* is what splinters me into fragments on the floor at his feet.

"I'll get sick." The whisper is out of my mouth before I can take it back. My eyes stay glued to the mist drifting against the window outside. There's no way I could handle seeing the disgust on his face at the pitiful state I'm in. Surely, all Raven's preconceived notions about me have just been confirmed because he storms out and slams the door behind him. The lock turns aggressively, and I'm once again on my own.

This time, tears roll in silent tracks down my face.

But before he can return and force a feeding tube down my throat, I drag myself out of my makeshift nest on the floor. Picking up the plate, I carry it across to place it with the growing pile of untouched meals and make my way into the bathroom.

That's where I stay for god knows how long.

I sit on the tiled floor and let the tears consume me at the same time as the hot water scalds my naked body. Hair plasters against my face and shoulders, and I don't even care. There's nothing I want to do other than wallow right here with my knees huddled against my chest and the wretchedness of my bloodline eroding my sanity.

When I've purged myself of every last sob and run through all scenarios I can imagine for trying to escape—none of which results in anything but my brains being splattered all over the wall—I crawl out of the shower and put on another one of the big masculine-smelling shirts from the folded pile stacked on the vanity. Avoiding the fogged-up mirror as I do so.

For once, I'm glad for the steam. I don't need to witness my puffy, swollen state of dejection.

Defeat weighs me down as I unlock the bathroom door and head back into the bedroom, but I pull up short in the doorway. The nest I had been wallowing in on the floor for days now has been tidied up. My bed has been remade for me. Sitting on the end of the blanket is a tray containing a bowl of salad greens and chicken, plus an assortment of freshly cut fruit. Beside it is a steaming mug of black coffee and a pot of herbal tea. There's also a notepad and pen.

I fall on the salad with a whimper. The thought briefly crosses my mind that maybe they've intentionally poisoned me with this offering, but hunger is a savage bitch and doesn't care right now. Rather than exercise any form of caution, I practically inhale everything in one go.

It's only once I've devoured every last scrap of food in front of me that I realize there's something written on the notepad. Peering closer, I see neatly printed handwriting in black ballpoint that fills the topmost page.

"Write your list."

CHAPTER 8
Raven

The easiest thing would have been to put a bullet between the cunt's eyes. To be over and done with it.

I told Thorne there was no sense in bringing her here. Despite his grand plans and schemes he's got in that big brain of his, it's all going to turn to shit.

I can smell it.

She's Noire blood.

Which means we should have just chopped the bitch up and shipped her remains off to one of the pig farms.

But then again, the thirst for vengeance is feverish in my bones. When I heard that her father had been dealt with, my first emotion wasn't relief that the monster who killed my sister was gone. But instead, it was jealousy. Thick and aggressive and demanding to be let out to play.

I wanted to smash something, or someone, into a pulp.

It churns inside me to think that anyone else got the opportunity to hack that piece of shit apart when I should have been the one to feast on his howls of agony for months on end.

So, this girl with her fucking purple hair and big doe eyes is going to have to suffice. I'll bet she bruises easily, too.

The call I've been waiting on tonight comes through as I'm pacing the perimeter of the compound. The voice is a familiar metallic-sounding scrambler, giving me instructions on who my target is and which round of the fight they need to be taken out in.

My entire fucking life has been one endless cycle of blood and death. I'm soaked in the gore of all the bodies I've buried for the Anguis. But it allows me to inch closer to the ones I want to gut with my bare hands.

This particular underground fighting ring is overseen by the council. They use it to dispose of their corpses through setting up fights where the guy is already fucked before he even steps through the ropes. In these cases, they're marked for death in advance, and the cocky bastards all willingly enter the fight—a death match, no less—thinking they stand a chance of winning. They're usually rich smackheads and junkies with gambling debts bigger than their bloated egos. All it takes is a few blows to the head and chest, and their body gives out before they've even hit the ground.

A broken neck and severed spinal cord are easy enough to deliver as they go down.

Putting rich idiots who think they're gods in the ring with me is like feeding a lamb to a tiger.

I don't care. I get paid.

And I never lose.

They're usually all the same. Lords and earls and sick assholes who owe bad people even worse debts. With daddies in powerful places inside the Anguis who can't even save their sorry asses. The world is a far better place without them; most of them turn out to be pedophiles, sadists, or abusers. None of them have an interest in anything but their own greed and hedonistic lifestyles.

But I'm the last face they see.

I wonder if they remember me in the hell they are bound for.

The scars run deep, and the pain slices further with each day I have to play my part. We're all here hiding in plain sight. Keeping ourselves on the inside of the very Household we're out to seize control of.

Thorne and Ky might do so with cunning plans and using secretive information they gather from the security team like chess pieces. But I'm forced to wear the mask of death. My role is one that has always been born of fury and stoked by the rage at what happened to the only good thing in my life.

How she never got to see a day beyond her fifteenth year.

And I'll never forgive the Noire bloodline for what they did to her.

"Confirmed," I speak into the phone as the details are finalized. The line goes dead immediately.

Anticipation swirls in my stomach. I can already feel the crunch of cartilage and bone beneath my knuckles.

"Tomorrow's fight?" Ky's voice calls out to me from where he stands in the pool of light glowing on the outside patio.

"Mmm." I acknowledge and roll my shoulders before walking over to join him. He's got a beer bottle in hand and takes a swig as he studies me with those green fucking eyes that see right to my rotten core.

I swipe the bottle off him and tip it to my mouth. When I hand it back, my eyes linger on his bare torso, all muscled shoulders and strong chest. He's always looked damn perfect. Some kind of golden glimpse of good to light my darkness, no matter how many times I've tried to push him away because that's the asshole I am.

"Some prick who dug himself a hole that he'll never get out of. Guess his favors with the Anguis have run out."

Ky's gaze is still on me as he rolls the beer against his lips. I see the hint of a smile crease his eyes as he smirks around the rim. My cock wakes up at the thought of having his mouth on me tonight.

He turns to head back inside, dangling the long neck between two fingers as he goes, but not before giving me a wink.

"That's why it's a lucky thing you don't lose then, isn't it, baby."

CHAPTER 9
Fox

"What if I refuse? You're going to drug me again, is that it?" My brat has come out swinging tonight. If these assholes wanted me dead, they would have seen to it by now. I've been here over a week, and they've left me cooped up with only my simmering pot of rage for company. They obviously need me alive for this plan of theirs, and I've long moved beyond the *blubbering on the floor in the shower* stage of grief.

Right now, I'm a rattlesnake, coiled and letting my warning to stay away echo loud and clear.

There are three insanely gorgeous psychopaths standing in my bedroom-come-prison, all wearing suits with such perfection it should be criminal. Each man is armed to the teeth with glimpses of guns strapped to their sides, barely concealed beneath the bespoke tailoring fitted to their muscled figures.

Fuck all of them and their stupidly hard abs.

"Put the dress on, Foxglove." Thorne might be standing inside the room, but he is barely present. Azure blue eyes glued to his phone in one hand, while the other is tucked loosely in his pocket. His tone is commanding, as is his presence, but I'm in no mood for this asshole's bullshit.

Raven—or Ven, as I've discovered the others seem to call the wolf boy—is like an immovable mountain at my door. Folded arms sit across his barrel chest, and a fresh assortment of bruises and cuts decorate his face. The asshole stares me down as if I plan on making a break for it in my nearly threadbare gray t-shirt that comes down to my knees.

He'd likely snap my spine just as easily as looking at me.

Then, there's the third member of this ominous squad of death. Ky looks even more Viking-like than ever with his sun-bleached hair gathered in a top knot. Along with Thorne, he's stayed away until now, and seeing him again for the first time in a week has left me certain that is a very, very good thing.

He's intensely attractive—with bronzed skin and moss green flecks in his eyes—in a way that tempts a secret part of me to overlook the fact he stole me, drugged me, and locked me away here.

And my body knows his eyes are gliding all over me with a heat to his gaze that feels impossible to ignore.

My arms fold over my breasts on reflex because, Christ almighty, I do not want him to see my nipples hardening beneath the thin material of this shirt.

Which brings me back to the very reason they've all let themselves in here unannounced and proceeded to bark orders at me in the first place. There's an event at Noire House this evening, and I am to be their sacrificial offering for the night's festivities.

Next to the three of them, I look homeless. What the hell kind of sorcery do they think I possess to get myself ready for a black-tie event with barely five minutes' warning?

"So this is your plan?" I gesture around the bedroom with my chin. "Lock me away in here, keep me against my will until the moment I'm useful, like some sort of pet goldfish in a glass bowl? Drug me if I don't comply, and then what...all have your way with me?" Those final words slip out without meaning to.

My mouth clamps shut immediately.

The atmosphere in the room flips in an instant.

I'm still not entirely certain they won't try and force something, considering their plan to *own me*, as Thorne so eloquently put it. And that little outburst seems to finally snag his attention.

His head whips up, and those impossibly blue eyes drill into my own. I'm squirming inside my skin within a second of his scrutiny. Fuck, why couldn't I just keep my mouth shut? Thorne flicks his cool, indifferent gaze down the length of my body. Judging me with every quiet moment he takes in my appearance.

Before speaking, he pockets his phone, then rubs his jaw slowly with his thumb. "That's not our style." There's a hint of mockery in his voice; I'm certain of it. "If any of us need a fuck, trust me, we're all well taken care of."

His words slap me, hard. There's no hiding the way my cheeks start to burn. I should be sinking to my knees with relief that they're not interested in anything sexual during my imprisonment, so why, instead, is my skin currently crawling with shame?

"You want your mother's memory protected, don't you?"

At the mention of her, my eyes narrow. "I told you before to leave her out of this. Don't you fucking dare—"

"Please. Go on. Finish that statement." Thorne's teeth clench, and a muscle in his jaw tics with impatience.

"She's innocent in all this."

Raven makes a deep, threatening noise from his sentry point beside the door.

"If you want to keep her name clean, then I suggest you do everything we say." Ice drips from Thorne's tone; he's brutally cold in his demeanor, and I see exactly the type of man he is for the Anguis. "I would hate for certain information about how your mother sourced all those children for your father's *empire* to get out."

By the time he's finished speaking I'm ready to claw his eyeballs out. My hands shake, and there's a violence thundering like a stampede in my stomach.

"She. Had. Nothing. To. Do. With. It." It takes effort to grind out the words while attempting to keep my tone steady. My father was the sick, twisted general who deserved to lose his head. Not my mother. *Not my mother.*

We're in a tense standoff. Them in designer suits, and me, drowning in the ocean of their threats and this goddamn shirt that belongs to one of them.

The Viking speaks up for the first time. "Put the fucking dress on. Or we'll gladly drag you out of here in chains and parade you around in nothing at all if that's the style you'd prefer." For how lewd his threat is, his voice is smooth. Far too fucking smooth.

I don't doubt for a second that he'd make good on his promise. The sick fuck would probably enjoy every second of my humiliation, too.

"You belong to us now, so we at least need you to look the part."

I'm seething. Heat billows over me like a cloud at the insinuation about my appearance.

Fuck them all. They can do whatever they like to me, but I refuse to be belittled for the way I look. Not when these three men are the very reason for my current state of disarray. So, I do the only thing left for me: I rip the dress off the hanger and swipe up the bag of makeup they've oh, so generously provided me with and storm to the bathroom. Slamming the door behind me, I make sure to lock it before taking in my reflection.

My nostrils are flared, and my skin is flushed.

There's murder and hatred etched across the light blue of my eyes.

Right then, I make a promise to myself. There is nothing Foxglove Noire will not do to get out of this mess.

These men want to own me and throw me back into that world? Then, they'd better be prepared for the moment I burn them all in their beds.

CHAPTER 10
FOX

No one tells you how the most minuscule detail might finally break you in two.

I was perfectly fine throughout the entire duration of the drive to tonight's event, keeping my fury hidden away beneath a placid layer of composure. Quietly watching on, I studied the way we left the compound where I'm being held captive—managing to remain unaffected when faced with nothing but vast darkness stretching before us. We followed a winding, lengthy gravel road, passing through an armed sentry with imposing high gates that indicated the moment we left the grounds and re-entered the outside world.

From what I can tell, the house where I'm being held is miles from anywhere. I'd be trekking for days if I did try to escape, and even then, I'm almost certain to get shot on sight by the ruthless-looking security team dressed in combat gear manning the only exit.

This place might be cloaked in thick forest and perpetual mist, but it is a fortress all the same.

We drive for what seems like an age. Maybe an hour? Thorne is in the front with the Viking who drives us, while I'm locked in the back seat with a rabid creature. Wolf boy bristles with the energy of a frayed wire. He toys with a knife in tattooed hands, sending me a not-so-subtle message: *don't try anything foolish.*

I make myself as small as possible, wary of whatever malice he might unleash at any given moment. There's no mistaking how this man detests me. Out of the three of them, I'm sure he'd gladly slit my throat right here and bury my body in amongst the thick cover of the surrounding pines.

Actually, I'm certain he wouldn't even bother with that much effort. He'd probably push me out the door, bleeding, while the car was still rolling. Leaving my carcass to be pecked apart by his feathered namesakes.

Eventually, we reach a series of all too recognizable winding roads as we descend into the devil's mouth itself. My heart rate begins to race the moment ornate iron gates appear before us, illuminated by the vehicle's headlights.

The entrance to Noire House, in all its familiar, disgusting glory.

My home for the better part of seventeen years.

A hundred-room mansion, rumored to have been built by a king, furnished with chandeliers, priceless antiques, and grotesque people loyal to my father.

We make our way through the grounds, following the lengthy driveway, and finally pull up with gravel crunching beneath the tires.

That's when my eyes fall on the sight that nearly breaks me. Of all things, it's the ornate gold door knocker in the shape of a wide serpent's mouth—completed with bared, glinting fangs—that has me breaking out in a cold sweat.

I don't understand why. Maybe it's because I saw that damn thing every day. Maybe it's due to all the times I heard it knock and prayed it wouldn't be someone at the door my father would sell me to this time.

Like I say, no one prepares you for that moment some insignificant detail threatens to drown you in a tsunami of terrifying memories.

Each of the men exit the vehicle, but I'm frozen in my seat. Fear and an all-consuming panic keep me rooted in place until my door is wrenched open and a huge hand roughly reaches across my lap to unbuckle my belt. I'm grabbed by the upper arm, and I numbly follow the sight of the calloused palm pressed against my tattoos, up the length of a suit jacket, until I find its owner.

The Norse devil himself.

His touch is warm and grounding in a way that it has no right to be, considering that only an hour or so ago he threatened to have me shackled and dragged through here naked.

"Come." It's all he offers, and I really don't have a choice in the matter. He tugs me to my feet and guides my arm to lock around the crook of his elbow, leading me to my doom. Thorne's imposing figure moves in front of us, and on my right side, I'm flanked by a prowling wolf in a suit.

To onlookers, it might look like a familiar gesture between lovers. With my arm tucked around his and our bodies nestled together as we make our way toward the vast frontage of Noire House. But, in reality, his touch is a reminder of my purpose here tonight.

With every stride forward, the crushing weight of what they are forcing me to do against my will bears down. Nausea rolls around my stomach like I'm being tossed at sea in a storm.

The sound of rushing blood fills my ears. My fingers feel numb where his hand loosely covers mine. There are people everywhere milling around and making their way inside, all dripping with couture gowns and diamonds.

I remember these events.

The terrible people who frequent them. Ones who hide amongst the elite members of the Anguis.

Whispers start before we reach the first step. They only intensify as we ascend the short flight of stone stairs and reach the imposing front doors.

Holy shit...look.

It's really her.

The Noire House heir.

I assumed she was dead.

No, that was Giana, the girl's mother.

The bitch ran away; she deserves to have her tongue removed.

By the time I set foot in the cavernous foyer, my palms are sweating and the commotion crackles around me like wildfire. People outright stare and talk about me as if I can't see the way they sneer down their noses. Others gawk at me with eyes bugging out of their heads, as if I'm some sort of celebrity idol in the flesh.

It's a struggle to focus on anything in the dimly lit space, with glinting reflections of the ornate chandeliers and lanterns hanging from the walls whirling around me.

Like wisps of smoke, my three captors vanish into the crowd without so much as a backward glance. Leaving me stranded on unsteady legs amongst the sea of vultures.

They cut imposing figures by my side as I entered the mansion. Now that they've disappeared, I might as well be naked without them to shield against this glare of unwanted attention. Those pricks will be watching my every move for the rest of the evening to ensure I comply with their demands, but right now, they're testing me. A trial whereby they're throwing me in the deep end to sink or swim and won't lift a finger to assist me until my lungs are heavy with water. If they decide to help at all.

So, I give in to the overwhelm and flee for just a moment, making a quick escape to the bathroom that I know is located behind the main foyer.

Pushing past the murmurs hidden behind glasses of champagne, I round the corner into the marble-clad alcove, and that's when it hits me.

With astonishing clarity, I now understand why Thorne's face seemed so familiar to me.

This is where I first saw him. Right here, in Noire House, at a party not too dissimilar to this one—a gathering of my father's associates and other loyal Household members. At a time when a much younger seventeen-year-old me had attempted to hide within this very alcove, I encountered an equally younger Thorne.

He'd been an imposing sight even then, dressed entirely in black, and so fucking powerful it took my breath away. The difference in our ages felt so much more pronounced. Me, having barely passed my mid-teens, while he would likely have been in his late twenties. I don't know exactly how much older he is, but at a guess, I'd say there are nearly ten years between us. At that moment, those piercing blue eyes had locked onto mine, and I'd found myself transfixed. Watching him fuck the face of some waiter knelt at his feet. Standing in the shadows with a hand gripped in the man's hair and in total command of each deep thrust forward.

That night, I'd been desperate for an escape. Rushing to this secret space hidden beneath the grand staircase. Needing to evade the wandering hands and leering eyes of men more senior in age than my father, who wanted to purchase me and own me. The kind of men whom my own flesh and blood were hungrily entertaining offers from and threatening me with on a daily basis.

Thorne had studied me with painful clarity, choking the man in front of him with his cock. The picture of unaffected calm. Meanwhile, the naive teenage girl version of me had been utterly hypnotized by him. Unable to look away, even though I'd intruded on something so private.

"Either finish what he's started or get the fuck out of here."

I remember his growl. The way he taunted me.

After he'd tossed those words in my direction all those years ago, the spell had been broken. Turning tail, I fled. Running as far and fast as possible from such an alarmingly beautiful man.

His dismissive tone had stung like a bitch but also left me shaken up in a way I'd never experienced before.

Until the day he walked into my tattoo studio, that is.

But now, as I hover here alone in that same spot with the ghosts of that memory, I can't help but wonder...does he remember me? Has he known I was that same girl this whole time?

God, who am I kidding? Of course, he wouldn't recall such an insignificant moment.

With a shudder, I do my best to shake off the past and push through the door to the bathroom, trying to shove aside all memories of how my body responded to him back then.

I most definitely do not feel anything but pure hatred for him now.

CHAPTER 11
Ven

There's a power void swirling through the shadows of Noire House.

It hungers for a new mistress.

Thorne and his brother have been angling to take over for years now, and this little bitch is going to give them everything they're owed. Everything they've suffered for until now.

I'll proudly stand beside them as they continue to rid this world of the filth that has multiplied in this place. Fuck it, I'd gladly be the one to dispose of the corpses for them one by one. All they need to do is ask.

Being a Calliano in this world has been hell for both of them, yet they've risen through the ranks of the Anguis by stealth and pure determination.

Tonight, a glittering show of wealth from those very members of their secretive ranks is on display. I've taken up my vantage point overlooking the foyer on the floor below, while Ky and Thorne will be doing the same.

Our role within the Anguis is to provide elite-level security. We're the ones these assholes entrust with their lives, and yet they have no idea we're actually planning the downfall of Andreas Noire's rotten empire.

Hawke is here somewhere, too, but he'll be keeping a low profile. He and his partners are in charge of the other face of Noire House. A side reserved for hedonism and excesses and catering to all manner of sexual appetites that could ever desire to be fulfilled.

When required, on nights like tonight, the mansion is open to only a select few when it is all glamor and displays of power for the members of Anguis. At other times, these very same people return and use it as the den of iniquity it has become notorious for.

Noire House is a sex club frequented by only the most exclusive and wealthy of Port Macabre. Where tastes run wild, and discretion is paid for in multimillions at a time.

But there is a hidden level to this place. One that is drenched in the blood of innocent lives. That is the legacy of Foxglove Noire's father, and the trafficking rings he coordinated while the rich and wealthy of Port Macabre turned a blind eye upstairs. That is the underbelly that we are here to tear apart piece by piece from the inside.

My own motives are personal. Emotional. I have my sister's life to seek bloody retribution for.

Ky's reasons are murkier. They come mostly out of loyalty to the Callianos. And to me, I suppose, after everything we have been through together.

Thorne...well, his motivation to destroy Noire House and take control comes from somewhere even darker. Born of a hatred for everything he and his brother were sold into. He keeps his cards close to his chest, even from the two of us. But I know abuse when I see it.

Both of the Calliano brothers have suffered at the hands of the Noire Household.

From my vantage point on the upper landing, I watch her

lilac hair swept up on top of her head re-emerge from beneath the gilded staircase. Loose curls fall down either side of her face. In amongst the sea of blonde and brown and black hair, she sticks out from a mile away. Not to mention the way her tattooed skin is in stark contrast to the endless suit jackets and designer gowns.

The others have taken up their positions, and now we get to enjoy the spectacle. The girl has no idea what tonight is about or why all these people are here. Little does she know it is all for her.

Her fucking funeral.

She's being surrounded now. There's a throng of seedy, old men grabbing her by the shoulders, all looking her up and down like she's their meal ticket to greater power. The ones most loyal to Andreas, and likely entrenched in his foul schemes.

Of course, amongst this glittering show of wealth, there are Household members of similar age to Foxglove Noire herself. Noire House and the Anguis have collected loyal followers through bloodlines, through initiations, and in our case... through being bought.

This isn't just a room filled with balding men, far from it. However the lure of Andreas Noire's heir arriving back among their fold tonight is attracting the most hungry, while other House members are content to sit back and watch the spectacle unfold.

Each of those swarming close pretends to offer a hug, pressing against her ear to no doubt share their sympathies for the death of her father. But I see their true intention with every hand that wanders a little too low on her back and embrace that lingers a fraction longer than necessary.

They all think they can collect her. Add her to their roster of women and men. That's the thing about this world we all inhabit and the way we choose to live our lives. The Anguis expect devotion to only the *Household* each person serves. Not to any particular individual. Arrangements and contracts and alliances form the foundation of any bed of power.

Empires don't succeed by following the fickle wants of the heart or lust racing through heated blood.

This world is no different. Power is the ultimate goal of the Anguis and its members.

Many of us defy convention with our partnerships. Whether that is a result of nature, or nurture, who fucking knows. But we all live by a code that ensures we don't rely on one single person or conform to monogamous expectations. Not only is it dangerous to do so, but in a life such as ours, placing the burden of trust on one single partner would be insanity at best.

It is rumored that the foundations of the Anguis were built by encouraging multiple partnerships to foster power. To spread allegiances and maintain control. But there are too many in this modern iteration of the Households who use polyamory as an excuse to abuse others. Too many men and women in the Anguis have taken the notion of not committing themselves to one person, and twisted and distorted it until the very concept is rotten to the core.

My eyes narrow on one particular man who hangs off to the side, with slicked-back, graying hair and a thin mustache. He hasn't touched her, but his beady gaze is intensely fixed on her curves. There's no mistaking his interest in what he sees as prime meat on offer this evening.

I know exactly who he is. Massimo Ilone. One of her father's right-hand men, and key player in the trafficking rings they controlled together. He's already marked for death in my eyes. It's only a matter of time until I drain the life from his corpse and toss the bastard into a pit.

There's a tall blonde woman whose name escapes me, but she has her by the shoulders now. Touching her face and talking like they're old friends. With every interaction like this, the girl is turning as pale as the moon hanging in the night sky.

She thought it was possible to escape this world?

Well, here she is right back at the sick and twisted heart of it. All these people gathered here tonight have been informed of her intention to step into her father's shoes...and the upcoming ceremony.

Everyone except her, that is.

Another associate of her father, a man with a large gut and reddened nose, clinks his glass to draw the attention of the crowd. A hush descends around the room as everyone eagerly awaits the announcement coming any second now.

Thorne has orchestrated this all to perfection. Using every powerful connection and blood-stained debt he's been able to accrue over the years, all leading to this moment.

"Welcome, our Gathered." The man bellows. "Tonight, we are here to celebrate the return of the Noire House heir to her rightful place among us."

There are cheers and glasses raised as the room's energy whips into a frenzy of anticipation. I watch the girl's shoulders shrink in on herself. She's glancing anywhere but at the sets of eyes all fixed on her. The tall blonde woman has her clutched to her side with fingers like talons, red nails indenting her tattooed shoulder.

"I'm sure you have all been eagerly awaiting the news, and I can confirm that tonight is one we have been looking forward to for many years." He reaches out with stubby fingers and pinches Foxglove's jaw. It's supposed to look like a friendly gesture—an old friend of her father's treating her like a member of his family—but I see the way he intends it as a threat, only to her. A reminder that she ran away from this world.

"A Pledging ceremony." The woman's voice is shrill and grating to my ears as she announces the words with triumph.

The girl's eyes turn into saucers.

Now she knows the truth of it.

Murmurs and whispers rocket through the crowd. There hasn't been a formal Pledging ceremony in Noire House for decades. It's an archaic ritual, one born of the old ways, and is only reserved for the elite families.

I have no interest in fucking this girl surrounded by these perverted assholes looking on. But for the sake of Thorne's plan, and the desire for vengeance sizzling in our veins...we have all agreed to play our part.

Claim her body. Claim her bloodline to the House.

Take every last piece of her power, and do so by force.

What it entails is just as twisted as these sick fucks all are. There's nothing more to it than perpetuating the predatory intent of men. The kind who have used the excuse of rituals like this one over the centuries as a way to claim their conquests and parade their fragile masculinity in front of the Gathered.

From here, I can see the wheels spinning in Foxglove's head. Yes, little bitch, it means the ultimate humiliation in front of the council as one by one, her body is owned for all to see. We don't believe in things like marriage in our world, but the old ways are carved in blood and stone. A Pledging ceremony is the final piece that will sign over Foxglove Noire's life to us in the eyes of the Anguis.

When she is spread out and fucked in public, in front of the members of the council, that cedes everything to us. It gives Thorne power over everything in Noire House. It means she is ours to do with what we like, which means if we decide to end her life, not one of them will blink an eyelid.

Judging by the way the bitch looks like she's about to throw up, it's safe to say she's come to that realization all of her own accord.

Wave after wave of onlookers and finely dressed assholes surround the girl. They're congratulating her and simpering all over her as if this ritual is something worth celebrating.

My eyes catch Ky's for a brief moment across the other side of the room. He taps out a message on his phone, and my own vibrates inside my pocket.

Time to go.

I couldn't fucking agree more. My skin is crawling with ants being in close proximity to this crowd.

Another buzz.

Eyes on Thorne?

Scanning the upper levels, I can't see him. But there's no doubt he will be watching on like a black cloud.

You collect the girl. I'll find Thorne. Meet you at the vehicle in 5.

I nod in Ky's direction rather than waste time replying to the message. He shakes his head with a rueful grin before bringing his phone to his ear. No doubt dialing Thorne.

While I tuck my phone back in my pocket, I look down at the spot where the girl had been just a moment ago. But she's not there. In fact, I barely catch a glimpse of her purple hair before she disappears into the corridor at the back of the crowd.

Foxglove Noire grew up in this place and knows it like the back of her own hand. If she's trying to make a run for it, I'll gladly hunt the bitch down and drag her back to our compound by her hair.

The cunt thinks she can escape us?

I don't fucking think so.

My long stride carries me down the staircase to the ground floor and in the direction of the doorway she disappeared through. There are too many goddamn people in my way, but I ease my way among them, maintaining my usual low profile.

When I slip behind the partially cracked door, the long hallway stretching ahead of me is paneled with heavy oak timber. There's only an occasional lantern casting a dim glow; this is not an area where the assembled guests tonight are supposed to be.

I'm scanning for a glimpse of movement or light beneath any of the closed doorways as I stride down the length of ornate carpet. All it will take is for a moving shadow to hint at where she might have fled to or attempted to scurry away and hide. Although this is my act of toying with her—it isn't really necessary, if I need to, I have more precise methods of locating her.

That's when I hear a noise. A scuffling and a low murmur.

It comes from behind me, in the room just off to my right.

The sounds are followed by a dull thudding noise. More muffled voices.

When I try the door handle, it's locked, and I could bet a fortune that the stupid girl has locked herself in here in a half-assed attempt to try and get away from us.

Maybe she's in there with someone, and I've caught her trying to run straight into the arms of one of her father's friends. Offering to suck his dick in return for being saved from us.

She's nothing more than a piece of Noire filth. It's laughable that she thinks she can get away from the three of us that easily.

A locked door never stopped me before, and it certainly isn't going to tonight. Ky or Thorne might use a more finessed method to gain entry, but I've got shoulders built for going ten rounds in the ring without breaking a sweat. All it takes is for me to throw my bulk against the wooden door, and the hinges splinter open.

The sight that greets me...well, that has me seeing red. A mist descends to cloud my vision as I take in the scene I've disturbed.

There's a greasy-haired Massimo Ilone, with his hand up the front of the girl's dress. Next to them lies a shattered vase and a plinth knocked to the floor. I can tell she's tried to fight him, but her efforts are pathetic. The asshole might be old, but he's too big and powerful for her, and in the dark, she would have been caught off guard too easily.

However, he's no match for me. The Anguis enforcer trained to end lives with my fists.

He's got her forced up against the wall; meanwhile, she's trying to push him off and frantically tilts her head away from his face. That's when her baby-blues snap onto mine as she hears me burst in.

I'm across the room in an instant.

My mind blinks offline, and instinct takes over. There's only the sound of his cries and yells filling the darkened room as I haul him off her, tossing the fucker to the ground. Knuckles connect with his jaw over and over as I straddle his chest and rain down punishing blows.

There's a mess of blood and split skin and broken teeth where his face should be.

He's unresponsive.

I don't care if he's dead.

The hits keep flying, and it's only the sensation of small fists grabbing at my arms and a soft body clinging to me from behind that prevents me from snapping the guy's neck with my bare hands.

"You're killing him."

She's yelling at me to stop, but all I can do is hiss in response. I don't want her fucking touching me. I don't want her scent anywhere near me. I don't want her body pressed up against mine.

Rising to my feet, I throw her off roughly and turn around to shove my face right in hers. "Don't think for one second I did that for you." Snarling, I jab a finger in the direction of the battered figure lying twisted on the floor. "I did that because you are the debt that we are owed and nothing more."

Big blue orbs glistening with unshed tears widen as she stares back at me; her pink lips gape. I take in the way her chest heaves and note that the girl's hair is disheveled, as if he grabbed those purple strands before I got to her.

But there's not one part of me that gives a fuck right now.

She's our property, and we're the only ones that get to hurt her.

CHAPTER 12
FOX

My night is a sleepless mess, replaying every moment from the evening before in my mind's eye until pale light creeps over the forest outside my windows. I watch until the sky brightens in streaks of purple and pink as dawn approaches. Once again, I'm drowning in an oversized t-shirt and echoes of their masculine scents.

It's like being tortured and antagonized and having my pussy teased all in one breath.

My head aches from the revelations of last night. A grotesque Pledging ceremony, of all things. Rage gnaws harder at my insides when I then think of how Massimo forced himself on me. I couldn't do anything to defend myself against either of the unanticipated hits that came my way.

Massimo Ilone has always been a threat in my life. One of the many contenders my father declared he would consider selling me to...for the right price. I guess last night, he decided he was going to take what he wanted without my father being in the picture anymore.

You'd think I might be shaken or hurt, but the sad reality is that I've had that exact experience before. Different man, different room at Noire House. Only, back then, I was a teenager, and at least I was fortunate enough that other members of the Anguis walked in before things went further than being groped through my clothes.

No one defended me or came to my rescue when I was a young girl, left alone in a sea of monsters. They simply laughed as I ran from the room, clutching my dress and fighting back tears.

And now, for some fucked up reason, I can't stop thinking about the way Raven nearly killed Massimo just for touching me.

I am not fantasizing about a man who beat someone to a bloodied pulp right after forcing me into a Pledging ceremony.

I. Am. Not.

This has to be the most archaic and patriarchal ritual of the Anguis. One that I thought had been cast aside.

I shudder thinking about all the women who have come before me. The ones who had no choice but to be put through a Pledging ceremony when the purpose was to impregnate them in front of an audience.

The worst kind of fear.

A Pledging ceremony is nothing more than a show of ownership. Claiming and taking from women, reducing them to nothing more than flesh to own, has been the case for centuries.

But it seems these men are intent on doing everything within their power to torture me and humiliate me. Forcing me to be degraded and treated like nothing more than a blow-up doll and a dumpster to rut into and fill with their semen in front of an audience. That's how they intend to take control of Noire House.

Right before they no doubt dispose of my body amongst these trees that I'm staring at from my bed.

How many other girls like me are buried out there?

I pause as that thought wanders aimlessly around my brain.

Why does the idea of them having other women here before me stir up something that has no right existing in my gut?

I'm sicker than I thought if I'm allowing myself to be attracted to these monsters. But then again, this was the world I was raised in. I can hardly blame myself for finding murderous psychopaths with a god complex attractive.

Biting my bottom lip, I sink beneath the covers, immersed in my nest of self-judgement.

My superpower of summoning them by thinking about their stupid faces is evidently in full effect this morning as I hear footsteps outside, and my door handle suddenly turns—surprisingly, with no unlocking noise this time. I file that little piece of information away for later.

But instead of my surly wolf, in strolls the gorgeous Nordic surfer himself. The asshole is shirtless, with sweatpants slung low on his hips, just to really fuck with my confused brain and unruly hormones. To make it worse, he's carrying two cups of coffee with him.

I sit up and drag my covers over my chest, eying him suspiciously.

"I hear a little Fox needs some lessons on how to use her teeth and claws."

That's the understatement of the year. Not that anyone spoke on the car ride back here last night, but Raven's bloodied fists and my disheveled state were rather obvious clues that something had gone down.

I'm guessing they discussed the details after I bolted straight for my room without looking back.

Ky crosses the space between us, making himself at home on the edge of the bed like he's done this a thousand times before. "Almond milk." He says as he hands me the coffee.

"Thank you," I mutter as I sniff at the fragrant aroma of roasted beans. Fuck, I could kiss him with how good this smells. Apparently, I am one easy bitch to please.

He studies me over the rim of his own mug. In turn, I try not to stare at all the bunched muscles on display, or at his crotch, or how his hair loosely hangs around his face. There's a slight curl to it, and some strands are a rich honey color, while others are bleached like white sand.

My horny brain immediately pictures him emerging from the ocean with rivulets of water trickling over every one of those indents on his chiseled torso.

"So, you're up for it?"

I must look as confused as I feel because I've completely forgotten what he's talking about. Lost in a trance of imagining the way I would run my tongue across his sun-kissed skin.

In an attempt to avoid my own sick fascination with these men, I take a long sip of my coffee.

"Get up. Get dressed. I'd like to teach you a thing or two." His green eyes have a knowing glint to them.

My pussy clenches. God, I practically have to shake myself to regain my senses. Clearly, the fact we're sitting on my bed, while both half-naked, has allowed my mind to spin off into dangerous territory indeed.

One where he's teaching me lessons of a very different nature.

The next gulp I take of my coffee burns down the back of my throat, dragging me out of horny-ville and into the present moment. Where were we?

Oh, right. Self-defense.

"I thought I wouldn't need any, seeing as I'm going to be locked in here for the rest of my life." Sarcasm is apparently my default setting when in fear of being caught out wondering how big this man's dick is.

He flashes a smirk that could make panties spontaneously combust within a mile radius. *Oh, it's definitely big.*

"You might belong to us, but that doesn't mean you're trapped in here."

I'm utterly confused, but can't help myself from buying into his scheme.

Then I remember last night and the flames licking at my core turn a more violent shade. "Why should I agree to do anything with you? It's the three of you who want to leash me and get your dicks wet, all for some obscene ritual before a hall packed with strangers."

He gives me an expression that falls somewhere between full of himself and indifferent.

"You're telling me that you spent the past few years of your so-called freedom never once expecting someone to come for you." It's not a question.

There's a slithering feeling along my spine.

He's right. Every day brought a new risk. I never knew if it would be the last one where I retained power over my own life.

"No." I answer honestly.

"It was inevitable that Anguis members would claim you one day. We happened to get to you first, baby girl." Fuck, I hate the way he makes that sound so alluring. I also can't stand the fact he's speaking the truth.

I'm refusing to acknowledge that he's just dropped a pet name on me. Nor am I ready to admit that my nipples have stiffened hearing those particular words roll off his tongue.

These men are dangerous assholes with control issues, and I have no business having conflicted emotions about what this entire situation represents for my life. But would I rather it were one of my father's foul associates who claimed me? Would I prefer things were different, and a group of those greasy, disgusting men forced me into a Pledging ceremony instead?

No. I most definitely would not.

In the worst-case scenario, I can hate-fuck these men. That, I can certainly do. Even if I do want to shove a gun down each of their throats, I can't deny how my body responds to each of them.

"I don't have any clothes to wear." It's about my only excuse left.

Ky gets up and crosses to the built-in wardrobe beside the bathroom door. With a flourish, he slides it open, and I nearly drop my coffee in my lap.

There are clothes in there. Ones that aren't man-sized. From what I can see, it's only a small assortment, but whatever, *anything* is a vast improvement on what I've had access to so far. How did I not notice?

More to the point—did these men have clothes delivered for me while we were at Noire House last night?

"Put these on, and let me give you some lessons." He rummages through a drawer then tosses a set of leggings and a sports crop in the direction of my bed. I'm so stunned; it's all I can do not to let them hit me in the face.

Our sweaty bodies writhe together.

Ky's big hands knead my flesh.

I'm panting and flushed beneath him.

There's a Viking between my thighs, and holy fucking hell, I can feel the outline of his cock pressing against my core.

He's big. Definitely, big.

"Better. But you still have work to do."

Clearly, Ky is able to keep his mind on the task at hand—which appears to be repeatedly flipping me onto my back and proving exactly how damn weak I am—rather than descending into a horny mess at the proximity of our bodies.

Or maybe this is his preferred form of torture because the asshole is still shirtless, and now he's covered in a sheen of sweat with abs glistening every time they flex above me.

His muscled frame is on full display as he sits back on his heels, still positioned between my legs. It's all I can do to lie here on the gym mat while I die quietly.

After a week of sitting around inside a small room, half of which I didn't eat for, and the other half I haven't slept for, my body is good for absolutely nothing. A fact that became painfully clear each time Ky pinned me down with ease.

Despite my best efforts to fight him off or defend myself in the way he carefully showed me—the man is surprisingly patient and explains things in a way that is simple to understand—I'm unable to do *anything* right, it would seem.

Maybe I'll be so exhausted tonight that my body might finally grant me a few uninterrupted hours of sleep.

I wave him away. "Just bury me here." My lungs burn, and my muscles are jelly. This gym mat surrounded by weight machines and workout benches seems like as good a place as any to hoist my white flag from.

A water bottle enters my field of vision as his golden Nordic glow looms before me.

"You're tougher than that." He shakes the bottle in my direction.

"Not in the face of being drugged or grabbed in the dark." The bitterness in my tone really shines through as I glare up at his stupidly gorgeous face.

Easing myself up to a seated position with a stifled groan, I tip the water down my throat and spill half of it over my chin. I really am doing my best to round out my efforts to look like a hot mess.

Ky shifts his weight forward to rest on both knuckles, bracing his arms on either side of my hips in a movement that brings us so close together I can feel the heat shimmering between our bodies. There's no stopping my pussy from clenching and throbbing at the sexual way we're positioned down here on the floor.

Oh, god. I'm more fucked up than I thought because all I can think about is him touching me and relieving the ache between my thighs that refuses to go away the longer I spend wrapped in his scent of cedar and the ocean.

"We don't have the luxury of playing nicely in our world." His voice has dropped low as he looms over me like a god. "But you already know that."

I do. I do already know that, and can't hide from my past or my future.

"You're not scared of us." He states it. Factually.

"Should I be?"

"Yes. You absolutely should." His masculine scent winds around me. "You should be running scared from all the awful, dangerous, terrible things men like us are capable of."

"Oh, yeah?" God. This man. Ky has this unsettling presence about him, one that makes me want things that I never thought of before. He's unraveling me in a way that comes with the force of a sledgehammer rather than a scalpel.

"Here's what I think..." Those green eyes of his are dappled with flecks of amber close to his pupils. "I think you're just as fucked up as we are underneath it all. A horny little bitch, who wants to be someone's plaything."

My mouth has gone bone dry. "Fuck you. Get off me." Heat flushes straight up my chest and neck.

Letting out a dangerous chuckle, Ky shifts forward, bringing us even closer together. Taunting me with that calculated movement, he forces me to drop back onto my elbows in an effort to keep a safe distance between me and those full lips. His wicked mouth twists into a smirk—a mouth that felt so alluring the day he kissed my hand.

I want those soft lips and the scratch of his beard on me, even though I shouldn't.

"Maybe I'll make you my little plaything, baby girl. Slip into your room at night while you're sleeping and see how wet your cunt is thinking about us. I'll bet you love waking up desperate and soaked, knowing I've had three fingers deep inside you. Wouldn't take long before you're whining and begging for my cock in all your dreams."

Beneath the sports crop I'm wearing, my nipples are hard, and the tight buds drag against the stretchy material. I can only hope to all that is holy in this world there's enough padding so he can't see exactly how my body responds to him. Or maybe I do want him to know. *Fuck.* My brain is a scramble of emotions and horniness and exasperation. A potent cocktail running in my veins that feels like gasoline.

I make an indignant noise somewhere in the back of my throat.

With a knowing wink, Ky gets to his feet and swaggers out of the gym with all the self-assurance of a man who absolutely intends to make good on his threat. My mouth hangs open as he leaves me swimming in a sea of filthy images he's conjured.

I can't stand how much he turns me on.

So much so, that I'm racing back to my wing to lock myself in the bathroom, ripping off the sweaty leggings and crop before I stand under the high-pressure waterfall head. My teeth catch my bottom lip in a brutal hold, and I slump back against the tiled wall of the open shower. Squeezing my eyes shut, I allow my hands to roam down over my aching pussy, gliding a finger inside, silently berating myself when I confirm how wet I am.

It's his fingers I imagine thrusting into me while I'm asleep. The picture is so clear in my mind of his big body leaning over mine in the shadows as he torments me.

Clearly, he's tapped into a dormant fantasy of mine because my pussy is slick and swollen, and I run my fingers up over my clit, spreading the wetness around. All it takes is a few firm circles around the aching bud, and my core is wound tight, ready for release.

In my vivid dreamscape, there are two other shadowy outlines now that appear. Both of them join Ky in my haze of lustful imaginings.

Each figure might only be a faceless mirage, but I know exactly who they are. Or at least, who they represent. They're positioned on either side of me, and all three of these dark figures play with my body while I'm sleeping. Touching, stroking, teasing me expertly, causing my body to be swept over the edge into such an intense orgasm I double over under the water.

Something hot and shameful sweeps up from my toes. How fucking dare they threaten me and claim that I'm nothing more than their possession to use as they see fit.

Even worse is the fact that Ky was right. A part of me does want to be used by them.

That's maybe the most terrifying realization of all.

CHAPTER 13
Thorne

Ky is circling like a shark. He's scented willing flesh, and now he's biding his time until he can move in for the kill.

No matter how many times I've warned him to stay the fuck away from the girl.

His cock is doing all the thinking, even if he denies it.

Which he doesn't.

There's too much going on for me to keep tabs on him and his bullshit all the time. But the fact he had her in the gym first thing this morning rubbing his dick all over her like he's marking his territory is a headache I don't need.

I'd tell him to go beg for a fuck from Ven and get whatever *this* is out of his system, but the surly asshole has disappeared. Most likely taken off into the depths of the forest, which can only mean that he's still purging last night's rage from his system.

His beasts always need their space to find their calm after he loses his shit like that. From the state of his knuckles and the fact Massimo Ilone most likely wound up in intensive care, if he even made it through the night, it's safe to assume he won't be back for days.

There's a place Ven goes to deep in the heart of this forest, and he's the only one who will know when it is time to re-emerge.

"...The Gathered are requesting increased security at this year's auction. After what happened to poor Andreas, they won't attend without assurances of their safety, Calliano."

The nasal voice on the other end of the line belongs to one of my contacts within the organization whom I'm forced to deal with in my line of work. This woman acts as a go-between for many of the security team members and the individuals of the Anguis whom they've been tasked with protecting. I guess she's a glorified secretary, but she acts like the world owes her a favor, and more than once, I've had to bite my tongue when dealing with her bullshit attitude.

Little does she know just how ill-advised it is to get on my wrong side.

"Of course. Consider it done." I mutter, pushing around some papers on my desk. There are a million things I'd rather be doing right now than listening to this woman, but it is all part of the show. The one I put on every day to stay hidden while our plan is gradually enacted. Piece by fucking piece.

"There will have to be amendments to the usual order of events." She goes into lengthy detail about shit I already know and have already taken care of with my brother. But if it makes her feel important, then I'll allow her to run that sour mouth all fucking day in order to maintain my cover.

I round the front of my desk to lean against the wood and pinch the bridge of my nose. The woman isn't even pausing for breath as she goes on and on about details that I'm already fully aware of.

As I listen, my eyes wander to the large floor-to-ceiling

window that fills one entire wall of my office and overlooks the central courtyard area. The space is closed in with a glass roof so that the area is not only secure, but keeps the place at a nearly tropical temperature. Even if the fickle winds of the coast bring endless days of fog and mist billowing through the trees surrounding us.

Life out here on the peninsula is isolated, which suits us for what we need, but the elements are harsh. I fucking hate the cold, so this is about as close as I'll get to a compromise while I still have to stay in this hell hole known as Port Macabre.

"...Each VIP will need a vehicle escort in addition to their regular security detail..."

Christ. The woman is like a bulldog decimating a bone.

Movement outside catches my eye. Cerulean water ripples across the surface of the pool, and that's when I see her. She swims into view, with her lilac curls forming a tangle on top of her head, casually gliding through the water.

I'm responding in one-word answers and confirming details, but only half of my mind is on the conversation at hand. Instead, I watch her gently swim up and down.

My mind is even further away from the phone pressed to my ear when she reaches the steps at the far end and starts to make her way out of the pool. Glistening droplets of water roll off her curves, and I go still. As if somehow she'll be able to sense my presence from where I'm hidden behind this fortress of glass and the wall of potted palms.

Whoever chose that fucking bikini to add to the selection of clothes we had delivered needs to be shot. At least she's locked in here and not somewhere that would have every asshole in the city trying to hump her leg. It's a pale blue color that matches her big eyes, and god-fucking-dammit it barely covers anything. The wet, thin material clings to every inch of her body.

As she turns around at the top of the steps I most definitely should be looking away. This girl is too fucking young for me to be staring with any sort of interest. I have no business watching the softness of her thighs and stomach and breasts. But there's no mistaking her hard nipples poking through the two triangles of fabric clinging to her rounded tits. And when my eyes drag down her soft stomach, over the inked design of a snake winding up her sternum, I see the high-waisted cut of her briefs has suctioned to her pussy lips. Every single fucking detail between her thighs is outlined.

Jesus.

I scrub my hand over my mouth. This is the point that I should move. The moment I go and sit behind my desk and attend to the reports waiting for me on my laptop. Not stand here with a hardening cock and a view of every inch of this girl parading past as she heads for her towel.

But I'm stuck here, still watching, and she's fucking bending over.

Her soft ass cheeks are rounded. The perfect curve to lay a handprint across that I bet would redden nicely against her fair skin. Just to add to this cock-tease of a show the girl is putting on, she reaches behind and rearranges the high cut that has bunched between her ass cheeks. As she tugs on one side, I catch the faintest glimpse of her pussy from behind. Soft and pink, and asking to be filled up from this angle.

Suddenly, I'm imagining sinking my cock into her tight, wet cunt while she's folded over that pool lounger. The worst part of me now craves to hear the way she'd moan my name as I wrap her purple hair around my fist and pound into her.

Fuck. My cock is fully hard and refuses to be ignored.

The heir to Noire House is collateral in our plan. That is all Foxglove Noire is. Nothing more. If I need a fuck, there are far less complicated places to go in order to chase a release. My brother knows the type of pussy, or cock, I like and can make arrangements that are exactly what I need.

"...You'll have that all finalized within the week, Calliano?"

My grip tightens around the phone at my ear, while my other hand has to readjust myself in my pants. All the while, I'm unable to take my eyes off the way her curves move as she slowly dries herself, completely oblivious to me devouring the sight of her.

"Yes. As I said, consider it done." I grit my jaw and hope this bitch gets the hint that we're finished here.

"Wonderful. I will send over the briefing notes."

"Great." My thumb jabs at the red end-call button the instant she starts to say her goodbye.

If I've been watching the girl hidden behind a glass wall, there are plenty of other vantage points in this place for someone else to do the same. And right on cue, Ky strolls out into the middle of the courtyard, sipping on a coffee and feasting his eyes on her figure. As usual, he's dressed in nothing but low-riding gray sweats, showing off all his pretty boy muscles.

There's no occasion when he feels called to wear a shirt. Ever.

She spins around at the sound of him approaching and immediately hides herself beneath the oversized towel. Interestingly, she doesn't shy away or run. Something has changed between them since last night, and I try to make out what they're saying, but as if Ky knows I might be watching, he positions them both so their faces are hidden. He doesn't look over this way, but I've known him long enough to understand every little mannerism of his.

I push my fingers through my hair. Then, whip out my phone to aggressively type out a text.

There are reports to be gone through.

Over the top of her head, I see his green gaze tick up toward my office window. A familiar grin creases the corners of his eyes. He digs his phone out of his pocket, takes one look at the screen before dropping his hand back down. The prick doesn't even open the message; he simply swipes the notification away with his thumb. Ky makes no attempt to move. Still sipping his coffee and standing there. Meanwhile, she's inches from him, looking like a wet dream, wrapped in nothing but a towel and the world's smallest bikini.

That means now.

I've sent the follow-up order within a second. He's always known how to push my buttons, but I need him to pull his weight and not spend the day chasing after pussy that is off-limits.

He doesn't even bother to read the text; instead, shakes his head with mirth in his eyes as he no doubt feels the second vibration come through in his hand.

Their little exchange must be over because she hurries inside while Ky saunters behind her. Only this time he shoots a look in the direction of my window before texting back.

Ok, Daddy.

For fuck's sake. I ignore his attempt at shit-stirring.

Just get it done.

Ky disappears from view back inside the kitchen, and it's at that point he sends his own follow-up text.

Just so you know...

She's definitely going to touch me first.

And when she does, I'm going to be eating her pussy until she screams.

Up to you whether you want to give yourself blue balls, or join in.

CHAPTER 14
FOX

Ky is toying with me. I can feel it on a cellular level.

He's so cocksure and charming that I know he's waiting for the moment I trip and fall on his dick. Three days of self-defense lessons with him have been hellish. Especially since he damn well planted that seed of an idea in my mind that he might touch me, and then backed right off. Playing the perfect gentleman. Keeping a respectful distance, all the while giving me the most *disrespectful* eyes.

Leaving me to spiral in my own filthy imaginings for the past few days.

I mean...a girl's gotta eat, right? And he is a ten-course degustation of temptation.

While there's still the lingering disgust at what is to come with this Pledging ceremony, my body is craving a release. There's too much damn testosterone in this place, even with all the glass walls and broody forest scenery outside to distract me.

Because now, I apparently have free rein around the whole compound to explore on my own. Including the outdoor areas like the pool and the enormous wooden entertaining deck that brushes against the edge of the misty pine trees.

They seem happy to leave me alone to my own devices. Probably monitoring my every move on security cameras, mind you. So I act the *obedient* captive and don't attempt to flee, even though there's a constant nagging in my mind that I'm fucked in the head and absolutely-definitely-should-be trying to make my escape. I should at least be *planning* one, shouldn't I?

To make matters worse, staying here is no hardship. In fact, it puts anything I've ever dreamed of living in to shame. The fridge seems to be perpetually stocked with the foods I requested on my list, and the open-plan kitchen has every appliance and modern top-of-the-line feature you could imagine. Half of them I'm too afraid to touch—in all honesty, I don't know what they do, or how to operate them.

I've explored as far around the square-shaped wings of the compound as I dare. The only places I haven't poked my nose into are situated on the opposite side of the central pool and glassed-in courtyard—which feels like being inside a tropical vision no matter what time of day you go out there. I've found myself spending more and more time either swimming, curling up on one of the loungers reading, or drawing.

The library that sits off the lounge is huge. In fact, this whole place is *huge* in its heavy-set masculine proportions. If I thought the windows in my bedroom were impressive, the day I casually wandered into the living space for the first time, I nearly shattered my plate all over the concrete floor.

I'm not even sure if you can call it a lounge. Double-height glass panels all finished in black edging form a pointed V shape at the top. The whole wall made of glass has a cathedral-like feel to it with the way it towers so high above my head. The vast window stretches the length of the room and honestly is like nothing I've ever seen before. It opens up the whole lounge to look out over the rolling forest outside.

Breathtaking doesn't even begin to do it justice.

There are deep-set soft couches in here that might as well be beds for how wide and comfortable they look. It's the type of space you could sprawl out in and lie down at full stretch, yet still have room for ten more people to do the same.

Everything is finished in dark shades of charcoal and stone gray, but against the vibrant shades of green rippling through the trees outside, it totally works.

At the far end is where I discovered the library, in its own alcove with floor-to-ceiling bookshelves, and a mezzanine floor with steps leading up to another reading area and books stacked as high as they can go.

From up on that midlevel, the view is astonishing. Rolling valleys stretch out beyond the limits of the trees closest to the windows. Off in the far distance, I can see a ribbon of turquoise coastline and recall them mentioning something about this place being located on a peninsula. Which would explain the fortress-like security gate we passed through the other night.

They can secure this place from the outside world with one entrance and exit point only. One road in. One road out.

It's smart. Tactical. I wouldn't expect anything less from the likes of Thorne Calliano.

Who, incidentally, I haven't seen for days now. He's like a whisper in the air, where I come across his scent and the faintest traces of him in the books I find on these shelves, or the missing coffee cup from the matching set in the cupboard. But otherwise, he's been a ghost in this place.

As for the murderous one...he initially went missing after the night at Noire House when he savaged that asshole. I haven't had the courage to ask where he went, or what he does when he's not here because I'm nearly one hundred percent sure he murders people for the Anguis.

Being in my father's world taught me one thing, and that was to recognize those who deal in death. Not in the way that

Thorne or Ky will do so if compelled to in their line of work, but for the likes of Raven it's different. I can tell his role is something *more.*

His soul is stained, and it shows in the deeply carved lines around his eyes.

Eyes and hands that have witnessed far too much blood.

For some reason, it doesn't make me want to hurl up my lunch at the thought of him probably snapping people's necks with his bare hands. Maybe I've got a kink for men who kill for a living.

It wouldn't be a surprise, considering the world I inhabited for so long—the one I'm still trapped in like quicksand.

Tonight, I settled in my newfound perch on the mezzanine level, with a small pool of light from a table lamp for company. Lying sideways in the oversized armchair with my legs dangling over one side and a book in hand, I've hidden up here for hours. After a while, I hear low voices downstairs. For the vast majority of today, I've been rolling around this place by myself, so the sound of the men being in the house feels a little strange. Being immersed in the pages of my book, I'd almost forgotten for a moment that they come and go like wild creatures in the night.

Curiosity gets the better of me as I sit up a little, which gives me a secret vantage point to spy on the level below since there's only a thin metal railing in the way.

Ky and Raven appear, both disheveled and half-naked in a way that unmistakably screams *we've just been fucking.* My thighs clench as heat snakes through my core. Ever the provider, it would seem, Ky holds two bottles of water and passes one over as they talk quietly between themselves. I really wish there was a way I could hear them, but I don't need to. Their body language tells me everything as I greedily soak up every little touch and signal of post-orgasm glow going on between them.

Ky lets out a playful laugh; his fingers push back his long hair, which is loose and mussed. Whatever he said causes the other man to scowl and grab him by the waistband, dragging him so close that their hips are flush with one another's. Raven bites Ky's lower lip and tugs on it slowly. Seductively.

An inferno races through my bloodstream, leaving my clit pulsing with a heartbeat of its own. I nearly let out a moan worthy of a porn star, barely catching the wanton sound before it escapes my mouth.

They're all muscles and strength and beauty together in a way that makes me breathless. I have to do everything to prevent myself from making a sound up here; there's no way I want them to know how long I've spied on this intimate moment between them.

Thorne's words fly into my horny brain. *If any of us need a fuck, trust me, we're all well taken care of.*

God, I want to be taken care of. In as many ways and places and positions as possible.

And the increasingly graphic dreams I've been having every night lately have featured all of these men. Now, the way I've just witnessed a new side to Raven—one where he oozed control and sex with that single commanding move has got my pussy tingling.

That's what I like the most when it comes to sex.

I *love* giving over control.

I *love* being used.

But unfortunately for my needy pussy, as quickly as they walked in, they're gone. Leaving me with flutters in my belly and turned on as all hell.

"WILL you tell me where we're going?" While I'm buckling my seatbelt, I give Ky my best *unimpressed* glare. He once again thumped me in the gym this morning, then announced with an air of mystery that I needed to be ready to go for a drive.

So now, I'm showered, dressed, and secured in the passenger side of their simply monstrous armored vehicle, similar to the one he drugged me in all of a couple of weeks ago—or at least I think it has been around about two weeks—and now we're headed down the gravel road leading away from the compound.

It's just the two of us. Alone.

My brain won't stop replaying the sight of his bottom lip being caught between Raven's teeth.

The temperature in here has skyrocketed a hundred degrees.

"You'll see soon enough," he says. Noncommittal as ever.

"Is this the part where you take me out into the middle of nowhere and dispose of my body?" I shuffle around in my seat to get comfortable.

All Ky does is rest one hand over the top of the steering wheel and the other on the gear stick in a way that shouldn't be attractive. But it is. It so fucking is.

In an effort to remind myself that I am still pissed off at them for what they've done to me, I snap my fingers in his direction. "Oh, no, wait...you can't do that yet; the three of you want to screw me in front of a room full of people first. You fucking creeps."

He keeps his eyes on the road ahead, but I see the way the corner of his mouth tilts upwards. We slow to a crawl as we pass through the security gate; the team stationed there in black tactical gear wear a *don't mess with us* air about them that indicates they've got everything from guns to rocket launchers at their fingertips.

Ky gives them a nod and a mock salute as we pass by.

Once we're out the other side, I pluck up the courage to keep pressing him. Out of all three of my captors, he's the one who has spent the most time with me. He brings me coffee and accompanies me to their gym. There's no hiding the way he openly looks at me with hunger, but for whatever reason, he's kept his hands and words to himself since that first day teaching me self-defense. Leaving me to be the one panting after him a little bit more day by day.

If there's any hope of getting at least one of them on my side in all this, I'll take my chances with the mischievous Viking filling the seat next to me.

"So what is it going to be? Fuck me, claim Noire House, and then get rid of my body?" Shifting my position to face him, I study the side of his face.

"I'd choose your words carefully, baby girl." Fuck. My face flames whenever he calls me that. Whether or not he means it as a phrase intended to taunt me, my insides do a little swoop each time all the same.

"Well, you're all the ones with this master plan to keep me prisoner and claim me."

"And...like I've said...you'd prefer if it was one of your father's many friends instead?" He drawls the words as if we're talking about something as mundane as the weather. The sight of his veins in his hand flexing as he grips the steering wheel is doing ungodly things to my sense of self-preservation.

I'm all but a melted puddle here in this expensive leather seat.

But I am one stubborn woman.

"I'd prefer it was *none* of you. I want to go back to my life." Chewing on the inside of my cheek, I watch him closely for any hint or flicker that he feels compassion for me in all of this.

"Then explain to me why you're panting and squirming over there."

Jesus. I swallow hastily in an effort to not sound exactly as he's just described.

"I'm not. You're all assholes who think you can get away with ruining my life."

Ky lets out a dark chuckle. "Is that so?"

"Yes."

"Well then, stop eye-fucking me, or I'll pull over and pound that sweet cunt of yours right here on the side of the road 'til you beg for mercy."

There's a strangled noise that comes out of me in protest. But he's already put the vehicle in park before I register where we are. For a long second, I'm frozen, thinking that he's about to do everything he just threatened me with. And I'm entirely conflicted about how that makes me feel.

Do I want him to fuck me right here in this car, out in the open? Would I even be able to fight him off if he tried? He's already proved just how easily he can toss me around in the gym with my pathetic efforts to learn self-defense amounting to nothing against this man.

There's a swirling sensation in my gut, and heat pools between my thighs.

A look of pure mischief twitches on his full lips, and he reaches over the middle console to unclasp my seatbelt for me. I flinch as the sharp noise of the buckle sounds like a gun going off in the thorny silence wrapping around us.

Oh, god. Is this the moment his resolve snaps, and he takes what he wants from me?

Ky braces one elbow on the armrest between us and his other hand on the dashboard. He's dressed in a white t-shirt, jeans, and a worn leather jacket, looking like the lovechild of temptation and illicit decision-making.

I shrink backward toward my door as he presses closer. My pussy is throbbing, but I'm also walking a fine line of terror at this moment because I have no idea what is about to happen next.

His green eyes darken as he surveys me for a long moment. I've quite possibly forgotten how to breathe.

"Keep lying to yourself. But I see you for the horny little bitch you are." That wicked mouth of his twists. "Now, get your ass out of the car. We're here."

With that, he's gone, and his door has slammed, and I'm left trembling in a state of unchecked arousal. Holy shit. I'm in way too deep and need to calm my goddamn hormones down. Am I ovulating? Because I swear each time this man gives me those mossy green eyes, I'm ready to climb into his lap. So before he can drag me out of the vehicle and discover just how much of a panting mess I've become, I rush to let myself out and follow behind him on slightly unsteady legs.

The sight that greets me as I exit the car is a warehouse, with big metal roller doors and nothing to indicate what goes on inside.

Probably torture.

A hit of salt air rushes at me, and glancing around, this definitely has the feeling of being near the port. It must be right on the outskirts of Port Macabre.

My eyes take a moment to adjust to the dim lighting inside, and the sound of the heavy metal door we just walked through clangs abruptly behind me. Everything about this feels ominous. But I'm also morbidly curious as to why I've been brought here.

It seems like a lot of effort to drive all the way down here when they could do whatever they want to dispose of my body amid the isolated forest out on the peninsula.

Ky walks over to flick on a light. The single bulb splutters to life, and I see a small stack of moving boxes. What this is all about, I can't possibly tell so I shoot him a confused expression.

"Boxes?"

"Open them up. You'll see." He shrugs. Leaning one shoulder up against the corrugated iron wall, with his arms folded across his chest.

"Why do I feel like there might be cobras in here. Or body parts." I mutter as I bump one with the toe of my boot.

"I'm pretty certain you'll like what's inside."

"Is it a box of hand grenades? Cyanide? Either will work perfectly for what I have planned for you three." I prop my hands on my hips.

Ky's lips twist into a devilish grin.

Nope. No. Not looking at *that* thank you very much.

To avoid revealing the way he's so effortlessly playing my body, I crouch down and dive into opening the first box. Fuck it.

As I pull open the cardboard flaps, my mouth drops open. Sitting at the top of the box is my tattoo equipment. All neatly packaged in protective wrapping. I shuffle some of the things to one side and see that the whole box is filled with familiar items from my studio.

There's barely a second before I fall upon the next box; this time, it opens to reveal clothes from my wardrobe. My own clothes.

I honestly don't know how to feel right now. Am I relieved to have my personal effects delivered here for me, or am I immensely pissed that these three men have wandered into my home and packed up my life without so much as a word.

No need to wonder how they got in. They've had my phone, wallet, and keys ever since the night they drugged me.

Oh, and being members of an all-powerful secret society would have guaranteed they could access whatever they desired from my life, too.

"Who...why..." I can't really form words. My brain is a little overwhelmed with everything at this point in time.

Ky scratches his jaw. "Because you belong to us now, and the *who* doesn't exactly matter, does it?"

"Oh, of course," I roll my eyes. "The great and powerful Thorne Calliano doesn't answer to anyone. He just does what he fucking wants."

The man before me bristles at the mention of that name.

"Listen carefully, little Fox. Watch your tongue when it comes to speaking Thorne's name. You know nothing about him or his life, and you'd do well not to forget that."

My curiosity perks up at the way this man is obviously willing to stand up for and defend someone so cruel.

"Then tell me. At least give me something to go on."

"It's not like you care. We're the monsters in this story, aren't we?"

"I think the Anguis are the true monsters. My father was, at any rate. Where you all fall within their plans and schemes... why you're insisting on putting me through this...that's what I really want to know." I huff, sick of biting my tongue. He wants to strangle me and dump my body among my meager worldly possessions for speaking out, so be it.

"Men like us had no choice whether to belong to the Anguis. You're a smart girl, you grew up in this world." Ky studies me harder. "You *escaped* this world. So, you know that not everyone who is part of it wants to be."

Chewing the inside of my cheek, I don't know whether to hold his gaze or look away.

"There are those of us who ended up among this world by force...and there are those of us who are determined to rid it of the rotten, hidden, festering parts concealed by men like Andreas Noire."

Ky doesn't give me time to digest his words, or consider the depth of feeling behind that statement. He's crossing over to the stack of boxes beside me. Bending down to pick one up, he's back to the usual mischief dancing in his eyes as he straightens back up.

He gives the lid of the box a tap. “Oh, and if you’re wondering about your toys, they’re all in here, by the way.”

With a knowing wink, he strolls out the door to load the box into the back of our vehicle.

Taking my stash of vibrators with him.

CHAPTER 15

There's a pretty girl with a pussy I can't stop thinking about on the other side of the compound.

One who spends her days wandering by the pool in a bikini that barely covers anything—not that I'm complaining, but the number of times I've fisted my cock over this girl is getting beyond a joke.

Fuck Thorne, and his dumb fucking rules.

The asshole probably won't admit it to himself, but there's no mistaking the way he carefully avoids being around this girl. And if there's one thing I know about that man, after spending half a life together, is that he will avoid something he doesn't know how to handle.

On paper, he's got his plan for revenge against Andreas Noire. In practice? He's just as caught in the intricate web of lilac hair and sexy tattoos and curves that beg to be bitten until she whimpers sweetly.

He wants her, too.

Don't get me wrong, she's smart. Funny. Gorgeous. Spending time with her is no chore. A beautiful girl who holds herself in any conversation? That's my weakness, and her name is Fox.

She turned all glassy-eyed, and that pouty little mouth of hers dropped open when I threatened to sneak into her room at night. Even if she can't, or won't, admit it out loud, she craves me just as much as I'm growing more and more feral for her.

Fox wants all of us. But that little secret she's keeping might take a little more massaging in order to have her brain climb on board with the idea. Her body has no problem with the concept, mind you.

So that's exactly why I'm standing over her like a vengeful shadow in the dark, listening to her soft, steady breaths fill the room. There's enough light to see by with the soft glow of moonlight slipping through a crack in the curtain. Enough for what I need at any rate.

Her door was unlocked. That wouldn't have stopped me, but it is certainly interesting to know that she doesn't try to prevent any one of us from coming into her room. We've got a key, yes, but if she was truly against the idea of us invading her space during the night...well...I'm sure this girl would get inventive.

And yet, here she lies. Sleeping soundly, with the covers half pushed off her soft body. Dressed in my shirt.

There might be sharp protests on her tongue when she's awake, but at night, the girl is leaving her door unlocked and wearing my clothes. Oh, yes. Fox is just as much of a perfect little slut as I'd hoped she would be.

It's like she's painted her body in a message just for my eyes. One that says she's more than willing for me to follow through on my promises.

Moving closer to the bed, I slowly ease myself onto the side of the mattress. Careful not to disturb her as I position myself next to her hips.

Thorne can go fuck himself. If he'd spent even a fraction of the time near her that I have, the asshole would be considered a saint for not indulging the compulsion to give her what she needs. There's no mistaking that our sweet little Fox enjoys sex. Her generous stash of toys gave away that secret. I suspect I already know what she'll enjoy the most, but there's plenty of time to explore that later.

Right now, I'm here with only one goal in mind.

I want this girl's pussy soaked and aching and swollen for me like a bitch in heat when she wakes up. In the morning, I want her staring at me over her coffee with pink cheeks and puffy lips from where she's been biting back the intensity of how turned on she is. This girl needs to be horny as fuck, dripping wet, and begging for my cock tomorrow.

Because she'll know it was me who came in here while she slept.

A filthy little secret that will only exist between me and Fox and the midnight hour.

Testing my weight by leaning one hand across her body to rest on the mattress on the other side of her hips, I wait to see if she'll stir at all. But sleep has a firm hold on her, and only her dark eyelashes fanned against her cheek move ever so slightly. Good.

She doesn't know it, but I gave her something in her water earlier this afternoon. Just enough to make sure she sleeps heavier than usual. I can't help but smile to myself, because I bet if I actually promised to drug her, to give her something she could knowingly take and give over control, she'd be panting within seconds.

With my free hand, I knock down the sheets covering her thighs and hiss in a breath through clenched teeth. The naughty little slut has nothing on underneath the shirt she's wearing; the material sits bunched up around the softness of her stomach.

I'm sitting here in the dark, staring at her glistening cunt.

She's trimmed, with just a small triangle of short curls left covering her mound. It's hot as fuck and suits her. Fox is the kind of girl who likes things artistically messy. That's why she loves tattoos and coloring her hair purple and collecting vintage jewelry. I'll bet anything she begs louder when you tug on those curls and lick her pussy at the same time.

Fortunately, my t-shirt is so big it hangs off her loosely. Taking the hem between my thumb and forefinger, I rub it together for a moment, planning my next move. I've been running over in my mind how I wanted to play this, and now that I'm here, she's like a playground of carnal temptation, and I don't know which part of her I want to claim first. The cotton is so fucking worn it feels like it'll tear, and for a moment, I contemplate cutting it off her body completely. But then the caveman part of me wants to do this with my shirt pushed up just above her luscious tits. Fuck, my cock jerks in my pants at the thought.

So I do just that, hooking the material and giving it a gentle tug to sit just above the swell of both her breasts. They're heavy and round and instantly pebble with the cool air of the room. Jesus, all I want to do is lean down and swirl my tongue over her nipples, to finally get a taste of her. But I can't risk doing too much in case she wakes up. I didn't drug her heavily; there was a fine line I wanted to maintain where her body will still feel and react to every little thing I do to her.

My mouth hovers as close as I dare without touching her skin, and I blow gently on the peak of her right nipple. In the moonlight, I can see the dusky rose coloring darken as the bud tightens into a stiff peak. Then, I repeat the process on the other side. Already, I can sense her body beginning to feel the ache flow through her veins. Those perfect lips that I can't wait to see swollen and wrapped around my cock are parted as her shallow breaths quicken ever so slightly.

I take my time. Teasing each one of her tits, over and over.

My cock is fully fucking ready to go by the time I draw back, and my pulse is thudding hard in my throat. She looks so goddamn gorgeous spread out like this, with her tattooed skin and flushed cheeks.

Before shifting down her body, I know exactly what will draw out her soft moans in her sleep—the ones I've been dying to hear for the first time. I let a string of spit fall from my lips to coat the tight bud of her nipple, then do the same for the other. The cold wetness coats the rigid points and pebbled areolas in a glossy shine.

The sweetest and horniest noise comes out of her.

I nearly lose it and decide to shove my cock inside her right then and there.

But being patient is what tonight is all about, even if I'm going to need to find Ven and fuck all of this tension out of my system for days.

So I grip my length through my pants and squeeze. It feels so fucking good and there's no way in hell I'm going to be able to go without stroking my dick for this next part.

When I carefully shift my weight back down toward her thighs, she's shifted around with the pleasure and arousal of having her nipples teased, and the best part of that is how her legs have spread wide for me. Her cunt is soaked. Every glistening part of her is on display, and I take a deep inhale to drown in the heady scent of her arousal. She's fucking perfect, and it takes a mountain of self-control not to pull my cock out and notch at her entrance.

We'll have to explore that fantasy another time.

Gritting my teeth, I give myself another firm stroke because now all I can think about is sucking on her clit until she's right on the edge, then sliding inside to fuck her until she wakes up with me buried deep inside her pussy.

The things I want to do to this girl...the things I want *us* to do to this girl.

Seeing Ven and Thorne fuck her too? Being able to feel her clench around my cock while Ven fucks me? And getting closer to Thorne, because he's always been that worse kind of forbidden fruit...Holy shit, that thought breaks me. I have to touch her, and right now, I'm beyond caring about being gentle anymore.

If she wakes up, she wakes up.

Repositioning myself, I use two fingers to spread her pussy lips, and the first touch of her silky, wet heat has me leaking a smear of pre-cum against my stomach. Her clit is swollen and pouting for attention—begging for my mouth. But instead of giving in to that particular temptation, I glide my fingers over her slickness, gathering it from her entrance and bringing it up to rub circles around the stiff bud.

Everything about Fox is soft and warm and so fucking delicate I'm stifling a groan.

My eyes devour the way she blossoms beneath my touch. Shifting her hips ever so slightly to give me better access. I snap my gaze up to her face. Those lips I want to fuck so badly it hurts are hanging open even more now, and she's making sweet little desperate noises while she's dreaming of coming all over my cock.

Christ. I want to scoop her up and take her straight to Ven and let him see this shit, too. He'd go fucking wild, I know it. Even if he hates what she represents, I know she's the kind of pussy he would go feral for sharing.

I slip my hand down and sink two fingers inside her. She's soaked and coats my hand, allowing me to slide straight to the second knuckle easily. As I press further, I can feel her pussy walls fluttering and clenching. Jesus. Fuck. I add a third finger straight away because this is just too fucking good to resist anymore.

Time slows down to a standstill as I'm lost in this moment. My fingers in her pussy and my cock straining the front of my pants, and her drugged body responding to me like the perfect little fucktoy she wants to be. Working in and out of her in a steady rhythm, her body rocks gently, but not enough to disturb her from sleep.

Her climax is building, drawing her body tight. I can feel her sucking my fingers deeper with each movement.

Even though my dick is screaming at me to keep going just so I can plunge inside her as she's still in the peak of an orgasm, I have to stop.

Inhaling deeply, I still my fingers and hold them there for just a moment. It's a possessive action, and it awakens something inside me.

A dark, coiling beast stirs within my chest—a sense of ownership.

With my free hand, I let my painfully hard cock spring free. Licking a generous track of spit across my palm, I begin stroking myself. Her heat and silky channel squeeze around my digits, as if her sleeping body knows how it would take no effort at all for me to line up at the entrance to her soaked little hole and slip inside with no resistance.

As my strokes grow faster, and my need to claim her fully beats incessantly behind my ribs, I contemplate all the ways I want to mark this girl the fuck up.

Leaving her a present to find in the morning painted all over her delicate, smooth skin sounds like the perfect way to go. But that glimmer of a thought gives me an even better idea for another time, one that I'm going to enact any day now.

Fuck. My balls ache, and my dick is ready to burst.

Just beside me, on the other side of her bed lie some folded clothes. I reluctantly drag my fingers out of her cunt and grab a pair of silky-looking black panties. Wrapping them around my cock inside my fist, I'm nearly there, and it's the moment I allow myself the first taste of her sweetness—licking her wetness off my fingers—that my release shoots out of me.

It feels like I'm coming and coming, and my heart pounds in my ears. Holy shit, the taste of Foxglove Noire and delicious ruination is better than I ever could have imagined.

As I tuck myself away, pocketing her panties with triumph and the taste of her pussy on my tongue, I take in the sight of our pretty little captive splayed out before me.

There's something hypnotic about this girl, and I'm going to find out exactly what that is. Seeing her bathed in the silvery glow that makes her skin seem unreal and her lilac hair shimmer against the pillow, I think I understand now why Thorne has been so determined to see this plan through.

CHAPTER 16
FOX

How the fuck is a girl expected to survive in this place?

I'm a raging mess of hormones and anxiety, which have all woven together to leave me feeling like I'm about to explode.

Not to mention, I woke up this morning after the most vividly intense sex dream I've ever had. If someone had breathed in the direction of my nipples, I probably would have combusted into a million pieces. My aching pussy and giant empty bed have one man's name all over them—there is absolutely no mistaking who is responsible for the complete mess I'm currently in.

Ky was in my room last night. I can't prove it, but from the way my body feels like I've been railed senseless, I know he made good on his threat to sneak in while I was sleeping. The only part that leaves me with a tiny fragment of doubt is that I can't help wondering why I didn't wake up.

Surely, I couldn't sleep through someone playing with my body and touching me that intimately.

But I can't escape the lingering question...if I'd woken up, would that filthy dream have turned into something more?

As if they all hear my horny brain doing burnouts, all three men appear in the kitchen while I'm quietly dying and brewing coffee at the same time.

Did I spend the past hour in my oversized shower, getting myself off again and again? Yes. Yes, I did. Apparently, three rounds with my favorite vibrator weren't enough to satisfy the ache that refuses to go away.

Which is why my pussy is one alert bitch when they descend on the kitchen like a pheromone-filled wet dream. They're all dressed in dress shirts and slacks and look the epitome of deadly charm.

This is the version of them I first met the night they drugged me, and I'm instantly on edge. Seeing them like this makes me wonder what *business* they're attending to today. Maybe they've got other girls they're busy kidnapping and keeping locked up in multimillion-dollar forest estates scattered around Port Macabre.

I would laugh if the idea didn't make me savagely jealous. Which is officially now the second most irrational conclusion I've come to this morning. It's not like I have a single claim on any of these men, and yet I've already fallen under some kind of non-existent dick spell.

I hate them, and yet I don't want anyone else near them.

Strange, isn't it, how threats of murder and forcing themselves on me have morphed into us standing around in a kitchen silently getting ready for our days. Mine will, of course, be filled with doing almost nothing, getting hornier by the second, while theirs probably involves seeing someone's intestines spill onto a cold concrete floor.

Or at least, I hope that's what they might be doing. My fluttering heart goes haywire imagining them going off to spend time with other women somewhere. God, I'm blaming the drugs they forced on me for the disappearance of my sanity. That bitch has clearly gone missing in action, leaving me panting after three men who I have no right to be eyeing up in their immaculately fitted button-downs.

I plonk myself on one of the stools at the large island in the center of the kitchen and cradle my coffee mug in my hands.

Normally, I try to make myself scarce before they appear, but today, I'm feeling like I want to observe them. Maybe it's driven by this weird streak of jealousy, maybe it's morbid curiosity. But I want to try and glean whatever tidbits of information I can about each of them. I'm already certain my greatest chance of wearing one of them down is going to be through Ky—the other two are more of a mystery. They're apex predators. Precisely the kind I need to study from a safe distance while discerning their patterns and traits, if I hope to survive this treacherous wilderness.

Thorne is stony-faced as usual, busying himself pouring three coffees. Raven aggressively makes enough scrambled eggs to feed a small army.

"You're not running away scared this morning then?" Ky directs the question at me while he sidles up beside Thorne and swipes one of the mugs before he's barely finished filling it. There's a scowl thrown his way, but of course, he shrugs it off with a smirk.

There's something I can't quite put my finger on in the energy between the two of them. It's a playfulness on Ky's part that feels like more than just brotherly banter. If I didn't know better, I'd think he was flirting.

"I've been trying to keep out of your way." I shrug. Burning holes in the side of Thorne's head with my stare. "Especially since I was instructed to *get out of your sight* and all."

The stone-wall doesn't rise to my challenge. Just stirs milk into his coffee with methodical precision. He's the asshole that took me and brought me here, yet he ignores me, or avoids me, nearly the entire time. I loathe how much I want just a scrap of this man's attention. His indifference feels like a punch to the gut.

"Wonder what could have made you bold enough this morning?" There's a knowing look in Ky's green eyes as he stares at me over the top of his coffee from across the kitchen. My body is officially a traitor and hums to life, soaking up every scrap of his suave attention.

"Thought it was about time. You assholes have been getting it too easy; now I need to work out how to make your life hell." I'm certain that my cheeks are cherry red based on the way he's smirking at me, but I hold my ground.

Ky takes a long, slow sip from his mug, then cocks an eyebrow at me. "Hmm, I thought maybe something had *come* to you in the middle of the night... something that made you change your mind."

I nearly spit my mouthful of coffee straight across the kitchen.

Oh, god. It wasn't just a wild sex dream.

He's definitely seen my pussy. There's absolutely no doubt whatsoever in my mind. He was in my room last night, and I'm equally turned on and mortified that he managed to mess with me. Not only that, but why the hell didn't I wake up?

I quickly avert my eyes, back in the direction of Thorne, who is glaring at his phone. He seems content to ignore our conversations and the accompanying minefield of innuendo I'm hopping around. Raven's back is still turned while he cooks, but I can feel the bristling energy rolling off him. He's like a panther, all lithe shapes and predatory movements, despite the fact his shoulders are big enough to fill half the kitchen.

He chucks plates around and throws eggs and toast at them, splitting the food into three portions, and I'm almost bemused by the domestic nature of it all. Wolf boy didn't strike me as being the cook out of the three of them, but now it makes sense as to why he was in charge of keeping me fed while locked away in my room. It must be his thing, and it makes my heart do a little skip at the notion that despite his murderous exterior and the brutish world he's been raised in, there's a man who cares enough about his lover and whatever Thorne is to him that he'll cook breakfast for all of them like this.

Even if it feels like he might bludgeon me to death with the heavy pan if I so much as glance at him the wrong way this morning.

Thorne grunts something that sounds like it could be a *thank you*, but it's hard to tell.

"Thanks, baby. It smells amazing." Ky swoops in like an eagle and grabs his plate.

I wriggle a little in my seat, more than a little turned on by the reminder that Ky and Raven are together, and I've seen both of them in their blissed-out, freshly-fucked state.

Being on edge and too turned on for my own good is a dangerous thing, this kitchen feels like it has shrunk to half its size. What I can only hope is that hiding behind my coffee might disguise the pink decorating my cheeks.

In fact, I should really just vanish off to the relative safety of my room. The food smells delicious, but none of it is for me, or is anything I can eat, so I'll just wait until they've left before creeping back in here to make something for myself. I've all but made the decision to cut and run, when I nearly lurch straight off the stool with a fright as Raven's tattooed hand swoops in front of me. A bowl is dropped onto the stone countertop with a clatter.

An assortment of sliced fresh fruit, nuts, and seeds stares back at me. Garnished with some kind of topping that looks like almond butter.

"Eat." Is all he barks at me, then proceeds to attack his own plate as if it's about to be taken away from him at any moment. Watching him hunch over his food reminds me of a beaten dog who will savage anyone who dares to come near while he's eating.

There's another little pang in my chest. He's obviously been through some serious shit in his life. No one is that protective of food unless they've had long periods when they've had to do without.

And now I've got the urge to give him my own bowl.

We sit around eating in silence. The men are all business, clearly with a schedule they need to stick to today. I can still feel Ky's eyes drifting over me every now and then, but I refuse to meet his gaze.

One thing I do not need is for my body to continue to betray me in front of all of them.

As they each finish their meals in record time, they quickly tidy up after themselves, and it seems an unlikely sight. From what I've observed, they don't have cleaners or maids running around, and I suppose it makes sense. Having outsiders allowed into their private fortress would only require an added layer of security or pose an unnecessary risk.

When you belong to the Anguis, the rules of *normal* life are no longer applicable.

They move as quickly as they arrived, with a silent precision that tells me these three have worked and lived together like this for a long time. There's an ease in the way they flow around one another that I'm quite happy to sit here quietly and absorb.

Except, before they depart, I find myself under the spotlight of Thorne's icy glare. He clears his throat. It's a quiet command for me to stay seated, or maybe it's a threat—although what it is that I've done wrong this time, I have no fucking clue—before he slides a slim package across the island toward me.

"We'll all be gone until tomorrow at the earliest, Foxglove. Use this to contact us, only if absolutely necessary."

My eyes take in the small, mysterious box, then dart up to meet his hard gaze, and I'm left without words.

Surely, this man is speaking in tongues. Is he giving me what I think he's giving me? Eyeing the item with suspicion, there's every chance this is a trap, and I'm walking headlong into it.

Thorne seems pleased enough with my silence. "There's an auction night coming up at Noire House, and you are required to attend. The Anguis will expect to see you there in exactly the capacity your father used to oversee those evenings in the past."

My stomach knots.

Of course, there's an auction. Of course, there is. And what he's asking me—no, forcing me to do—involves taking on the position of my father, who used to schmooze with his room full of pathetic followers, as women get sold off onstage. Meanwhile, the real trade was going on, hidden from view downstairs. The whole lavish affair of these nights acted as a cover for the fact he had children locked in the basement. The auction nights were always a distraction and a front for his trafficking operations. It makes me want to go clutch the toilet bowl whenever I stop to consider the way I unknowingly lived under the same roof as his sordid empire for so long.

Do they know about the reality of what my father did? Or, an even worse thought catches in my throat, could they also be involved...am I at the mercy of monsters worse than my father?

I can't even form a reply. Protesting against this is futile.

So I remain in my seat with my eyes lowered, like a pathetic little creature.

Thorne doesn't offer me any further explanation.

They just leave.

And once again, I'm surrounded by the echoes of their scents while outside, the drifting mist curls its ghostly white fingers against the window panes.

CHAPTER 17
Ven

It's long past midnight, yet sleep has no desire for my presence.

Ky and Thorne are still finishing up preparations for tomorrow's auction at Noire House. Allowing me to return to the compound and get on with the never-ending list of surveillance reports and bullshit for the Anguis...in peace.

There's also the matter of checking in to confirm what our little bitch of a prisoner got up to while we were gone. She doesn't deserve the level of trust Thorne gave her yesterday. Permitting her to have a cell phone? I warned him it was a shit idea, but at least there's every form of spyware installed, giving me full control over anything the cunt might attempt with the device.

With a single tap, I can see every time she's even glanced in the direction of the damn phone screen. The device gives me full access to her camera and audio, not to mention every action or keystroke.

Other than contacting our pre-programmed numbers, she's blocked from making calls, sending texts, or accessing the internet. I'm curious to see how many times she tried to do any, or all, of those things while being left alone for an entire day unsupervised.

As I open the browser on my laptop, what I'm expecting to see is a screen littered with a long list of keystroke actions, each should be recorded with a timestamp. But instead, all I see are a small handful of items. I can see that she unlocked the phone—not bothering to set a password or face ID, interesting—and she's looked through the three contacts added. Each of our numbers were already loaded into the phone. She spent the longest hovering over Ky's number, and that makes something in me sit up to attention. From the log on my computer, I can see that she opened up a text message to send to his number but didn't type anything, then closed out of it immediately.

The next move she made was to bring up the keypad as if to dial a number. But again, hovered over the phone without pressing anything before swiping out of it again.

After that, the device detected no activity for the rest of the day.

Curious. Foxglove Noire didn't try to contact the outside world, call for help, or seek out her friend. Maybe the girl is finally understanding her place in all this—that she's nothing but property and her very existence is ours to destroy piece by piece.

I'm almost fucking disappointed she didn't spend the day frantically trying to escape or run away or track down assistance. Her lack of effort, or fight is pathetic.

However, trust is a hard won commodity in my world. There's not one piece of my black soul that believes she didn't get up to *something* while we've been gone. I watch her on the cameras and the way the girl drifts around this place sets my teeth on edge.

There's an easy way to confirm my lingering suspicions, so I bring up the video feed from the day and speed through it to track her movements through the house. She sticks to her usual simple routine: gym, shower, and then spends the rest of the day floating between the kitchen, pool, mezzanine above the lounge as she always seems to like to do. At least now I don't have to deal with watching her curled up on her bedroom floor for hour upon hour like a wounded dog anymore.

Even if the girl did try to escape, there isn't anywhere she could go without us knowing. The tracker in her phone matches the one inserted at the back of her neck.

As I tap through the real-time camera footage, I notice that she's not in her bed. Her covers are thrown back and none of the motion detectors are alerting me to her location inside the compound. Both trackers indicate the same place, and from what I can tell, she's locked herself in the bathroom.

For fuck's sake.

The last thing I need right now is for this Noire House princess to be trying to slit her own wrists while she thinks no one is looking.

While the spyware allows me to access her camera to see what she's up to, I really don't care; I don't need to see what she's doing while she's concealed herself in the bathroom. But apparently we need to keep her alive and healthy, as per Thorne's orders.

I fucking told him we should install cameras in there, too, but he said it wouldn't be necessary. Now would be the perfect opportunity to let him choke on his own words.

I pull up the camera access showing me what her cell phone can see, and all I get is an image pointing at the ceiling, showing half a light fixture. It must be lying flat on the bathroom counter. Nothing to prove whether or not she's up to some shit in there that will require placing her under constant surveillance.

Christ, the simplest solution would be to let her get on with it, or I'll finish her off myself with a bullet. Thorne isn't here, he doesn't need to know the details. It'll be less hassle for all of us.

I move to exit the browser window, but that's when I hear it.

Her panting breaths.

I can't see anything, but the sound is immediately obvious to me.

There's the faintest whine and a hitch in her throat.

It's whisper soft. Barely audible. But inside the small, silent room, every tiny murmuration echoes off the tiles.

As my fists clench into blanched knuckles, hovering over the keyboard, what follows is far worse. The distinct sounds of movement and wetness hover in the air. Skin and sex and the act of plunging in and out. The exact kind of filthy noise that means she's fucking herself with either her fingers or one of those many toys.

Fuck.

I've never been into watching porn. Getting pussy or ass whenever I need it is never an issue, and the performative side of watching actors screw each other on screen with their fake expressions and exaggerated cries does nothing for me.

But this...the faintest hint of this girl bringing herself to orgasm? That has my cock hard and pressing insistently against my fly. Fucking fuck. Small, throaty noises, like she's biting back whimpers keep coming through the speakers, and I can't seem to turn the goddamn thing off.

All I can do is readjust myself and grip the edge of the table, imagining what her dripping cunt looks like as she pumps in and out of herself. Whether she uses two fingers or a fat dildo.

I'm unable to hold back the torrent of filth my brain is conjuring up, and one particularly vivid picture forms in my mind to fill in the unknown. A sight of her splayed out on the bathroom counter with knees spread wide, pinching a reddened nipple in one hand while the other impales up to her knuckle; thumb rubbing her clit.

There's only the rapid stab of my pulse in my throat and

surging cock, as I remain trapped here, followed by a whispered groan of pleasure before things go quiet.

My balls are tight, and my leaking dick wants to go finish what she's damn well started.

Slamming the laptop shut, I dig the heels of my palms into my eye sockets. Screw the little bitch for putting on a cock tease like that. Thank fuck Ky is out with Thorne right now because he'd sniff out her needy cunt from a mile away, and other than fucking his throat to shut him up, I'm not going to admit that my body reacted that way.

Anyone remotely interested in pussy would get hard at the sound of a girl fingering themselves.

It's got nothing to do with *her*.

CHAPTER 18
Thorne

There's a spray of blood on my boots and a body wrapped in plastic my team needs to dispose of.

Standing here in a drafty warehouse on the far edge of the port, all I can smell is the mix of copper and brackish water and fear.

Meanwhile, my phone has been blowing up in my pocket while I've been busy, and I know exactly who is responsible.

Wiping off the blood splatters, I toss the stained rag on top of the body. They'll be here shortly, so while I wait, I fish out my phone—ignoring all of Ky's messages for the moment.

Confirmed.

It's all I need to send to the unknown number to alert them that I've eliminated this prick. There's no telling what he did, or who he screwed over within the Anguis, but he'd run out of favors that involved keeping himself breathing. He was nothing but an informant, one of their low-level soldiers who ran deep in circles of filth. Someone who had tried—and failed—to become initiated as a member.

I have no issue with ending the lives of those who spend theirs abusing others. This fucker was up to his neck with the worst of the worst. Trading in minors and adults alike and doing business with Andreas Noire unbeknownst to the council.

Judging by his age, there's every chance he played a part in selling me and my brother to the animals inside Noire House when we were children.

Seeing the fear claw his face and knowing he pissed himself as I took my time carving him up was just another step toward our bigger goal. It doesn't bring me satisfaction to kill, but it does help me sleep better at night, knowing another piece of the rotten Noire empire has been dismantled.

And I'm in the necessary position to make sure their sickness dies with the last of them.

Hawke and I are getting closer to that goal every day.

Speaking of my brother, a message from him arrived while I watched this man bleed out. Details of the auction and lists of girls who will be on offer this year. He and his partners run the side of Noire House, most well-known to high society in Port Macabre. A sex club for only the wealthiest and most powerful, who pay their millions to join and become patrons and have all their desires catered for.

Of course, there's the hidden layer beneath it all that Andreas Noire ran and perpetuated from the shadows. His trafficking trade, dealing in the flesh of children and adults alike, because the man was a sick fuck who didn't care as long as the body had a pulse and could be sold for a profit.

His daughter will give us the opportunity to exact our own revenge since we can't give him the kind of gruesome send-off we had been planning for years.

As I'm scanning through the auction information, Hawke sends me a follow-up text.

Keen to buy anyone this time? Your dick is going to fall off if you don't get laid soon.

I tilt my head up to stare at the roof. Taking a deep inhale through my nose before jabbing at the screen to type my reply.

Fuck off.

My brother might be in the business of pleasure and fantasies being brought to life, but he doesn't need to meddle in who I do, or don't, have sex with.

Sure about that? You seem more tightly wound than usual these days.

Worry about where you're sticking your own dick.

I'm sure I can find someone with tatts…

I'll even throw in a cute little purple wig they can wear for you.

Are you quite done, asshole?

I'm busy.

Three dots bubble on the screen. But then disappear.

Thank Christ for that. Neither of us is in the business of talking just for the sake of it. We're carbon copies in that regard. And I don't need my own brother thinking he can stir shit or get under my skin.

Tires crunch to a halt just outside the roller door, and my team pulls up. Nodding as they file in past me, I give them the brief and prepare to leave them to their work. His body will vanish, just like all the others, and that's what makes us so highly sought after within the Anguis. There's an ocean of blood I've had to spill to secure this place at the heart of their organization. And this prick's death is nothing more than another step along the path I've been forced to walk.

"Got it, boss. You can head out." Mickey, one of my older men who looks like a mean bastard but has a heart of gold underneath that imposing scowl, inclines his head in the direction of the door.

"Check in with me once you reach the farm."

"Would I ever not? My woman and I would prefer not to wake up with you shoving a barrel down my throat...all for forgetting to send a text." Teasing me relentlessly for how much of a stickler I am when it comes to tying up loose ends is this man's favorite pastime.

But in this life, loose ends can spell death. *Or worse.*

"Yeah, and that shit makes you hard, Mick. Don't forget I know all the kinky shit you and Ella like to experiment with." I call over my shoulder as I leave the warehouse. His gruff laughter echoes after me as I step out into the chill of pre-dawn. Fog blankets the wharf in a murky shroud, wet concrete scuffs beneath my boots.

I'm so fucking tired.

As my heavy limbs slide into the driver's seat, the notifications in our group chat blare across the screen of my phone. There's no avoiding Ky when he's in this kind of mood.

Opening up the thread of messages, it's a one-sided conversation that Ky has been having with himself in there. *Of course.* It's a whole process to scroll up through the lengthy list of updates and scattergun of details he's been sending through while I've been steeped in the stench of death here at the warehouse.

I skim over most of the messages.

Talked with Hawke. He needs a higher security ratio for the main floor at the auction.

There's a whole lot more logistical shit he's banging on about that my brain can't handle right now. What I need is a shower and a fucking drink.

I've assigned four more bodies to the stage and placed five at the exits.

Should satisfy the Gathered. But it means we'll have to bring in some of the teams from Port for the night.

Ven leaves everything on read, as per usual.

You two are the most boring assholes I know.

Can't a guy at least get a single fucking reply?

Then I see the newest message that came in just before. The topic that I knew would eventually come up.

You know, if she's just a blood debt we're owed...

Inside the shirt I probably need to burn rather than wash, my shoulders stiffen immediately. Quick fingers tap out a reply.

Ven. Please fuck the brat out of him so we can get some peace around here.

Some of us have work to do.

Ven reads the message and once again doesn't bother to respond. I'm surprised he even opened it, to be honest.

Dots are bouncing fast and loose as Ky types. I start the ignition and am just about to pull away from the warehouse when his reply comes through.

You realize we have a pretty and willing little slut under our roof, don't you?

Or are you too blind to notice anything these days, old man?

No.

No...

As in, you don't realize?

Or, as in, you're not blind, and you HAVE noticed?

He follows that with all sorts of dumb fucking emojis like eyeballs and devil faces and eggplants.

Christ. There is no end to how far he tries to push me some days.

Don't fucking touch her.

Simple as that, Ky.

My teeth clamp together, and my knuckles grip the steering wheel until white ridges form. As I hit the accelerator and steer the car out into the deserted streets, there's another text that comes in.

Being the pain in the ass he is, Ky can't help but have the final word. His message pops up on my phone screen sitting on the passenger seat.

All I'm curious about is why we're bothering to keep her...especially if we're not going to play with her.

CHAPTER 19
FOX

"Thought I might find you up here."

A deep voice drags my attention away from the book I'm barely concentrating on. Of course, it's Ky who comes into view, wandering up the stairs. He's the only one who actively seeks me out in this place, and while I'm enjoying the freedom to do as I like these days, I'm hiding up here sulking.

A pang of missing my art and my life has become a record playing on loop.

There's not much point in setting up my tattoo equipment when I have no one to create a piece for. And there's only so many times I can tattoo my own thigh. All the boxes containing my possessions have been stored in the empty room next to mine. I really should spend a day unpacking, or at least sorting through my belongings, but it feels too raw to touch the shattered remnants of my world from before these three men came along and flipped everything unceremoniously on its head.

The concept of opening any of those boxed up items feels a lot like admitting defeat somehow. If they are emptied and the flotsam and jetsam of my life is re-homed somewhere inside my space, it feels like I rolled over for them and exposed my belly; conceding that my entire life is going to be spent locked away here in confinement.

However, if I leave those boxes untouched—sealed and with all the contents neatly packed inside—it's a strange sense of hope that bubbles up, one that makes it seem remotely possible that I might leave here with breath still filling my lungs.

"You've been hiding, little Fox." Ky smirks as he crests the top of the stairs.

I shrug and roll my eyes. "I'm sure you've got every camera in this place trained on me. Not to mention, I bet you're sick enough to have planted something on me." I close the book in my lap and tilt my head to one side, studying him through narrowed slits. "That's how all you assholes keep track of your possessions, isn't it?"

He scratches at his bearded jaw and lets out a laugh that is equal parts dark and seductive. Add that to the fact he's shirtless and wearing those slutty low-slung sweats of his hugging his trim hips; I'm defenseless against his onslaught of magnetism.

Embers start to flare up, burning low in my stomach like a wildfire.

He doesn't confirm or deny my suspicions.

I know, without a doubt, that this place is crawling with cameras. I've spotted many of them as I've spent my days mooching around in here. Although, I'm testing him with my jibe about putting a tracker inside me because that part is uncertain to me...but I should know by now not to shove my hand inside a steel trap if I don't want to risk losing a finger or two.

"I'll be here to train with you in the morning." Ky ignores me, closing the distance between us. He sets his phone down on the table beside me before reaching into my lap, picking up my book with a curious expression. As he does so, the backs of his fingers lightly brush the inside of my bare thigh, and that minuscule point of contact leaves my core clenching in response.

My heart is trying to climb out of my throat at his proximity. Being here with him this late at night feels too sensual—too intimate.

Like it would be far too easy to fall into a very tempting ambush.

"Is that all you came here to inform me?" I huff. Desperate to ignore the roar of my pulse inside my ears.

"Thought you might be lonely up here."

"You could have sent a text."

His lips twist. "Oh, but where's the fun in that? You wouldn't get to see my pretty face."

"You're ridiculous."

"But you're not denying it."

"I'm not denying what?"

"That you think I'm pretty, baby girl."

God, this conversation is veering into dangerous territory, fast. If I was smart, I'd be slipping past this man and taking myself back to my room as fast as my legs can carry me.

Obviously, tonight, I am not in possession of a single intelligent brain cell. What were we talking about again? Right... training with him in the morning.

I latch onto that point.

"Maybe I don't want that—to train with you anymore." Even as I add that last part on, my eyes bounce all over his torso. Because damn him, he is so fucking pretty. Not only that, but his cock is right at my eye level, with an unmistakable outline in the dark gray fabric. I dart out my tongue to wet my lips, and that small movement snags his gaze.

Ky tosses my book onto the table beside me, and the thud makes me jump a little.

The evening has closed in, and I've only got the small lamp turned on beside the armchair to fill the gloom, which makes his angular features look even more sinful than ever.

This spells danger to be here alone with him like this. Especially when there's nothing but shadows and heat wrapping around the two of us.

"Or maybe you do want it, and you're lying, baby girl." Those mossy green eyes of his draw me in every fucking time.

"No, I'm not—I don't." I'm spluttering. This conversation is clearly not just about self-defense lessons or training together in the gym anymore.

He leans over me, spreading those muscular arms of his wide, and grips the armrests. The move forces me backward until I'm as far as I can go, sunk into the soft cushioning of the chair. My strappy cotton dress that I threw on over the top of my bikini earlier today after swimming feels like it is going to burn to cinders.

"Your mouth keeps saying no. But your body gives away your secrets." Right on cue, goosebumps pepper my bare arms. I can feel the heavy fullness in my breasts with how turned on I am, surrounded by his intoxicating scent and charm.

I'm like one of those fish you see on nature documentaries, trapped in the glowing light produced by a deep sea monster. One that is designed specifically to lure their prey into row upon row of needle-sharp teeth.

"You're all sick. Just a bunch of depraved assholes who abuse women like me for your own selfish wants."

"Is that so?" He's looking down at me with hooded eyes and a quirk playing on his full lips.

"You know it is." I spit the words at him. Wishing I had sharpened claws to rake up that handsome fucking face of his.

"Then tell me why your cunt is getting wetter with every second you spend here with me? If I'm so disgusting, why are your panties wet?"

Fuck him. Because as much as it makes my stomach churn to admit it, he's right. I'm soaked, and I violently hate my body right now for responding to him—all of them—this way.

"Just leave me alone. Let me go."

"Little sluts go around leaving their door unlocked at night."

God. Oh, god. I had tried to forget all about that night, even though it was impossible to ignore how my body had been toyed with. Why the fuck do I not seem to mind that this man has crept into my room during the night and done god knows what to my body.

I nearly texted him about it the day Thorne gave me my own phone, but then immediately chickened out. It would have been just like Ky to deny it all and make me sound desperate. So I've been stuck not knowing whether any of it was real, or my own wild imagination, as I go crazy in this place.

But now, he's confirmed it.

"Don't you ever fucking touch me again." My teeth grind together.

Ky drops his face even closer to mine. The blond streaks in his hair are illuminated by the glow of the lamp, and his tanned skin loves the way the light falls perfectly across his body.

I'm fighting the whole way as this ship plummets to the bottom of the ocean. Taking me down with it while lashed to the mast.

"Was that why your pussy tried to suck my fingers deeper?" He whispers into the darkness. So close that the loose curls around my face tickle against my skin. "If you don't want us to touch you, then how come you gushed all over my hand?"

My stomach falls through the floor.

Yet I'm still waiting for the moment when I feel sick or violated to actually arrive.

Words are clumsy on my tongue right now. "There's no way in hell I'd let you touch me again. Stay away from me."

Ky straightens up to his full height, but remains standing so close to the front of my chair his shins touch the fabric. "Hmm... there's something just so damn sweet about pussy you're not supposed to touch." His eyes are so fucking hungry; he's devouring every moment I fight him and enjoying it like the twisted asshole he is.

A shiver runs right through to my toes.

"I bet that sweet little cunt of yours is aching right now."

He's not wrong. But I bite my tongue, refusing to give this asshole the satisfaction of knowing how easily I dissolve into a panting mess because of him.

"Go on then." Ky's eyes rake down my body, fixing on the spot just below the hem of my bunched-up dress. I'm sitting with my legs crossed in the chair, and it's ridiculous how easy it would be to slip my hand beneath the thin material of my bikini bottoms.

Fuck, he's nipped me between those deadly teeth of his, and we're headed in a dizzying spin toward something inevitable.

"In your dreams." I hiss quietly. Live wires spark in my core.

He lets out one of those dark chuckles again, knocking me sideways with a fiendish smirk. "Oh, no, I can assure you that it's all in *your* dreams, baby girl. I've heard the slutty little sounds you make in your sleep."

My teeth sink into the inside of my cheek to halt the whimper attempting to escape. "You're a pig."

"One that you're going to get yourself off while thinking about, so you might as well do it right here."

My brain is still putting up a fight, but my pussy is a horny bitch, and I can feel exactly how soaked I am. There's every possibility I might die of humiliation when Ky discovers how quickly I'm going to come the moment I decide to touch myself.

Because this is inevitable. There is no way this man is going to let me go until he gets what he wants, and the charming dickhead is right; with the state my body is in, I would be running straight to my room to take care of this *situation* going on between my thighs anyway.

Fuck him very much.

My body's reactions are shameless. Hard nipples. A slickness between my legs that is impossible to look past. Added to the infuriating ache that has been building steadily in my pussy since he waltzed up here half-naked and oozing sex.

I should be putting distance between us. Not dissolving at the sight of his hair tied in a messy bun, complete with wild strands haloing his savagely handsome face.

But Ky has no idea what the word distance even means. I'm not sure it's in his vocabulary.

"Is this what you perverts do for fun? I feel sorry for you that you have to force girls to play with themselves to satisfy your sick fetishes?" I slide my dress up the swell of my thighs so that it rucks up around my hips, and Ky's face lights up with the knowledge he's worn me down.

"Oh, but you love every moment, don't deny it." His cock strains against the front of his sweats. My greedy fucking eyes drop to the outline pressed against the soft material. If he's going to force this orgasm out of me, then the least he can do is show me his dick in the process.

"Looks like you need to do something about that." The impression his hard length makes has my mouth watering, and every breath becomes more shaky as I guide my fingers to slip beneath the waistband of my bikini bottoms, confirming how drenched I am.

The twitch on his lips is so cocky and provocative and deadly. "You want to see my dick? All you have to do is ask, baby girl."

"I hate you." The words have absolutely no weight behind them because I'm quickly biting my lip and stifling a moan when my middle finger swipes over my swollen clit.

"Fuck yes. You're a dripping wet little slut aren't you?" Ky pushes the waistband of his sweats down, revealing the full extent of the muscled v descending past his hips.

I'm rubbing faster circles as he takes his cock out, and Jesus, he's all the dreams I've had rolled into one.

Holy fuck. He's pierced.

My eyes widen at the sight of him. Long and veined and with a shiny piece of metal through the head.

"Like what you see?" Ky is so smug, it hurts. "Bet you're aching to know how good it feels."

Nope. I am not thinking about rubbing his piercing against my pussy. I am not.

"Such a shame I'm not allowed to touch you, and show you how good it would feel sliding through that wet cunt of yours. But I'll still make you come for me any time I want...and I'll do it just like this if that's what it takes." As he speaks, his fist glides up and down his length from root to tip.

Those words float through my lust-fueled mind, and I don't quite grasp his meaning. But he'll definitely make good on that promise, whatever it is, and right now, I'm lost in a sea of pleasure, so I don't fucking care.

I'll deal with the shame coating my skin tomorrow.

Right now, I want to come. Really. Fucking. Badly.

There's a tingling building from my toes and flowing up my body like white-hot sparks on a breeze. I'm already close, and Ky can tell.

"That's it. Come on your fingers like the dirty slut you are."

A low moan slips out of me by accident.

"Take your tits out." He's stroking his cock faster now. Those green eyes of his follow the desperate movement of my fingers below the fabric with unrestrained hunger.

His command is so filthy, I can't see straight. The thin cotton straps of my sundress have already fallen halfway down my shoulders, nearly exposing me. With my free hand, I tug at the two triangles of my blue bikini, and my breasts easily pop out on display.

Cold air pebbles my nipples into tight buds, with everything in this moment feeling hypersensitive. It only takes two more circles over the tiny bundle of nerves for my mouth to drop open and my entire body clenches up. The breathy noise that comes out of me is gasping and wanton.

Ky grunts, and while I'm still tugged under by the force of my climax, he shoves one knee onto the front of the seat, braces a heavy palm on the back of the chair beside my ear, and aims the head of his cock at my breasts. He fucks his fist and spurts hot cum all over my bared skin. My hard nipples are coated, and wetness slides down the soft valley where my tits are squeezed together.

I'm stunned and turned on and can do nothing but sit there as he paints me with his release.

For a moment, shocked silence keeps me immobile. Then I snap out of it and hastily cover myself up, wincing as the sticky residue clings to the inside of my bikini and the material of my dress. It smears against my heated skin and I grimace internally at the way I fell so easily into his net of come-hither looks and muscles.

As he tucks himself away, he makes a noise of approval somewhere in the back of his throat, then snatches up his phone.

With a quick tap on the screen, he glances back at me, and I really, really don't like what I see in his expression.

"Save that for later, baby girl. You're quite the pretty picture."

Still wrapped in the haze of coming down from my orgasm, a buzzing sensation comes from my phone where it has fallen down the side of my chair. I don't really know why I even have it with me. But my shaky fingers are grasping to fish it out of the crack between the cushion and the armrest, and I dread what I'm about to find there.

The notification lights up to reveal a new message from Ky.

It's a video attachment.

And the thumbnail on the screen is unmistakably a side-angle of my bare tits covered in his cum.

CHAPTER 20
FOX

Plunging beneath the water, I allow myself to get lost in that glorious weightless feeling. A sanctuary where my skin is caressed by a fine layer of minuscule bubbles; silence entombs me as I glide beneath the surface. Nothing quite compares to the sensation of being wrapped up in the quiet, buoyant embrace of the pool.

It's why I spend most of my days out here.

Not to mention that the place is a stunning tropical greenhouse, even though we're on a windswept peninsula and the world outside seems permanently shrouded in gray at this time of year. The summers in Port Macabre get stiflingly hot, but for now, it's autumn, and the forest is preparing to be claimed by winter's icy talons.

Much like I'm mentally preparing for the Pledging ceremony.

I don't care about having sex with multiple men. Nor do I care about being watched while enjoying sex. In fact, both of those things are sitting very high on my list of dream scenarios, considering my current situation in life and the three infuriatingly handsome men I'm forced to cohabit with.

But what sends my stomach curdling and a sick feeling running down my spine is the Anguis. Their archaic rituals and methods of controlling women and the twisted fascination they have with owning another human being like cattle.

Their customs and my father's empire are grotesque.

Pledging ceremonies and inspections fall amidst the archaic, ritualistic nonsense of a group like the Anguis. Perpetuating legacies of ownership and control of women in the elite Households. The kinds of practices passed down from days of kings, queens, and oligarchs. Women in positions of power who were forced to have witnesses to confirm their first fuck, and to give birth on a platform in front of a council to ensure the baby—and a bloodline—was not swapped at birth.

Stupidly, I believed these sorts of things were no longer used, even within the folds of this secretive world.

I don't want that to be my life, and yet these men are intent on forcing me to live through everything my father stood for.

How can I reconcile hating them for what they're putting me through while at the same time being intensely attracted to them?

When we're here at the compound, I am *almost* tempted to forget who they are and what they are entangled in as part of their secretive society. However, there's no forgetting. And I would be a fool to think for one second they care about anything more than revenge on my father or getting their dick wet. Or, as Thorne has made abundantly clear, he doesn't even consider me worthy of the latter.

Ky, on the other hand, is now a very present force in my daily life. Ever since our moment two nights ago, he's inserted himself in every way that he can until I can't turn around without him being there. If he isn't dragging me to the gym, he's texting me and flirting relentlessly, or he's like a shadow watching me from his spot on one of the stools in the kitchen.

Not that I am complaining. A shirtless Nordic surfer god is anything but a hardship to endure being around.

But other than doing his best to make me blush, he doesn't make a move.

Heated looks and wicked grins are thrown my way, but only ever from a distance.

Unless he's showing me things related to learning self-defense, Ky doesn't touch me. I still can't figure out what he meant the other night when he said that he's not supposed to.

He obviously did the night he snuck into my room, but I guess shooting cum all over my tits maybe doesn't count. He didn't actually *touch* me, technically speaking, in amongst our dirty little moment together.

Jesus, every time I think about what he did—what we both did—I'm a horny, flustered mess. I've watched the video he took at least a hundred times. While at first, I was spitting mad that he'd recorded me without my permission, I can't deny that it's filthy and degrading and turns me all the way the fuck on.

I bite my lip as I reach the far end of the pool. Has he replayed it, too?

An even dirtier thought crosses my mind. Did he send it to the others to watch?

Just allowing that door to crack open a fraction in my devious brain—imagining Thorne or Raven watching that video and wondering whether they might like what they see—sends a throb straight to my clit.

Throwing my head back with a frustrated growl, I let my body fall beneath the surface. Taking my sex-crazed mind and dunking her underwater.

That bitch needs to cool the hell down.

This meeting is dull as fuck.

Tell me what book you're reading.

And what color panties you're wearing.

Are they lace or silk?

Or...are you bare?

ROLLING MY EYES, I leave him on read. Ky is out with Thorne on whatever important murder-business they are required to attend to for the Anguis. I'm not answering him, even though he successfully tugs a smile out of me with his cheekiness. Not that I'd ever admit it to him, but Kyron Harris has absolutely got a charming aura and swagger about him that lets him get away with murder.

Quite literally.

Wolf boy has been a scarce sighting, like a rare species, a mythical creature who only appears once every now and then to feed on the souls of unwitting victims. So, considering that my three captors are all otherwise engaged, once again, I'm going to be rolling around the house on my own.

The auction is tomorrow night, and to ease my mind a little I'm planning on getting my outfit ready and doing some beauty pre-gaming. If I'm to be paraded in front of the Anguis once more, I've decided that I want to do so with the confidence of a woman wearing a suit of armor—one that comes in the form of looking and feeling my best.

Last time, I barely had five minutes to prepare. This time, I am determined to be ready with sharpened claws. While I was sitting by the pool this afternoon, I tried to list out all the little things Em would always bug me about remembering to do. Painting my nails, trimming up down there, moisturizing, deep conditioning my hair. All the tedious little girlie things that are one hundred percent the reason why Emerald Kirby is a rising star in the plus-sized modeling world, while I own a tattoo parlor where I can get away with wearing the same ripped black jeans for a week. Hell, I'm so useless at anything fussy like this. They're all the things I far too easily forget because, in my natural habitat, I am a low-maintenance bitch who regularly forgets to shave her legs.

Don't leave me on read, baby girl.

Those two broody assholes do it to me all the time.

Not you, too.

Ky follows up his little plea with a line of watery-eyed emojis. It's so ridiculous; my resolve breaks, and I start typing back something cheeky and maybe a teeny bit flirty. I bite my lip trying to think of a reply as I flip my towel over my shoulder and wander toward the kitchen.

A little harmless flirtation never hurt anyone, surely?

Only, that irresponsible line of thinking is rapidly erased when I round the corner and bump straight into a firm wall of muscle cloaked in black and blood.

I nearly drop the phone with a scream.

"Fuck. You scared the shit out of me." I'm clutching my towel and phone against my chest, heart pounding, and being stared down by Raven. His glare is pitch black, and one cheekbone is framed with the yellowing evidence of an old bruise.

He narrows his stare, dark hair hanging across his equally dark eyes, and tension crackles off him like a frayed wire. Threatening to spark and burn the whole place to the ground around our ears. He's got dried blood caked all up one side of his face, and the smell of woodsmoke and pine trees clings to him like he's been out in the forest. Or perhaps he's been burning bodies on a funeral pyre.

In one hand, he's fisting a jet-black motorcycle helmet. His other hand, with bruised and bloodied knuckles, is clenched by his side. A silver chain glints around his neck, hanging over a well-worn black t-shirt.

Raven looks like sin and sex and the worst decisions a girl could make.

"Did you just get back?" I swallow heavily. Nerves are prompting my mouth to move, when I know in my logical mind I should back away slowly and leave him be.

One side of his upper lip curls.

Shit.

"I'm going to..." This is absolutely the moment I make my hasty exit. So I duck my head and move to go around him while making doubly sure to allow a wide berth. Like a good little captive, I'm ready to scuttle off toward the kitchen and leave him well the fuck alone.

If only that was possible. I don't even make it one step before his tattooed hand collars me. As he pins me beneath a tight grip, my head thuds against the glass wall at my back. His strong fingers and thumb dig in at the sides of my throat.

There's nothing but malice filling his uncaring eyes. This man hates me with the force of an inferno fueling his rage, and even though he might offer me food and tolerate my presence here, something tells me he's in the mood to spill blood tonight.

And most likely, I'm his next victim.

His fingers tense around my windpipe. The kind of firm hold that tells me everything I need to know about how many times this man has watched the life drain from someone's eyes. But I'm not truly afraid. If anything, his tortured path is exactly why I chose to run away; he can't see past his own need for vengeance to understand that.

I don't judge him for that. I'd most likely do the same in his position.

He's boring holes through my skull with such ferocity in his expression that it sucks the air from my lungs. Without needing to say a word, he's telling me the story of his hatred with those void-like, soulless eyes.

My hands fall limp by my side. I'm holding a fucking pool towel and a cell phone, and I'm dressed in a crocheted coverall thrown over my bikini. What a way to draw in my final breath.

"Just...make it quick. Please." My voice rasps under the crushing weight of his palm.

Every ounce of his disgust for me pours forth, and the worst part is, I can empathize with him.

"I'm sorry for what they did to you. I'd hate me too if I was in your position." Something in me wants to try and tell him precisely how much I'm on his side, no matter what these men have threatened me with since they took me as their captive. If this is my last moment, I at least want him to know—even if he refuses to believe me.

He drives me harder against the glass, and I wince. Closing my eyes in defeat, the dull thud of my pulse sounds in my ears, and my lungs burn with the lack of airflow.

Just when I'm certain things are going to turn fully black, I feel it.

There's a gentle pressure as he sweeps the pad of his thumb across my cupid's bow. My eyelids flutter open and I'm staring at two eyes with fire smoldering in their dark depths. He traces along my bottom lip, this time pressing down on the middle for a long second.

It's over as quickly as it began. Raven shoves me away, leaving me spluttering for air. The man vanishes into the depths of the darkened house like the cloud of night he arrived wrapped up in.

While I'm left clutching my neck and struggling to regain my senses.

What the fuck was that?

More importantly...why did he let me go?

CHAPTER 21

FOX

If only Em could see me now, the girl would be deafening my ears like a screeching banshee. My best friend would be a proud lioness licking my face, telling me that I look like a sex kitten.

Because even I can acknowledge when I look good, and I'm particularly pleased with my efforts at donning my armor tonight.

This dress is a buttery soft fabric that molds to my curves like a dream. It's simple. Black, with a halter neck and a long flowing skirt that hits above my ankles to show off the satin bows tying my cute wedges in place. They're peep-toed, revealing my deep crimson polish that matches my fingernails.

Red for luck.

Or to represent the bloodbath that tonight might become if I'm not careful.

I don't give a crap if everyone else is teetering around on spindly heels; I'm going to be on my feet all evening, and past experience has taught me well that seductive skinny stilettos are for looking at, not for walking around in for any length of time.

While recovering from my run-in with Raven last night—trying to keep my mind occupied with anything other than fucked up thoughts about how it felt to have his hand around my windpipe—I ransacked through the boxes of all my things in search of this exact outfit. I knew if I was going to be thrown into the pit of savages, well, this was exactly what I needed to don in the face of impending battle.

Feeling like myself is the only way I'll be able to handle standing amongst their kind, plastering on a fake smile to appease this insanity.

Although I haven't yet had anyone else fully appreciate my efforts this evening, as Ky was required ahead of time at Noire House to get things prepared.

I hate that seeking out his approval, or some kind of reaction, was immediately where my thoughts drifted.

As for the other two, fuck knows where Raven has been. I thought I heard his motorbike sometime in the early hours of the morning, but that could have been wishful thinking on my part. I can only guess his absence is for the same reason.

Which brings me to the third of my murderous captors, Thorne, who succeeded in trapping me inside this silent car with him, only to promptly ignore my existence for the duration of our drive to Noire House.

Fine by me.

Even if I can't help sneaking a look at how faultlessly he fills out a suit as he folds himself into the car.

Christ. I'm reminded all over again why I fell for his stupid tricks in the first place. He's a work of art and a broody asshole—my worst kind of weakness.

As we pull into the gateway and enter the Noire Estate, I finally break the silence. If I'm supposed to follow their rules, I should at least have some idea of what they are.

"Is there anything I need to know about this evening?"

His massive hands flex around the steering wheel.

"Act as your father would have."

Ok, well, that gives me almost nothing.

"I don't know what he would have done. I never actually attended an auction."

"But you knew about them." He grits his teeth.

"Knew about their ulterior motives? Knew about the fucked up shit my father was hiding? As a teenage girl trapped in a world she had no choice but to be in?" My hackles rise, and I have to breathe slowly through my nose. "No, of course I didn't. Until the moment I *did*." The ominous facade with endless rows of windows comes into view as we wind our way along the snaking drive of the estate grounds.

"I don't buy that for a second."

Whatever. This man can think I'm worse than shit on the bottom of his shoe and I'll never change his mind. When it comes to men like Thorne Calliano there's no point wasting your breath trying. "Once I found out, that's when I ran." Looking out at the heavy, masculine exterior of the mansion I spy the familiar sight of gothic peaks and iron finishes.

He doesn't reply.

"I know you won't ever believe me. So why bother, right? You hated my father, but I can't begin to tell you the depth of my disgust for that man. So this is me telling you, I don't know how my father would have acted. I spent most of my time actively avoiding his presence." Blowing out a heavy exhale, I smooth the material of my dress over my lap. Trying to plead my case is more than a lost cause, it's like spitting into the face of a hurricane.

"You know enough. Be the heir to Noire House." His tone is final, and he pulls the car to a stop outside the front steps. There's a valet to greet him, and as he exits the car, I can see the woman in question is more security than actual valet. Thorne clearly knows her as they immediately clasp shoulders in that familiar bro-hug style that men tend to do with each other.

While there's nothing sexual in it, a little prickle of heat builds at the back of my neck seeing him with another female for the first time.

Fuck's sake. What is wrong with me that I'm this territorial over someone I can't stand to be around for longer than is absolutely necessary.

So I do exactly what the catty bitch inside my chest wants to do. Thorne Calliano wants me to be the perfect example of the heir to Noire House? Well, she is someone who does not tolerate anyone putting their hands on her property.

I slide out of the car, making sure to sweep my loose curls over one shoulder, and then slam the door with enough force to have the woman's head pop up and turn my way. She's dark-haired, fierce-looking, and absolutely stunning. The quintessential femme fatale you see cast as the heroine in movies.

Which is probably why I'm spurred on to round the front of the car and extend my hand in her direction, inserting my body between the two of them.

"Foxglove Noire." I purr, feeling Thorne stiffen beside me when I purposely brush against his torso. "You'll take care of my vehicle, I presume."

"Good evening, ma'am. Of course, it would be my pleasure." The other woman steps back with the keys she's been entrusted with, a bemused expression in her eyes as they bounce between me and Thorne.

"Thank you, you're too kind." Laying it on thick, I do my best impersonation of the rich assholes who frequent this place. Before she can get in the car, I stick my leg out through the slit of my dress, revealing my entire thigh and quite possibly my lace thong, but I don't fucking care. He wanted a show tonight, he'll get a fucking show.

"Thorne, baby, can you retie my bow for me? It feels a little loose." Fluttering my long eyelashes, I pout my lips a little and give him a coy look.

He returns it with one that says he wants to strangle me.

The woman holding the car keys chokes a cough into her fist. Yeah, she has most likely never seen anyone treat the great and powerful Mr. Calliano this way, and I'm eating up every second of this power struggle.

Will he give in all for the sake of his plan?

I nearly keel over when the mountain standing in front of me sinks down onto one knee, all the while keeping his steel blue gaze fixed on my face. He wraps a calloused palm around my offered ankle and tugs it toward him with a firm yank. The command in that one singular movement has a straight line to my pussy. His fingers drag over the sensitive skin as he takes the silk tie and unravels it with a painfully slow tug on the bow.

"Wouldn't want you hurting yourself tonight," he murmurs through gritted teeth while deftly re-tying the silk, and somewhere along the way, I've forgotten how to make use of my lungs during this entire interaction.

"Thank you, baby." The words feel heavy on my tongue. He continues to hold on to my ankle for a long moment; his fingers brushing over that sensitive spot that makes my knees go a little wobbly. And when he finally straightens back up and offers his arm to lead me inside the doors to the mansion, I don't even notice that the woman and our vehicle have long departed.

We've barely made our way into the foyer of Noire House before Thorne shoves a mask into my hands—one that is a skull designed to cover my eyes and my nose—and promptly evaporates like mist in the wind. He's lost to the crowd, and once again, I'm ambushed by every slimy asshole who pertains to be a friend of my late father.

They all wear similar skull masks that only partially cover their faces, as is the tradition of the Anguis. Most gatherings such as this, they will adorn themselves with a skeleton-like covering. It doesn't disguise their identities, but is an adherence to just one of their many inane society rituals.

Conformity. Reverence. Devotion. All in the name of the Anguis.

One by one, I'm pulled into hugs that linger too long and submit to hands that wander too freely over my body.

But I smile politely and greet them like they're the exact people I had hoped to see tonight. All the while, biting back nausea with every moment spent suffocated by their proximity.

"It is such an honor to have you here." One woman with horsey teeth and bleached hair strokes my arm. It takes everything not to flinch away from her touch.

"Here, let me help you with that, sweetie." Another woman swipes the mask from my hands and starts fixing it over my face for me.

Their presence is cloying and overwhelming.

Murmured words swirl around me. *Condolences for Andreas. We miss your mother terribly. What a shame to leave you all alone. Noire House mourns the loss of your father.*

God. I just want out from their insipid fawning.

"The selection for the auction looks wonderful tonight." A man with a flushed nose and dense eyebrows stares at me over his champagne.

"Will you be taking the opportunity to choose someone who fits your tastes, Miss Noire?" There's another man who I remember as being one of my father's friends, leering at me from behind the soulless eye sockets of his mask.

"I don't intend to place any bids tonight, no," I reply. My eyes scan the room, but the crowd is thick and surging toward the main hall upstairs, where the auction must be held.

Someone tries to press a glass of champagne into my hand, but I don't want to accept a drink from anyone in this vile place. My nerves are on high alert and after the calm of the forest at the compound, this feels oppressive and menacing.

God, I really am fucked if I'm finding myself eager to get back to the house where I'm being held as a goddamn prisoner.

"I'm sorry to interrupt, but there's someone asking for you." A warm palm wraps around my elbow, and with a flick of a hand, the unwanted drink is shooed away. My Viking steps in between me and the men who are busy staring at my breasts. He's a vision in his suit, earpiece in place, towering over me as always with a twitch threatening the corner of his lips. His mask disguises one side of his features behind the hollow cheekbones and sunken eye socket of a skeleton.

"Of course. If you'll excuse me, gentlemen." I've never been more relieved to see him, and my fingers itch to take his hand.

Ky nods at them all before gesturing for me to head in the direction of the enormous staircase. He trails behind me, and I shiver under the weight of his heated gaze as I make my way up the stairs.

There's no shame in the way I'm soaking up his attention on my ass right now.

"Holy shit. You could have warned me *that* was what you were going to wear this evening." His long strides catch up to me, and he hisses in my ear as we reach the upper landing. "I'm going to be fighting off packs of assholes from getting near you all night."

I bite back a small smile and glance at him coyly over one shoulder. "Well, I thought the idea was to assume the role of the Noire House heir?"

"If you look like that..." He stops mid-sentence, eyes ticking up to something that catches his attention, and I follow his line of sight.

What I see is Thorne, standing over by the far wall of the

landing. There are half a dozen people milling around up here, but they're all making their way into the auction.

But that's not what steals my attention.

He's with a girl.

Neither of them have a mask on.

Jealousy slithers down my spine. Is he trying to mess with me for my little performance outside?

I must be a fucking masochist because I can't stop staring at his imposing shoulders fitted to perfection inside that tailored jacket. My eyes are glued to his every movement, as if I need to prove to myself that it really is Thorne.

The girl is all over him. Her hands roam across those muscles encased in expensive fabric that I so badly want to touch.

But he hasn't invited me to.

And yet here this bitch is, drooling all over his suit and damn near humping his leg. Everything in her body language screams, 'This man fucks my brains out seven days a week and three times on Sunday.'

A familiar curdling sensation rises inside me. Shame and a sense of feeling more pathetic than ever. Obviously, this girl's bed is where Thorne Calliano disappears to during all those times when he's not around.

He's even told me that his sexual appetites are well taken care of, for Christ's sake.

I'm almost snarling—hypnotized and with a band cinching tighter and tighter across my chest—as his big hands reach for her. His thumb glides up her bare arm until he reaches around to cup the back of her neck.

There are a thousand reasons why I should look away.

Right now, I can't think of a single one.

Maybe I want to see it with my own eyes. See the way he takes her mouth, and that'll be the beginning and the end of this stupid infatuation festering behind my rib cage.

"Spying, are we, baby girl?"

The voice right at my ear has me stumbling. One heel wobbles beneath me, and it takes everything not to tip over.

Fuck. My head snaps up, and I'm looking into Ky's forest-green eyes, finding only mocking there. This asshole lives to see me suffer, I'm sure of it.

So, I do what any self-respecting woman in my position would do.

I go down swinging.

"Thorne can screw whoever he likes. It's none of my concern." My words are not elegant. I sound petty and a little too high-pitched. I'd love nothing more than to find an uncorked champagne bottle, pop it myself, and guzzle straight from the neck.

Maybe then I'll use it to club these men over the head and bash their skulls in. Or, perhaps swing it at their nuts.

Ky's gorgeous lips twitch. He looms large over me, even in heels, and props a suited shoulder against the pillar. As he scratches his trimmed beard on the uncovered side of his face, he glances over toward where I've been burning holes in the back of Thorne's stupid dark curls.

As I watch on, that's the moment it happens.

His head lowers and she opens for him. Blossoms and unfurls like a spring flower caressed by sunlight. Being good and obedient and all the things Thorne clearly wants in a woman. A knife stabs and twists in my belly as I'm unable to look away from the point where their lips touch. He wraps a hand beneath her jaw, and devours the bitch.

My pulse thunders so loud in my ears, I can't see straight. Thoughts of savagely tearing them apart and screaming in his face cross my mind for half a second. But I'm owed nothing by this man. I'm his captive. His payment in kind.

Why would he have any reason to look at me as anything more than a possession?

CHAPTER 22
FOX

My only means of escape from this hellfire is to bolt headlong in the direction of the auction.

A lump of burning coal sits in my chest, and I can sense that Ky is following me, but I can't bring myself to look at him.

Part of me wonders if he brought me up here simply to force me to witness that. But I also don't understand why, unless this is all part of their sick fascination with punishing me. Raw humiliation tingles through my veins, leaving me with a pit where my stomach should be.

Oh, how quickly Thorne flipped things around on me after my little power play outside.

He's a master at these contests.

Clearly, I have a lot to learn.

As I'm walking blindly toward the heavy double doors up ahead, I plow into an imposing figure. Blinking up at the familiar-looking suit jacket in front of me, I'm not sure what I'm seeing.

Thorne's blue eyes narrow on me from behind a skull mask, and he steadies me by my shoulders. Once he notices the point of contact between us, his big hands drop hastily away from my skin as if my touch is poison.

By this point, I'm a seething mass of emotions and utterly confused. He couldn't possibly have gotten over to this side of the room before I did...barely a second ago, he had his tongue shoved down some tart's throat.

I'm in the midst of trying to collect myself when the very bitch I want to grab by the hair and hurl down the stairs pops up by my side. She's all starry-eyed. Slightly flushed.

My gaze takes in a raft of details that I wish to hell didn't make her seem like the perfect little fucktoy to sate the appetite of Mr. Calliano. Dark, curious eyes. Hair like midnight falling in soft waves down her back. Full cherry lips. A tiny, bombshell package, a little shorter than I am.

Fuck her. She's a picture of flawless beauty, with curves for days and an air about her that says she owns the place. *I could take her.*

"I can't believe Thorne has taken this long to introduce us; I've been dying to meet you." She gives me a smile. One that I have no intention of reciprocating as I stare back with unbridled disdain. Who the fuck does this skank think she is?

Polyamory is the norm in the world we inhabit. I'm all for it. But there is not one single cell in my body that would be ok with sharing Thorne with this woman. With *any* other woman.

He scowls at Ky and barks something at him about needing to hurry up, before turning on his heel, striding through into the other room. Ky gives me a wink but remains by my side.

She watches the range of emotions battling with my face and then glances at the back of Thorne's shoulders stalking away from us.

It's only a beat before her hand flies up to her mouth. "Oh my god, he is such an asshole." She looks mortified.

I'm about ready to put my self-defense lessons to work and punch her in the vagina.

"God, I'm sorry, this is the worst introduction ever. I'm Poe, by the way, and I'm guessing he didn't tell you?" She gives the man beside me a withering look. "He didn't say anything, did he, Ky?"

My Viking shrugs, his eyes dancing with mischief.

"Tell me what?" I bite out.

She makes a noise somewhere between a laugh and a groan. "It's best if I show you."

As this bombshell before me turns around, I see her face light up like a ray of goddamn sunshine. Walking toward us from across the room—and the source of her visible swooning—is a carbon copy of Thorne.

What the actual fuck?

"Haven't you got shit to be doing, fuckface?" The Calliano-doppelganger scowls at Ky, and holy shit, he even sounds like Thorne.

"I'm running point for Fox this evening." Ky smirks. "Foxglove Noire, meet Hawke Calliano."

"Twins." The girl named Poe gives me an apologetic look.

Oh my god. My face takes all of a second to turn beetroot red, and I'm more than a little stunned.

I'm also relieved.

Though we're not examining the reason for that right now.

"Miss Noire." Hawke extends a hand that looks so much like Thorne's it's a little freaky. But as I take his palm in my own and give him a firm handshake, I notice the watch on his wrist is completely different. Then there's the tiniest scar beside his left eye. However, at a glance or from a distance, when you're being a jealous psychopath, they are exact replicas of each other. The likeness is more than a little eerie, to say the least.

He's also studying me with that same brand of wary indifference that Thorne has when he looks at me. I'm guessing his motives for revenge against my father align with his brother's. Which, by extension, means that he has no trust in me either.

"Come with me, Fox." Poe has glued herself to my hip. "I have an idea for a way that we can teach Thorne Calliano a thing or two about learning to communicate."

THE LITTLE WOMAN NAMED POE, whose full name is rather endearingly *Posey*, is a force to be reckoned with. She managed to efficiently dispose of Ky and has taken me through to the auction staging area out the back of the hall, going through the rear entrance to neatly avoid the entire crowd.

There's a burlesque show going on to warm them up prior to the bidding, so we're able to talk as she fusses over some of the final details.

"You run the club with Hawke?" I'm seated on a chair beside a makeup mirror and a row of large bulb lights, surrounded by gorgeous women who are all dressed in outfits that leave next to nothing to the imagination.

Some are only in lingerie and heels.

Others wear what might be loosely termed as dresses, but they're made of latex and feature tight bodices and matching collars.

Poe is evidently in her element, ensuring all these gorgeous women are suitably ready for their turn onstage.

It's odd to see someone feel so at home here when I lived under this roof for years and couldn't wait to escape.

"We do, and our relationship includes our two other partners, Grey and Angel, who we are also *with*. But Hawke isn't bi like his brother, he's only with me—Grey and Angel are both bi, though." She huffs a stray curl out of her face. "God, it gets so fucking complicated trying to explain the whole thing, but I know you understand."

I warm to her quickly, even though I'm still a little turned inside out by the whole twin-reveal thing.

"And you all run the club side of operations at Noire House?" I'm watching her as she checks off her list of girls for the auction, giving them various sets of instructions verbally as she goes.

"That's our role." She gives me a knowing look over one shoulder. One that says she knows what I know about Thorne Calliano's plans for the Anguis and my father's legacy.

"And you play your part in that." I finish for her, and she nods. We both are aware of what can and can't be said in places like this where the walls have ears.

"Your mother was Giana?" Dark eyes turn somber as she ticks off something from a run sheet.

Lump forming in my throat, all I manage is another nod in place of a reply.

Poe twists her lips. "I never met her, I only came to Noire House for the first time a little over a year ago and she'd been gone a long time before that. Well, that's what I've been told, anyway."

She doesn't offer apologies or condolences or any of that meaningless shit that won't bring my mother back. Which is a relief, to say the least.

"It's been a long time." Offering a shrug, I adjust myself in the seat.

"If it's any consolation, I know what it's like to come into this world...unwillingly." She offers me a sealed bottle of water from the table in the middle of the room. The space is supplied with all the things these girls might need before they're paraded out on stage and purchased for outrageous sums of money. "And strange as it might sound, it turned out to be the best thing I could have ever hoped for."

"Really?" Swigging from the bottle, I can't help but wonder what her story is. But we don't have time to get into any further details because there's movement, a flurry of feathers and sequins, as the burlesque performers bustle off stage. The main event is due to start any second.

"Ready?" Poe looks at me and flashes a wide, conspiratorial grin.

I bite my lip, then smile back at her.

"As I'll ever be."

CHAPTER 23

Thorne

"Welcome to you all, our Gathered, for this evening's annual auction of pleasures." The woman on stage commands every fragment of attention from the sea of skull masks filling the room. Her black bodice and fishnet tights glitter with diamonds set against her dark skin, and she has the audience eating out of the palm of her hand from the moment the spotlight falls on her.

My brother pays Keisha a fortune for her work here in the club, and she's worth her weight in gold. Her intel alone has been crucial to unraveling most of the trafficking operations we've been able to get to in the past year.

"Tonight, all successful bids will guarantee the winner a full twenty-four hours enjoying the company of your chosen prize...*exclusively*." A ripple of eagerness rolls through the crowd. "And while you have paid for the privilege of the company of these stunning jewels, of course the nature of how your time is spent is entirely your choice." Keisha winks and drags a finger seductively up the length of her thigh and then over her bodice. Catcalls and whistles ring out as the anticipation builds into a crescendo.

My brother, Hawke, and his partners Poe, Grey, and Angel run this side of Noire House. Between them, they manage the trade in consensual sex and pleasure that the mansion has become renowned for around Port Macabre. Coordinating these annual auction nights is all part of their repertoire to keep the customers satiated, their interests stoked—providing yet another opportunity for hedonistic escape.

Before Hawke and I had reached the levels we now have within the Anguis, and long before he succeeded in taking on the running of what is now one of the country's premiere sex clubs, it used to be nothing more than a sordid fuck fest. But the council, and even the elite members knew there was no way they could keep a lid on their secrets if things had been allowed to continue in the way Andreas Noire encouraged for so many years.

Which is why he sent his trafficking underground and established a formal club—a false frontage that kept his secrets concealed.

No one asks questions when they're balls-deep in the delivery of their perfect fantasy. All the while, the innocent have suffered the worst of the worst at the hands of certain members of the Anguis while hidden away.

While we're up here tonight, our team is intercepting the trucks bound for Noire House containing the real trade that was intended for the isolated basements deep in the bowels of the mansion.

Andreas Noire is dead, and from now on, there will be no more lives being bought and sold through this place.

Instead, we use these auction nights to plant people with those we desire information on. Another step in our plan to thin the herd of scum still hiding like cowards within the Anguis.

These women who are going to be auctioned tonight are the savviest, smartest individuals I know. It's only due to their business being in sex work that makes them stigmatized by society at large. When the reality is, they're more than capable of intellectually flogging every one of these pompous assholes. And they'll do so while wearing eight-inch heels.

In the months leading up to one of these nights, Hawke's team trains new recruits who go on to work at the club. If we get lucky, some might go undercover for the long haul, feeding back information on the Households and high-level members. Over the past few years, that has been our means of discovering many of those responsible for the trafficking rings we've destroyed from the inside.

I watch as the girls parade out on stage, each more gorgeous than the last—if that's what you're looking for. They're intelligent as fuck and can easily run rings around the likes of Andreas Noire's loyal followers and their flaccid dicks.

As I maintain my position overseeing the floor, the night draws on with a procession of bidding wars. These people should really feel ashamed for spending the amounts they have tonight. Men and women dropping eye-watering sums on something as frivolous as a night of sexual fantasies without so much as a second thought. But to them, money is no object. Lust and power and gluttoning themselves on pleasures are their ultimate cravings.

"Lastly, we have a very special treat for you all...a late addition to tonight's bounty on offer. One that is *not* listed on your bidding cards," Keisha announces, whipping the crowd into a frenzy as she gets set to open the bidding on whoever this final girl is.

From my vantage point overlooking the room, I narrow my eyes on Keisha. The run-sheet Hawke had provided didn't account for a bonus auction entry.

"For the first time ever in the history of Noire House, we have an elite Household member available for you to bid upon." Her voice is hushed into the microphone, and I can feel the visceral shift in energy ripple through the masked men and women seated in the hall.

Curiosity stirs.

Lilac curls swing into view as she emerges onto the stage. Still dressed in her black gown and heels from before, only now everything has been intensified—a darker shade of lipstick added; more dramatic eye makeup peeks out. Those bright blue eyes of hers are accentuated beyond belief despite the skull mask covering the upper half of her face.

She's wearing that fucking dress like a second skin, with her every curve caressed and highlighted beneath the sultry lighting on stage.

My fists curl by my sides. What the hell is Foxglove Noire doing, willingly entering as a piece of flesh to be sold off to the highest bidder? There's going to be a feeding frenzy any second now. Of course everyone in this room wants her, that much is obvious from the electric tension sparking in the air.

They're salivating.

I'm seeing red.

Some perverted old cunt thinks he can buy her and molest her and do whatever he wants with her? I'm not about to stand by and let that happen.

That girl belongs to me.

My jaw pops under the force of my teeth clenching together, and before I can make a move, Keisha announces that bidding has officially opened.

Everywhere I look, numbered cards fly up in the air immediately, and wild sums of money are yelled out in a cacophony of bids.

Ten thousand.

Twenty-five.

Forty large.

The sums being offered race past fifty thousand in a blink.

It's already at eighty thousand and climbing before I can unclench my fists or try to formulate a plan.

Moving through the seated attendees, I head toward the row of high rollers closest to the stage and rip some asshole's bidding card right out of his grubby hands. Ignoring the protests and shock from the table when they can tell, even hidden behind my mask, that I'm not one of *them*.

It crumples slightly inside my fist as I shove it in the air and bark a number at Keisha that makes more than a few people gasp. Eyes are on me, and that's the last fucking thing I need or want.

"Ohhh, I see we have a real contender here this evening." She gives Foxglove an appreciative look over, before gesturing toward me. "Five hundred thousand, for a night with the rarest jewel of them all."

Big Bambi eyes filled with the brightest blue imaginable are looking straight back at me. Growing wider by the second as she takes in what is happening.

Poe might be the brains behind this auction tonight, but if this goes sideways, she's going to find herself in a living hell. Hawke had better get his woman on a fucking leash and under control. I don't know what she thought putting on a stunt like this would achieve.

My feet carry me right up to the edge of the raised dais, so close I can feel the heat of the lights, and I've now officially crushed the numbered card tight in my grip.

I'm getting ready to drag Foxglove off that platform, by her hair if necessary, when I hear a noise behind me.

"Five-fifty."

"We have another contender." Keisha hums into the microphone, giving me a wicked look.

There's murder in my veins and an itch to rip my gun from its holster as I turn around. Seeking out whoever the cunt was that dared to place a counter-offer against me. Without looking back at Keisha, I've already announced my next bid of six hundred, which she repeats for all the crowd to hear. The hall falls into a hush, only punctuated by noises of intrigue.

The man who raises his number and outbids me by another fifty thousand is a face I know well. He's one of the men who has, time and again, purchased minors from Andreas Noire. He's a notorious sadist and pedophile, and my skin crawls just looking at him, with his thin face hidden beneath the mask of the Gathered and his graying comb over. He might be taking part in their ritual of wearing these masks for occasions such as this, but I would recognize him anywhere.

Ivan Victore is involved with the worst of the worst, the ones we are coming for next. And this whole scenario threatens to blow our hard work out of the water.

I'm the figure usually watching on from the shadows, while Hawke is the one those assembled tonight will be familiar with. And yet here I am, forced to stand in the middle of this sea of vile monsters and publicly bid against one of their own.

When all I want to do is put a bullet in this man's skull and set fire to this place with the likes of him and all Andreas Noire's accomplices locked inside.

This time, I raise the offer by a further hundred thousand. I've lost track of the total, but I know we're inching closer to a million. I couldn't fucking care less.

Knowing the monster this man associates with has me damn near crawling out of my skin. A thousand tortured memories come flooding back, and I'm fighting the urge to lunge across the satin tablecloth in order to tear out his throat with my bare hands.

He purses his thin lips, considering my bid. Then the man shifts his head to one side, looking first at me and then at the stage over my shoulder. There's no mistaking the way his eyes flick up and down, taking in the girl being paraded behind me. For a moment he drums his fingers on the card before finally, giving his head a slight shake and then sinks back in his chair. The asshole is the picture of relaxation; raising his glass to me in salute, and the applause filling the room confirming my victory is only a dull roar.

My skin feels like it's on fire beneath my suit. Forget tearing his throat out, I want to rip this man's head clean from his shoulders and shove his balls down his snapped windpipe.

Foxglove Noire has no idea what I'm capable of, and right now, it is taking every ounce of my self-control not to do something that will ultimately fuck up the plan we've been working toward for so many years.

The ghosts of the woman who claimed to be her mother echo everywhere in this place, and I'm heaving in deep, sawing breaths. Feeling strangled by this suit, the holster caging my shoulders, and the clouds of thick perfume filling my nose.

I stalk along the outer rim of the stage following her every move as my prize is guided toward the steps by Keisha. She reaches the top of the stairs, and that's when our eyes meet. Ky and Ven have appeared, lingering back ever so slightly, but they're here all the same. I don't need to look their way; they'll know this shit show wasn't on the cards for tonight.

No words are required for them to know how fucking furious I am.

The girl starts her descent, but pauses when she reaches eye level with me. Shoulders set, her face is filled with defiance, but I also detect a wariness there. She's intelligent enough to know that I hold her life in my hands, and that it would be beyond stupid to provoke me in any way.

"Thorne..." A little swallow hints at nervousness lying barely below the surface.

"Shut the fuck up." I hiss through gritted teeth, and she visibly blanches at my tone. "Get her out of here." Out of my sight. Whatever. The order is thrown in the direction of Ky and Ven, because I don't trust myself. Spending a second longer in such close proximity to the one person I want nothing to do with at this moment, there's a chance of doing something I might come to regret.

Without a second glance back at the girl I supposedly purchased for the better part of a million, I leave the heir to Noire House—the cunt everyone in this room wanted to purchase tonight—standing on the steps...alone.

Telling every single person watching on just how much I *don't* want her.

But making it abundantly clear that I *own* every single part of her.

All I want is to escape these sick bastards.

Thorne Calliano is the most callous and calculating asshole I could ever have the misfortune to meet.

I blindly race through the mansion, wrenching the mask from my face, coated in a blanket of sweat and humiliation. My only goal is to disappear into the garden outside.

Behind me, I hear Ky calling out my name—his deep voice echoes down the stairwell and off the marble flooring. I want to put an ocean of distance between myself and that room full of people who witnessed my shame served up on a gilded platter for all to see. Every cell in my body vibrates with a special kind of loathing and disgust after what he just did.

I *especially* want to put as much distance between me and Thorne as possible.

When he started bidding, it played perfectly into the plan that Poe had come up with while we sat together backstage. Only, there's no accounting for someone being a black-hearted dickhead with nothing but a toxic, malefic sludge running through his veins.

As I push my way through the doors at the back of the foyer and make my way down the familiar corridors of my childhood, I don't give a fuck if some slimy man tries to drag me into one of these side rooms tonight. I already feel cheap and used and discarded.

Thorne dropped an unfathomable amount of money simply to buy me out of that auction, which was what Poe assured me would happen, only to spit in my face with the way he cursed at me and stormed off in front of the Gathered.

Whatever he has planned for ruining my life and making me pay for my father's sins, he's certainly off to a flying start.

Consider him the victor this time around. My humiliation has been laid bare, much like I will be at the Pledging ceremony.

"Fox." Behind me, Ky's voice is close. Curt. But I don't dare stop. Tears sting the back of my throat, and if there's one place I've ever felt safe here, it's outside these walls, lost in the heart of these gardens. A place that became my refuge so many times as a child and then as a teenager. Running in this all-too-familiar direction feels like I've stepped back in time, and now I'm trapped in a loop from my past, one that seems intent on infecting my present and future.

"You can't run forever." There's taunting in his voice now. Hearing it makes my insides scream, and my skin crawls at the notion he's obviously laughing at me, too. This whole clusterfuck played perfectly into their plan to skin me alive in front of the Anguis.

Parading me around as their pet and their possession was all part of their vengeance. I guess they've already succeeded twice now on that account.

The chilly night air hits my skin once I burst through the set of French doors, but I don't pause. My rushed steps carry me straight toward high hedges. Walls of topiary illuminated by the glow spilling from the upper windows of the mansion.

There's a formal garden out here, not a maze as such, but it is filled with towering lengths of greenery trimmed into immaculate rows, and in the light of day there are endless alcoves and hidden corners. To the uninitiated, it would be easy to get lost, especially in the dark, but I lived here for years and spent as much time as possible in these secret hideaways.

If there's one thing I know how to do successfully on the grounds of Noire House, it is to disappear.

These assholes can hunt for me all night long and they'll be lucky if they so much as catch a whiff of my scent. Unless they *have* put a tracker in me like a part of me suspects. Well, in that case, I'm as good as a fish snagged on the end of a lure. Every time I try to escape they'll just reel me back in, foul hooked, with a barb of shiny metal gouged through my cheek.

"Wouldn't want to get caught out here in the dark, would you?" Ky calls out. His voice draws in closer, off to my left and running parallel to where I am. So I change direction abruptly, heading for where I know there is a large fountain and narrow openings between the hedges I can slip through if I shimmy my way between them.

"Where do you think you're going, hmm?" Ky taunts.

His cruel laugh rolls through the night air. Following after me, nipping at my heels like a ghostly apparition. Even through the dark his presence envelops me with his cold, ruthless menace.

Another eerie chuckle makes my fine hairs stand on end. "There's nowhere you can hide."

My palms are clammy as all hell and the pressure of blood rushes in my ears.

"What do we get if we catch the little slut?" He crows amidst the blanket of darkness. Raven has remained silent, worryingly so, and that flips my already heightened emotions into something more panicky. All in the space of a few heart-beats, the energy has morphed.

Now it feels as though they really are on the hunt out here.

Do I want to know what happens if they catch me?

"Run all you like. You can't escape, not from us." The threat rings out across the shadowy pathways and neatly ordered hedgerows. It's almost pitch black, and the only reason I know where to go is from years of memory coming back in a flood. At this point, it's more instinct and a desperate sense of self-preservation than anything spurring me on.

My heel catches on a stone on the paved footpath, and I lurch sideways, but instead of falling to my hands and knees, I crash into the firm row of foliage. It rakes across my skin as if I've been scraped by hundreds of fine teeth, leaving a bitch of a sting radiating down the length of my arm.

A gasp rushes out of me, and I slap my hand over my mouth. The noise would have sounded like a firecracker going off in this enclosed space.

There's no time for me to stop and think. Instead, I rub my scraped shoulder to ease the burn and carry on.

Reaching the end of the long hedge that I'm following, I round the corner, preparing to bolt deeper into the walled garden. That's when rough hands grab me from behind, covering my face and my torso. My heart is about to leap out of my throat, and I make a noise like a feral tomcat, struggling against the fingers digging into my cheeks and the curve of my stomach.

It's Ky. There's no mistaking his body and scent and the heat radiating off him against my back and shoulders. Even as I writhe to fight against his grip, a shudder passes over my bare skin pressed along the length of his torso.

"I've always wanted to chase a pretty little slut through these gardens and fuck her." His mouth is right at my ear, and his breathing is heavy—not with exertion, but with anticipation.

Holy shit. My brain and my body are at war over how to react. His words ooze with twisted fascination that feels like a drug. Adrenaline floods my veins to form a potent concoction of liquid gasoline merged with white-hot sparks. Each attempt at a further struggle only cinches my body tighter inside his clutches.

Once again, I'm reminded of exactly how pathetic I am when it comes to defending myself. My futile attempts at learning have gotten me nowhere if this is how easily a man like Ky can overpower me.

That thought draws a snarl out of me. Fuck this. I refuse to go down without a fight, and he hasn't pinned my arms or legs. So I kick out at the inside of his foot with my heel. I don't connect properly, but I'm pretty sure I connect with something solid and manage to bash his ankle bone. Following that, I thrash backward with my elbow, aiming for his groin or his stomach or anywhere really that might do some damage.

His hold on me loosens, not by much, but just enough that it incites me to keep resisting, and I bite down on his fingers covering my mouth. There's wetness over my lips instantly, and a coppery taste springs onto my tongue. But I don't linger to contemplate the fact I just drew blood; instead, I make a run for it. There's a menacing hiss that surges behind me as I sprint toward the deeper, darker heart of the garden. A place where the hedges tower higher and the faint moonlight barely reaches the footpath in front of me.

Only, in my haste and panic, I've forgotten a vital detail. Ky isn't hunting out here alone.

I barely make it a further ten feet before a figure looms up ahead. The wolf himself materializes out of thin air like an apparition. His silver chain glints at me, while the rest of Raven blends into the night like he's composed of shadow and malice rather than flesh and bone.

He doesn't reach out and grab me, but his presence causes me to falter. As my brain and body collide, understanding dawns upon me in a chilling sweep along my exposed skin, I draw up short and stumble.

That's all it takes.

A hand roughly fists my hair and yanks my head backward this time. Ky's short beard grazes the side of my jaw while his other hand is hungry and demanding, grabbing at the material of my dress covering my stomach. The action digs into the softness of my flesh at the same time.

Behind me, I'm surrounded by the solid wall of him.

He's pinned me in place, facing the shadowy figure of Raven, who stands before me like a nemesis from the dark.

"Get your filthy fucking hands off me." My growl is punctuated by a wince as he tightens his grip on my hair. The sting radiates across my scalp like a thousand pinpricks.

"Such a desperate slut. Don't you think she makes a good prize for us, baby?" Ky ignores my protests and speaks to the man standing in front of me. Oh, god. The way he's talking so casually, like I'm not even here...there's no reason why that should send a flood of arousal through me.

"Thorne doesn't even want her, but she's begging to be stuffed with cock." He carries on. Tugging my head against his chest, forcing my back to bow as a result of his brutal hold.

He doesn't want me.

Ky's words remind me of exactly how and why I've ended up here like this, and I'm pulsing with a special kind of fury. One fed by the cocktail of every emotion I've been through in the past weeks since they came after me.

I'm a tempest ready to take down the entirety of Port Macabre.

"You're pathetic." Spit flecks my mouth, and Ky chuckles darkly against my ear.

The proximity of him and heat from his mouth sends sparks of goosebumps erupting across my skin.

"What do you say, baby? I think it's about time we taught

the slut a lesson for trying to run from us." Raven still isn't replying, but I sense him shifting in the lengthy shadows. His presence draws closer, and tension winds tighter in my stomach.

"Wouldn't you love to have her perky tits bouncing in your face while she rides my cock?"

There's a whimper forming in my throat, but I swallow that bitch down. "I'm your worst fucking nightmare. Let me go."

"Oh, I don't doubt that for a second. Our mayhem and fury and revenge all wrapped up in one pretty little package for us to ruin."

His free hand roams over my body in a possessive claim. Ky explores me with the determination of a man who has been denied and tempted for far too long without respite. Whatever held him back before now has evidently dissolved into the inky blackness enveloping the three of us. I'm fighting the urge to cant my hips as his searing hot palm explores my figure. First sliding over my covered breasts, then down to cup my pussy through the soft material.

"Don't touch me." Lies fall from my lips as I squirm beneath his brutal hold. Following the curl of his fingers, I'm subtly rocking against the heel of his palm within a second.

God, I'm nothing more than hunger and need.

"Jesus. I guarantee she'll beg for your cock so pathetically, baby." Ky presses harder, heat radiates from my pussy straight through my dress. "Just the way you like it."

CHAPTER 25
FOX

This shouldn't be turning me on.

I'm angry right down to the depths of my soul.

But these men can make me feel something else, and tonight, I want to reach for anything that will replace the humiliation of the auction. Whatever I can clutch onto, other than this current sensation of unwantedness, I plan on grabbing tightly with both hands. At my core, I'm exhausted. Sick of the overwhelming sense of being out of control. Let them do whatever the fuck they want to my body and make me forget all about the wretched state of my life.

Even if it might spell my ruin, I choose to play by their rules.

"Please don't make me do this." There's a small part of me tucked away that might actually mean those words. However, she's been overruled by the horny devil currently behind the wheel. The one who wants to fuck all thoughts of Thorne Calliano out of her system.

Ky clicks his tongue, then shoves me down onto my knees. The slit in my dress allows the material to bunch up, and my skin scrapes heavily against the cold, rough footpath. He readjusts his grip at the base of my skull and positions himself in front of me.

"Are you going to force me?"

He tilts his head to one side. "I bet you'd like that a little too much." I can practically hear his wicked smirk.

There's an unnerving energy radiating from Raven, who stands beside him; everything about him feels predatory. With Ky, I know there's a twisted sort of match we're both playing, but with him...I'm not sure if it's a *game* or if he would actually force me against my will. He's unpredictable, and that sends a shudder down my spine.

A fresh flood of wetness coats the inner swell of my thighs. I can't help squeezing them together.

"Stick your tongue out, slut."

Well, shit, this is really happening. Dutifully, I open my mouth, and straight away, Ky uses his free hand to shove his middle and ring finger in before I come to my senses and change my mind. Pressing down so hard and so far back that I start to choke, saliva rapidly pools at the corners of my mouth.

Ky makes a disapproving noise, a tongue clicks from behind the skull mask, while his fingers rock back and forth, making me gag.

"You willingly put yourself in that auction. What were you planning on doing, hmm? Going to spread your cunt wide for any perverted old fuck who decided to buy you?"

I make a rough sound around his fingers. Spit runs down my chin and my eyes water.

That results in a hypnotic tilt of his head. "We're going to use you exactly how you were willing to be used. Did you think putting yourself in that auction would save you from us?" His masked face is mostly hidden within the shadows, but I know there's a snarl curling his lips. I can hear it.

"We own you, sweetheart. And you're going to obey us for the rest of your life, so you might as well make yourself useful."

My knees howl like a bitch, while my clit throbs at his heartless words, and I don't understand why my body is reacting this way. So eager for his cruelty.

"Thorne purchased you and didn't even want you...but your cunt has been paid for, so go on and be a perfect little whore for us, baby girl." He lowers his fierce, Viking features to mine, and I can only see black in his normally green eyes. "You're going to be nothing more than a hole for us to stick our dicks into at the Pledging ceremony, so now's the perfect time to break you in. Our own dirty little toy."

Tears fall down my cheeks, no doubt taking my makeup with them. The worst part in all this, is that Ky is right. I willingly got up on that stage, and there was every risk that Thorne—or either of these men standing before me—wouldn't succeed in winning the bid for my body. Poe had assured me she had a foolproof plan, that Hawke would step in if needed, but the whole point of the evening was to sell pleasure.

I offered myself up in return for cash. Turns out I'm about to reap the consequences of my actions with the very men who already claim to own me.

"Take my cock out." When Ky speaks next, I'm nothing but the perfect slut who obeys. Fumbling with his belt and zipper in the dark until I free his erection; that silver barbell glints at me in the faint moonlight as it bobs in front of my face. The sight of him makes my mouth water, and I can hardly see his expression, but I look up at him with pleading eyes all the same.

He pulses his two fingers against my tongue.

My pussy clenches, imagining what they would feel like repeating that same movement while shoved deep inside me.

"Be a good little whore for us, and you might even be allowed an orgasm tonight." Just at the point that my jaw really starts to burn, Ky lets me go. But it's only for a second, barely long enough for my throat to work down a swallow before he strikes. Replacing his fingers with the pierced head of his cock, which I greedily take into my mouth.

He's smooth and velvety, invading with the abundance of cocksure energy that comes so naturally to him. The unfamiliar sensation of metal glides over my tongue as his musky scent fills my nose. Fuck, he fills me perfectly, and the taste of him leaves my eyes wanting to roll back in my head.

"Goddamn." The grunt of dark pleasure in his voice does indecent things to my insides. With heat pooling low alongside the unrelenting ache in my pussy. What I want to do is plunge my hand between my legs and rub my clit while he fucks my throat. However, I haven't been given permission for that, and I suspect he's testing the precise extent of how *good* I'm willing to be for him.

For them both.

"That dirty fucking mouth." Ky holds my hair on top of my head and thrusts his hips forward. "So damn pretty like this."

I do my best to gaze up at him, lapping and slurping around his thick length, focusing on breathing through my nose as he picks up the intensity and hits the back of my throat. Over and over. His grunts filling the darkness are the sexiest fucking noise, and this filthy scene we're creating right here is exactly what I've been starving for. To be used by them and treated like their perfect plaything.

But it isn't long before he pulls out, leaving a long trail of saliva hanging down my chin. He swipes away the mess with his thumb, bringing it to his own mouth.

A whimper of protest escapes me, while my knees are scratched the fuck up; my thong completely soaked.

"Enough of a show for you, baby? Let me see you fuck our slut's mouth." The taste of Ky still lingers on my tongue, and yet I'm a shivering mess in anticipation of what Raven will be like. What his cock will feel like in comparison.

This time, I don't move to take him out. I sit back on my

heels, obediently waiting. There's an unspoken line in the sand here, where this man only does things on his terms. I suspect he's still coming around to the idea of having anything to do with me—the person who represents everything he hates—let alone fucking me.

Silver flashes on his fingers as he undoes his belt. The clank of the buckle has my clit pulsing like some kind of automatic response to this man. Anticipation of what might come next leaves me panting.

How far will he be willing to go if I can prove to be good enough for him?

Raven looms out of the dark, still hidden by the night and the skull covering half his face, but even so, the heat of him draws near. He's got his cock in his fist, and holy fuck. This man is thick and veined, and the head is swollen with a glisten of wetness already formed at the tip. I lick my lips and once again stick out my tongue.

There's no preparing myself for him. One hand collars my neck from the front to hold me in place as he drags the fat head over my bottom lip. Smearing pre-cum, before shoving his cock in my mouth without warning.

I don't have time to adjust. It's rough, and he uses me; taking his pleasure with firm thrusts that hit the back of my throat straight away. He has me gagging around his length and quickly turns me into a drooling mess.

When movement stirs behind me, I can't help but moan with my mouth full of his gorgeous dick. God, I hope this is the point where someone fucks me because I'm going to combust otherwise.

"Help me move her," Ky says.

Raven's cock slips from my mouth with a wet pop. My dress gets shoved up, and I'm being repositioned with an arm banded around my middle to hoist me off my knees and onto my feet. I reach out and grab onto Raven's thighs for support. I'm not sure if he'll even allow me to touch him like this, but it's the best I can do considering the circumstances.

Ky is a man possessed, tugging the drenched scrap of fabric to one side. "You're soaked. So fucking desperate for this, aren't you?"

Leaning over my back, he bites down on my shoulder, and the shock of the sting causes me to jerk beneath him. The frantic pulse between my legs only intensifies.

"This gonna get you off, is it? Knowing you can't fight against us must do it for you."

My eyes slam shut as I focus on taking a few steadying breaths, absorbing the blow of his crude words.

That's when he chooses to strike. His heat and powerful frame disappear from where he'd been up against my spine a second ago, and his mouth covers me from behind. Every scrape and bristle of his beard has me gasping. Slutty sounds burst out of me—he's ditched his mask, and his tongue dives into my wetness. As he tortures my pussy, I slide my lips back over Raven's cock, working him like it's my only job to make this man come down my throat.

Like my life depends on it.

Which, in a twisted way, maybe it does.

I'm shaking as Ky works me with his tongue, and his short beard scratches against my sensitive flesh. He's licking and sucking and swirling in all the right places as he eats me out until there's no way I can hold on any longer.

Moaning around Raven's length, I really should have known better, the asshole isn't doing this for my benefit. Ky pulls away just as I'm teetering on the edge. Instead of tumbling into an orgasm, my ass stings unexpectedly with a searing pain.

A smack.

At the same time as the sharp crack blooms across my ass cheek, the cock in my mouth blocks my airway. A muffled cry of pain escapes as a result of the joint force of the slap and need to swallow around his tip at the same time. Sensation roars through me like a stampede and my clit throbs with a heartbeat of its own.

Raven's hips draw back, allowing me to suck in a couple of shaky breaths, but his fingers exert more force, tightening around my throat. He gives me no warning before his hips shove forward again, finding a punishing rhythm. I think he's getting close, and I'm floating away on the torrent of sensation, overwhelmed by what they're both doing to me.

Several more sharp strikes rain down on my exposed ass cheeks. Searing heat coats my skin and I'm growing wetter by the second, feeling his palm imprint itself on my flesh.

"You wanted some stranger to do whatever the hell they wanted to you for twenty-four hours?" Ky punctuates his gruff words with more stinging slaps, alternating from one side to the other. "Now you get to face the consequences of trying to escape us, even for just a short amount of time."

The wolf in front of me, who fills my mouth with his cock over and over, doesn't care about my bruised lips or my muffled protests and cries. He's taking every ounce of what he desires, wringing out his pleasure while maintaining a tight grip on the front of my neck.

The sensation of him holding me like that alone causes my pussy to ache. Apparently, I'm a whole different level of slutty for Raven flexing his strong fingers around my windpipe.

Each time his cock hits the back of my throat, he lightly squeezes, making low, filthy noises of pleasure.

I'm nothing but theirs to use, and I've drifted off into that perfect space where I let go and give over command of my body.

In a normal world, especially inside the club, there would be limits and safe words and aftercare. But everything in our lives is fucked up. So I enjoy the way they're giving me exactly what I need, in its own twisted way.

"Jesus. Fuck." Ky grabs my hips from behind, and the head

of his cock presses against my entrance. "You better come at the same time I do, baby." He grunts at Raven.

"Hurry up and fuck the slut already."

Shit.

It's the first time the other man has spoken, and his voice is a deep, gravelly tone that hooks in behind my ribs. His words are rough and crude, and absolutely should not feel like he's given me a shiny star for being a hole he can use to get himself off. But I'm hanging onto those words like they're comprised of gold dust and not at all like they're spoken to me while he fucks my face in a darkened garden.

Ky lets out a hissing noise of pleasure as he sinks inside me all the way to the hilt. I'm so fucking wet he glides in easily. His hips meet my ass, and he holds there for a moment.

"Christ, she's so fucking tight." He digs his fingers into the fleshy part of my hips. "Our perfect toy to play with whenever we want."

His cock is stretching me, and I'm being dragged toward the orgasm I've been denied until now as he begins to pump his hips.

I'm moaning desperate noises around Raven's cock. Incoherent sounds that are something like *yes* and *please.*

"Come for me. Show us who you belong to."

There's no stopping it. I'm coming. The feel of Ky's length dragging against my inner walls and the way his piercing is hitting just the right spot has me tumbling straight into my climax.

By this stage, I've lost all technique with Raven's blowjob, he's using my mouth to chase his release, and his cock kicks before the salty tang of his cum bursts across my tongue. Obediently, I swallow down every last drop. Grunts and a dark-sounding noise fill the air as my throat works, and that must set Ky off.

"Fuck. *Fuuuuck.*" His cock sinks deep, then pulses, and he fills me up, thrusting as his release jets inside me.

Everything from tonight hits me at once. I'm limp and groggy and more than a little messy. My knees smart, my jaw aches, and as Ky slips out of me, a track of wetness runs down my thighs to add to the residue coating my tongue.

Ky swipes the flat of his hand through the mixture of my arousal and his cum, before reaching around, covering my mouth with his palm, and pressing two fingers past my lips.

"So goddamn sweet. Taste us, baby girl."

Without hesitation, I do as he says. Licking at his palm and swirling my tongue all over his fingers while he hums a dark sound of approval.

"That's it. Clean up every last drop."

Holy fuck. The coarse edge of lust to his words leaves me spun out of my mind with pleasure and the overwhelm of sensations...trying to maintain some kind of grip on my sanity. Can I rationalize what just happened? Should I?

Somehow I suspect there is no need for rational thought where Kyron Harris, or these other men are concerned.

Sounds around me blur and turn fuzzy as it becomes tempting to curl up and sleep right here in the gravel. I think the two of them might be talking to each other over my head, but I don't catch what they're saying. At least, for the moment, I'm floating on a cloud of euphoria, with my body humming a tune I could very much get used to. All thoughts and feelings from earlier have flown away on orgasmic wings, and heaviness lures my eyelids closed.

The comedown will arrive soon enough, but for now, I'll happily hide out here...a little while longer.

CHAPTER 26

Ky

The urge to keep this girl tucked up against me for the rest of the night is all-consuming. But she needs her own space to properly decompress after everything that happened at Noire House this evening.

After the garden-fuck-fest, Ven and I got her back to my car, where she promptly curled up in the front seat and went to sleep. Not that I'm surprised.

Tonight was...a lot.

Finally, getting to fuck her and share her with Ven, well, that was an unexpected turn of events. There's no way that's going to be the only time it happens either. The feel of her tight, velvety channel gripping my cock while she fell apart is going to be hard to ignore anytime I look at her from now on. I've never experienced anything like her. Our new toy is the hottest goddamn cunt I could have ever dreamed of.

And she's all ours.

Fox had better get used to the idea that this wasn't a one-time-only thing.

Besides, I could see in Ven's eyes that he would have fucked her, too, if we'd had more time. But as it was, we messed around in the gardens long enough for one night.

He took off on his bike to head back to the compound, leaving me to drive the girl home on my own. Which was absolutely fine by me. A girl covered in my cum and smelling like filthy sex in the front seat of my car? I'm already imagining all the ways I can have her looking exactly like this over and over again.

Used and gorgeous.

Looking like she belongs to me. *To us.*

Although there's one dick in the equation who needs to get his head out of his ass.

Reluctantly, I put her in her own bed—rationalizing that even if I can't force her to sleep in mine, yet, I'll at least help her change out of her dress, wipe off her makeup, and make sure she wears one of my t-shirts.

She's half asleep and so damn pliant, I'm permitted to do whatever. Fox doesn't seem to care. My dick stirs at that little bit of further confirmation as to this girl's *likes.*

After all that's done, I go seeking out the man himself.

I find Thorne sitting out on the large porch by the back of the property. The skies have called a truce and cleared, revealing a carpet of stars littering the inky black vista above us.

He's got a beer that he's nursing. I spy another one sitting on the floor beside his foot and swipe it before collapsing into the chair across from him.

Fuck, he looks so somber and angular in the warm amber light coming from inside the house. The glow pours over the wooden decking like honey, offering just enough illumination to sit out here with only the quiet of the forest for company.

"Hawke sent through the details of who has been assigned to which targets." I twist the lid off my beer, and it lets out a satisfying hiss. We'll be working through information gathered as it comes back from the girls won at the auction over the coming weeks. For some of them, it might become a longer-term assignment, but we'll only know more after the next twenty-four hours are up.

Thorne nods and tips the neck of his beer back.

I can't help watching the way his throat bobs as he swallows.

It sends that same old familiar feeling of longing whirling inside me. One that I've learned to smother and shove down and do my best to ignore for a very long time.

After a pause, he drops his head back to rest against the top of the chair. Staring up at nothing in particular with a heaviness coating his shoulders.

He's ditched the suit and wears a pair of sweats with a long-sleeved t-shirt. Even though the autumn night is crisp, his feet are bare. While Thorne always looks like a fucking perfect specimen of muscle and power, I soak up any opportunity for a glimpse of him like this. When he seems most himself.

"You fucked her." He states. Keeping his eyes turned to the night sky.

"She needed it." I shrug. It's the truth. There was nothing we did tonight that Fox didn't want us to do with her. Even if her mind isn't fully on board, yet.

"Ven, too?"

Using my bottle to hide my smirk, I wonder if Thorne realizes how transparent he really is underneath all that bullshit he wears like a shield.

"Do you want me to draw you a fucking diagram or what?" I tease.

Thorne growls.

"Or would you prefer photos instead?"

His head snaps up, and his eyes are ice cold. Or maybe they're burning hot. Glaring with that look he's given me ever since I was a skinny little kid and the Calliano twins saved my life.

Whatever. He can try to intimidate me with those gorgeous eyes all he likes. Either way, that little detail grabbed his attention, even if he's trying to persist with this charade that he's not interested in Fox, for now.

Not that I have any photos from tonight, mind you. Of course I don't, I was too busy chasing a pretty girl in the dark to be recording anything, but I'm not going to tell him that. Fuck, I wish I did, though. Ven looked so good fucking her mouth; I almost lost it seeing them together like that. But I do store that little piece of information away for later. It seems our mighty Thorne Calliano might be more of a voyeur than I thought.

I decide to leave him to it, but not without stirring shit first, because I am who I am.

As I walk past, I bump the neck of my beer against his. "Thanks for buying her for us to play with, by the way."

His sapphire eyes narrow on me.

"Shame you didn't get the chance to feel what a tight pussy worth a million bucks feels like when she comes all over your cock."

CHAPTER 27
Ven

I've thrown enough punches at this goddamn bag to leave me doubled over, dry heaving.

One corner of our custom-built gym is set up for me to train in. With boxing equipment and heavy ropes, shit that I can hit hard.

By the time I've put myself through a punishing workout, some of the tension has been purged from my system. But I'm still on edge.

What I'd usually do at a time like this, when my blood feels like it's going to burst from my body in a torrent, is head for the forest. There's an isolated cabin hidden away deep in the trees off one of the dirt access roads, only accessible by hiking in on foot or taking my bike, and not even Ky or Thorne know where I disappear to when I'm up there.

Just the way I fucking like it.

It's better than me risking losing my shit at them or hurting them...or worse. They get it, and they don't question me, but even though I want to vanish into the mist right now, I can't leave.

A phone call is due to come in, providing the details of my

next target. The when. The where. The who. So, until that happens, I'm stuck here at the compound with a leash on my patience that is threatening to snap at any moment.

If I wasn't so keyed up, I'd roll out my muscles and use the sauna. But I can't be fucked with any of it, so I settle for a hot shower instead. Afterward, I can slip away for a long drive somewhere on my bike and at least wait out the call in a wide, open space where the creatures in my mind can roam freely.

At times, being here inside these four walls feels like being stuck inside a cage.

Even though I know that isn't my life anymore.

The rainfall shower head starts steaming a few seconds after I flip it on, and the tiled walk-in bathroom begins to dampen as the heat from the water takes hold.

"You look like you could use a hand in here, baby." Ky strolls in just as I'm stripping off my top, and his grin is a mile wide.

I toss the sweaty singlet at him. "Yeah, you can wash that for me."

He's never shied away from my darkness. Always coaxing me back to the light, time after time, when he's got more than enough of his own shit to deal with.

"Tempting. But I've got a better idea."

As I lean back on the vanity in front of the mirror, I cross my arms. He's in the mood to mess around, and I can't ever seem to deny this man.

"Planning on being a good boy for me, are you?" My cock wakes up at the sight of him, shirtless as always and fresh out of the pool from the look of it.

"The best." Ky's green eyes dance over me and I don't hate the way he openly admires my body. He's gorgeous, but for whatever fucking reason, he seems to be able to look past all my shit and stays, even when I tell him he'd be better off without me.

"Your cock gets a taste of fresh pussy, and now look at you.

Desperate for a fuck wherever you can find one." I taunt him. Knowing fully well he loves it when I'm like this.

Ky shivers, closing the distance between us. His thick length is already hard against the front of his swim shorts, and his tanned skin is damp. I don't know how he manages to look rugged and pretty all at the same time, but his long hair is tousled and wet, and I want to sink my fingers into it while he's on his knees for me.

"Hmm." He reaches for my shorts and runs a hand over my hardening dick beneath the fabric. "I can tell you now, you'll feel the same way once you know how she grips your cock like a dream." His palm cups me and squeezes until I let out a hiss.

"You say that like it's a foregone conclusion."

The gold flecks in his eyes glint with mischief.

"It's only a matter of time, baby." Over the top of my shorts, he works me harder now. Rubbing and teasing while his other hand does the same to himself. We're standing chest to chest in the swirling cloud of steam while the waterfall of the shower pours in the tiled area to the side of us.

Ky's gaze drops to my mouth, and that's my fucking weakness. I hate kissing, but with him, he makes it seem like the most natural thing in the world.

"Let me take care of you," he murmurs, and who am I to say no to an offer like that.

"Are you going to beg for my cock?" I reach up and grab his jaw. The way his short beard cuts into my skin is so fucking addictive. Feeling that firm scrape and scratch is a sensation I find myself chasing, and I crush my mouth against his.

I love it when he's like this. My good boy who bends for me and never breaks.

We're nothing but teeth and licks and hard nips at each other's lips and jaw. I suck hard on his tongue, and Ky absolutely melts for me.

Yeah, he fucking loves it when I do that.

The darkest part of me eats up every drop of his groaning pleasure against my mouth.

He fumbles to get rid of both our pairs of shorts. When it comes to the two of us, we always seem to be starved for one another.

His rough palm wraps my rigid cock, and he makes a satisfied noise in that deep, commanding tone that rumbles right through me.

"Shower. Now." I bite down on his bottom lip, plant one hand on his chest, and shove him backward.

Ky takes up a spot against the far wall, grabbing a bottle of something soapy and squeezing a few pumps into his hand.

"Get that big dick of yours over here." He arches for me against the wall, and his pupils are blown out. I'm buzzing beneath my skin as I cage him in, with my arms pressed on the tiles on either side of his head. Spray from the water pounds down and hits my back while the faint scent of sandalwood soap twines with the steam.

He grabs both our cocks and firmly grips them together.

"*Fffuck.* Yes." God, his firm grip makes all the blood run to my groin. I drop my head forward against the crook of his neck. "Just like that."

With long, firm strokes, Ky works both of us at the same time. Rubbing our cocks together and letting the slick glide of the soap build us both into a frenzy.

I sink my teeth into his neck.

We're both panting and grunting. The sounds of us chasing our release together echo around the dark tiles on the walls and floor.

"Jesus. *Ungggghhhh.*" Ky's fist strokes us harder and faster. The pierced tip of him rubs delicious friction against the throbbing head of my cock. Each time his hand runs over it, tension climbs, locked and loaded at the base of my spine.

I bite my way down the column of his neck, scraping my

teeth over his Adam's apple. He whispers all sorts of unintelligible curses of pleasure as I rake over his skin, squeezing us both together even harder.

My spine stiffens. Lust races through my veins.

"Ven...fuck..." He shudders; the husky edge to his voice is the most erotic thing.

"You'd better come for me, right fucking now," I growl against his throat and that does him in. We're both bucking against one another. Our wet bodies move in sync, and at the same moment, as his hips surge forward, skin slapping against skin, he pulls an orgasm out of me that leaves me seeing white spots behind my eyes.

Cum shoots all over our abs and his hand as we unload in unison with gasping breaths.

It's a few minutes before either of us can move. Ky strokes my wet hair off my forehead, and I'm too lost in the moment to do anything but enjoy the way he touches me.

Just for this long second, among the pounding comfort of warm water against my back and gentleness from the man in front of me that I certainly don't deserve, my eyes drop closed. But it's only fleeting; we know neither of us can remain suspended in time, that kind of luxury doesn't belong to men like us.

We both shower off properly. The little shit is still eyeing my dick like he's ready for round two, although anything he had in mind gets cut short when a text arrives from Thorne, apparently needing him for something.

"That asshole really needs to get laid," Ky grumbles as he types a reply on his phone.

I tug a fresh shirt on and find some pants. He's wrapped a towel around his waist and disappears off to his own room with a shake of his head and more muttering to himself. Something about being cock-blocked inside his own house.

Grabbing my phone, I head in the other direction. My feet

carry me toward the kitchen, only to find the Noire House succubus herself—the mayhem who has entered our lives—in there, filling a glass with ice and water.

Wearing nothing but her workout gear.

If what she has on could even loosely be termed that. It's a bra and some minuscule, skin-tight shorts that leave absolutely nothing to the imagination.

This slut is as bad as Ky for never putting clothes on.

She's all soft curves and tattoos, and the stretchy fabric molds to her ass cheeks. Her back is turned to me as I slip into the kitchen; the sound of the tap running, mixed with the music she's got playing on her phone, conceals my footsteps. And maybe it's the fact I'm still floating a little, so soon after Ky dragged an orgasm out of me, but I lean against the counter right behind her with my arms crossed.

Might as well take this opportunity to remind the girl she's not safe to let her guard down, especially not around us.

Fox turns the tap off, picks up her phone, and as she turns around, ends up nearly hurling the glass at my head with a screech. I quickly reach out and grab her fist inside my own—preventing the glass from falling and smashing into shards all over the polished concrete. We don't need that sort of a mess to deal with.

"Holy fuck." Blue eyes glare up at me. "Warn a girl next time you want to play stalker, would you."

I run my tongue across my teeth. Not giving her anything, but I let her hand go once I know she's not going to drop the damn glass.

She points a finger at me with her free hand, the one clutching her phone. "You know, you're going to have to learn to talk to me, especially if you're happy to fuck my mouth and shoot cum down my throat." Her tongue pokes against the inside of her cheek as she puts on a pouty little glare.

I meet her with my own stern expression. But as we face off

in the small space in this kitchen, there's laughter in the fine lines creasing around her eyes. Pink flushes high on her cheeks, damp hair frames her face from where she's obviously just finished her own workout.

"I think that should earn me a *hello* at the very least." Her lips tip up, and she flashes me a crooked smile.

That shit doesn't affect me, but it's exactly why Ky chases after her like a panting dog.

My mouth twists as I stare right back. She's got fire; I'll give her that. So, I give a bit of rope and allow her to be playful with me for the moment. What can it hurt. She choked on my cock like a fucking dream.

Keeping my arms folded, I lean forward, getting right in her face. "*No*."

Fox's smile widens to show off a row of white teeth and her nose scrunches ever so slightly, making the silver of her nose ring catch the light. "There. That wasn't so hard, was it, wolf boy?"

I arch an eyebrow at her, but all she does is saunter away. Taking herself off to the lounge and settling down in a spot on the large couch facing the kitchen.

Time evaporates as I can't seem to take my eyes off this girl. Before I can make a move or remember what I damn well came in here for in the first place, the sight through the other end of the large open-plan space from where I'm standing leaves me stock still, my jaw tightening.

She's bending forward. Right where she knows I can see her. That sports bra of hers is thin as fuck, and her heavy tits are bulging over the top.

And Christ, now all I can imagine is sliding my cock between that soft flesh and leaving her nipples glazed with my cum.

Her tight shorts cause my already lust-charged blood to rush straight back to my groin. As she straightens up and readjusts the high waistband, I'm devouring that spot between her soft thighs, picturing her cunt leaking with the evidence of me pounding her hard and filling her up. I'm imagining what it would be like to have her wrapped around my dick when she's already a mess and dripping with Ky having already spilled inside her.

Jesus.

Fuck.

There's no denying she's putting on a show right now. Or maybe she isn't, and I'm just whipped into a frenzy, knowing there's a fight coming and a target I'm due to eliminate with my fists. Whether she realizes what she's doing or not is irrelevant. The girl knows I'm here, and she knows exactly what kind of nightmare creature she's toying with.

As I watch on, because I can't seem to move from this spot, she relaxes back on the couch. Her painted fingernails reach into the glass, and she plucks an ice cube out. With slow, sensual movements, that little frozen square gets rubbed across her pouty bottom lip. Back and forth, back and forth, as her eyes roam over the page of the book she's picked up with the other hand.

My nostrils flare as I devour the way her fingers drag the rapidly melting cube to trace the column of her neck, and further down to glide across the swell of her breasts.

Her mouth hangs open, and I don't know what the fuck she's reading, but one thing is clear, I'm turned on as all hell by this little exhibition.

Even though I shouldn't be, I'm hard and furious and can't seem to fucking get away from this performance.

I don't want her.

I don't.

And at the exact moment she slides her fingers lower, to glide the trail of wetness over the serpent tattooed on her sternum, my phone explodes in my pocket.

The buzzing is like a chainsaw going off, slicing straight through whatever spell had suffocated me. I finally manage to tear myself away from the kitchen island, not bothering to look up at the girl and confirm whether she knows I'm still here.

When I see that unknown number flashing on the screen in my palm, I know the time has come.

The blood on my hands never stops.

CHAPTER 28
FOX

For the first time since I've been held here, my three captors are gone.

As in *fully* gone.

Ky at least had the decency to text me and let me know they were required to go away for a few days, although when I pressed him for more details, he said he couldn't tell me.

The occasional delivery has been dropped off to the house by burly ogres outfitted in combat gear—part of the team I saw manning the gated entrance. They leave me fresh produce and groceries. All the things I asked for with my list. In fact, as I unpack everything into the double-door fridge, I can't help but notice there only seems to be the foods I eat in here.

Are they really intending to be gone that long that they've cleared all their own items out?

Whatever, I can't be bothered trying to fathom what goes through their heads. They all have their secrets and mysteries, and I'm just their vengeance against a man who is rotting in hell.

So I fill my days with a horribly simplistic sort of routine that makes me feel one part house cat, one part forest hermit.

After waking up, I make use of the gym, cook for myself, explore a little in the woods closest to the house, and spend the remainder of my time in and around the pool. My notebook is overflowing with sketches and tattoo designs, and at least my creativity seems to be thrilled with all this space and time on my hands. Even if the circumstances leading to my artistic endeavors now bursting at the seams are less than ideal.

On one of the days, I find myself feeling oddly bold enough to properly snoop through their bedrooms. Ky's is first on my list to explore. It's surprisingly tidy yet also feels somewhat unlived-in. I suppose he and Raven might share the same bed most of the time? It's near impossible to get a read on their situationship, but I can tell their feelings for each other run far deeper than merely being fuck buddies.

Or enjoying *sharing* other women together.

God, the memories of the gardens and being with both of them sends a flood of heat to my pussy.

I quickly shake my head free of any thoughts of their impressive dicks. For all I know, the two of them have been busy railing multiple women in the time they've been gone from the compound.

Annnnd now the jealous bitch is back, sitting on my shoulder whispering in my ear. Reminding me that men like these monsters are only interested in a fuck wherever they can find one. What they did with me that night was only because Thorne had purchased my body to be used. I mean absolutely nothing to them. That fact has been made abundantly clear.

Continuing my nosing around, I poke through Ky's drawers and discover a few extra tees that smell like him. Immediately, I grab a couple to squirrel away with me. The others I've been wearing on repeat have lost the heaviness of his scent, and unfortunately, I've Stockholm syndromed my way into craving having him pressed against my body.

Yup. I'm seriously fucked in the head.

My phone is in my hand, and I pull up the text message thread he's been blowing up. I've ignored his latest, leaving him on read for now. It's all he deserves after purposely trying to rile me up while he's not here.

A smile plays on my lips as I read back over our most recent exchange from earlier today.

Admit it.

I won't do anything of the sort.

With you, I never know what you're after.

You know you want to.

No. I really don't.

Go on. Admit it, baby girl.

There's nothing I need to admit to.

Yeah, but you miss my pretty face.

Remember when you called me pretty.

Right before this moment.

(Screenshot attached)

When you looked like the sexiest goddamn thing dripping with my cum.

Just thought you'd want to check in with the object of your blossoming adoration.

Oh. My. God.

KYRON HARRIS.

You've got such a pretty mouth and a naughty little tongue. I'm still thinking about how incredible you looked down on your knees for me in the gardens.

Thinking about it, aren't you?

Like when you licked the cum off my hand.

That was so fucking hot.

How wet are you right now remembering how good it felt to be filled up?

Sorry. I can't hear you over the sound of my vibrator.

Tease me all you like, baby girl.

Record yourself when you come.

I like it when your hair looks freshly fucked and you're all heart eyed for me.

Especially when you're moaning my name.

There are other messages there, too. Ones from the past few days that I haven't answered. Ky asks me all sorts of things. He digs and pries and fossicks around, wanting to know about my art and how I got into tattooing in the first place. My texts are littered with screenshots he keeps sending of tattoos he wants me to do for him. Apparently, he's got lots of ideas but has never found the time to sit for them.

Gnawing steadily on my bottom lip, I debate with myself whether to reply or willfully ignore the whole thread. He sucked me into his devious little game of flirtation, but talking about more personal things—about my creativity—feels much more dangerous somehow.

This man doesn't want to get to know me. There must be some catch, and I'm not prepared to wander straight into his next trap.

I tuck my phone away before I do something insane, like ask him when he'll be back.

God forbid. He'd never let me live it down if he got a sniff of an idea that I might be currently stealing his t-shirts in an effort to cling onto his scent.

Next to his room is one I presume belongs to Raven. The bed is neatly made, with a simple plain charcoal cover and matching pillows. There aren't any personal effects that can be seen. I don't linger for long; it feels like intruding on something...sacred. Also, if I'm honest, the prospect of what might happen if he were to show up unexpectedly and find me here uninvited leaves me more than a little terrified.

What does strike me as I cast a final look around, is how everything feels so impersonal. Like these men didn't have anything before moving in here. There's no clutter or odd little pieces forming the debris of life that you might expect to find accumulated over time.

It makes my throat tighten a little to wonder what circumstances they all came from before landing here on this mist-covered peninsula.

Lastly, I fully indulge my curiosity, following her to the wing I haven't dared to set foot in, yet. This is Thorne's domain, and it honestly freaks me out to explore this part of the house. But at the same time, I'm dying to know if I can find anything—some infinitesimal detail—that might go toward unraveling his plan for making my life a living hell. I'm bound in proverbial chains here for as long as he deems me to be useful, so maybe, just maybe, there might be a key hidden away among the expanse of glass and concrete.

I can fuck Ky all I like, and maybe Raven too, but that won't change the fact Thorne is holding threats over my head against the memory of my mother and Em's safety.

My teeth grit together on reflex as I recall how callous he has proved capable of being. Using my only real weaknesses with the precision of a surgeon. Having me dutifully obeying him because the man is a maestro in the art of manipulation.

Thorne Calliano is vile, and I wish to hell there will be something here for me to use in my favor. But of course, I'm left frustrated and jiggling a securely locked doorknob instead of turning his office upside down. He's far too calculating to leave his shit unguarded, and I end up standing with arms crossed, silently cursing the sealed door for an untold length of time.

I'm painfully aware of the fact that the biggest danger to me isn't a secret society or the looming darkness of my father coming for me anymore...the biggest threat to my life inhabits these four walls.

Irony is a sadistic bitch.

Further down the hallway lies his bedroom. The door is cracked open, and I seize the opportunity with both hands. No fucks are given as I push inside and find myself in a space finished with wood textures and verdant green soft furnishings. It's like the forest has reached out with long mossy branches extending inside and made itself at home. While the rest of the spaces in this building might be made up of concrete and glass and shades of charcoal, in here, there is a softness I wasn't expecting.

The presence of the trees and earthiness reflected in the decor filling his room is a visceral thing.

Dare I say, this space feels calming. *Grounding.*

I quickly huff out a breath. Jesus. No. There can be no good that comes from starting to romanticize this man based off of how at-ease his bedroom makes me feel.

Rifling through his wardrobe proves that he really does live in expensive suits, with everything meticulously stored and organized. I mess up some of his ties, just because I can.

I'm busy pulling out drawer after drawer. I don't know what I'm looking for, but maybe it's his humanity that he might have shoved in here, buried along with his matching pairs of socks. There's a selection of workout gear, sweat pants, and long-sleeve tees. The navy blue material snags my eye, looking soft as a feather, and before I know what I'm doing, my fingers dig into the fabric, pressing it against my cheek.

It feels like being wrapped in a warm embrace, and the deeply satisfying essence curls through my blood. His scent of citrus and wood lingers, mixed with laundry powder. My eyelids drift closed, and for one fluttering beat of my heart, I allow myself to imagine the soft cotton is his palm cupping my jaw. Images of how it looked from afar when his identical twin held Poe's face that night at the auction flow into my mind, the moment when I thought it was Thorne touching another woman.

How would it actually look if it were the man in question himself holding someone like that?

Butterflies begin to riot around in my stomach. The tiny traitors.

I'm more of a disaster than I realized if I'm letting myself get tangled up in knots over Thorne Calliano. As that thought springs to mind, it prompts me to wake the fuck up from my weird little wardrobe-reverie. I drop the sleeve like it scalded my flesh.

He is nothing more than a master manipulator and irredeemable asshole. A man whose ribs I would happily acquaint with a knife if given half a chance.

I blink and stare at the room around me. Daylight has drained away and it suddenly feels as though the evening shadows have crept in unannounced. While I've been consumed with my efforts to snoop around, it all happened quicker than I noticed. There's an ominous silence and the darkened forest looms outside the floor-to-ceiling glass windows occupying one whole wall, exactly as they do in my own room. Now, standing amongst a wardrobe full of men's clothes, I can't help but feel like someone is watching me from the lengthening shadows.

My skin prickles with goosebumps, and a sudden movement out of the corner of my eye makes me jump. The thundering pulse in my neck doesn't make any attempt to slow down, even when I see it's only a bird flitting through the gloom.

All of a sudden, I'm very aware of just how deserted and isolated I am out here on my own.

My vulnerability is laid bare in lurid detail.

Before I can hyperfixate on that fact, I contemplate hurrying to my bedroom, but instead decide I'm a big girl. Now is not the moment I'm going to run scared. What I will do instead is brush off whatever freak-out I'm having and take myself for a pleasant little nighttime swim. The courtyard is aglow with warm lights scattered throughout the foliage, and the pool itself takes on a luminescence with the underwater lighting. Being out there feels warm and cozy and a hell of a lot safer, besides, the water is calling my name.

For a second, I even think about skinny dipping since I'm technically here alone, but I don't really fancy an awkward encounter with one of those gargoyle-looking guards if one decides to appear out of the blue. So bikini it is, and after quickly changing, I plunge into the heated water with a sigh.

But that damn crawling sensation over my skin follows me, even below the water's surface.

Stupid. So goddamn stupid. I'm uneasy as all hell because there's an ever-present impression of being watched. But the glassed-in courtyard only reflects back the twinkling lights and greenery each time my eyes dart from side to side. The rippling surface of the water sluices around me as I swim from one end to another while my eyes ping pong around the courtyard. Logically, I know there's nothing and no one able to get to me here —this place is an impenetrable fortress. Not only that, but even from where I'm positioned in the pool, I can see straight into the kitchen, where I left more lights than necessary blazing.

This is one of those moments in life when I have to give myself a stiff talking to. The darkness outside is unnerving. It's quiet. And I let a stupid bird flitting through some trees have me halfway to shitting my pants.

Just thinking about how uneasy I felt while standing in Thorne's room has my pulse ratcheting up again.

Would convincing these men to let me have a weapon of some kind, you know, for the times when they're not around make me feel better? I suppose I could always stash one of the knives from the kitchen...God, I'm such an idiot. Why didn't I think of that earlier?

As I duck dive under the water, I'm contemplating whether to scurry to the butcher's block filled with all manner of big, sharp implements that could easily carve a hole in a man's stomach, when there's a muffled, plunging noise behind me.

It sends a pressure wave through the water that tosses my body a little, and panic races through every limb like a frozen gale. My blood turns to ice within a second.

There's a silent scream that bubbles out of me as I thrash to try and turn around, but it's too late. My arms are pinned by my sides as I'm grabbed from behind and dragged right to the bottom of the deep end of the pool.

It's impossible to determine which way is up. They say when you get tossed around by heavy surf that the force of the waves overhead can be so disorienting that your panicked brain gets confused. Everything is dark. You try to kick toward what you believe to be the surface, only to hit your head on the rocks below and drown.

Right now I'm surrounded by shadows and water that threatens to fill my burning lungs.

There's a hand clamped over my mouth, pinching my nose. Another roughly cups my pussy.

Everything morphs into a grim kaleidoscope of distress as I struggle against the nightmares of what it might be like to drown at the hands of a psychopath. One who wants me dead in the act of seeking revenge.

I see myself floating face down in the water, while the members of the Anguis stand around my corpse sipping champagne.

But there's enough fight left in my bones that I twist my body and scratch at my assailant's arms, which only rocks my clit against the fingers holding me tight.

When spots blur the edge of my vision, we breach the surface; the rough hand covering my mouth and nose finally decides to let go.

Sweet, warm air rushes into my oxygen-starved lungs while I hack up a chestful of pool water. It runs out my nose and splutters from my mouth, mixed with saliva. Somehow, I've thrashed my way toward the edge closest to the steps. Desperate fingers search for the tiled lip to heave myself halfway to safety as I cough and gag.

I've barely had time to catch my breath before powerful fingers grab my jaw and pull me back down into the water.

This can't be happening.

Only this time, instead of being sunk to the bottom like a stone in a lake, my body is forced to twist around.

Demanding lips seal over mine, stealing my ragged breath and claiming me in a punishing kiss.

CHAPTER 29
FOX

My Viking takes command, kissing me like he's never going to permit me to draw breath again.

He's feral and desperate, and this is the rawest side to him I've witnessed.

There's every chance I'm kissing back someone who has just put countless bodies in the ground. But this man is giving me no choice in the matter; he keeps our mouths pressed together as his tongue slides over mine. The sheer terror from moments before writhes and transforms into a dragon inside me, winding a coiled tail around my insides and breathing fire through my limbs to scorch away any lingering fear.

Ky turns me into a savage beast. One who starts scratching at him, my nails dig themselves into his wet skin, leaving long trails of reddened welts and hopefully drawing blood in the process. I'm desperate to chase his touch and match his wild intent as I hook my legs around his waist and bite down on his lower lip.

There's a venomous noise that comes out of him, the kind of intoxicating sound I drink down. As he nips me right back, his fingers sink into the softness of my hips, holding me so tight I hope to god there are bruises painting my skin in the morning.

"*Fuck.*" I dig my claws into his scalp. "*You.*" I hiss while pulling his head back. Tangling my fingers in his hair. He fights me every inch, keeping those glowing forest-colored eyes on me.

"Miss me, sweet thing?"

"You tried to kill me, you psycho."

"Fuck yes, give me that fire." He nips at the edges of my lips, then runs his tongue over the sting. "Haven't thought of anything but fucking this needy cunt again."

God. The mouth on this man.

Ky hums and nudges his nose against mine. "Having you fight me makes for the sweetest flavor of dripping wet pussy."

He dives back in, leaving me no time to focus. Slanting our mouths together, and this time, every seductive moment is clear, and I'm almost certain he breaks my brain like the cocky asshole he is. Ky moves slower, but no less intensely or roughly. Everything from the scrape of his beard, to the skill of his tongue, to the nip of his teeth tugging on my bottom lip.

Well, holy shit. If I didn't already know this man could kill me, I think he might just be trying. My body aches for him right down to the heart of my bones.

"I didn't think you would ever kiss me." I pull back, panting against his mouth. My fingers cling to the nape of his neck. There's a slight desperation in the way I dig in and hold him tighter, tangling my hands in his hair. While I'm certainly not ready to admit it out loud, I don't want him to ever stop putting his mouth on me.

"Things were a bit rushed the other night." He brushes his lips and stubble along my jaw. "If I'd known that was the first time I'd get to taste you, I might have done things differently." When he draws back to look at me, his eyes gleam, filled with golden flecks and wicked thoughts. "Or maybe not. It was hot as fuck."

"Oh, yeah?" Well, I'm needy as fuck right now, unashamedly grinding my pussy against his torso. Ky walks us slowly through the pool, and the sensation of water as it glides over my exposed skin is so delicious I could melt on the spot.

"Mmm, Christ, the flavor of your cunt tastes like *mine.*"

Oh, god. He's definitely trying to kill me.

His big hands knead my ass, crushing my body against his own. I get the impression he's running from whatever devil has consumed them during the days they've been gone.

For a moment, I wonder if the others are back too. My brain stalls as I consider whether they're inside right now, watching our every move through the endless vista of glass surrounding this courtyard.

That seed of an idea turns me on even more.

"Rub that pussy all over me, baby girl. I've been dying to get another hit of your sweetness."

I preen at that admission. This man has a veritable sex god keeping him satisfied already, yet he still wants me. He wants to call me *his.*

"Tell me what you would have done, then. If things had been different..." My neck arches to give his mouth access. Ky chuckles against my throat, before scraping his teeth and sucking down on my pulse point.

"You want to hear it?" He teases me with a finger dipping beneath the gusset of my bikini. Stroking along the outer edge of my pussy lips from underneath.

God, that feels insanely good. "Mmm, that's a much better idea." I hum. "Show me instead, naughty boy."

When he pulls back and hits me with a ferocious look, I bite my bottom lip.

"You're a slutty little tease."

I am.

I absolutely am a slutty little tease. And I love how powerful I feel in his strong arms while being a good girl for him. "Show me what you want to do to me."

Ky's lips curve into the kind of lethal smile that should make me want to fling myself out of this pool and run.

Apparently, I have zero sense of self-preservation.

The vivid green in his eyes reflects the lights beneath the pool's surface. Every inch of him looks like some kind of water-born deity—a mer-god cut from a fairy tale, with his wet hair pushed back and smooth skin caressed by rivulets and droplets.

Strong fingers pinch the sensitive flesh at the outer edge of my pussy, making me jump. His mouth devours the cry of pain mingled with pleasure that I let out, and his tongue dives back into my mouth with raw hunger.

I'm clinging on for dear life, ready to be consumed by this man.

There's no more waiting, or teasing. He hoists me out of the pool like I'm nothing more than a feather and sets me on the edge, with water sheeting off my body and a torrent of lust filling every space possible beneath my skin.

"Slide your panties aside. Show me your cunt." His gruff command makes me shudder. Rough hands press my knees as wide as they'll go, spreading me obscenely for him.

"Ky." My breathing is choppy and his name comes out as a throaty whisper.

I do as he instructs, my clit throbbing. Bracing myself on one hand, I use the other to pull the wet material to one side. It's all I can do not to buck toward his mouth, with how intensely the ache is building inside me.

I've already had an incandescent preview of how this man can make me come as quickly and effortlessly as breathing.

"Look at you. Pink and swollen and messy for me, baby girl." As he lowers his face, I'm a flurry of small, pathetic noises.

Trust me to fall apart the second Ky gives me the full force of his undivided attention.

"Please." I really am a desperate slut for him.

His teeth bite down on the fleshy part of my inner thigh, followed by a swirl of his tongue over the spot, easing the sting. Giving me a lewd preview of his skills in that department. All I want to do is grab his head and ride his face until I scream this place down, but instead, I keep holding the fabric to one side as my pussy gets wetter and wetter by the second.

"Fuck. You're dripping." He keeps his eyes on mine, kissing a line toward my clit. His lips are soft as he works his way closer; the scratch of his beard has my pulse galloping until, finally, *finally* he fastens his mouth over the aching bud.

My back arches as the rippling pleasure spreads throughout me. "Oh. Oh, my god."

The porny way my voice catches in my throat makes him hum against my pussy before he sets to work and licks me everywhere. Right from as far back as he can reach, swirling around my entrance, and then up to my clit. Again and again.

Rasping his beard against the sensitive skin, his gravelly voice vibrates against me, "The prettiest little thing."

Somewhere out there, Daddy Universe is smiling down on me because, holy shit, this man eats my pussy like he's been sent from the stars.

Can I be addicted this fast?

I'm aware on some deep-seated level that it's a very, very bad idea to even contemplate getting attached to Ky. However, any coherent thought scatters and is replaced with scalding desire, and the race toward the edge of pleasure consumes me.

"Oh, fuck. Oh, god. Right there." Ky adds two fingers shoved inside my pussy, while his tongue flicks my clit. I'm about to detonate.

He adds a third finger, curling them to find the perfect angle, and that's what tosses me headfirst over the edge. I clamp down around his fingers inside me and come on a long wail with my head thrown back.

"That's it. Good fucking girl." His praise washes over me, and I crumble. Forget addicted; I'm a squishy ball of putty in his hands to mold and shape as he likes.

Which he proceeds to.

His big hands and plush lips are on me, everywhere, tugging roughly at the ties on my bikini top and bottoms until I'm exposed to him. Shifting up my body with a deep groan, he takes one of my nipples into his mouth and sucks down. I'm arching and moaning and begging as he works me with his tongue. The feel of his beard against my skin is so fucking good, while his rough fingers pinch and pluck at my other nipple. Squeezing roughly in a way that drives me wild for him.

My breasts are always so sensitive after coming, and the attention he's giving them is making me want to climb him like a tree.

"Please. Please, Ky. I need you inside me." There's nothing left for me to do but beg.

Ky squashes my tits together, running his tongue over the expanse of soft flesh exactly where he marked me with his cum that night. "Christ. I want to fuck every part of you."

Oh, god. Yes. I'm more than on board with that idea.

"Put your hands around my neck." He shifts now to scoop me up and drops us both into the water. His cock notches at my entrance, and he guides my back to press against the wall of the pool.

The surface of the water laps at my sensitive nipples.

Ky presses the head of him just inside. Breaching my entrance and then slowly pumping the pierced tip in and out. My eyes drift back in my head.

"You want to know what I plan on doing to you?" He asks.

My moaned noise of agreement is about all I can muster. "Yes...I want..." But then awareness prickles through me. Am I out of my goddamn mind? What the fuck am I doing? I try to push him away, but his cock is already pressing into me and there's nothing I can do to stop this.

"Stop. Wait." I pant.

Ky's features are a mask of feral intent. His lips twist into more of a snarl than the usual smirk I've grown so used to seeing. His cock is still part way inside my channel.

"We didn't use protection before. We can't..."

He collars my throat with one giant hand. Cutting off my words.

"You think any of us want to bring up a child in this world? Each of us took care of that years ago."

I'm struggling against him, which only grinds my hips and sinks his cock deeper, and my brain can't fathom what he's saying. Fear brews in my chest. Having unprotected sex—not once, but twice—when I'm not currently on any form of birth control would be among the stupidest things I've ever done.

Fingers flex against the spot where my pulse thuds harder than ever, and with that small touch, it's as if the words magically unscramble in my brain.

Each of us took care of that *years ago.*

Oh.

Ohhh.

Suddenly, the notion that these men have all chosen to have a vasectomy is the hottest goddamn thing I've ever heard.

"And another thing you need to understand..." He bites the shell of my ear. "Is that we have never fucked at the club without using protection. But when it comes to fucking you, I won't have anything between us."

I dig my teeth into my bottom lip.

"I know your darkest fantasies, baby girl...even the ones you won't admit to yourself."

Trying everything not to whimper and concede that he's right, I bite down harder.

"We're all clear, and we know you are too." Ky runs his tongue over my pulse, driving me into a frenzy. "You think we wouldn't already have discovered everything there is to know about our property?" He rasps against my ear, and a shudder rolls through my body. Something about the way he's meddled with my brain, calling me *his* and telling me that I'm their *property* has ruined me completely.

My resistance melts.

Ky feels me give up my fight and uses the opportunity to drag his cock up through my slit and the metal rolls over my clit, before sliding back down to nudge at my entrance. His piercing is like a miracle and feels so fucking good that I can hardly stand it. Fireworks and lightning bolts rock through me every time that metal bar brushes over the sensitive bundle of nerves.

"You're going to let me fuck you raw, baby girl. I want to see my cum spilling out of you every time."

My body is a horny little devil, begging for him to get inside me *right fucking now*.

He tugs on the patch of trimmed hair down there, hard enough to make me gasp and buck against him.

"Who owns this pussy?" There's so much heat simmering in his green eyes as he looks at me; I'm a tinderbox waiting to catch fire.

I cry out with a whimper when his cock slams inside me. "You do."

"Try again, baby girl." He bites my bottom lip between his teeth, tugging roughly while his hips pulse short thrusts, staying buried so fucking deep that his piercing hits a magical spot I can never reach on my own. One that dissolves my body into liquid pleasure.

"Say it." He grunts as he lets my bruised lip go.

"All of you." I'm sure my nails are scratching him up as I dig in and hold on. But he doesn't seem to care at all.

This time he slides right out to the tip and pauses. "Who gets to fuck you?"

"You. All of you." He slams inside me again as soon as I confirm what he wants to hear. A low groan of pleasure breaks from him as I say the words he's evidently been waiting for. "I want all of you."

That admission stokes Ky's intensity. He's fucking me with a brutal rhythm now. My spine rocks against the hard tiles, and the water laps at my burning hot skin.

"That's right. All of us." Each snap of his hips sends me spiraling higher. "We *all* own this pussy."

There's nothing but desperate whimpers and moans coming from me. My nipples rub against his hard chest, and the force of him moving against me leaves me with no choice but to cling tight to his damp shoulders.

"Including Thorne." It's a statement. Not a question. Not a request. Just telling me with all the confidence of the type of man Ky is.

Meanwhile, my brain has vacated the premises because it takes me a moment to process what he's saying. But I can't deny the first answer that swarms my brain with buzzing intensity.

"Yes." I screw my eyes shut. Admitting it out loud leaves me feeling more exposed than ever.

"You want him too?" The pace of his thrusts slows, and this time, he's asking. Maybe even genuinely. Even though I know they consider me their property, and he's forced me to consent to allowing them all to fuck me, right now I get the feeling he might actually care about my answer.

Or I could be imagining things.

"Yes." My needy whimper is breathy and filled with lust.

"Such a good fucking girl." That spurs him on, each drive of his hips intensifies in pace as his thumb finds my clit. He pulls back to watch the place where our bodies are joined. "Look at your cunt, swallowing my cock like you were made to take me. That's it. Just like that. Take every fucking inch."

Holy fuck. I'm done for.

We're both caught in the tide dragging us under. He grunts darkly as his length swells. My own climax builds and as I cry out Ky drives forward, cursing against the crook of my neck; his cock pulsing and filling me while my pussy clenches around him.

He praises me, coats me with beautifully filthy words as he fucks me right through our joint orgasm. I'm nothing but a bright spark, and he's the center of my world right now.

My tormentor and my captor.

And as he takes care of me, first carrying me to his shower and then to his bed, where he worships me for the rest of the night, I have to admit to myself that my Viking has become something so much more.

CHAPTER 30
Thorne

A pig can chew through human bone and flesh like butter.

We keep our stys well away from Port Macabre, but they make it a piece of piss to ensure someone we want to disappear does so, without a trace.

The past few days have been gory to say the least.

We finally were able to move in on one of the largest trafficking operations that still existed after the intel we received from the night of the auction at Noire House. Trucks were intercepted that night, while members of the Anguis gorged themselves on pleasures of the flesh, allowing us to act swiftly and ruthlessly.

This isn't an act of taking prisoners or dispensing justice.

This is an elimination.

One by one, Hawke and I have been able to take these operations down, and we're closing in on the final target. But that is also the one posing the greatest risk, controlled by a black shadow that has plagued our lives for decades.

They've been hiding in plain sight for years now, and they

know we're coming for them. Which will make it all the more satisfying the day we blow them apart.

I've got half a mind to sew a grenade inside their leader's chest while still conscious and pull the pin out through a hole in their windpipe.

The ring we've just decimated gave us scraps and morsels of intelligence. Random pieces of information we managed to pull from the men and women during torture, but nothing revolutionary. Most of it was their final attempt at evading the inevitable consequence of their foul existence.

Abusing children and profiting off willingly inflicted exploitation...they can lose their heads, and their tongues, for what they've done to countless innocents.

Ven's methods of extracting information are effective, to say the least. The man is a master of his craft. And after three days straight without sleep—days that bled into nights as he removed teeth and tore out fingernails and sliced away chunks of flesh—he's finished what he came here to do. For the time being, at least.

Ky, the team, and I took care of the rest.

The Anguis have made Raven Flannaghty their executioner for too many years. It's the least we can do for him to give his tarnished soul a break from embodying the Grim Reaper for a change.

I'm standing in front of the rusted sink in the packing shed, surrounded by the stench of blood and manure, scrubbing the caked evidence of death from beneath my fingernails. I want to bathe in bleach until the stink of piss and shit from their bloated corpses has been eliminated from my senses.

There's a small square of mirror hanging from a crooked nail on the shed wall in front of me. It's cracked along one side, with spider web lines reaching across the glass, cutting my reflection into pointed fragments. Mud splatters line one side of my face. Most likely blood, too. Trying to scrub the worst of it off with the tattered cloth hanging beside the basin seems futile.

Outside, the moon is high, and the night air is crisp. There's not even the usual sound of the barn owls for company. Just horrific, repetitive, crunching as the pigs get to work on the bodies.

Drying my hands on the rag, the familiar buzz of my phone emits from the pocket inside my Kevlar vest.

It's Hawke.

Reports are starting to roll out. Our media contact packaged it up nicely.

He attaches a link to an online article, which, when I tap it open, reveals the breaking news report that reads about a prominent politician who has died in his sleep. That's the pretty little bow we put on things to satisfy the public at large, but it sends a silent warning to all those he might have been associated with that someone is coming for them.

They know the target on their back gets larger with every day they still wake up breathing.

In reality, that man was torn to shreds by the time Ven was finished with him. Nothing more than strips of burnt flesh and hollowed crevices after gouging out his eyeballs.

On your way?

Will be there in a few hours.

The aftermath of a stealth move like this requires Hawke and I to work together without the risk of phones being tapped or walls listening in on private conversations. Which means that from here I have to head straight to Hawke's place, when I'd much rather be making my way to the compound. But we've got days of work to get through before the next gathering of the Anguis rapidly approaches.

Without realizing I've done it, my thumb hovers over the contact name I have yet to utilize.

Foxglove.

The last time I spoke to her was at the auction night, and for some festering fucking reason, I keep mindlessly pulling up her name on my phone as if I'm going to do something with it.

My thumb starts typing as I run my other hand over the back of my neck.

There is an event you need to attend.

No. I quickly delete the entire line of text.

You will be required at Noire House. Dress accordingly.

Delete.

I trust you have received the food deliveries I arranged while we were gone.

Fuck. Delete. Delete. Delete.

I will be seeing you at the upcoming event. Ky is currently on his way back to the compound.

Jesus Christ.

"Fuck this," I mutter out loud. Jabbing furiously at the arrow that will erase all evidence of whatever the fuck it is I'm trying to say.

Blowing out a long breath, I swipe out of my texts and resume thumbing through the full article sent by Hawke. That's when another message arrives, only this time it's from Ky and has been sent to our group chat.

He and Ven left earlier this evening. I knew Ven would disappear into the forest, but Ky...there's no need to guess where, and who, he headed straight for.

What he's sent is a video attachment. The thumbnail is too blurry and dark in the tiny image on-screen to make out what it might be. But I already know.

Ven hasn't read the message. I doubt he'll turn his phone on for another day or two.

My free hand scrubs over my mouth and my thumb hovers over the video. This is the part I wanted to avoid, like the fucking plague. The whole reason I threatened him not to touch her, because now he has, it's like opening a can of putrid worms.

She's gotten under his skin without even trying.

It won't take long before the infection spreads, my immune system is already hard at work fighting it, but the pull and desire and dizzying kind of need to own this girl in every way imaginable is already there. It's sitting right behind my rib cage like a stuck knife. One that digs in deeper every time I try to fucking draw breath.

Standing here in the deep shadows of a drafty shed, hours away from the compound, I'm at war with myself over a goddamn video clip. The screen dims, and I quickly tap elsewhere on the surface to illuminate it again. An eerie blue glow is the only light to see by.

After the hell that the past few days have been, my resolve shatters. I click play.

What I see on screen is a lot of Ky's naked chest.

A pan down follows, showing me a wet, tangled heap of pale purple curls.

Delicate, red-painted fingernails rest lightly over the toned muscles of his stomach.

I work down a heavy swallow as the silent clip shows off a grainy, dark video of a naked Foxglove Noire curled up asleep in his arms. There's not much to see because Ky's bicep is in the way, but I can see enough. As he continues to film, it shows the spot where his other hand cups her bare pussy.

Clenching my jaw, the brutal grip I've got on my phone tightens even further.

And Ky cements himself as the most infuriating asshole and

brat I've ever had to deal with when he swipes two fingers through her slit. The video only shows a blurry, dark outline of the spot between her thighs, but it's there, and I know it's there all the same. He then brings those fingers close to the camera and the glow illuminates a sheen of wetness coating them—god-fucking-damnit, it could be her cum or his or both of theirs—before the camera jostles a little and all I can see is the lower half of Ky's face now filling the screen.

His short beard comes into focus, the corner of his lips tip up in a taunting smirk, and he sucks down on his fingers.

My stomach clenches at the sight.

The video plays on a loop and I don't make any attempt to try and stop it.

I'm trapped, unable to do anything but devour the way their bodies look twisted together in the dim lighting, and the thought rushes into my mind before I can stop it.

They'd both look even better in my bed.

The moment my thumb taps on the save video button, his next text comes through.

> Daddy's missing out on the sweetest pussy he'll ever taste.

CHAPTER 31
Ven

Her scent is the first thing that accosts me when I enter the compound.

A lingering floral calling card that doesn't belong here. *Pear blossom and coconut and honeysuckle.*

Even when I reach my own room the fragrance fills my nose, and I can't tell if it's the fact this girl is so deeply entrenched in every corner of this fucking place, or whether she's actually been in here.

I dump my helmet inside my wardrobe and rest my forehead against the wooden frame. Throwing myself in the river and spending a night beneath the stars washed away some of the stain of what we've had to do these past few days. But my devils enjoy the clear skies and sleeping amongst the creatures of the night best. It calms them after they've been whipped into a frenzy of blood lust, or at least, seems to satiate them long enough that I can return to the compound and bear to be contained by concrete and glass walls once more.

Normally that would be the case. Tonight, however, I'm still teetering on the edge.

And the presence of that girl is stirring up something dark within me.

I still don't trust her, even if Ky is happy enough to empty his balls inside her over and over. There's a venomous snake slithering beneath her tattooed skin, and it might sink its fangs into us yet.

Thorne isn't immune to her, as much as he acts as though he's indifferent. The fact he didn't reply to Ky's message last night is evidence enough. Probably has whatever's on that video saved in a hidden encrypted folder on his phone somewhere. I know most of Calliano's secrets, and he's desperate to fuck her every hole.

I saw the message come in but didn't watch it. Maybe I will later, or maybe I won't even bother. It's not that I care who Ky chooses to be with outside of the two of us; what matters is that we're there for each other in a way that goes beyond stroking his cock and fucking his tight ass, and that loyalty is the most important thing to me.

He can stick his dick in whoever he wants, as much as he pleases. But in our life, and our line of work, there's a rare occasion we can trust anyone else. So, for the most part, we only share girls or guys occasionally at the club when the mood strikes.

This world wasn't made for his and hers matching towels and promises of death-do-us-part.

That's why we enjoy the freedom of picking who we choose to bond with, and you'd be surprised how many people are quite fucking capable of caring for and being intimate with more than one person.

Intimacy. I chew over that word like a piece of grit. Something I've never been good at. Yet somehow, Ky and Thorne both tolerate my bullshit, and in exchange, I tolerate theirs.

I'VE BEEN LURKING HERE in the shadows of the kitchen for a while now. The glass walls around me reflect back an eerie pattern of grim lines and cracks of light from where the moon shines into the central courtyard.

The whiskey I've been nursing is nearly finished, and as I'm draining the last, there's a rustling sound to my right. My eyes fall on the source, and she's dressed in one of Ky's worn shirts, looking at me as if I'm about to tear her limb from limb.

Probably because there's every chance I am.

"I'm sorry—I didn't know you were in here." She's stuck halfway between the kitchen and refuge. Definitely not far enough away from me to be considered safe.

Fight or flight hasn't kicked in, thanks to her sleep-addled state.

Slowly lowering the glass, I rest it on the stone top of the counter and lean forward on both hands, eyeing her fragile form. She'd be so fucking effortless to break. I can already hear the crack of bone snapping beneath that smooth skin.

"Out here, creeping around at night again." I watch on with faint amusement as her eyes go round, taking in my partially hidden appearance. There's only a glow from the clock on the oven lighting one side of my face.

I hope when Foxglove Noire looks at me, I'm akin to her worst nightmares. Because everything in me says that this girl is a risk.

Her life might belong to us, but that doesn't mean we can trust her.

She told Ky she wanted all of us—he's already regaled me with every detail of their night together over text—but I'm not buying that bullshit line for one second. This girl has no idea what that means, and my inner monsters certainly aren't settled enough to want to be tamed at present.

If there's ever a time she's going to discover what kind of wolf I really am, it's now.

"Um, I wanted some water." She tucks a strand of hair, then goes to move around the counter to the left of me, but I'm there before she can make it close to the cabinets. Snatching her wrists, I've twisted them together behind her back within a second, even as she lashes out, trying to avoid my grasp.

Ky's been teaching her fuck all when it comes to defending herself.

"I think you came in here looking for something else." I sneer at the side of her face. There's no holding back on the ugliness; let her fucking witness it all and run away screaming.

"Let go of me." She struggles again, feebly, and my fingers dig in around her wrist bones. Pinning both together in one hand, I use my other to shove her head forward against the cold stone bench top.

"You're just a dirty slut walking around looking for her next cock to tease, aren't you." My clasp on her wrists intensifies, yanking them higher, dragging out a yelp of pain. The force turns her face to one side on the counter.

"You're a fucking asshole." Her pathetic attempts to struggle against me continue. "Fuck you." Her voice goes straight to my dick.

"That's what you want, isn't it? To fuck all of us."

She goes still beneath me. I can almost hear the exact moment her stomach plummets through the floor. This stupid bitch didn't think Ky would tell me what she said, and it's almost laughable that she seems shocked by my words.

"I lied. Told him what he wanted to hear, that's all."

She shivers beneath me, with her ass sticking out and her front bent over the counter. Looking every inch a warm, willing hole—desperate to be filled.

My tongue runs over my teeth. "I don't think you're that good at lying." I tsk at her through the darkness. The sound sends another tremor underneath my punishing grip.

"Get your hands off me." Her words might pretend to be acidic, but they're weak. This girl is useless against my years of training and fighting and ending lives. She knows I've got her trapped, and it'll only be at my mercy that she leaves this kitchen tonight.

"Oh, I think you're the type of nasty bitch who enjoys it exactly like this."

There's a tiny growl that comes out of her, but she doesn't try and argue with me and fuck, I'm losing control on whatever has been stemming the tide until now.

"I think you're walking around here wearing almost nothing, hoping someone is going to fill you with cum."

This time her choked growl sounds more like a whimper. "Don't you dare lay a hand on me."

I lean my weight forward more, and it forces the outline of my hard cock in my jeans against her ass, while the edge of the stone counter digs into her hip bones.

Why do I find myself drawn to this girl and wanting to find ways to suck out her pain and poison all in the same damn breath. She's a giant temptation for me. The tiny, breathy edge to her voice when she struggles paints the sweetest backdrop to her protests.

"It's always the same tune with you. Those threats of yours mean nothing when your cunt is dripping wet and begging." I hiss at her ear. The loose hair fallen from the bun on top of her head brushes the side of her face.

"I don't want this."

"Do you think I care what you fucking want?" My teeth grind as I shove her harder against the stone.

"I'll scream for Ky."

Like hell she will. That drags a menacing laugh out of me.

"If you were going to scream for help, you would have done so by now. Rather than stick your ass in the air hoping someone is going to come along and fuck it."

Her body goes rigid.

"You wouldn't." Her voice is raspy, and every inhale grows more and more erratic with each passing second.

"Wouldn't what? Fuck your ass raw until you bled? Break your cunt in around the shape of my cock while you're crying for mercy?" My hips thrust slowly, jarring her pelvis against the cutting edge of the stone. No doubt she'll be bruised as shit after this.

"Let me go." I can see her biting that bottom lip of hers so hard it's all puffy and swollen.

I dig my phone out of my back pocket and pull up Ky's number, laying it screen-up right beside her face.

"There you go," She sucks in air through her teeth. "Your precious Ky is right there if you want to call him for help." His name is illuminated on my phone, alongside the big glowing green button. All she has to do is make an effort to reach out and tap once.

She doesn't flinch or twitch.

Dirty fucking girl.

Bending closer, I take a hit of her fragrance. "You're ours to use how we like, and you might just be my favorite victim."

"*Please, Raven.*" She says my name like it will mean something.

I give a slow shake of my head into the darkness. Running my finger down her bare arm, she shivers for me and goosebumps pebble beneath her tattoos. "Not a chance. You're ours to play with whenever we like, and your pathetic little screams won't save you."

With a shove at the back of her head, warning her to stay down, I move my hand around to fist the back of the t-shirt hanging loosely over her ass.

"You're our little whore now. Just accept it."

She makes a feral noise of protest beneath me. "*Don't.* I don't want this."

"Hmm, is that so? Time to see how much of a liar you really are."

As I drag the material up over her hips, she's got on a pair of high-cut panties. They're white cotton and lace and look innocent as fuck. My cock starts leaking at the sight of her rounded ass cheeks with only a strip of fabric to separate them. Bared like a feast in front of me.

"Please. Please, don't." She starts squirming against my hold, and with one boot, I kick her feet to spread wide.

"We own you...which means we own every one of your orgasms." I shift my hand around to cup her covered pussy. "And I bet you get off on that."

"No." Her defiance is commendable, but her body betrays her. As I expected, there's a giant wet spot beneath my touch where the fabric is soaked right through.

I smirk into the night. Rubbing a thumb roughly over her panties and pinching her through the wet material. Once I've gathered enough of the dampness on my fingers, I bring them back around and shove them under her nose. She recoils with a hissed-out curse as I force her to scent her own arousal.

"Well...what do we have here?" Keeping her pinned in place, I drag the damp pad of my thumb over her bottom lip so she can't evade the reality of what her body craves.

"You're sick." It's a little disappointing that she doesn't try to bite my fingers off.

"Says the slut who's dripping wet. Now show me what a good little whore you are."

My fingers find the front of her sodden panties again, pressing hard over her clit. Fox tries to fight back the moan of pleasure that wants to come out. Judging by how drenched she is just from being held down, her pussy must be a swollen mess already.

"Stop." She thrashes and turns her head the other way. All it does is buck her hips against my hand.

"No," I growl. My fingers bear down on her, working in short, sharp circles, and I know this kind of pressure is going to have her falling apart immediately.

"Don't—" Fox begs, but her cheeks are flushed, and her ass grinds against my hard cock.

It only takes two more circles against the spot directly over her clit when her body seizes up, then quivers beneath me. A broken noise falls from her lips as she tries to swallow back her moans.

"Again." My voice is heavy with the need to free my cock and pump into her, besides, my shadows have yet to be satiated.

"I can't. Please, stop."

It's as if she thinks that won't make me push harder. So, of course, I do—ruthlessly rubbing over the bundle of nerves even though she's overstimulated. This girl is going to come for me again, and I'm going to drag it out of her with fangs.

"You're ours, and that means you're going to come when we fucking say so." She breaks apart under me. This time unable to hold back the wild noises and sobs bursting out of her.

Beneath me, her body goes limp as her orgasm rocks through her, then subsides. I let her wrists go, planting them on the counter beside her head. She's boneless and doesn't do anything to try and stop me this time as I free my cock and tug her panties to one side.

Impaling her with one shove, she's fluttering and clenching around me straight away as I push forward, right to the hilt. The force of my intrusion makes her eyes squeeze shut. But not before she makes the tiniest of whimpers against the bench-top...a noise that sounds an awful fucking lot like pleasure.

Her cunt is the tightest, wettest, silken glove. Swollen with the afterglow of the orgasms she's already given me, and she's not doing enough—or anything—to make me stop. Her hot cunt clamps down around my length, sucking me in deeper.

My hands grab her hips, each thrust is determined and sharp. Pumping into her with gritted teeth as she sobs beneath me. Her fingers try to grab at the smooth counter while her body slides against the stone surface, and she fully submits to it all.

It's a heady rush. One that I haven't experienced in god knows how fucking long.

But I'm not done yet with showing this girl who she truly belongs to, so I reach around and shove my hand down the front of her panties. Touching her properly this time, and Jesus, she's so warm and pliant it makes my balls tighten immediately. Her soft pussy is wet and slick beneath my fingers; straight away I brush against her clit eliciting a breathy little gasp. This girl might say one thing, but that tiny pouting bud is desperate for more attention.

When she feels what I'm doing, she gives another pathetic attempt at fighting me, but all it does is sink my cock at a deeper angle—one that has her gasping loudly into the dark of the kitchen and clenching around my length.

"Better be quiet, don't want anyone to hear how much you love getting bent over and used like a little fucktoy."

Her cunt tightens around my dick immediately.

"Fuck, you love this, don't you." Hips punching forward ruthlessly, skin slaps against skin. "Don't make a sound. You'll have to keep quiet, or they'll know you're out here getting pumped full of cum like a proper little whore."

She makes a strangled noise. Biting down on one hand, her teeth sink into the fleshy part of her palm in an effort not to moan. Her pussy has my cock in a vise grip, leaving me pounding harder, intensifying the way I've trapped her hips.

She might pretend not to like what I'm doing, but her body is betraying her little lies every step of the way.

"Such a dirty girl. You wanted to be fucked by all of us; well, now you know what it's like to be owned by us." With each thrust, I punctuate my cold words. "Maybe you should have thought about what it's like to belong to *all* of us before walking around with nothing on." As I sink my cock deep, I pinch down on her clit this time and she shatters.

My balls draw up, and my hips jerk, and I'm unloading into her. Hot streams of cum fill her tight cunt, and I keep hitting as deep as possible while she lets out a string of muffled cries against her palm.

Christ. A few white spots crowd my vision as I find myself bent over her, breathing heavily.

I'd planned to pull out and walk away, leaving her there marked up and damp with freshly-fucked tears staining her face. But something stops me, and I don't know what it is, but for a moment, I'm struck immobile by the glisten of wetness coating her long lashes. Even in the dark, I can see the pink blossoming high on her cheekbones. Her lilac hair tumbles around her nape and jaw in the places where her curls have come loose.

The only sounds filling the darkened kitchen come from our rough breathing, and the racket of my pulse as it begins to recede in my ears.

My cock twitches, still buried deep inside her. More than interested in all the ways to explore using our new toy.

Though I decide that can wait, instead, I pull out with a grunt. Holding the cotton to one side, I watch with rapt fascination as I see the welling of cum at her swollen entrance. She can keep that evidence against her skin, proving exactly how much she enjoyed every minute of getting bent over and used. This girl needs to remember who she belongs to now.

"These stay on," I say as I readjust her panties to keep my claim right there.

She doesn't move, and I suspect it's because I've fucked all the fight out of her.

I shift at her back, hooking the long hem of Ky's shirt back down, then tuck myself away. My eyes are fixated on her curves as I do so, following the slope of her thighs where the t-shirt ends right below the soft flesh of her ass cheeks like a goddamn invitation for round two.

"Just go. Leave me alone," Fox whispers brokenly.

Which is what I absolutely plan to do, but not before I've picked her up and carried her to her bedroom. I stand over her until she pees, ignoring her protests. It's only upon threats of taking her bathroom door off its hinges permanently that she finally relents. Her eyes won't meet mine. *Good.*

She seems lost in a quiet daze as I settle her beneath the covers of her bed.

Standing back, I'm a statue beside her mattress as she rolls over, turning her back on me. For whatever reason, I stay firmly rooted there and keep watching as she drops into sleep almost instantly. Her sooty lashes rest across her damp cheeks while her breathing turns shallow, shoulders rising and falling in slow succession. Because if there's one thing I know for sure now, is that my demons are quieter than they've been for a long time.

And I don't know what to do with that information.

CHAPTER 32
FOX

I have a serious problem.

I'm sicker than I thought.

The way Raven claimed me last night and forced orgasm after orgasm out of me might have broken my brain. I hate him for what he did, but not more than I hate myself for enjoying it. Afterward, when he watched over me, I couldn't even look at him, because...what the fuck is wrong with me.

A man forced me to have sex, even when I said no, and called me a dirty slut.

But I liked it.

Possibly more than liked it, even.

Turns out I'm more of a freak than I dared admit to myself before knowing these men. The sense of disgust in how much my body enjoyed last night crawls across my skin like spiders.

He's right. I could have called for Ky. He gave me every opportunity to get away, or seek help. But, instead, I let him use me...shame scalds my cheeks when I think about the fact that I came harder than I've done in a long, long time.

If ever.

The imprinted memory of his rough hands and cock buried

deep inside me leaves heat rushing to the tips of my ears. Not to mention that when I woke up, I discovered a glass of water left for me on my bedside table, alongside a silver foil packet containing a couple of painkillers.

Something inside me says it is a dangerous idea to allow myself to believe it was *him* who left them for me while I passed out asleep.

Although, it appears that my body is now finely attuned to the presence of both Ky and Raven. Both men watch over me tonight from the edges of the ornate ballroom at Noire House, looking like gods poured into their jet-black suits. I can feel the weight of their possessive gaze over me; however, as per the terms of their plot for revenge, I make my way through the crowds of Gathered. *Alone.*

That doesn't mean they're immune to this lingering desire that seems hell-bent on captivating all of us. My naughty Viking nearly had me bent over the hood of the vehicle tonight before we'd left the compound. For a moment, I thought they were set for another round of sharing me when I caught wolf boy looking at my ass like it was his next meal, but instead, he shoved Ky into the vehicle and made sure I was secured in the backseat.

In all honesty, I wouldn't have made a single peep of protest if they'd chosen a different course of action. My pussy has been tingling since the moment I saw them suited up in all their handsome, murderous glory tonight.

"Babe, you're living up to your name...a stone-cold Fox. Look at that dress." A gentle voice cuts through my thoughts as Poe sweeps up to me, glittering in her own silvery gown with delicate metallic chain straps. She looks like a gorgeous badass, immediately offering me a glass of champagne as she holds her own in the other manicured hand.

This is absolutely the only person I would even consider accepting a drink from in this place.

"The whole thing looks amazing." Even though Noire House was my home, there were entire wings I never set foot in. This ballroom was only a place I glimpsed on occasion. I never did come to an event held here when I was younger—mostly because I was too afraid of catching the eye of one of my father's friends.

But even knowing what this place represents, I can't help but admire the way Poe has worked magic to create a stunning club and event—working to erase the stains of the past. It's my father's friends intermingling with the Anguis in attendance that turn the whole thing rancid.

"Thank you. Although I gotta say, I much prefer when it's simply the *club*, rather than the pretentiousness of these do's the council insist on us putting on...you'll have to come sometime." Her eyes drift to where Ky and Raven stand talking with Hawke. Two other gorgeous men, who I assume must be Poe's other partners, are with them.

The reason I know it's Hawke and not Thorne is because the man in question has been a ghost for nearly a whole week now. Apparently, he's supposed to be in attendance tonight, but so far, he's made himself scarce.

"The club?" I take a sip of my champagne. "Do you think they'd allow me to?" My eyes dart between Ky and Hawke where they stand together talking. There's something so different in the way they interact compared to how he behaves with Thorne.

In the couple of times I've seen him around Hawke, I can see the brotherly banter sitting front and center in their dynamic... but with the other Calliano brother, the energy swirls in an entirely different direction, and there's a thought that sways on the outskirts of my brain, but I don't put a voice to it.

"Allow you to?" Poe scoffs. "It's your inheritance. Your club by all rights. Tell you what, fuck whatever they might say; I'm sending you our guest registration right now." She whips out her phone and starts typing. This girl isn't afraid of these men, and it gives me a little dash of courage in my own quest to learn how best to survive them and their world.

Almost immediately, my phone vibrates inside my clutch.

"How..." I pull it out and see there's a message from a new contact and Poe is smirking at me over the bubbles dancing in her champagne flute. "How did you get my number?"

She mimes zipping her lips and chucking the imaginary key over one shoulder. "Thank me later. Better yet, even if you never fill out that form, promise you'll come and at least tour the club with me, ok?"

"You're trouble." I shake my head and quickly save her contact.

"I'm the tame one. Just wait til you meet my bestie, Rita. That's when you know the night is going to get really wild."

At the mention of girlfriends and nights out, my heart stalls a little. I miss Em something shocking, and I have no idea if I'll ever see her again.

I deflate like a worn-out helium balloon, and Poe's brows crease together as she notes the shift in my body language.

"I don't know if girls like me get to have *girls' nights*. When you're just a means to exact revenge against a dead man, your life ceases to exist."

Poe cocks her head. Her eyes fill with what I can only hope is compassion rather than pity. I don't know her full story yet, but I get the impression she at least understands...even if her circumstances of entering the world of the Anguis were different.

"I don't know what to tell you, Fox...but has Thorne only mentioned your father to you in all this?" There's an expression on her face that's hard to read.

I'm busy trying to form words when there's a noise from the crowd as someone calls out Poe's name. There's a group of what must be her club regulars waving her over and she gives me an apologetic smile.

"Sorry, Fox. My VIPs are a horny bunch to keep satisfied. I bet they want the inside goss on plans for the next club open night." Before I can grill her about what Poe meant by her cryptic statement about Thorne, she's gone. Swallowed up by the sea of dinner jackets and gowns.

People I have no interest in speaking with spot that I'm isolated from the herd once more and come up to me in droves. All the while, I drain my glass and smile as they talk about my father as if he wasn't a festering boil of a human.

My clutch vibrates, and I quickly excuse myself to check the message. It's another from Poe.

Sorry, I shouldn't have opened my big mouth.

If Thorne wants to tell you…he will.

Tell me what? I want to text back and demand answers because I'm so sick and tired of all this bullshit and secrecy. But then the string quartet in the corner strikes up and I've immediately got a slimy old man with dyed hair and a leering smile filling my vision, asking me to dance.

And because I'm here to be punished, I have to say yes and do so with a gracious smile.

I LOVE how I look tonight. Secretly, I swooned like a heart-eyed schoolgirl when I heard Ky's low whistle, catching the way he devoured every inch of my figure the moment he laid eyes on me. I'm in a floor-length velvet gown the color of obsidian, with a thigh-high slit and a soft draped scoop of fabric across my breasts.

But there's no worse feeling than having this creep lay his hands all over me under the pretense of the occasion. He's doing little more than making a brash attempt to feel up the Noire House heir in front of his pathetic band of Gathered.

He'll probably be front row at the Pledging, too. Angling for the best position to watch me spread my legs.

What I can't explain is the difference between how I enjoyed Raven forcing himself on me last night and the sickening feeling rising in my throat the longer this man paws at me.

I can't cause a scene in here, not in front of all the Anguis. I'm playing the dutiful part of my father's heir, after all. By going along with their plan, I'm protecting Em and safeguarding my mother's memory from their sick lies and twisted, false claims. But my skin is crawling, and my chest grows tighter with every turn around the dance floor.

Eventually, the man groping me speaks up. "Do you remember me?" His face smiles serenely at the room, nodding periodically at whoever looks our way.

"Yes." I force a smile. His face is familiar enough, but right now his name evades me, and I'll gladly do without knowing it. In fact, I would happily go without ever seeing his leering expression ever again.

"Andreas and I had plans; you may or may not have been aware of these sorts of things. Especially considering your lengthy absence from Noire House."

His beady eyes flicker down to look at me and I want to vomit.

"Well, my father isn't here now, and I'm taking his place as the last remaining Noire." Lies, but I don't need him knowing that.

"You'll be needing a steady hand." The man's teeth are

polished white against his overdone fake tan. "A naive girl like you knows nothing of this world. What you require is someone who can successfully guide the Noire seat and this Household within the Anguis."

"I am more than certain I'll do just fine."

"There will be expectations of you as the Noire heir to fulfill certain *duties*."

Ew. If he's suggesting I get knocked up in the name of Noire House, no thank you.

"Wouldn't want a pretty little thing like you to end up beyond her depth with the Anguis. Your father made certain of that."

I bet he fucking did.

Just as I'm starting to fall apart at the seams, a shadow looms large over my shoulder. Our movements halt abruptly.

"If you'll allow me, Crane."

Miles Crane. The name rears up in my gut like a bull ready to charge. I remember him, or more to the point, I remember being threatened with the prospect of being sold to him as a teenager.

But I don't have time to roll into horrid memories of my father's schemes, the sudden recognition of this man is not what captures my attention. The deep, velvety voice and solid wall at my back isn't either of my so-called protectors who I arrived here with tonight.

It's Thorne.

His palm comes to rest against the curve at the base of my spine, and sparks begin to soar from that tiny point of contact.

"Of course, be my guest, Calliano." The sleaze steps aside, gesturing the length of my body with a disgusting look on his face as if I'm already his to lend to Thorne for a twirl around the floor. I have to fight every urge that wants to spit in his face.

Thorne comes to stand in front of me, and I'm never prepared for this man, it would seem. He's dressed in black to match Ky and Raven, with his hair tousled and jaw looking fine in a coating of stubble.

Where the fuck has he been all this time?

I want to slap him and kiss him and have his hands on me all at once.

"Good timing. I think I was about to be the evening's ritual sacrifice to appease the Gathered."

Thorne steps into my body and wraps my hand inside his massive palm, while the other snakes around my waist. I nearly gasp when the weight and heat of his possessive hold feels as though it might burn through the fabric of my dress at any moment.

"He deserves his tongue cut out for touching you like that." The gruffness in his voice makes my thighs clench.

Well, fuck. Murderous, possessive Thorne is my kind of temptation, it would seem.

"Any time you want to bring me that vile man's tongue, would be a wonderful thing." We don't exchange civilities or greetings like normal people might do after not seeing each other for an extended period of time. It seems almost laughable —the first words we've spoken to each other in a week, or since the moment he left me on those steps the night of the auction, are about dismemberment.

Because *nothing* about this life is normal.

Our bodies move intuitively with the music, and of course, this asshole knows how to dance. He's smooth and suave and smells so fucking good I want to melt. His giant paw dwarfs my hand inside his while holding me steady. There's no escaping him, and maybe it's because I haven't seen him for days; I find myself perfectly content to be held by him. Clearly, my hormones are acting like lusty bitches again, since not one single fiber in my being wants to flee his presence.

We're both silent. His stormy blue eyes focus on the room over my head. Meanwhile, my mind spins in furious circles, clutching at the right words to ask him where he's been, what he's been doing...and possibly the most desperate answer I'm searching for of them all; I want to know *who* he's been doing it with.

Rather than reveal the full extent of my budding jealousy, I bite down on the inside of my cheek.

I doubt he would concede to giving me an honest answer, anyway.

Thorne is a tempest of mystery, and I suspect that is exactly how he has survived in this world long enough to get to where he is now. Even while exacting revenge against the finely dressed predatory scum lurking in this very room.

What I decide to finally settle on, is a thread I'm now itching to pull at since my brief conversation with Poe a moment ago.

I know they harbor the same hatred for my father as I do. While there are mountains of secrets and untruths, along with threats issued by these men, what I know is that they are against what my hideous bloodline represents. And if they're willing to go to extreme lengths to seek revenge on Andreas Noire—while being monsters in their own right—they're at least the type of creatures I can find it within myself to come to an understanding with.

This world doesn't operate on the simplicity of identifying whether someone is good or bad. Everyone has their own version of darkness lurking within.

"What did my father do to you?" I ask. Nothing like coming right out with it.

His jaw lines with tension, arms stiffening even though we're still swaying in time to the music.

"I've already told you, Foxglove. Don't ask questions about things you don't want to hear the answer to."

I roll my eyes and let out a petulant sigh.

"We have a common goal here, Thorne." My head tilts back

so I can study his cheekbones and his handsome profile, but his eyes remain busy scouring the room rather than meeting my gaze. Despite that fact, I keep pressing because I know he's listening; it's merely his instinct to be wary around these vultures at all times. "Everything my father did and represented is the worst kind of disgrace against humanity. You know enough about my life to understand why I ran from him. Let me help in some way."

There's a steel wall in front of me. He's impenetrable and doesn't react or look at me. Yet, something about that spurs me on. I don't actively seek to push this man's buttons, but the mounting tension and probably the glass of champagne gets the better of my tongue.

"Why won't you let me help?" With a huff, I try to pull away from him, and that seems to be the key to finally attracting his attention.

Thorne's fierce eyes are suddenly on mine. Blazing and filled with years of savage disgust for everyone and everything my father hid within these walls.

"I don't trust you." His voice is low, barely registering above the music. Each word reverberates through my bones.

"What will it take?" I'm being sucked under by the intensity of his stare. Whereas before, he was searching the room, right now, he's searching my very soul. Ransacking through every cell, looking for evidence to prove that I'm no different than my father.

I swallow heavily, and his eyes flit down to the exposed column of my throat. "What can I do to show you...prove to you...that you can trust me?"

The harsh planes of his cheekbones seem to grow more severely defined. His strong hand flexes over my fingers. And as I'm trying to remember how to breathe in his presence, he leans down so that his lips brush the edge of my ear.

"You don't fucking get it, do you? We wanted you to suffer. We wanted you writhing in agony and wishing you were dead."

My heart lurches to the back of my throat. "And now..."

Thorne takes a deep inhale. "You're a parasite. An infection in my blood that I can't get rid of."

He removes his hand from my waist, lifting it to finger a curl of my hair. As he does so, his knuckles graze the side of my face. That infinitely small point of contact sends a jolt through me, shooting right down to my toes, in a way that I will now forever associate with this man. Being near him is like standing naked and wet in the middle of an electrical storm.

Every fine hair on my arms stands on end.

Thorne studies the lilac strand, rubbing it back and forth between his thumb and forefinger. We're moving together around the dance floor, but the whole world feels like it's dropped away, leaving only the two of us locked in this moment.

Dangling on the edge of vulnerability.

My whisper floats up between us. "Let me help. Please." *Let me in.*

As he pulls back to look at me, there's strain painted all over his handsome face while conflicting emotion lurks behind his eyes. A tic flickers in his jaw, and I'm preparing myself to become reacquainted with his cold, hard shell, when he abruptly stops moving.

The song hasn't finished, which throws me off guard. I collide with his massive chest and an audible puff of air rushes from my lungs. It's only his bulk being in the way that prevents me from sprawling across the marble floor.

"We're leaving." He announces. Seemingly content to ignore the way I'm plastered against his torso.

My brain is still trying to fathom what is happening. He's either so pissed off with my line of questioning that I'm in serious trouble, or something in my pleading has finally gotten through.

A thought that terrifies and excites me in equal measure.

Either way, we're moving. Fast. Thorne Calliano wastes no time, keeping my hand wrapped in his warm, calloused palm, he tugs me behind him.

We head toward the edge of the dance floor, cutting through the crowd and making an arrow-straight line for the exit.

Apparently, when this man decides to move, there's not a moment's pause, and I'm a little uncertain what the urgency is.

CHAPTER 33
FOX

Thorne opens the back door of the vehicle for me and helps me step up. As I slide into the spacious backseat, he doesn't shut the door behind me in the way I've come to expect. Instead, his bulky frame follows me like a muscular shadow and the space shrinks by about three feet.

The others are hot on our heels, with Raven driving and Ky making himself comfortable in the passenger seat, having already ditched his suit jacket on the way out. He quickly rolls his shirt sleeves up his forearms, catching my line of sight in the rearview mirror as he does so.

There's pure mischief in his eyes when he snaps me checking out his veined forearms.

I duck my head and go to shift further across toward the other door, but my progress is halted when a heavy arm bands across the front of my waist. The unexpected contact makes me jump, and Thorne uses that to his advantage. Scooping me off the leather and settling me sideways in his lap.

"What are you doing?" With fists clenched, I push against his chest. Quite honestly, right now, I feel like a startled rabbit about to be skinned alive and made into slippers.

"I don't know," he murmurs. His eyes have darkened, and that heavy-lidded gaze drops to my mouth.

Holy ever loving fuck.

This must be a fever dream. Maybe they drugged me again, and I'm hallucinating. Because there is no way Thorne Calliano is holding me in his lap, staring at my mouth like he'll starve if he doesn't get a taste.

My wretched heart leaps into my throat, pulse tripling in intensity.

I'm apparently squirming, because a solid palm lands on my leg to prevent me from moving. His fingers wrap the outside of my thigh while a thumb presses down on the soft inner flesh.

"Thorne…" I hesitate. Darting my tongue out to wet my lips, steely eyes track the small movement.

His pupils bloom.

Every molecule of air gets sucked out of this tiny space in an instant.

Oh, my god, he's turned on.

"Let go of me." I don't know if I mean from his lap, from his compound, or from the intensity of his stare.

No matter how hard I try to argue otherwise, my body yearns for him in a way that must surely be insanity. I've found myself tangled in a web between the three men filling this vehicle, and right now, I'm gladly allowing them to spin their devious threads tighter and tighter.

Heat rages through my body and all I can feel is the overwhelming presence of *him* assaulting me. I want to turn around and straddle his lap. I want to throw my arms around his neck and lose myself in his lips. I want to guide him inside me and put on a show for my wolf and my naughty boy, whose two sets of eyes I can feel searing into me from their positions in the front.

As soon as we pull out of the Noire Estate grounds, Thorne strikes.

He twists my body so that I'm now seated directly on his lap with my back against his torso. There's no hesitation or lingering debate going on inside him now as his fingers hook the slit up the side of my dress and yank at the material until it rucks up around my hips. With predatory ease, he slides two rough palms up the inside of my thighs and spreads my legs to fall on either side of where his knees are spread wide. Holy fuck. I'm a live wire beneath every inch of skin his touch glides over with fierce, possessive strokes.

It's as though he's been calculating exactly how and where he's going to imprint his hold on me, and this is finally the moment his plan comes together.

His muscled chest presses against my back, and the hardness of his cock juts up against my ass. Jesus. They're all big, but this man might split me in two.

Thorne expertly avoids the space between the junction of my thighs where I'm already aching and throbbing to have his rough hands on me, *right there.* A delicious rumble flows from his chest when he realizes I'm shifting and trying to chase after his fingers. Issuing a low noise of warning, and being every inch a controlling asshole, Thorne grabs my wrists and wrenches them behind my back.

My brain is too fogged with unrestrained desire to react.

It's only when cold metal kisses my skin that I'm broken out of my horny daze. He clicks a set of handcuffs around my wrists with the efficiency of a man who has done this a thousand times before.

I open my mouth to protest and curse at him, but Thorne is a master at this kind of ambush, and I'm nothing more than a fumbling, incompetent student. Two fingers hook the corner of my mouth before I can get my words out, and with the other hand, he slides a hot palm up and over my rib cage until he reaches the curve below my breasts.

Drool quickly collects at the corner of my mouth, and I'm

arching like a cat in heat as he teases my nipples through the velvet material of my dress. Without a bra, I'm able to feel every point of contact, and Thorne uses that to his advantage. Thumbing with an expert touch over my sensitive, hardened peaks until I'm making desperate noises against his fingers.

An ache starts to build in my shoulders thanks to having my arms crushed against his ridiculously hard muscles. The metal of the cuffs chafes and digs into my skin.

Thorne presses his fingers deep and firm against my tongue. "I don't need a brat, Foxglove."

Fuck him for the way he says my name and the fact that every time he does, it makes my pussy clench. Not only that, his voice makes me want to sink to my knees, worship his cock, and say thank you for the privilege of having him fill my mouth.

"I need a good girl who craves the feeling of submission. Are you going to be a good girl for me and let me finger this pussy whenever I want?"

Oh, my god. Yes.

I make a humming noise around his fingers. There's a mess of drool down one side of my face, and the thong I'm wearing just burst into flames.

"Are you going to be an obedient little slut, who knows exactly who owns her, and opens her legs for us all?"

Fuck. Thorne Calliano has effortlessly tapped into a part of my brain that has been begging for a master.

His mouth is hot at my ear. "Is that a yes?"

I nod frantically against his two fingers. That seems to satisfy him because he lets my mouth go, allowing both hands to now wander freely.

Over the wild thudding of my pulse, I hear Ky shifting around in the front seat.

"Jesus," he mutters as I catch his reflection in the rearview. There's an anguished look of arousal on his face.

All I can see of Raven is the back of his wild hair and the whites of his knuckles gripping the steering wheel.

"You're going to come on my fingers, while that wet cunt of yours drips all over me, and then when we get back, we're going to fuck you until sunrise."

Who is this person, and where did they bury the body of stern, silent Thorne? This man has a filthy mouth on him, and he wants to fuck me, and I'm so relieved I could weep.

He's completely scrambled my brain and body, flinging my sanity out past the point of no return. So, I say the only thing I can think of as his hands roam over my tits, squeezing and pinching at my begging nipples.

"Thank you, Daddy."

Thorne makes a feral noise, and his hips give an involuntary thrust beneath me. Oh, yes, he's definitely a Daddy. I've never called anyone that before, but it slipped out, and now that I know it affects him, it's my new favorite thing. That and the direction his hands are moving in. He slides them lower over the curve of my waist until he reaches the crease of my thighs. With one firm tug at the side of my thong, he rips the soaked lace off me.

"*Ffffuck.*" Ky sounds like he's dying in the front seat. Which only gets worse when Thorne tosses him the scrap of fabric coated in the evidence of my arousal. "You're such a dick." Squirming, he readjusts himself like he's going to crawl out of his skin.

"Got something to say?" Thorne growls and fuck me this man is so unfairly hot. "You've already disobeyed me once when it comes to her pussy, so you can sit there and listen to me finger fuck her until she screams my name."

Hearing him be possessive over me shouldn't be turning me on. But I'm a writhing mess, desperate for him to uphold that promise and touch me properly for the first time. Even if I have to beg for it.

"Did you like having both their cocks, hmm?" Thorne turns his attention back to me, sucking my earlobe into his mouth, and I nearly levitate off his lap.

"Yes." God, yes. My head drops back against the crook of his neck. At this point I couldn't care less about the way my shoulder joints burn or how the cuffs dig in relentlessly.

"Do you really think you can handle three of us?" His tone is rough but laced with unchecked arousal.

"I want all of you." My breathy voice doesn't even sound like me; the only noise in this car is my frantic breathing and tiny whines as his hold digs against the softness of my thighs, almost to the point of agony.

He's got me panting and lifting my hips, and the man hasn't even touched me properly yet.

"You're ours. We own you. So no other man, or woman, fucking touches you. Do you understand me, Foxglove?"

Jesus. A wanton noise escapes me that is something of a cross between a *yes* and a *fuck yes*.

"This needy cunt is ours anytime we want."

"Mmmm...Yes." I nod.

Finally, finally...Thorne's thick fingers start to move. Brushing across my overheated skin, before he spreads my pussy lips with two fingers. I nearly fall apart right then and there when Ky readjusts the mirror so he can see exactly what is happening back here.

These men are going to be the goddamn end of me.

"Oh, shit. Oh my god." Moans fall from my lips as Thorne begins to fondle my pussy. Taking all the time he pleases, spreading my slickness around, exploring right from my entrance up to my aching clit and back down again.

His cock presses more insistently against my ass.

"We're your gods now. And you'll only call out for us when you're being a good girl spreading your legs."

Ky's head hits the headrest with a thud. His hand is on the

fly of his pants, and he's squeezing. "Christ, Thorne. I'm going to blow just listening to you say that kind of shit."

"She's so fucking wet, Ky. I think our plaything enjoys you watching her."

My heart is pounding in my throat.

That's when Thorne goes in for the killer blow. He plunges two thick fingers inside me, and starts rubbing my clit with the heel of his palm.

"Look at your greedy pussy. Dripping all over my hand and letting me sink right up to my knuckles."

"Fuck. *MmmFuck.*" I buck against him, trying to give him better access and leverage and to chase the liquid pleasure pouring through my veins like gold.

"You're going to let me play with this sweet little cunt all day if I want. Listen to how desperate you are just for two fingers."

The car is filled with the obscene sound of my wetness as Thorne pumps in and out of me. I can't stop the noises bubbling up, and I turn my head to the side, moaning into the crook of his neck. My lips are wet and plush against his warm skin, and the feeling of his stubble beneath my mouth adds to the sensations hurtling through my body.

"That's it. Be a good fucking girl and come for me."

What mere mortal could resist a command like that. Certainly not me when his intensity picks up. The heavy pressure of his palm against my clit sends me shooting off into the stars as he fingers me mercilessly.

As my mouth opens on a silent cry, I can taste the faint hint of sweat and his scent from the side of his throat, where my lips press hard against his skin.

"Oh, god. Daddy. *Yes.*" I break apart on a whimper and a gasp while clenching around his fingers. Pins and needles shoot along the length of each arm, and I don't think I can feel my toes anymore.

"Make yourself useful, Ky. Get back here and clean our little slut up."

"Thank fuck." His voice from the front seat is hoarse.

I'm not sure if this is one reason they have a vehicle of this size, but despite his massive shoulders, Ky threads himself into the back seat with the skill of a gymnast.

"Screw you all," my wolf mutters as he fists the rearview mirror and levels me with a piercing glare. One that promises all kinds of wicked deeds once he's no longer trapped in the driver's seat or in control of this vehicle. "That's the last time I drive for either of you horny dickheads. Next trip, I'm taking her, and you can both walk home."

"I promise I'll make it up to you, baby." Ky's green eyes devour my body as he responds to Raven. Now that he's moved into the back seat, it feels like an oven in here. His gaze pauses on where I'm still spread wide in Thorne's lap, fixating on the place where his fingers part my pussy lips. My clit is swollen and exposed, and I can tell I've made a mess of his pants.

I drag my bottom lip between my teeth as I see how hard Ky is. The outline of his cock strains behind his fly.

"Well? Don't just fucking sit there. I told you to clean her up."

CHAPTER 34
FOX

Don't just fucking sit there. I told you to clean her up.

Well, fuck. Thorne is going to dom Ky, too, and even though I'm still reconnecting with my body after that orgasm, his words send a fresh flood of arousal straight through me.

While I suspect these two have never explored this unspoken *thing* between them before, if it takes sharing me to help them find their way, I'm the most enthusiastic participant they'll ever find.

Right now, I really wish I could see Thorne's face, to soak up his expression while Ky shifts his position in the back seat. My wolf's attention flickers between the deserted road up ahead—illuminated only by our headlights—and what's unfolding in the backseat.

What I do hear is Thorne's breathing becoming more ragged, revealing the first glimpse of his composure breaking the moment Ky lowers his head. But not before he pauses, hovering close to my hip, while giving me the filthiest wink.

"Let me live between these thighs, baby girl. I'll happily lick your pretty little cunt anytime."

His mouth fastens over my pussy, and I'm arching—whimpering with every wicked flick and suck. This man can kiss like the devil himself and uses every inch of his tongue to work me into a frenzy. The scruff of his short beard scrapes my skin, and it's pure bliss.

I'll never experience anything else like this man between my legs, of that I'm certain.

"Oh, fuck. Ky." My teeth sink into my lower lip as he feasts on my pussy and swirls his tongue over my clit. Sending me flying headlong toward another climax.

"Be a good boy and make her come. I want our girl nice and loose when we fuck her." Thorne's voice is dark and gravelly as he nips my earlobe. The vibration of him speaking shoots through my body and whatever he said makes Ky falter for a moment, losing his rhythm.

"Whose name is she going to scream out this time? Yours or mine?" The man hovering over my pussy is playing with fire. Taunting and teasing the limits of Thorne's patience.

Holy fuck, it's scalding hot being between these two men.

"If you think I won't edge you until you're whining for relief, you're gravely mistaken, *Harris*."

"Sounds like a good time." Ky's lips twitch, then he attacks me with sinful expertise, sucking on my clit until I'm begging. Incoherent. A smoldering blaze.

The man at my back brims with power over both of us.

"Ride his face and make a mess of him." Thorne shifts his hand and digs it into Ky's hair. Holding him against my clit in exactly the way I would want to if I had use of my hands, except they're still cuffed behind my back. Seeing his strong fingers flex in Ky's blonde strands is the moment I fall apart. Crying out as my pussy clamps down, and I'm jerking against his face. Meanwhile, Ky works me through the rolling waves with his stiffened tongue, continuing to massage the sensitive bud.

My body and brain are on two different planets. I'm only

distantly aware that we've arrived at the compound. Does this vehicle have tinted windows? Whoever was manning the gate probably had a front-row seat to my pussy on display.

Whatever.

Two orgasms already tonight...was absolutely worth it.

THREE WILD CREATURES surround me en route to one of the massive couches in the lounge. Clearly, we aren't going to make it more than a few feet inside the house, what with the avalanche of tension threatening to bury all four of us tonight.

Ky hadn't waited for an invitation as we parked up. Just hauled me off Thorne's lap and slung me over his shoulder. By the time I'm set down on the cushioned edge of the sprawling couch, he's already tossed my heels somewhere, and he's working to get rid of his shirt with record speed.

Raven prowls in behind him. Jacket now gone, and he's loosening his cuffs. Between the two of them, they look carved from marble in the silvery moonlight streaming through the floor-to-ceiling windows. Only the ghostly outline of the forest edge looms behind them, and it almost feels as though we're right in amongst the trees.

The last one to arrive is Thorne. He's carrying his suit jacket and tosses it over the back of one of the chairs.

Holy shit. This is actually happening.

My legs are a little shaky, but I'm going to need at least one of them to help get me out of this dress—especially if they don't plan on uncuffing me any time soon. I stumble while attempting to get to my feet, and even though my body feels lax with pleasure, I can't help wincing a little when Thorne's hand grabs my hip bone in an effort to steady me.

Which becomes immediately clear, was a mistake.

"Are you hurt?" He removes the cuffs quicker than I can blink, and his eyes are furious. Thorne scans over me with rapid, scrutinizing sweeps of his gaze. It's as if I'm made up of pixie dust and might disintegrate if one of them breathes too hard in my direction.

Hastily, one hand goes to rub at my wrist, and I shake my head. But Thorne has me manacled in his grip within a second.

My blood quickens.

"It's nothing." My eyes fly unbidden to Raven. I don't know or imagine he particularly cares if I'm hurt or not, but I don't want him to think for one second I wouldn't want that kind of experience from him—with him—all over again.

"What the fuck did you do to her? I'm gone for less than a fucking week..." Thorne follows my line of sight as he growls in the direction of the others. My fingers grab his hand and hold him there, pressing down against the bruises on my hip bone from where my wolf had me bent over the stone countertop last night.

"It's ok, I'm fine..." If anything, I'm a little flushed with embarrassment.

"What?" Thorne's steely eyes search mine before that cold, firm gaze roams over me once more.

"I liked it," I admit. My eyes flit back over to Raven, who is silhouetted by the forest and glow of the moon.

He chews that piece of information over, glancing at Raven and seemingly putting two and two together. "What parts specifically."

Oh, god. He's going to make me come out and say it, much like Raven forced orgasms out of me.

"Being forced." My pulse flutters wildly and I have to wet my lips before continuing. "I've never explored that part of myself before, and while I've fantasized about it on my own, I never really thought I'd ever get the chance in person."

You could slice the air in here; it's so thick with desire and tension.

"And you enjoyed it." He states again. No—demands to know.

"It's fucked up. I guess I'm more broken than you bargained for." My eyes drop to the side.

That stirs up a hornet's nest of bristling muscles and clenched jaws. Suddenly there are three men crowding me, each wearing a fierce expression.

"No. It's not, baby girl." Ky tugs on a strand of my hair before rubbing it between his finger and thumb. These three all seem to be obsessed with my hair.

"Your mayhem matches ours. Nothing is wrong with you."

"Who made you think that?" My wolf isn't touching me freely like the others, but he's stepped close enough that I can see the scars on his lip and eyebrow. His words are low, sounding out a warning.

Like he's already planning who he needs to dispose of.

Well, fuck. That's made me horny for this man all over again.

"No one. I just..."

I don't know how to finish that statement. After a life of being threatened by my father to sell me to some disgusting sadist who *would* force themselves on me over and over and over without mercy, it feels like I'm messed up in so many ways, if that is something I actually admit to enjoying.

But that's the thing, it is these men who make that fantasy come to life in a way that makes my insides light up with desire.

Only these men.

Thorne reads all of that and more in the story playing out behind my eyes. Sliding fingers into my hair, he guides me to look at him and take in all his masculine beauty. Harsh angles caressed lovingly by deep shadows. "Your pleasure belongs to us. No matter what form that comes in. Do you understand?"

There's a shaky exhale that leaves my body. But I nod, because I do believe that he understands this part of me. "Thank you."

Out of the corner of my eye, I can see Ky has fisted the front of Raven's shirt, and even though his green eyes are still on me, he's starting to undress him.

My throat bobs at the sight.

But Thorne still holds near total command over my attention. "Your pleasure is ours to provide."

He lets go of my hair and uses that hand to slowly knock the straps of my dress off each shoulder. One by one.

"Ours to take when we want to."

The velvety material slides down my body. Baring me to them completely. My tits are heavy with desire, and my nipples pebble between the glide of the fabric over the sensitive buds now being exposed to the cool air.

"And ours to control."

With a powerful, veined hand, he cups my breast and pinches one of my nipples. Heat and pain shoot off in a race against ecstasy, darting on a wild course through my bloodstream.

He guides one calloused palm over my bruised hip and proceeds to back me up against the wall of vast windows overlooking the forest. The cold surface presses against the length of my spine, and I'm so small against this vaulted cathedral of glass. Like an ant who might be squashed beneath a heavy boot at any moment.

"Yours," I murmur. Entranced by the magnetism of this man and completely at his mercy.

CHAPTER 35
FOX

Thorne is all-consuming as he leans over my naked form.

He's still clad in his dress shirt and trousers as his hands press either side of my head; those powerful forearms and chest cage me in. Behind me, I feel the quiet tapping of rain against the window, and there's a dappled effect to the moonlight drifting across the room. Rivulets of water start to bead and slowly drip down the glass. Somewhere between the moon and the droplets, an eerie glow is cast like a silvery net everywhere I look.

My eyes dart over to where the other two are in various stages of undress. Fucking hell, this is every outrageous fantasy of mine come to life, and it just so happens that the men who want to punish me also desire me.

I guess we're all as fucked as each other.

"Eyes on me." Thorne rumbles. The sound is like honey coating me from head to toe, and my stomach does a swan dive in anticipation of what's to come.

One finger hooks under my chin, and he tilts my head back

so that I'm swimming in his azure-blue gaze. He looks down at me with so much furious longing that I'm suspended for a moment, not knowing whether he's going to kiss me or kill me.

"I don't mind sharing your body, Foxglove. But when I'm fucking you, I expect every ounce of your focus to be on me, unless I give you permission otherwise."

Well, shit. Yes, please. This man can tell me what to do all day and all night long.

Those hands he uses to probably murder people are so careful with me, and my entire body hums. Desire radiates like a solar flare from that singular point of contact below my chin.

With Ky, he's like being inside a whirlwind. My Norse god filled with wicked promises.

Being with wolf boy is every dark edge of mine being lured to tangle with his menace.

But with Thorne? It's like I'm melting for one drop of praise from his lips or feather-soft brush of his fingers across my skin.

"Take me out." His command is quiet and firm.

My hands seek out his belt buckle; each clank of metal as it comes undone beneath my shaky fingers sends a spark straight to my clit. The buzz of his zipper descending causes goosebumps to erupt down the full extent of my arms. And then I'm biting my lip as I carefully push down the waistband of his briefs.

Oh. My. God. Thorne's cock is thick and long and veined along the length of him. It bobs up against his stomach, and at the base, I can see his trimmed dark hair.

I must be signaling every dirty thought of how I want to drop to my knees and take him in my mouth because the man in front of me makes an impatient noise.

"There's plenty of time for that later."

He grabs me under the ass and lifts me to wrap my legs around his hips.

"*Thorne*." I gasp. Feeling the swollen head of him pressing insistently at my core.

"Put me inside you." The instruction is gruff, leaving a trail of shivers dancing across my skin.

"Yes, Daddy."

He makes the sexiest grunting noise hearing me call him that, and I have to bite my lip.

With one hand clinging to his shoulder, I reach down and wrap my fingers around his cock. He's velvety beneath my grip, and the sensation of me touching him for the first time causes Thorne to let out a hiss of pleasure. Knowing just how much I affect this man sends me floating on a glittering cloud, feeling all-powerful. Even if I'm the one completely naked and at his mercy to be used by him as he likes.

I wriggle slightly in his hold, fitting him to my soaked and swollen entrance.

"That's it. Guide me in. Right there." The moment the tip of him breaches me, he takes over.

"Shit. Even after stretching you around my fingers, you're so tight."

I throw both arms around his neck, and my mouth hangs open as he presses my spine up against the windows.

"*Oh, ffffuck*." I moan as he pulses his hips, allowing me to adjust to his size, and the fat head of him feels so fucking good working that delicious spot.

Thorne makes a feral noise, like he's barely hanging on by a thread, then his eyes drop to my lips.

"You're mine." His voice is a murmur.

My reply is only the faintest whimper.

He slams his mouth over my own, and that has me done for. Thorne is kissing me, and my soul decides to vacate my body.

This man tastes like the sweetest kind of torture because now I know what his lips feel like, plush and firm and demanding; there's no avoiding the knowledge that I'm going to want this again and again.

Thorne groans into my mouth, and as his tongue invades, his cock pushes deep inside.

My back slams up against the window, and he starts thrusting into me with the weeks and weeks' worth of pent-up tension that has been building between us.

All I can do is cling to him as my breasts bounce and drag against his shirt, and my pussy spasms around his cock. The drag of him against my inner walls is unreal, filling me so goddamn perfectly, and leaving me lost to anything but the sensation of him.

He consumes every part of me. Nibbling and licking at my lips, his powerful body stroking me with each determined shove forward of his cock. The pleasure is addicting as I'm stretched around his length, and Thorne hits a spot that feels so fucking intense and soul-destroying.

"Fuck, you feel like you were made for this." He says in my ear, before burying his face in my neck.

My fingers tangle in the short hair at his nape as I mumble a response.

I don't know how long we're lost in that moment, when all I can feel and taste and think about is him, but all too soon, the cool glass leaves my spine as I'm lifted off the window. Part of me wants to protest, while part of me can hardly catch my breath. Thorne carries me across the room with his cock still buried deep inside me. Between the orgasms he wrung out of me in the backseat of the car, to how well he's filling me, I'm not sure if I'll make it through tonight.

RIP my pussy if all three of these men intend on fucking me like that.

As we reach the enormous couch, I catch sight of the other two, who are completely naked, and my mouth goes dry at the sight of them. They're both half-lying, sprawled out side by side, and are in a prime position to watch us fuck up against the window. Ky is tucked under the crook of Raven's arm and he's leisurely pumping both of their dicks. Two sets of darkened eyes rake over my nakedness as I cling to Thorne.

"Holy shit, you look good together." Ky croons as he comes toward me, brushing my hair to the side before dropping a hot kiss on my neck. "I'll watch that show any day."

Thorne's cock pulses inside me.

"I'm not done with her yet." He growls at Ky, who chuckles, then licks my ear.

"Don't worry, Daddy. You can still have your turn."

My eyes find my wolf, who sits with one arm thrown over the back of the couch and a knee raised. Exactly like I hoped, his entire chest is tattooed to match the ink crawling up his neck and down his arms. He's a fucking masterpiece, and I'm a little awestruck, staring open-mouthed at his naked form.

Could he be convinced to roam around in nothing but sweats all day like my Viking does?

Ky pinches my ass, making me gasp against the man carrying me—whose thick length is still deep inside my pussy. "Stare all you like, baby girl. Just watch out when the wolf finally catches you."

If I didn't know better, a ghost of a smile tugs at the corner of Raven's lips.

Thorne turns us both and sets one knee on the edge of the giant L-shaped corner of the couch, setting me on my back against the cushions as he pulls out. When he straightens up, I'm treated to another sight of his dick, and if a girl could die from voyeuristic pleasure, I'd surely be six feet under right now.

"You assholes have had your chance to fuck her already; that pussy is all mine tonight." He unbuttons his shirt while glaring at the other two.

Ky is already looming over me with glittering eyes. "God, you look good getting railed, baby girl." He drops his mouth to cover my breast, and my spine bows up as he sucks down. I thread my fingers into his hair, holding him in place as he flicks his tongue and plays with the sensitive bud before shifting to the other side. Grazing his teeth over the hardened points, he takes one and bites down gently.

My blood turns to fire, and I cry out with a loud moan.

"Dirty girl. You like when I play with these gorgeous tits, don't you?"

"God. Yes."

He sucks the other into his mouth and then does the same thing. I'm flying high on the mix of pain and pleasure running red hot through every cell.

Beside me, Thorne slides into the corner up against the cushions; his palm runs over my other breast, and he pinches hard while Ky nips at my flesh. Ungodly noises burst out of me as both men torture my nipples.

My eyes are glazed with lust and desire as I stare up at Thorne, waiting for his next command. Because I know there's one coming. He's running this entire show tonight, and the other two seem content to let him assume that role.

"Has anyone fucked your sweet little ass before, Foxglove?"

Well, shit. Hearing those words causes my body to tense up in a rush of excitement laced with uncertainty. Ky's tongue slowly runs over my aching breast, hovering, waiting to hear my answer. There's electricity zapping around the room as I try to find the right words in my dazed state.

"Yes, but not in quite a while." I stammer. My tongue feels too big for my mouth.

"You didn't enjoy it?" Thorne's brow creases.

Oh, god. This feels like the worst time to talk about my less-than-stellar experience with past attempts at anal. "It's not that I didn't like it...I just don't think I was prepared very well." My eyes bounce between him and Ky.

This feels like I'm on stage, under a spotlight...*naked.*

The wheels in Thorne's mind turn rapidly. "No one goes near her ass...tonight." He jabs a finger at Ky and Raven. Part of me exhales a relieved sigh, while the sluttier part of me wails in disbelief.

My Viking gives me a filthy look. One that promises all sorts of devious exploits once we move beyond tonight. Then his weight disappears and he flops back under Raven's shoulder.

But before I can get too distracted with thoughts of all of these men filling me, Thorne pinches my nipple, eliciting a sharp jolt of pleasure. "Be a good girl and get on your knees. You can worship their cocks since you're gagging for them."

And because I really am, I crawl over to where my Viking and my wolf are lounging side by side, looking like sin. I settle myself between Ky's spread legs and take him in hand. In this light, a faint dimple pops, hidden below his short beard, and it nearly kills me.

What I'm a little less certain of, is how Raven feels in all this. He's been sitting back quietly, watching everything unfold between the three of us, and all of a sudden, I'm a little unsure. Does he even want me to touch him?

After our experience in the kitchen, caution seems like the best approach.

"He doesn't bite, baby girl." Ky's cock throbs in my hand as I slowly stroke him from root to tip. "Much." He cheekily adds the last part and I'm preening with satisfaction when that morphs into a deep groan in response to the moment I flatten my tongue and take him in my mouth.

If I'm going to have any chance of taming this wolf, I'd better put on the performance of a lifetime. So I take care of Ky, bobbing and sucking and hollowing my cheeks, while my body incinerates under the heavy weight of both Thorne and Raven watching me put on a show. Both men devour the sight of me naked and hovering on hands and knees over Ky's cock.

Before long, fingers dig in my hair, and I'm roughly yanked

off him. A long line of spit trails between my swollen lips and that unreasonably sexy piercing. How one person can be so hot is criminal. A heady rush engulfs my limbs as it's Raven who now demands my attention, dragging me over to kneel beside his hips. I hungrily suck him down next.

With me in this position poised above him, he doesn't have as much dominance as the night in the gardens, but he still fists my hair so tight it stings my scalp. I'm humming with pleasure as his salty taste and masculine scent consume me. The feel of him against my tongue and in the back of my throat at the perfect angle is a powerful thing.

"*Ffffuck.*" He drags me off him after a while and glares at me with eyes as black as his heart.

"Our perfect little slut who loves being shared." Ky leans forward and consumes my mouth. Kissing me and experiencing the taste of all of us combined.

But I don't have time to melt beneath him like he's tempting me to. The next thing I know, Thorne tugs me back into his lap, cradling me in his powerful arms, and I find myself settled back against his gloriously naked chest.

Clearly, he's had enough of sharing for the time being.

"You like to watch." He brushes his hot mouth against the side of my neck.

"*Yes.*"

"You want to watch them together?"

I'm nodding. Lost to the depths of desire.

"Then get on my cock, Foxglove."

A shudder ripples through me; there's no doubt this man could compel me to do pretty much anything at this point in time. He guides me so that I lift up and then sink back down on him, reverse cowgirl style, with my back flush to his chest.

Beside us, the other two are already well on their way to fucking. My Viking is lying on his back, while Raven kneels between his thighs. He's got a bottle of lube and is pumping his cock and covering Ky's ass. I'm shivering and so turned on I can't see straight. Behind me, I hear and feel Thorne's heavy breathing as his hands roam across my tits and down to my pussy.

"Oh, my god," I whisper as I watch Raven push Ky's legs upwards, and he starts to slowly work himself inside. Prepping him first, then adding a second finger. Once he seems satisfied with the writhing, groaning mess he's reduced Ky to, he begins to gradually press forward with his thick cock.

Time stretches out as I'm transfixed by the sight of these two men together. I'm clenching around Thorne, and we're both panting as we get a front row seat to enjoy them fucking right beside us. It's beyond any fantasy. My body is a live wire as every greedy, voyeuristic part of me takes intense pleasure in this moment.

I want that.

I want them...all.

Raven's movements are slow and sensual and seem to be in complete contradiction to the ruggedness that I know these men are capable of. I'm dancing on the edge at how insanely hot they look together and the fullness of Thorne's cock inside me. While I rock my hips, he cups my pussy and spreads my wetness up and over my clit, rubbing slow, soul-destroying circles.

Watching Ky's gorgeous face contort with pleasure as Raven fucks him is captivating. Glimpses of strong lines along their shoulders. Stomach muscles rhythmically bunching and contracting. Soft grunts and groans of pleasure fall from their parted lips. Locks of unruly dark hair fall in Raven's eyes as he bears down. The indents at the side of his sculpted ass flex with each thrust forward.

These men all rule over my attention in different ways.

Thorne continues to slide his fingers over my soaking wet core, finding the perfect spot to have me gasping as he rolls over the sensitive bud. I'm slick and messy and he dips down to tease around the place where we're joined before dragging back up to circle over my clit again.

I'm quivering—whimpering with unrestrained pleasure.

We're all so electrified by the moment that it doesn't take long before Ky starts to beg louder.

"Oh, fuck. Right there. Don't stop." Tipping his head back reveals the pulse beating heavily in the side of his throat.

His fingers dig into Raven's tattooed shoulders, and then his cock spills between them as ribbons of cum spurt everywhere, covering their stomachs. My wolf growls, lunging forward to dig his teeth into Ky's Adam's apple, and his own release claims him.

There's no chance of me holding on any longer as I lose it and fall apart. This time, my orgasm sweeps me far out to sea, and I'm sure I must black out a little because the next thing I know, I've been flipped onto my back, and Thorne is between my legs, pounding me with gritted teeth as our bodies slap together and he strains to hold his bulk off my body.

"*Oh God*, Daddy." I hook my legs behind his ass, clinging to him, whimpering into his neck and sucking on the sensitive spot just below his ear. "Come inside me." That must be his only weakness because my whisper against his skin undoes him entirely.

"*Fffuck.*" His hips stutter, and he lets out a deep grunt as he thrusts deep; his cock pulses and fills my pussy with cum.

We're all disheveled, sweaty, rolling together in a tangle of limbs. Ky twists my face so he can sloppily kiss me before slumping back toward Raven. And then Thorne is kissing me again, sliding his tongue deep and slow in my mouth, soaking up the fact he's reduced me to a placid lake of pleasure beneath him.

Even though my wolf doesn't kiss me or touch me, his legs

brush up against mine, and I'm certain I don't imagine feeling the faintest graze of his knuckles along the outside of my thigh.

It's messy and perfect, and there's a thing inside my chest that tries to speak, but I hastily shove it aside.

I can't fall for these men.

Can I?

CHAPTER 36
Ky

"Stop looking at me like that."

My snappy little Fox is concentrating hard as she inks the design into my upper thigh. I'd been wanting a piece there for a long time, and who would have thought we'd end up with our very own tattoo artist, held captive under our roof.

"Like what?" I tease. Hooking at the front of her singlet when she pops her head up to glare at me.

"Like you can't keep your dick in your pants for five minutes." Fox waves the tattoo gun in the direction of my crotch, before going back to work. Her gloved fingers press my skin taut and she methodically works on the shading around the skull and feather design she drew for me.

It's not my fault I can't get enough of this girl. But I've had to share her with Thorne, the two of us coming to a truce of sorts. One where we each agreed to have her in our own beds for a night over the past couple of days. After all of us fell asleep in the lounge together—the night he finally woke the fuck up and admitted how badly he wanted her in the first place—we decided to give Fox a chance to have a little more time with us separately.

Besides, Thorne was a man possessed—intent on keeping her to himself like a damn caveman. So, hence, some temporary ground rules on *sharing*.

Which meant I got to have her in my bed all to myself last night, and fucking hell, this girl is my new favorite drug. I'm enchanted...and it's not only the way my cock wants to be buried inside her constantly.

We lay in bed and watched old-school horror films together on my laptop, and she bundled herself up against me with those lilac curls tickling my skin. Then melted for me while I simply enjoyed losing hours in her kisses, tasting her lips with her soft body draped on top of mine.

Not to mention how perfect she tasted when I had my mouth on her pussy this morning while she was still sleeping. Followed by the feeling of my cock slipping inside, slowly waking her up to my gentle thrusts in and out of her silky channel. Well, that might just be the way I intend to start every day.

She fucking gets off on it as much as I do because the way she clamped down on my dick...well, her cunt squeezed me harder than any other time she's climaxed while I've been inside her.

And I know she's still thinking about this morning, too. Pink spots appear, coloring high on her cheeks.

My girl adjusts herself in the chair and leans over me, studiously applying the ink as the quiet buzz of the machine fills the room. Trying to evade the situation, like she's not replaying those exact same memories over and over.

Hearing Fox moan and feeling her clench around my length while she's still drowsy with sleep...there's no feeling like it. Knowing it gives her what she desires and fulfills the fantasies she has makes it a thousand times hotter.

"Is Raven ok...with all of this." Fox doesn't look at me, but I see the way she's gnawing on that lower lip of hers. "He's been gone a few days, is all."

What she means is that he's been gone ever since the night we all fucked in the lounge, and I've been curious to see how long it would take her to pluck up the courage and ask the question. She's still wary of him, which is only understandable on her part. But Ven will always be more wild than tamed. That's a part of who he is, and there's no sense in trying to rationalize how he handles anything.

"He'll be back." Is all I say. Truth is, I honestly don't know when he'll reappear, and that's something that has come as a lesson to make peace with over time.

Fox is studying the artwork on my leg mighty hard. Refusing to look up at me. "I don't want to come between you two or anything."

Ahh. There it is.

"Baby girl." I brush her lower lip with my thumb, pulling it out from between her teeth. Wide blue eyes snap up to meet mine. "You know well enough that we're all creatures who won't tolerate anything less than what we want."

"That doesn't answer my question." She pouts. Concern furrows her brow as she dips the needle head of the machine in her ink.

"Wait til I tell him you're already missing his grumpy ass."

"I'm not." Fox huffs.

My smirk widens, and I pick up my phone. "You're so cute. I can text him now if you want."

She whines and nearly drops the tattoo gun trying to swat at me with her free hand.

"Don't you dare. I'll tattoo a big hairy ball sack right here on your leg if you do."

Laughter roars out of me.

Fox's scowl darkens. It's adorable.

"Your secret is safe with me." God, she's pretty when mad. It makes something in my chest glow to know that her first concern is for my relationship with Ven, over and above whatever she might be exploring with each of us individually.

"Just promise me that you won't let my being here ruin things for you both, ok?" She wipes methodically at the freshly laid ink. Removing the excess from my skin.

I shrug. "Ven and I have always been open with sharing other partners. This is no different."

"But you haven't had them *living* here and in your bed every night." She's arching an eyebrow at me, but there's enough of a question there that I get the feeling she's also more than a little curious about our past.

"No, you're right. There hasn't been anyone else living here except the three of us." Ever.

She twists her lips. "So you would usually only share with others at the club?"

"If it ever happens, it has been a one-time thing, and only at the club," I reassure her. Because for some reason, there's an urgent need inside me that wants to spell it out loud and clear. To have her under no illusion—there hasn't been anyone else in our lives who has even come close to the way I'm feeling about this girl.

"And Thorne...he never *shares* with either of you two usually?"

At the mention of his name I can't help but shift my weight a little in my seat. The tips of my ears heat.

"No. That hasn't happened before."

"Oh."

Yeah. *Oh*, is right indeed. Watching Thorne fuck our girl into submission that night is now permanently seared into my memory.

I've seen his cock numerous times before. But that was always when we were younger, and scattered in amongst those inevitable moments that come with living together as *brothers* when we would be around each other in various states of undress. It became clear to me pretty damn quick as I got older that I never once reacted in the same way to Hawke while growing up, and the two are fucking identical twins.

But no matter how many stolen glances I might have cast his way over the years, I've definitely never seen Thorne in a state of arousal like that.

Now I know what his dick looks like when it's hard and veined, and it feels as though he intended to alter my brain chemistry for good.

I swallow heavily.

Fox seems to be more than a little curious about the layers to our lives that I've shared with her. There's a silence for a few minutes as the machine hums a high pitch frequency, and she shades in the eye sockets of the skull design.

"Are you still sharing?" She asks quietly. Eyes averted.

"No." I tell her with all the sincerity I can pack into that one little word. I don't dare examine why, or what it means, or that I can't stand the thought of going a single day without hearing this girl's voice and getting to brush my lips against her soft mouth.

But here we are.

Fox is perfection, and she's ours.

"So, none of you have plans to visit the club anytime soon?"

"Baby girl, other than in a professional capacity, we haven't been to the club for a long time." My mind tries to quickly calculate how long it's actually been for any of us...eight months? Maybe more? "And unless you say the word and want to go, I can tell you right now, none of us will be going again."

Her blue eyes lock with mine. "You would want me to go with you?"

"It is technically *yours,* you know." The urge to grab her and kiss that bewildered expression off her face is incredibly strong.

I'd follow this girl anywhere she asked me to, even though she seems intent on disbelieving me on that front.

A furrow forms in her brow and I see the tiniest flash of fear arise before she hastily looks away. "Would you want to share me with others...at the club, I mean." Fox goes back to intently focusing on my tattoo.

Oh, fuck that for a joke.

The low growl comes out on instinct. "Look at me." It's almost impossible not to launch up off this seat, but I don't want to destroy the art she's inking into my skin.

Wide eyes meet my own.

"You belong to *us*. You're *mine*. Understood?"

Her plush lips press together, and she practically glows hearing the possessiveness in my voice. God, I want to see the way she lights up like that every damn day. It's followed by a tiny quirk that tugs at the corner of her perfect mouth.

"So...that's a no on the sharing, then?"

A laugh barks out of me. "You're lucky I'm the one who enjoys stirring up shit around here; if it was Thorne, he'd take that bratty attitude and punish your sweet little ass."

There's zero remorse in her gorgeous smile, and I selfishly eat up every radiant drop of her satisfaction. If there's one thing I know, it's that Fox is stunning at any time, but especially so when that flicker of relaxed happiness blesses her features.

I might just make it my mission to find out the myriad of ways to make it happen every damn day.

"I'm deadly serious, no one else touches you, Fox." My finger hooks a curl of her hair, tugging gently toward me so I can drink in another hit of those bright blue eyes that haunt my dreams.

"Ok." She gives me a soft look. One that immediately has my obsession with this girl spiraling high amongst rainbow fucking clouds.

My girl goes back to working on my ink while I'm preening

like a puffed-up goddamn peacock at the thought of getting to keep something so unbelievably special, like I've won first place without even trying.

Fox pauses to wipe my thigh, and dips the needle in more ink. "Well, you can all enjoy keeping your dicks to yourselves for a little bit." She hits me with her best *no-nonsense* expression. "I started my period this afternoon."

Seeing how serious she looks has me biting my tongue to prevent myself from falling apart with laughter.

Oh, this girl has a lot to learn about the creatures who wander this place at night.

CHAPTER 37
Thorne

The black screen illuminates in front of me, with the lines of ominous white text that have consumed my thoughts all day.

It's an encrypted message. One that Hawke and I have run through all our known codes to confirm the source, and yet I already know exactly where it originated from within the Anguis.

What I want to do is invite them to the basement at Noire House and interrogate them one by one until I have every blood-soaked piece of evidence I require.

But I have to bide my time.

Foxglove Noire has enemies slithering within the walls of her father's Household, and they want her dead.

Little do they know, she's already bound to serve a different master who decides whether she lives or breathes. And I'm in no mood to entertain any fucker who thinks they can get away with threatening what belongs to me.

Even though I have to endure exactly that.

I knock back another gulp of whiskey as I sit here in the dark, surrounded by the raging thoughts of gory retribution clouding my mind. The words on the screen are imprinted in my memory; I've read them so many times.

"The heiress Foxglove Noire is a traitor. Those like her with poisoned hearts will lose their tongues and their heads before the serpentine moon rises. The clock will strike, and her blood will spill, clearing the bloodline for the true heir."

It gives no clues, other than the usual bullshit the Anguis like to spew. Their followers get off on speaking in riddles and prose as they practice their arcane rituals.

What makes my stomach churn is the open threat against her and the connection to the Pledging ceremony.

It isn't supposed to happen like this.

Our plans are coming together, and this confirms that moves are finally being made—but it's not how Hawke or I anticipated things might go.

We have to be wary.

If we think for one second we know what this snake will do, then we've already lost.

It leads me to wonder if they're planning something before the Pledging, or choosing to wait until the night itself. Whatever the case, I don't want to take any undue risks before I can put my teams onto making sure her safety is ensured.

The mere fact they were able to get this message sent to me while here inside the compound is enough to have my teeth grating. It doesn't guarantee that they could reach her in here, but it's a lingering menace. The meaning of which is spelled out in bold letters.

We know how to get to her.

So, my only option is to get out ahead of this threat—one that wasn't supposed to be happening like this—and hide her away somewhere safe.

Even if I have to drug her again to ensure the girl complies.

These endless tests and demands to prove our loyalty are driving me to the brink.

If I have any hope of exposing the scum responsible and getting to disembowel them slowly while feeding them their own putrid organs, I have to temporarily get her secured. And I know a location that will be the safest possible.

Draining my glass, I fish out my phone and send a text to our jet pilot informing them of our flight plans—well, a time when they need to be ready to depart at least, they won't know the actual destination until we take off—followed by a coded message to Hawke.

It won't mean anything to anyone except him, but my twin will know where we're heading.

That means I've got three days to set plans in motion with my teams and operatives scattered throughout the Anguis. Which, in my world, is more than enough time to put enough distance between us and the threat against the girl sleeping just down the hall.

CHAPTER 38
Ven

There's a moment, right as the life finally drains from a person's eyes, when they've given up the fight. It's a look of resignation as they accept their inevitable fate.

Sometimes, I catch a glimpse of it as I'm kneeling on their windpipe in the bowels of some underground fight ring headquarters. While my victim lies bleeding beneath me, coated in the grime of their existence.

Other times, I can only imagine the fleeting glimpse that might appear as their neck snaps, and they crumple to the ground. Lifeless, before they've even hit the rotting floorboards below our feet.

I tug my helmet off, feeling the sting as it scrapes over the fresh cuts along my nose and eye socket. The asshole I had been tasked with eliminating tonight was scheduled to be dispatched in the fifth. Which meant taking enough blows to make the bout look believable for the drunken hordes baying for blood.

The stench of piss and mildew and vomit still clogs my nose, even after traveling for hours. Usually, the long rides like this one will clear some of the filth away.

But tonight it feels like it has embedded itself into my very bones.

I swing my leg off the bike, and I can still taste ash and gasoline on my tongue from where I stopped to burn my clothes.

There's a dull ache in my brain, not from the fight, not from the blows landed—from the unease at returning for the first time after so many days away.

When I left the compound four days ago, the others were curled up asleep in the lounge together. Thorne saw me leave, I know he did, but he was too invested in holding Fox tight in his arms.

Something shifted that night, and it has kept me on edge ever since. I can't put my finger on it, and maybe that's the thing that has my skin feeling like it's crawling. Uncertainty and distrust are foes I know well.

I learned the hard way never to put faith in anyone bearing the Noire name.

My sister paid for entering their poisoned world with her life.

Initiations, such as the one I've just attended to oversee some of the new members who have made it into the ranks of the Anguis, are so often the same formula.

Blood. Death. Fealty.

That's all they require in their holy trinity of fucked up allegiance.

But for the likes of me, my sister—Thorne and Ky, too—we weren't given a choice. Children like us were a commodity bought and traded. The offspring of junkies and desperate people who found themselves in even more desperate circumstances. There's no trying to guess what motivates someone to sell their own child.

We don't know anything about the people who offered us up into the jaws of darkness.

All we know of life has been driven by the environment we were raised in. All we have ever known is the way a society such as the Anguis has rooted itself in our ligaments and tendons and bones, whether we choose to accept it, or not.

Sucking in a deep inhale, cool air inflates my lungs.

It's late.

My soul is fucking worn to tatters.

The sliver of a moon hangs low in the sky above the blackened outlines of the trees coating the hills around the house. Jagged silhouettes enticing me to steal away into their peaceful embrace.

So, when I walk into the kitchen, in search of a whiskey and my sanity, I'm less than impressed to find Foxglove Noire perched on a stool scrolling her phone. She's got something heating in the microwave and a packet of pills beside a glass of water on the counter next to her.

At the sound of my entrance, she whips around. Looking startled for a moment, then her mouth forms a small O as her eyes drop. Taking in my bloodied and bruised appearance.

I bare my teeth at her.

She wants to try and be cutesy by calling me a wolf? Well, the girl can have my fangs while I rip her throat out.

"What happened to you?" Her mouth speaks words of concern, but it's the rotten Noire heart at her core that I can't bring myself to look past.

"Nothing."

"That doesn't look like nothing." She stands from her stool as if to cross over to me, but wisely stops herself.

"Part of the job."

"Those cuts need cleaning." She chews her lip then decides to take a step closer, and once again, there's nothing but one of Ky's oversized tees adorning her curves. I'm guessing she sleeps in them all the time now, and to be honest, if this girl is in the kitchen dressed like that, I'm more than a little surprised Ky isn't here panting after her.

Shrugging Fox off, I cross to the cabinets on the other side of the kitchen, fishing out a bottle and a glass. My knuckles are battered, and there's a deep bruise forming below my ribs, I can tell. No doubt that's going to hurt like a bitch in the morning.

"Let me help." She's followed me around the island in the kitchen, trying some foolish attempt at bravery or some shit.

"Leave me the fuck alone." As I pour myself a drink, amber liquid sloshes over the rim and onto the bench. She's still there, but shrinks a little in the face of my bark. Just because I fucked her and she choked on my cock and put on a show in front of us with Thorne...none of that means shit.

If anything, it's every reason she should be staying the hell away from me.

Whatever's inside the microwave has long stopped turning, and it lets out a shrill series of reminder beeps. That seems to startle her out of the apparent interest in my cut-up face, and she huffs at me. Pushing past to wrench it open and take out a soft bag. With a forceful slam, she turns on her heel and moves over to scoop up the packet of pills and the water.

But the way she winces as she gathers her things is unmistakable.

I know a wounded creature when I see one.

Before she can make it another step, I've rounded the stone counter and blocked her path.

"What's wrong with you?" I grab her hand and turn the packet over, seeing that it's rapid-action painkillers clutched in her fist. The contents of the microwave turn out to be some kind of heated wheat bag, the warm, earthy scent wisps between us.

"My ovaries are trying to kill me. Not unlike you are, too." She snaps at me. "Have it your way; sort your own damn cuts out. Better yet, let them get all gross and infected. I'm going to bed."

My eyes drop to where she's cradling the bag against her lower stomach with her free arm.

"You're hurting."

Those baby blue eyes do an exaggerated roll as she tries to wriggle out of my hold. "Like a motherfucker. So please, do me a favor and get out of my way. I'll gladly leave you to drown your sorrows in peace."

Maybe it's the bloodlust still running hot through my veins, or the way this lilac-haired scrap of mayhem has upended everything. Or perhaps it's the sickest part of me that can scent a suffering animal from a mile away. Stepping aside, I allow her to pass by, and then stalk directly behind her.

I crave the power to control her pain.

I want to own it, and breathe on it, until those embers flare into a glowing inferno.

I also want to control the precise moment she experiences exquisite relief.

She looks over her shoulder at me with a frown and makes a frustrated noise. But her pace quickens ever so slightly, following the glassed-in corridor in the direction of her bedroom. My boots are a heavy, thudding echo in contrast to her uncovered feet padding silently on the concrete floor.

Fox's bare legs and ass are a feast for my eyes as she tries to scurry away from my looming presence. Darting another look over her shoulder at me, this time fear flickers in her wide eyes.

That sight alone sends a rush of blood to my cock.

"Leave me alone." Her words hang in the dark on a whisper as if she doesn't want to risk anyone else hearing. I suddenly wonder if Thorne, Ky, or maybe both, might already occupy her bed. How appealing that sounds right about now startles me.

But as she ducks into her room, the patch of soft light spilling from the ensuite reveals an empty bed with rumpled sheets tossed to one side.

Probably for the best, considering the plan I've quickly decided on since abandoning the kitchen.

She tries to bolt for her bathroom, but her movements are slow, more labored than usual. This girl is no match for me, even during the best of times, and at this moment, she's easy prey.

Before the door can slam in my face, I've blocked it with a heavy palm. Confusion mixed with concern lines her delicate features, and I surge through the doorway. Crowding her body up against the vanity, she backs away from me.

"Take your pills," I grunt. Letting my eyes roam at will. Already, Fox's body is responding to me even if that brain of hers won't shut up and stop protesting—denying what she truly craves. Her nipples form stiffened points beneath the soft fabric, and goosebumps paint her forearms.

"Get out." She's run out of room, crammed against the edge of the counter with no escape.

"I'll shove them down your throat for you if you don't."

"You're disgusting." Her eyes flash, then roll. *Brat.* Fox makes an exaggerated effort to pop open the silver foil casing of two white capsules, downing them with a large gulp of water.

Then she sticks out her flattened tongue to show me.

This girl can be sweet when she wants to be. But I prefer her sour side.

"Sit on the counter." I take a step forward and relish the way her body shudders.

"I'm not in the mood for your bullshit."

"Don't make me ask twice, little Fox. Because I can assure you I won't be asking the second time."

"Why..." Her brow furrows as her words trail off. A hasty swallow makes her throat bob, and she looks mighty nervous all of a sudden.

I cock my head to one side and study her in silence.

Her bratty attitude from a second ago evaporates in an instant.

"Oh, no." She shakes her head and holds up her hands. "Nope. No way. I've already told Ky and Thorne this...I have my period."

Her protests are eaten up as I close the small distance between us, and lean both hands on the edge of the vanity outside her hips. Our noses almost brush, her tiny fists clench and fly to my chest in an attempt to shove me away.

"I don't fucking care." My low snarl comes from somewhere deep and primal in my gut. "I just ripped a man's ear off tonight with my teeth, and I've been soaked in blood since sundown. Do you really think a little bit of yours will put me off?"

She's panting and still pushing back, but I see the pain she's experiencing has drained her face of color, and right now, this Fox is in no position to hold up an extended argument with me.

"Raven."

"Fox." I echo.

"You can't be serious."

Oh, she has no fucking clue.

I run my nose along her jaw, inhaling the subtle notes of fear lingering between us, before pausing at the shell of her ear. "When it comes to pain, nothing controls it like a deep fuck and coming as many times as I'm going to tell you to."

Her breath catches as I draw back, finding her blue gaze. This girl is looking at me like she either wants to stab me or sink to her knees.

Probably both.

"But—"

"Sit." I've already picked her up and dumped her on the polished marble before she can continue arguing with me.

Fox covers her mortified expression, making small groaning noises. "You're killing me. This is so many kinds of wrong."

That makes me pause. My hands catch hers, and for a

second, our fingers intertwine as I drag them away from her face. She's all delicate, smooth skin beneath rough calluses. A petal with the misfortune to flutter onto concrete.

Leaning down, I make sure to hold her widening eyes level with my own. "Nothing about enjoying pleasure is wrong. When everyone is consenting, there is nothing to be ashamed of."

She wears a thousand expressions trying to fight each other for parity as her mind wrestles with that information.

"But you can't possibly want...to do *that*." Her voice shakes.

I'm about done with explaining myself to this girl. So instead, I shove her t-shirt up her thighs and tap for her to shift from side to side so I can lift it above her hips. Fox's mouth hangs open as she watches me work the soft fabric up her stomach.

"Stay still." I nudge her shoulders to slump back against the mirror.

Her pulse is like a hummingbird's wings in the side of her throat.

Then I drag the hem all the way up to sit over the top of her breasts, exposing their heavy fullness and perfectly hardened buds. Both furl tighter under my stare, and the dusky rose-colored skin surrounding her nipples pebbles.

"Hold that there. I want to see your tits while you come on my tongue."

"Oh my fucking god." She's squirming, her voice a husky whisper of disbelief.

My eyes rake down her soft stomach, over the snake sitting at her sternum, and lower to her tattooed thigh. The point where her hips crease around the edge of the high-waisted black panties she's got on.

"What do you use?" My hands land on her knees, and I settle her thighs wider.

She stares at me like I've got three heads.

"You've got about five seconds before I find out. So you can either answer me, or I can discover for myself."

Her mouth opens and closes before she rediscovers her tongue. "*Jesus*. I'm wearing period underwear, ok?" As she speaks, my fingers curl beneath the waistband, and her stomach caves on reflex.

Right now, I'm a man on a mission, there's a fire licking flames through my core as I ease the thick cotton down over her hips. Fox makes tiny noises somewhere between a protest and a whimper, and I feel the heavy weight of the gusset as I slide them down her legs.

With my eyes on hers, I rub my finger and thumb over the wet inner layer of material. She must be past the heaviest days, but it's unmistakably fresh blood beneath my touch.

With lips parted, a delicious quiver races the length of her body.

I keep my gaze fastened on hers...and suck the pad of my thumb into my mouth.

CHAPTER 39
Fox

Holy fucking shit. My insides turn to knots as the wolf standing between my thighs runs his tongue over the pad of his thumb.

His thumb covered in a smear of blood.

My blood.

I'm trapped somewhere between disbelief and the most primal kind of arousal I could imagine. When I hobbled my way into the kitchen tonight to reheat my wheat bag and find some painkillers, I could never in a thousand lifetimes have imagined this is where I'd end up.

About to have Raven do god-knows-what to me while I'm spread out beside the washbasin, bleeding.

"Come on my tongue first, and then you can have my cock." He settles himself with his shoulders wedged between my thighs, and I'm coiled as tight as a spring. This feels like a million different kinds of wrong; it's unfathomably dirty and yet, he's staring up at me with glittering eyes. It makes no sense to my brain, but for some reason he wants this. Under the intensity of his gaze, I somehow feel like a queen on a throne made out of marble tile and mirror.

I'm sure there's no air in my lungs, or my breath has stalled somewhere in my throat as he lowers his head. All the while, a torrential downpour of intrusive thoughts assault me. Worrying about how I'll taste, or what I smell like, or what he'll think of...

And then his mouth closes over my clit, and everything goes blank.

My wolf is eating me out for the first time, and of course, it's while my pussy is coated in crimson.

His tongue laps and swirls around to explore every inch of me. As he licks and sucks with torturous precision, my body is so hyper-sensitive it feels like I could shatter at any moment. I've always been a horny mess during my time of the month, but I have never entertained the idea that someone else might enjoy my body in this particular state. The bundle of nerves he's working are unbelievably aroused and more responsive than ever. Meanwhile, every glide and lick along the ruffles of my pussy sends sparks flying down toward my fingers and toes.

I buck and writhe beneath him. Panting and gasping and whimpering all sorts of unintelligible noises.

His mouth makes the filthiest wet sounds as he presses my knees wider, and his tongue explores *everywhere.*

As the crest of the wave begins to rise, he must sense it from the way my muscles tense. It only drives him to pin me down with greater force. He's merciless, continuing his onslaught. The part that finally hurls me over the edge is when he looks up from between the junction of my thighs—with dark crimson highlighting his cheekbones—and while I'm trapped in his gaze, sucks down on my clit.

"Oh, fuck, Raven, I'm—"

I fail to get any other words out. My climax roars through my ears while I quake and fall apart on his tongue, just as he commanded. Entirely consumed by the carnal, dirty scene he painted.

My wolf strikes quickly, shifting up my body, and he takes my breasts in both hands. Pinching my aching nipples and covering them with his hot, bloodied mouth. As he moves between the two, he smears the evidence of me all over my skin, and it feels like I'm being branded anew. Claimed by this man again in the most primal anointing possible, where my blood serves as a ceremonial oil and this bathroom counter stands in place of an altar.

The last time it was his cum filling me while forcing my body to accept him. This time, it's the way he's taken the most intimate part of me and uses it to leave the evidence of how easily I bend to his will smeared in bright red streaks across my tits.

"Oh, fuck." My eyes clamp shut as he bites down on one of the tight buds, and brilliant sparks of pain melt into liquid pleasure.

"Open your mouth." His voice is pure sin. I blindly open wide, sticking out my tongue, and that's when I feel it.

He spits onto my tongue.

A coppery tang fills my senses, and I'm a moaning, pathetic mess. It's beyond dirty. There is no way in hell this should be turning me into a pool of lust.

Raven hasn't even made an attempt to kiss me, or shown any interest in doing so. Yet he just spat my own blood into my mouth.

The sickest part is that right now, in this tiny bubble of desire, it feels like the sexiest thing I never knew I needed.

This man is going to be the end of me.

I'm nothing but his to control from that point onward. He's officially broken my brain. I'm lost in a slutty fantasy where Raven is my nirvana, and I'll gladly crawl across crushed glass naked for him. All he needs to do is snap those tattooed, silver-ringed fingers.

He slides me off the counter and spins my body, pressing

down between my shoulder blades to bend me over. The cold marble feels wet against my bare breasts, and I can only assume —with a rush of embarrassment—it's a result of the mess I've made.

Raven's wild reflection appears behind me, and his bruised and cut-up face is coated in streaks of brickish red. He undoes his pants, and there's a chaotic rush of pleasure currently coursing through my veins. My limbs feel like they're levitating.

Wolfish, hooded eyes meet mine in the mirror and holy fuck. I'm done for.

Raven grips my hips and presses the fat head of his cock at my bloodied entrance. Licking his lips, he holds me—no, chokes me, with his stare in the mirror's reflection and starts to slowly push inside.

A curl tugs his upper lip. "You taste like the sweetest kind of torture."

As my whimper tumbles out, he sinks in, filling me all the way, and my eyes roll back in my head. We're both making animalistic noises, and my wolf fucks me deep and slow from behind. Holding my hips at the perfect angle so that his cock hits every delicious spot, reducing me to nothing more than squirming, arching cries beneath him.

I want this. Every day. I don't want him to stop. He hunches over me, with one hand braced against the mirror and the other pins me in place by the swell of my hip; thrusting in the most carnal, yet sensuous way.

"Watch yourself." As if he detects that I've drifted off on wings of pleasure, he yanks my hair to tilt my chin. Our eyes lock as the glass fogs with each of my panting breaths.

"Raven...oh, god." I suck in a ragged inhale.

"See the way you love taking my cock. How much you fucking love this."

A sob falls from my parted lips. He picks up his pace,

growing more forceful, eyes darkening as he demands every ounce of my attention.

It's utterly hypnotic and filthy, and my back bows on instinct, letting him angle further inside me. I'm struggling to focus on his devilishly handsome features, but at the same time wanting to be such a good girl for him.

"*Ffffuck*. Yes. Milk my cock." Pure, gritty sex coats his voice.

I'm drowned by the unfiltered desire evident in his words.

"Feel the way your cunt wraps around me. Every time I move you're trying to squeeze and hold me in tight." He digs ruthlessly into my hip, and everything around us in the bathroom starts to fade as my blood throbs with need.

"Keep those eyes open and fucking watch." I hear his voice grow rougher as I do exactly what he says.

This time, my climax winds its way around my throat and pours through me like a steady waterfall. I'm crying out and clenching around him as his cock pumps into me. He falls into his own release before I've finished coming on shuddering waves. The sticky wetness of my blood and his cum combine to make a hot, slick mess at the spot joining us.

I lie beneath him, nothing more than a limp noodle. Vaguely, I'm aware that he pulls out and murmurs something about staying still. Little does he know I couldn't move, even if I wanted to. I don't think my brain functions anymore, either.

Did I just plummet to my demise and allow myself to fall for this man?

After a few moments, he scoops me off the marble and tosses the t-shirt bunched around my neck into a heap somewhere before leading me over to the bath. Apparently, while I've been lost in the depths of my besotted-with-Raven-trance, he's started filling the tub with bubbles and steaming water.

My eyes are glazed with the high of my orgasms, but I can still manage a moment to devour the gloriously naked sight of him. While I'm busy ogling his inked body, Raven lowers himself while it's still filling before gesturing me to follow.

"Come here."

That low, commanding tone should be illegal.

"Straddle me. Fuck yourself down on it like I know you want to."

Jesus. He's still not done.

My lust-addled brain looks down and sees that he's still erect. And his cock is covered in the coppery red evidence of being inside me. The man just pumped me full of cum, and yet he's already hard again.

"You're actually going to kill me," I mutter. But follow him obediently and sink down over his length. As the warm water coats my skin and surrounds me in a cocoon of bliss, I melt further. My head finds its way to nuzzle against his chest.

"A good way to go." His deep rumble presses against my ear.

Oh, fuck no. Now is not the time for this man to discover how to make jokes. I've already succumbed to his devious clutches. If he develops a sense of humor, I might never claw my way out of this abyss.

But then he's straight back to being the perfect mix of wicked and depraved.

"That's it. Take all of me. Ride my cock." He guides me to roll my hips in a gentle motion that feels like I'm flying high above the forest outside, blanketed in a starry coat gifted by the night sky. Raven coaxes me and lets out low, smoldering groans that vibrate from his chest through into my body. Throwing my arms around his neck, mouth tucked in the crook of his shoulder, I give everything over. He slips one hand between us, rubbing my clit, until we both come again on a slow, undulating wave. One that picks us both up and tosses us over the cliff together at the same time.

I don't know how long we stay entwined, but he seems content to leave his cock buried deep inside me. Surely after that, I must look like a complete disaster between my blood and his cum, but I couldn't care less as my body slumps over him in a boneless heap.

Meanwhile, I'm completely ignoring any concerns as to whether he might loathe my clinginess. Right now I crave being held. Warm palms rest over my hips, holding me in place. He doesn't exactly caress me, or cuddle, but seems uninterested in permitting me to move off him either.

The pain from earlier has completely melted away.

Maybe my wolf's has, too.

"Did you actually bite a man's ear off tonight?" I mumble against his throat, my body nestling itself into his torso.

Even though I can't see his expression, the faintest hint of a laugh ghosts through his lungs beneath my ear.

I want to bottle the sound and keep it tucked away somewhere precious. This man might as well have given me the keys to the golden kingdom.

Every inch of me knows I can't allow myself to catch feelings. Not for someone who barely speaks to me and hasn't attempted to kiss me.

He is murderous, aggressive, and if I was in my right mind, I would run a mile from his particular brand of psycho.

And while it absolutely shouldn't, hearing Raven Flannaghty laugh makes me more than a little giddy with delight.

Like the pathetic fool I am.

CHAPTER 40
Fox

My anxiety has been ready to spike through the roof of this private jet for the past twenty minutes.

Firstly, having Thorne Calliano issue me with all of five minutes' warning earlier today that he'd already packed a bag for me, and that we were going to be leaving, that was enough to have my blood pressure rising.

Secondly, he wouldn't give me any details about where we were going, or why, or for how long.

And now we've sat seemingly waiting here on the tarmac for some unknown reason, and the tension is enough to make me feel like a boiled frog.

Just as I'm ready to climb the walls, I spot movement out the window. Sleek black vehicles almost identical to the ones owned by my men pull up. Three are in a cavalcade, and two muscular-looking security or armed guards—it's hard to tell from here amidst all the black they're wearing—jump out, one from the front vehicle, another from the one at the rear.

Out of the middle, a third equally *serious* man exits from the driver's side. The three talk together for a moment before opening the back door.

I gasp, because a short figure is bundled out wearing a black hood over their head and what looks like ill-fitted black track pants and a hoodie.

"What the fuck?" I say out loud. Silence greets me, and somehow, I didn't even notice that none of my men are within earshot.

In fact, when I glance up, the cabin is empty.

That's when I notice them all having a fucking murderers anonymous reunion outside on the tarmac, with whoever their hooded victim is, clutched by the arm.

Crap.

I'm no idiot. I know they're in deep with whatever fucked up shit they're required to do for the Anguis, but it flips my stomach to think this prisoner might be destined for a bullet through the back of the head and a shallow grave somewhere on the outskirts of this private airstrip.

Unease rolls through me, and I chew the inside of my cheek.

Then the unthinkable happens. My men part, and the hooded figure is led, or more aptly, dragged toward the steps to the jet.

My eyes widen, and I start to squirm in my seat. Rubbing my palms against my dress, I can't drag my eyes away as they draw closer.

My heart starts to jackhammer as the two figures hit the stairs, and I'm caught, not knowing what to do, ending up frozen in place in this luxury leather seat as they enter the cabin.

Straight away, muffled sounds of protest—a woman's voice—come from beneath the hood. Oh, god, whoever that is under there, the person is also gagged for some reason, and my stomach turns queasy.

The bulldog with a sharp jaw and scowl etched between his eyes shoves the hooded captive into the chair opposite me—that's when I realize they're cuffed, too.

He reaches down and unshackles the person's wrists, and I see feminine hands and chipped nail polish, which only drives my anxiety higher.

"What the fuck is going on?" My nerves feel shot to all hell.

At the sound of my voice, the figure across from me stiffens, then starts yelling incoherently against their gag. Not frightened noises, but ones filled with fury. As soon as the cuffs are released, her hands fly up and wrench the hood off.

"Oh my god...Em?" My shriek pierces the air. Launching forward at my best friend, she blinks at me like an owl. Wild hair halos her face, mascara smeared in dark circles below her eyes.

"What the fuck did you do to her?" I shout at the brick wall of a man who stands with arms folded and the cuffs dangling ominously from one hand.

Easing the gag out of my best friend's mouth, I drag it down her neck and cup her face in both hands.

"Are you ok?" I'm torn between wanting to hug my friend and gouge out the eyes of the man who brought her here like this. "Stay the fuck away from her." I hiss in his direction.

Em seems to blink back online after staring at me in shock for a moment. "I'm fine, babe." She works her jaw to ease the tension after being gagged for god knows how long. "Or, at least, I will be once I get rid of my psychopath wardens." Her eyes flash with fire as she runs a hand over her disheveled hair and glares daggers at the man.

A throat clears. Thorne stands in the doorway and jerks his head in the stranger's direction. Summoning him outside.

"Run along, then." Em narrows her eyes.

Before he moves, he weighs the cuffs in one hand and runs his tongue across the front of his teeth. Looking all too pleased to click them back around her wrists. "Don't say I didn't warn you about the consequences of being a hellhound." His voice is a quiet threat in the small confines of the plane before he's gone, following Thorne down the steps and out onto the tarmac.

"Ugh, thank god. Screw him and his stupid little games." She rubs at her wrists.

"Em, what the fuck is going on, are you hurt?" I take in what she's wearing, and the fact she's turned up looking every inch a captive, and my mind starts racing.

She shrugs my question off and instead latches onto me with a tight hug. "Fuck me, it's so good to see your face. Don't even worry about *that*...he's just a temporary test of my sanity."

I squeeze her back, still in complete shock at the fact my best friend is here, after convincing myself I might never see her again. "Are you sure you're ok? It doesn't look like it, to be brutally honest."

Possible kidnapping and being forced here against her will aside, Emerald Kirby does not wear baggy track pants and oversized hoodies. Ever.

"Oh, what, because you're sitting here all glamorous on a private jet? Please, I'll take my little kidnapping role-play any day over luxury seats and private air travel." She giggles. At least her sense of humor is still intact. Surely, that's a good sign? "Apparently, my protection squad don't know the difference between being bodyguards or brutes with egos the size of Saturn."

A few puzzle pieces slot into place in my mind. Thorne had threatened Em's life when they first took me; maybe this is his twisted version of making sure no one gets to harm my friend unless it's on their orders, of course.

But I can't go revealing anything because otherwise, her life is most likely to end up in far more danger than it's worth.

"They didn't do anything to you... like, drug you?" My eyes dart back toward the empty doorway.

She gives me a funny look, but then shakes her head. "No, babe. Honestly, despite how this might look, I'm fine."

Something tells me my friend is hiding her own secrets right now, and I'm not exactly sure where to start with my own teetering pile of lies I'm perched upon.

I've never told her about my past, and she has never pressed me for details.

"So, my woman of mystery." Em settles back in her seat and readjusts her hair into a bun, before crossing her legs. Seeming entirely unbothered by the circumstances she arrived in. "One minute you were busy telling me about your whirlwind romance with Mr. Calliano, the next minute you lost your phone, and now we're here, looking like you're about to jet off to somewhere fabulous."

I stare at her with my mouth hanging open.

"What's going on with you lately? You've been avoiding my calls like the plague, but at least getting a few text replies here and there let me know I wasn't going to see you pop on late-night news after finding your body floating face down in the river."

My brain is struggling to catch up. Em doesn't look pissed off, more an eerie sort of calm. It's almost as if she's only half present with me here.

"You got texts? From me?" Repeating her words back to her only results in an arch of an eyebrow. Confusion runs rampant because I sure as hell know I'm not the one who has been texting my best friend.

"Of course, and call me ridiculous for even saying it, but I suppose I can forgive you for leaving me with barely one-word answers...even if it was all because of a *guy*." Em does an exaggerated roll of her eyes. "I'm truly happy you finally met someone, so here's me doing my best to be supportive of you, bitch."

She's grinning playfully; meanwhile, I'm still stuck trying to make sense of who has been pretending to be me.

Was it one of my men? They're the ones who took away my phone, after all.

"Yeah, that was shitty of me, I'm sorry." Fuck. The words feel numb on my tongue. Everything in me wants to blurt out the truth, but I'm terrified of the thought of my best friend getting tangled in the web of the Anguis.

"Ok, well you're gonna have to spill the juicy details and clue me in on this so-called whirlwind romance. One that has been important enough to have you leaving town *and* disappearing off the face of the earth."

"Uhh..." For whatever reason I've forgotten how to form words.

"Dick so good, you're tongue-tied?" Em fans herself.

Oh my god. "Thorne's a very private person." Is the first excuse I first settle on. "His line of work means he has to be very discreet." Shit, I'm painfully aware that I'm fumbling my way through this.

"Oooh, like NDA's and shit? I get it." If my best friend suspects I'm lying, she's being a real champ about not yelling at me and telling me to go fuck myself.

So, I do my best to answer as many questions as I can within murky shades of the truth: things like why I haven't returned her calls—because the cell service is shitty where I've been staying—and how I could move my entire life to Port Macabre without telling her—because it was the only way Thorne and I would have an opportunity to get to know each other. You know, because of his *work*.

Christ almighty.

The lies flow freely amongst tiny grains of facts.

Recapping the part about how I met Thorne Calliano that night at my tattoo studio is easy enough. It's the truth, and she helped me get ready for our 'date' after all. I have to gloss over the part about being drugged and kidnapped while I try to pretend that we spent the evening falling head-over-heels for each other like loved-up teenagers at some fancy black-tie gala.

Em cranes her neck to look out the window at the group of

men outside before turning back to me. "And the other two? How do they fit into this cozy little picture?"

Once again, I'm left with nothing. But my face flames immediately and gives me away like a traitorous little hussy.

"I mean, I don't have binoculars on me or anything to study closely...but they're certainly not hard on the eye."

Right now I don't know whether I want the ground to swallow me whole, or to at least reveal some fragment of the insanity my life has become.

The relief of sharing some small part with my best friend sits high in my chest. That much can't hurt to tell. Even if it is only a tiny sliver of the truth.

"Well..." I fidget with the ends of my hair, studying the purple strands. "Let's just say I'm exploring something new."

Em's face cracks into pure, unrefined glee.

"Please tell me you're exploring *all* of them."

I nod, my lips twisting in a hesitant smile of my own. "I am."

"Thoroughly and regularly, I hope."

"You're something else, you know. Send you in here gagged, handcuffed, and with a hood over your head, and yet you're more concerned with my sex life."

Smirking at me, she swivels around to get a better look out the window. "Don't judge my idea of a good time. Besides, we're here to focus on you, remember. Mostly the part about how my bestie scored the dick jackpot of sleeping with three men. At. The. Same. Time."

"Are we?" This woman is giving me whiplash. Something about Em's energy feels odd, and I can't figure out for the life of me why she won't give me a straight answer.

"So is it orgies twenty-four seven, or exclusively one dick at a time on the menu?"

"My NDA says I'm at my confidentiality limit." I shake my head.

"Oh my god." Em gives me a stricken look. If I didn't know better, her favorite shade of lipstick was just obliterated from the face of the earth. That girl is a slut for her lipstick collection.

"What?"

"You're not on birth control." She leans in like we're both in on some great conspiracy and grabs both my hands in hers. The fierceness in her expression makes me fight back a small laugh. The first real one I've felt able to let go of since our strange little rendezvous began.

"I'm not?" I quirk an eyebrow at her.

"Foxglove Marlina. One does not fuck that many men and be careless. I raised you better than that, bitch. Are you kidding me right now?" Her eyes are saucers. She's whisper-yelling at me, even though the men in question have continued to make themselves scarce, and we've got the cabin to ourselves.

"Don't worry, I'm being careful."

"Babe, I know your body struggled with being on birth control, but surely you could give it another try? Find another brand or doctor?" Em is spiraling. "How does it even work with figuring out condoms for three dicks? Do you have an entire garage stacked full of bulk-order super-strength rubbers?"

Now I'm actually laughing. I shake my head. "Let's just back away from the ledge, ok...they've all had the snip. I'm safe."

Em's jaw slackens, and I reach up to push her mouth closed. She slaps my hand away, still firmly in the land of disbelief.

"All of them? You're serious?"

"Swear on my life."

She slumps back on the seat across from me. "How is this real? Last I checked, you were living in the same city as me, in a committed relationship with your drawer full of toys. Now you've got three gorgeous specimens of male running after you like you hung the moon and the stars, and you've moved halfway across the country without telling me?"

She's right to sound more than a little incredulous. Em

doesn't know anything about the Anguis, and I'll gladly ensure that doesn't change.

I don't dare tell her the real reason they're in my life.

I'm also carefully side-stepping the part where she's drawing conclusions about them feeling a certain way. *This is just their revenge, and fantastic sex. That's all.*

"You know I'll always support you, right?" Em gives me a firm look.

I nod. "Same goes for me with you, babe."

She sighs heavily. "I only want you to be happy. And if they make you happy, I'm good. But if they hurt you in any way, be prepared for me to turn up with a machete to hack their dicks off, and an army to bring you home, ok?"

I can't argue with that because if our situations were reversed, I would be threatening the exact same thing. And judging by the state she arrived in, I'm still not entirely convinced I don't need to storm the castle to save my friend.

Although, there's absolutely no chance of Em, or anyone for that matter, extracting me from my own situation. Right now, I'm trapped down the rabbit hole and I don't think I'm ever going to be leaving Wonderland unless it's in a body bag.

We get to spend a little bit longer together, where Em expertly side-steps any and all of my questions about what is going on in her life, and I tiptoe around what I can and can't tell her of my own.

But Thorne appears, and his presence signals that our time is up.

Our hugs goodbye bring copious tears, and as I watch my best friend disappear down the steps of the jet—at least this time allowed to walk away of her own accord—I honestly don't know if I'll ever see her again.

The strangest part is that Em continued to breeze on about plans for the summer and when we can next see each other again, while all I could do was bite the inside of my cheek so hard, I tasted blood.

"It isn't what it looks like. She's safe." Thorne ushers me back toward my seat and explains quietly that he's having her moved somewhere as a precaution. I don't even think I hear half of what he tells me. My eyes are glued to Em, watching her cross the tarmac outside the jet. I press myself up against the oval window and follow the black cavalcade of armored vehicles containing the most precious person in my life pull away.

I only caught a brief glimpse of my men exchanging words with one of the other guys who looked like he belonged in a SWAT team who was in one of the vehicles that just left. He looked gritty and all business, complete with armored vest and dark glasses to go with his black hair.

I'm really hoping he's a ruthless cunt who will protect my friend with his life.

Apparently, he's one of the men the Callianos trust the most, or so Thorne tells me as I slump into my seat and we prepare to take off. I suppose I should be grateful he's changed his tune about threatening my best friend and degrading my mother's memory.

Grateful.

What a fucking joke my life is.

CHAPTER 41
FOX

I find myself sunk against Ky's warm chest, curled in his lap, while my sand-covered toes dangle over the side of our shared deck chair.

Could this be paradise? Possibly, if there weren't so many goddamn secrets lurking in the long shadows.

But on the outside, this location looks every picture-perfect inch as though it were a dream. A tiny, off-the-map tropical island with a private helipad and not another soul to be seen.

The only structure to be found is an airy wooden cabin nestled upon white sand and an expanse of moonlit ocean, as far as I can see. Waves gently lap against the shore barely thirty feet from where the wide glass bedroom doors and wooden shutters open up onto a deck.

It's nothing more than simple, sun-bleached timbers and whitewashed concrete. Above me, palm fronds swish amidst the occasional creaks of dizzyingly tall, slender-trunked coconut trees.

But the ominous question that hangs over this entire idyllic scene is why we're here in the first place.

Thorne sits on the other side of the small fire pit, while my wolf lies on his back, hands tucked behind his head.

Shadows kiss every single muscular outline and indent. Making my mouth water.

This man leaves me perplexed at every turn. Raven flew us to this island in a helicopter from whatever unknown landing strip we'd arrived at, leaving the jet and the pilot waiting for us when we eventually return to the mainland.

Yes. He actually flew us. While I sat with my headset on in complete shock for the twenty minutes or so we were in the air, taking in the *whomp* of rotors whirling and vision of endless aquamarine waters stretching below.

Raven rides a sinfully hot motorbike, knows how to fly aircraft, and murders people for a secret society.

Why is that the biggest turn-on ever?

"You want something, baby girl?" The weight of Ky's attention falls on the side of my face as I gaze at the other two gorgeous specimens of muscle. I angle my neck to turn back toward him, and he holds out a slice of mango for me from the plate of cut fruit at his side.

I reach out, but he pulls back, keeping it away from me, shaking his head.

Oh, he wants to play? Well, I'm stuck here in tropical utopia and the sight of these three men—shirtless and caressed by firelight—is stoking my hunger.

My hand drops to my lap which draws out a devilish smirk. He brushes the edge of the slice across my bottom lip, the fruit bursting with sweet flavor and soft flesh. Sticky juices run down his fingers as he pops it into my mouth.

I close my lips around his offering and suck down on him. His mossy green eyes are more amber in the warm glow of the flames, and the way he looks down at me turns molten while I clean every drop off his fingers.

"That fucking mouth of yours." He hums his approval and

slides his forefinger back into my mouth and I suck him further in. Feeling more than ready to entertain my Viking's schemes.

His eyes flick up over my head. Then his voice is hot and sinful when he whispers in my ear. "I think Thorne looks hungry, baby girl."

A riot of sparks explodes in my stomach.

With hooded eyes, I look over his way and melt beneath his ferocity. Thorne's stare is fixed on the place where Ky's finger presses down on the pout of my bottom lip. There's no mistaking the way he likes the image of the two of us together, and in the firelight, I can see the outline of his hard cock pressed against his shorts.

"Go on." He slips his finger out of my mouth and straight into his own with a crooked grin. Handing me the plate, his knee nudges me to move. I dutifully cross over to Thorne's chair, feeling three sets of eyes track my every step from the shadows.

"Hi," I say softly. It seems so pathetic really, not knowing what to say to this man. He successfully leaves me tongue-tied simply by glancing in my general direction. But Thorne readjusts himself in the chair and moves his arms wider to give me room to sit.

Whether it's the turmoil of today or the tropical heat winding through my blood, something makes me bold, and I decide to straddle his lap. From the way his dark eyes glitter, I assume I've pleased him. Knowing that, well, it does something wicked to my insides.

As fucked up as it might be to admit, I miss being in his bed. My feeble little heart pouts and feels like it's been forever since last spending time with him as intimately as this. Even though it has barely been a week, I quickly discovered that a night spent in Thorne Calliano's arms is a temptation I will fall for every time.

He fucks like nothing I've ever experienced before, and I

only drown a little bit further with every opportunity to catch a glimpse behind his shuttered exterior. Having his cock buried deep inside me from behind while his raspy voice is up against my ear, being possessive as all hell, is far too addicting for my own sanity.

You're mine.

You belong to me.

I want you in my bed every night.

Jesus. I'm an absolute mess for him. For all of them.

With Ky, it's like the thrill of playing with fire. With Thorne, I never know if I'm going to lose a piece of my soul. And with Raven, well, I might end up bleeding out on the floor.

"Are you going to tell me why we are here?" I settle myself with my knees on the outside of his big thighs.

The fine lines around his eyes crinkle a little, but that's all he gives me.

"Is Em really going to be safe?" I press. A subtle nod comes in reply.

God, there's no telling whether my best friend will actually be protected under the watch of his *people*. But surely it can only be a good thing to not involve her in this world—to keep her as far away as possible from the Anguis.

Not that the man beneath me is giving an inch where my questions are concerned.

Ignoring his broodiness, I carry on. "I'm under no illusions. This isn't a holiday. Are you planning to bury my body out here? Seems like a lot of effort to go to." Digging my teeth into my bottom lip, I pick up a slice of fruit between my fingers.

Thorne still doesn't reply but reaches up to grab my wrist. Holding me steady as his soft lips close around my offering. When his tongue flicks against my fingertips, that wonderful throbbing intensifies between my legs.

His hard cock presses against my core, and I'm fighting every urge to start grinding down on him.

"We don't bury bodies." Those azure blue eyes of his lure me in when I should really know better.

"Fuck, Thorne. Just tell her." Ky says. "She should know."

The man beneath me is a locked vault.

"Something needed to be handled. It was safer you weren't around."

It's less than nothing to go on, but I stupidly glow a little at the notion that this man put my well-being somewhere high enough on his blood-soaked agenda to fly us halfway around the world. He could be lying through his teeth, mind you.

"Your friend is being guarded by the only men, outside of these two and my brother, who I would trust with my life," he adds.

Cocking my head to one side, Thorne must hear my thoughts immediately protest in response. *Hood. Gag. Handcuffs.* Hardly looked like protection to my eyes.

"What you saw shouldn't alarm you. In fact, your friend is being guarded while she continues to work and travel. They will ensure she can't be targeted, I promise you that, Foxglove." That's all he seems willing to volunteer.

I'm fighting a smile. All I can do is take what he's saying at face value, and if that's the truth, then I'm more than a little relieved. Considering where we started out at the start of all of this...when he threatened her life as a means to keep me in line.

"What?" He glares at me in the flickering shadows of the fire.

"Thank you."

"No thanks are required. I protect what belongs to me."

Oh, god. Chalk this round up to Thorne Calliano. He took me by force, told me he owns me, and here I am thanking him for protecting me. When, in his mind, I'm nothing more than the equivalent of an asset to keep hidden away like a valuable painting until the moment I become useful.

"Well, even so, how can I thank you properly?" My breasts

ache with the nearness of him. Thorne's heat and scent overwhelm me, and it drives me to distraction the way this man will silently study me without touching my body in the way I want him to.

Thorne Calliano is a king when it comes to edging.

This time, he picks up a piece of fruit from the plate and bites half of it before guiding the other piece to my mouth, and I greedily take him between my lips. My eyelashes flutter heavily at the feel of him against my tongue.

Behind me, I can feel the dark presence of my wolf watching us. Even though he's hidden by the dancing flames, I sense his intensity all the same. I might just be a slutty little possession to him—and I'd be a fool to forget he's a complete asshole—but for whatever fucked up reason, I want to please him, too.

Even more so after the sight of him in command of a helicopter earlier today. If I thought Ky's strong hands gripping a steering wheel of a car was hot, Raven has managed to level that up a few thousand notches.

The memory of what we did last time the two of us were alone together back at the compound lives rent-free in my mind at this stage. I'm pretty sure I spent the past couple of days wandering around in a trance replaying that night on loop. No one has ever treated me like he does, and I think I'm more than a little addicted to his brand of poison.

I want him to join us, and I want *more* between all four of us this time.

Maybe I'm officially out of my head, but the breathy words slip out before I lose my nerve entirely. "How can I thank *all* of you?"

Ky's warmth appears behind me; there's no question my naughty boy is on the same page, with his fingers stroking through my hair. Leaning forward, I suck Thorne's fingers past my lips once more while my soaking-wet pussy presses against his cock.

"Doesn't her sweet little tongue feel so fucking good?" Ky's murmuring while standing behind me. I know he's talking to Thorne, but the edge to his voice tells me those words are meant for Raven as well.

God, I love it when he starts running his mouth.

"That hot little cunt of hers feels even better." He's all mischief, and Thorne's cock kicks beneath me. Oh, this man is the devil, intent on winding our solemn protector up, too.

"Sounds like our little slut is wanting to be filled." Ky's strong grip tightens in my hair, and I moan a little around Thorne's fingers. He presses down on my tongue, and I'm certain my eyes glaze over at the delicious thought of having all of them at the same time.

My Viking wets his lips, then strikes. Dragging me off Thorne's lap, which makes me squeak, as the plate tumbles forgotten into the sand.

"I'm going to get our girl wet," Ky announces, tossing me over his shoulder. "If you assholes want to join in, you'd better hurry up and move."

CHAPTER 42

FOX

There's an open-air shower attached to this cabin. One that swirls with faint hints of lemongrass and hibiscus, with a wide wooden bench off to the side of an adjustable shower head. It doesn't even need a door; you can stroll in here straight from the ocean.

Ky doesn't wait to undress me once we set foot in the private alcove. As soon as he tips my body upright, he pins me against the concrete wall. Flipping the shower on, the cool spray of water soaks us both.

I'm wearing a bikini beneath a thin cotton dress, and the material is see-through and plastered to my skin within seconds.

His hot mouth devours mine, and I moan against his lips. Everything inside me is begging to be stroked and teased and pleasured; I can only hope that my other men are wanting to join in on this, too.

Ky licks and sucks his way down my jaw and neck, feathering his tongue over my pulse point, before he grabs the edge of the fabric covering my breasts with his teeth and tugs on it roughly. My tits pop out, with my nipples already hard and wanting.

"Oh, my god. Ky." I breathe as he closes his mouth around the furled bud and drives me insane with his skilled mouth.

Tonight, he seems more intent than usual to be on me, and quickly descends my body. His powerful fingers dig into my hips, restraining me against the wall.

"Gonna have you on edge every time you so much as look at me. This sweet little cunt will be weeping and aching, going insane for my tongue and my cock. I'm gonna have you as fucking desperate for me as I am for you."

"Fuck, Ky. Please." Trying to find purchase, I squirm, threading my fingers in his hair.

"So pretty when you beg, aren't you." He grunts and lifts one of my legs, throwing it over his shoulder. Ky tugs my soaked bikini bottoms aside, and his mouth fastens over my core. If it wasn't for his punishing hold against my hip, the force of his actions would almost knock me over. There's no teasing or going slow with this moment. His tongue is hungry and everywhere, and water trickles over my exposed breasts, tracing the valleys of my body as I get lost in the pleasure his mouth is building.

"Holy shit." Legs shaking, my eyelashes flutter closed as I grind against the friction of his beard and the effortlessly wicked way he stirs me into a frenzy.

"This is all mine." He growls against my core. "Come on my tongue, baby girl." Then he spears into me, and I can't help the loud cries bubbling up.

Ky works me so hard and fast the room spins on its axis.

As he moves back up to suck on my clit, I hear a noise. My eyes pop open and there are two vengeful gods standing before me. Both devour the sight of my half-naked body with strain on their faces and an inferno raging beneath their hooded eyes.

Raven drags his thumb over his lower lip, and Thorne's gaze drops to where Ky's face is buried in my pussy.

I lose it.

My orgasm races up through my trembling legs, and I buckle with the force of the waves tossing me about. My Viking continues to lick and suck and nibble at my pussy lips as my body quivers from his attentions.

"Christ. I need to feel your cunt gripping my cock." Ky swoops up and makes quick work of ripping the sodden clothes off me. I'm no help at all, already limp and aching for more.

Just as he said I would be.

He guides me to follow his path, dropping backward onto the wooden bench, sitting with his back against the wall. Splaying his knees wide, Ky maneuvers me to straddle him. I've managed to come back to my body a little, and the feel of his cock sinking inside me as I lower down is a perfect fullness, ramping up my desire once more. His piercing drags against my sensitive inner walls, and I'm damn near clawing at his chest to keep my balance.

"Ky. *Ffffuck.*" I whimper. His lower stomach rubs against my overstimulated clit, and I don't know if I've wound up biting off more than I can chew. Who the fuck do I think I am to handle all of these men at the same time?

One of them is overwhelming enough. Let alone three who all look guaranteed to eat me alive.

"You want more?" Ky ducks his head, taking one of my nipples into his mouth again, moving slower now that whatever frenzy consumed us moments before has passed. This is more like the teasing and torturing I've grown accustomed to from my naughty boy when we fuck.

"Yes." Liquid heat gushes through me as he tugs gently on the stiffened peak with his teeth.

"One of you two had better help me out here unless you're just going to stand around tugging on your dicks." Flicking my nipple with his tongue, he pins me with a cheeky grin, and I shiver.

Ky's eyes roam hungrily, and he groans. "Fuck. Yes. Squeeze my cock just like that. Our girl loves the idea of being filled up."

A muscled torso presses against my spine; Thorne comes up behind me, and the outline of his hard length is unmistakable. My teeth sink into my bottom lip, knowing that he's willingly joined in without me having to plead for his attention makes me swoon in double time.

"You're going to be a good girl and take all of us, Foxglove." Thorne runs his nose along the curve of my shoulder and up my neck. Goosebumps tumble down my arms and his lips graze my pulse point.

"Yes, Daddy." My back arches into his touch, and he rumbles a noise of approval.

Fuck. I don't even know where my wolf is, but I can feel that he's here.

"Ky, you need to lie back. Keep her on top." Thorne drags his fingers down my spine until he reaches my ass. Then slides his hand lower; a featherlight glide of his fingers getting me used to the sensation of being touched there, but it's enough to have my pulse kick up all the same.

Beneath me, Ky is already moving. Keeping himself buried deep inside me, he shifts us so that he reclines along the bench, flat on his back.

"I think our little slut is going to look damn perfect with all her holes filled." Ky holds my thighs to keep me steady, and his cock pulses inside me. The image of all of these men using me is carnal and filthy, and I want it so fucking bad.

"We need you nice and relaxed. But if it gets too much, you tell us." Thorne twists my face around to look at him, and I nod quickly. At the same time, something cold and wet drizzles over my ass, followed by fingers smoothing over my skin and the click of a cap. Well, aren't these men always prepared for an orgy.

"Words, Foxglove."

"Yes. I understand." That satisfies him, and he lets my face go, but as I turn back toward Ky, that's when my eyes snag on Raven.

Holy shit. He's naked, and every tattooed inch of him is right fucking there as he fists his cock.

Thorne's fingers start gliding over my ass, and it feels electric beneath my skin. Having him take such careful control of my body is a sensation like no other. I find myself quickly grinding back against his hand as he rims around my hole, then dips a finger inside.

"Oh, god." I let out a moan of pleasure.

The heat swirling around us picks up in intensity. Ky shifts and rolls his hips beneath me and I'm grinding on his cock and Thorne's hand.

"You want more?" His voice is dark and gritty behind me.

"Please, Daddy." Oh, god. Yes, please.

That's when Ky glances up at Raven. Their unspoken language passes between them, and his lips curl into a wicked expression.

"Get it wet for me." My wolf's voice is a low command.

"Anytime, baby."

And oh, fuck. Suddenly I'm treated to the sight of Raven's thick cock dragging over Ky's lips before he shoves into his mouth. He's so close that I'm consumed by that familiar musky scent, and I flick my tongue out to glide over my lips.

Thorne presses harder and works another finger into my ass while Ky's piercing rocks against the perfect spot deep inside me, and I can feel the build of my next climax racing up to claim its hold.

"Ven." The man behind me grits out as he starts scissoring his fingers. "You going to fuck her throat or what?"

Dark eyes snap to mine. This is a tango we're already familiar with, and he wastes no time, pulling out of Ky's mouth on a wet pop. Then lining up in front of me.

I watch, captivated and panting as he lazily strokes his length, before digging one hand into my hair.

"Such a filthy little toy." The way his words grate over me makes my entire body clench. "Perfect lips to suck my cock while your other holes are being filled."

Ky groans beneath me, and Thorne draws in a ragged breath. This wolf is playing dirty and none of us are safe.

The gasp I let out is the opportunity Raven takes to push past my lips and into my mouth. With my damp hair tight in one hand, he pumps his hips and holds me still for his pleasure.

I'm moaning and gagging as he fills my mouth and taps the back of my throat, reducing me to a riot of sparks about to shoot off and explode in the night sky.

There's nothing I can do but let them all work my body, causing everything to pulse and throb. The pleasure they're drawing out of me is a delirious thing coursing through each limb with giddy joy.

"Fuck, yes. Just like that." Ky groans beneath me as I clench and flutter around him. He slips a hand between us to play with my clit, and I'm teetering on the edge of falling apart.

"Don't swallow." Raven's command is low and sharp, and the only warning I get. His hips punch faster, hitting deep, before a grunt precedes the salty burst of his release coating my tongue.

I obey him. Of course I do. Half out of my body with pleasure thanks to the skills Thorne and Ky are demonstrating, working my pussy and my ass.

But I'm completely unprepared for his next move. My wolf sweeps in, tattooed fingers curled tight in my hair, to capture my mouth with his own.

Fuck. Holy, fuck. He's kissing me.

Raven rips my sanity apart with a searing hot kiss, and of course, he chooses to allow our lips to find each other's for the first time when I have a mouth full of his cum.

Well, shit.

This man is filthy and terrifying...and I decide right at that moment I can't get enough of his madness.

We exchange tongues and saliva and the tangy evidence of him before he draws back. Ravenous eyes consume me for what feels like a moment suspended in time. Then he turns and fuses his mouth with Ky's, and the sight of them kissing and sharing the taste of him sets off my fluttering orgasm.

Ky is groaning against his lips and digging his fingers into my flesh as his hips rock up from beneath me. His cock swells and jerks before filling my pussy. All the while, Thorne pumps his fingers in and out of my ass with a steady rhythm. Quiet, filthy words are whispered in my ear, and there's nothing I can do but dissolve while biting back cries of pleasure.

It feels like Thorne is watching this all unfold and taking his time to savor the performance we're all putting on...for him.

Because maybe, in some way, we are.

CHAPTER 43
Thorne

Jesus.

This is not exactly how I thought tonight was going to go. I expected Foxglove to be angry, maybe even try to escape us after seeing her friend, Emerald.

But as usual, Ky was right, and he's going to be a self-satisfied little prick about it.

He convinced me that she needed the chance to see her friend, and while we were at it, our team was able to run some reconnaissance as the two girls talked.

Now, we're all falling into bed with lust racing through our veins, and it's like we've done this dance with one another a hundred times before.

Ven and Ky have shared plenty of girls between them at the club over the years. In all that time I've never felt compelled to join them.

Not until now.

Not until her.

At the sight of our purple-haired beauty being filled by the two of them, Christ, I'm barely hanging on.

But everything feels so...right.

"Get on Ven's cock so I can eat your sweet little pussy, baby girl."

My dick twitches at the way Ky has taken to calling the shots tonight, and there are no complaints from me. She's already dripping with Ky's cum and had a mouthful of Ven. If they want to play with her a bit, just the two of them, I'll gladly sit back and enjoy watching, for now.

Ven props himself against the headboard of the bed, guiding her over his cock with her back against his chest. She's so fucking pliant after two orgasms in quick succession, and even though I'm sure he's threatened to slit her throat more than once, she gladly goes to him with a smile in her eyes.

It makes me wonder exactly how close they've gotten.

Her pussy is glistening. A swollen and pouting invitation. My balls tighten, seeing her splayed out like this, with the spot where Ven's length sinks inside her, capturing every inch of my focus. Cum wells at her entrance stretched around his dick, slicking them both and coating her thighs.

Ky falls on her like a man starved.

I don't blame him.

Fucking hell. Fisting my cock, I sit back and take in the sight of the three of them groaning and filling the room with filthy, wet noises. I've sat back at the club plenty of times before, content to watch others fuck, but nothing has come close to the scene I can't drag my eyes from.

They're the hottest goddamn thing I've ever seen.

Ky's abs bunch and flex as he licks her pussy, and Ven sucks down on her neck until she arches and moans. Her gorgeous face flushes with pleasure as one hand digs into Ky's hair, and she clings to Ven with the other.

One thing I know about Raven Flannaghty is that once you have his attention, there's no leaving his clutches.

This girl is never going to escape him. Even if she tries.

I spit on my hand, stroking my cock, and that's when her

eyes flutter open. Everything collapses into the smallest tunnel. Our gazes hold, locked together across the room. She's everything. Stunning and magnificent and the best part of all of us. Her mouth drops open the moment she's tugged under again.

Good fucking girl.

She reads my lips as I mouth those words, falling apart so beautifully under Ky's tongue while riding Ven's cock.

"*Ffffuck.* Holy shit, Thorne. You need to get over here and fuck our girl." Ky's breathing is ragged. As he drops kisses all over her soft thighs, and Ven hisses through gritted teeth.

He's barely holding it together. I see it when his eyes drift to meet mine.

"I need you, baby." Ky's talking to Ven now, and my stomach does a rapid tumble at the immediacy of this next part. One where there's no avoiding how close together we're all going to be.

I wasn't jealous seeing Ven fuck him the night we were last all tangled like this, but the realization dawned on me that what I thought I wanted...well, turns out that has evolved.

The other two move Foxglove, and I cross over to join them on the bed; kneeling, then wrapping my arms around her from behind. Taking over Ven's position at her back.

She turns, giving me a blissed-out sigh over one shoulder.

Something that has no right to be there clatters around inside my rib cage.

I cover up whatever the hell is going on inside me by tugging her earlobe between my teeth. "You're going to come all over my cock, while Ky fucks your ass." Greedily, I soak up how my raspy words have her quivering in my arms.

The soft whimper of a *yes* in response makes my dick throb, and my gaze finds Ky. He's right there, with green eyes that burrow straight into my soul.

CHAPTER 44
Ky

Thorne Calliano is a man I have had many thoughts about over the years.

Most of them are steeped in longing. Some of them are desperately miserable. Others—more and more frequently of late—are borderline obscene.

Right now, there's only one going through my mind.

He's here.

Not only that, but his cobalt eyes are on me, and I know exactly how Fox feels whenever she looks his way. My whole body comes alive whenever that man so much as glances in my direction, and yet I've never gotten this close to the edge of becoming something *more* with him.

What I want to do right now is dip forward in order to kiss them both.

Only problem is, Thorne is about as hard to approach as Ven. And this is already pushing him into new and unfamiliar territory.

The last thing he needs is for me to unload years of sexual attraction on him like a horny avalanche.

But fucking our girl in the ass while our cocks rub together through her thin inner walls? That sounds like an incredible idea.

"You're doing so good, baby girl." I help ease her down on top of Thorne. Eating up the sight of his shoulders flexing and the way his dick is so fucking hard. This man is a masterpiece to look at, and right now, I'm in heaven with him and our girl beneath me, Ven at my back.

Out-fucking-standing.

Fox is so out of her head with pleasure, and wet with my cum and her own, that she takes Thorne's fat cock easily. Her body flattens against his broad chest, and she buries her face in his neck.

It's dirty and perfect, and they look so goddamn good together.

Ven shifts behind me and passes me the bottle of lube while he works some over himself and my ass as we adjust our positions.

He reaches around and grabs my cock, stroking me from root to tip, making my head dip between my shoulders. "*Unnghhhh*. Baby." I'm always such a goner for him the moment he handles me like this. He's a gorgeous asshole and knows it, too.

"Those are some hungry fucking eyes you've got there." His voice is gravel at my ear, and he bites down on my neck. "You sure you're going to be satisfied just fucking her?" He whispers the last part so only I can hear, and I shudder at his perceptive words.

He lets out a dark chuckle. Squeezing my dick, and then reaches lower to tease my balls.

I grunt a curse at him.

Yeah, well, I see the way he looks at Thorne, too. So he's hardly one to talk.

Ven thinks he's a sealed fortress. But I know more of his secrets than he cares to admit.

"You going to fuck me good, or what, baby?" My teeth clench as my hips thrust into his hold.

"Get inside her already, Ky." Thorne looks like he's struggling not to blow. I'm right there with him. Our girl is messy and whimpering every time I stroke over her sweet little hole, and even though Thorne prepped her earlier, she's going to be so fucking tight.

"Just breathe for me. Tell me if you're ready." Like a good girl, she clings to Thorne's neck, and nods.

"*Please*. I'm ready. Please, Ky."

I fist my cock, taking over from Ven, and press against her ass. Working her gently and watching her shiver with pleasure as the initial resistance gives way slowly and my cock starts to sink deeper.

"So fucking good. Breathe with me, baby girl." My movements stay shallow, with small pulses easing past the ring of muscle, and she's the hottest, tightest thing I've ever been inside. Sweat beads on my forehead, she's so full with Thorne already seated deep inside her pussy.

"Fuck...Ky...It's so much."

"That's it." I croon, barely keeping my head with how incredibly tight she is.

Fox moans and tosses her head back. "I want you in me."

"Such a filthy little thing, aren't you." I feed her a few more inches. "I love that dirty mouth when you get all demanding. Give it all to me, my good girl."

"Mmmfuck...*baby*. Just like that." She shudders beneath me.

Going slow and holding on and not hurting my perfect girl are about the only things I can focus on.

At this point, I'd fucking crawl just to hear her call me baby again.

"You're taking us so well. You gotta relax for me, Christ; I'm nearly half-way."

Both Thorne and Fox make a groaning noise—half pleasure, half disbelief.

"Fuck. *Fffffuck.*" Thorne holds my eyes as I work deeper, and I know he can feel it.

"That good for you too, hmm?" I can't help but feel a wave of cockiness that my piercing is rubbing Thorne through her inner walls, and he's straining to keep it together because of me.

"Jesus," he grunts, and all of a sudden, my hips drive forward to sit flush against Fox's ass, and we all let out a deep groan of pleasure.

"That's—Shit. Holy, shit." Thorne's composure is hanging by a thread.

I can tell Ven is laughing to himself behind me. This fucker is enjoying every moment of watching us all panting and writhing, waiting for him to join in.

"Christ, you feel so fucking good." I can't help but start shifting my hips against Fox, and she's moaning and clenching as I move inside her. I'm fucking both of them. Fox *and* Thorne. Holy shit. Both of them are incredible and as I get lost in the stormy blue of the eyes before me, I think he knows that's what I really mean.

You both feel good.

"Please." She's breathless and begging for us to get there faster, tightening around both our cocks.

"Nearly there, baby girl."

"You're taking us so well." Thorne pushes her hair off her forehead. "Give me that perfect fucking mouth." She whimpers, sliding her tongue against his, melting into him.

Behind me, Ven presses forward, and it's so fucking good I'm not going to last long. None of us are.

"Oh, fuck. *Ungghhhhh.*" Slutty little noises burst out of me as he shifts more, working his cock deeper, with each motion rocking us all together.

"You good?" Ven checks in with me through gritted teeth.

"Just move. Goddamn, baby. Fuck." With each movement of his hips, my balls are growing tighter, and Fox is squeezing my dick like the tightest fist imaginable.

"Holy shit." Thorne pants against Fox's mouth. His voice is a hoarse whisper. "That's it. Good fucking girl." She's splintering apart and her climax is the final straw.

I'm pretty sure I feel Thorne jerk at the same time her pussy ripples around him; he unloads inside her with a grunt and heaving chest.

"Oh, god. Ven." His hips start pumping harder, chasing my release that is building so goddamn fast as he groans in that deep, sexy fucking way he does when he's about to come. "Don't stop. Right there." Hitting that deliriously good spot, my body lights up as my spine stiffens. All the blood rushes to my dick and I'm soaring high, flying past stars.

"Ven...fuck...fffuck."

"You want me to fill this ass up? Then you better come for me while I'm owning you, my pretty little slut."

"Oh, god. *Baby*." I'm gasping. My cock thickens and throbs and fills my girl for the second time tonight. His thrusts and filthy words tip me over the edge.

Ven's cock surges and unloads inside me, following right on the heels of my own orgasm, and we dissolve into a mess of groans and sweaty limbs and cum.

The four of us float around in a daze for what seems like forever. Each coming back down to our bodies one by one.

That was so fucking hot.

I can't wait to do it all again.

"You did so well; you were perfect." Thorne is busy checking in with Fox, gently stroking her hair and sharing hushed words of praise, which earns him a loopy grin of pleasure in return.

God, she's stunning. Flushed and messy and dripping with

the evidence of us, a cloud-like dream who cushions all our jagged edges.

Ven gives me a quick kiss on the shoulder as he pulls out of me, the first to find it within him to move. He drags me off her, because I sure as shit still haven't quite rediscovered the use of my limbs. Scooping Fox's languid body up, he quietly smuggles her off to the bathroom, where he makes sure she gets properly cleaned up, and pees, all the little attentive things that make him the way he is. He takes care of our girl in the only way he knows how.

Despite my own hazy fog of pleasure filling my head, I find my way to the outdoor shower. While I'm in there with my head bowed under the water, the back of my neck heats as Thorne comes in to join me. It feels like the most natural thing in the world for us to both be here like this together, and I shift over, giving him space to wash under the wide spray of the showerhead alongside me.

We don't talk. But we don't need to either.

Beneath the water tumbling over his angular cheekbones and firm jaw, he fixes me with solemn eyes. Such a familiar sight, yet this time, they're filled with years of agony—all the unbearable things he and Hawke have been through, and I see it.

I see that he can't take it out on Fox.

She's not the one responsible for what happened to him. Or to any of us.

His silent nod is confirmation enough, as he grabs a towel and I do the same, following him back into the darkened bedroom.

I slip into the cool sheets, where Ven lets me take over, grabbing hold of our girl from one side, while Thorne wraps around her from the other. She's long since passed out already, and her soft breaths as she turns and cuddles into me makes my heart grow about ten sizes inside my chest.

This girl might belong to us, but now, she's truly our possession.

More than a thing that we own or control. She's tunneled in and embedded herself right in our rotten bones.

Whatever happens from here on out, I know Fox is going to be at the heart of all of us.

Of that, I am absolutely certain.

CHAPTER 45
Ven

"Those secrets of yours are piling up like bodies over there, Calliano."

I stretch my legs out and glance sideways at the man filling the seat beside me.

Over in a spot close to the turquoise water, Ky and Fox are cuddled together in a hammock laughing, and it looks like a scene from a fucking picture book.

Only it isn't.

We're here because there's a threat against our property, and Thorne knows shit about whatever is going on that he's choosing not to reveal.

I'm far from an open book, but when it comes to this girl... there's no way in hell I'm going to let him get away with thinking he can run this gig himself.

"Takes one to know one." He grunts at me. But digs a hand in his hair, observing the other two as closely as I am. As if they might vanish from right under our noses, stolen away from us, if we dare blink for a second too long.

"What's the latest from Hawke and the teams? Have they uncovered anything to trace the encryption?"

"Nothing." Thorne looks just as frustrated as I am. The Anguis are culpable of turning a blind eye to the scum of the earth, and it has my teeth on edge that whoever made this threat knew exactly how to reach us in the one place we have always been safe.

It doesn't make sense.

Tapping my thumb against my thigh, I put a voice to the thought I've been turning over in my mind since leaving Port Macabre. "The fight night might be the perfect opportunity, you know."

"How so?"

"Use it as a spectacle. Jab whoever this is in the ribs. Flush out some information."

We have to leave here tomorrow, whether we want to or not since I'm featured on the title card for a fight night held at Noire House. Where the Gathered will soak themselves in the gratuitous violence of watching two men beat the shit out of each other and then lose themselves in an evening of hedonistic pleasures at the club afterward.

Blood. Violence. Sex. The foundation upon which the Anguis built their temples of power.

I'm guessing that whoever is attempting this threat will be in attendance. There's no doubt in my mind they'll be fixated on the little Fox's every move.

Possibly this so-called 'true heir' they claim will be revealed might be among the crowd, too.

"It seems risky."

"There are three of us. You really think someone could get past us all?"

A peal of high-pitched laughter bursts from the direction of the girl in question. She's squirming, but it's all for show; there's no genuine attempt to get away from Ky's taunting or riling or whatever he's up to. Probably both, seeing as how his hands dig into her soft curves and his lips hover at her ear.

That asshole has rarely been without a cocky smile in all the years I've known him, but lately, it's like he can't stop beaming.

"She needs to be kept safe," Thorne mutters beneath his breath. He's reluctant to admit how much Fox has gotten under his skin, and I can see the conflict raging inside him. He's stuck with the reality that he doesn't have a choice but to let her in... or lose her.

"Which is exactly what you'll do. But you'll achieve nothing by keeping her away from the fight night. We need to push whoever is planning shit into making a wrong move."

He stares at me with those cold blue eyes of his. "And you think by parading her around some more, it'll do just that?"

I shrug. "It'll force their hand at the very least." Turning my attention back to Fox and Ky in the hammock, I try to block out the dull thud of my pulse intensifying in my ears. There's something that tightens inside my chest whenever Thorne and I spend time close like this. Having his eyes on me isn't anything similar to how it feels when I'm with Ky.

"Or it might be unnecessarily setting her as an easy target." He scrubs a hand over his jaw.

"Sure. Or, it might piss off whoever this is enough that they start getting sloppy. So far, they've hidden behind encrypted threats sent by message. But they might take a swing and give us something much easier to trace."

"You know how risky that shit is." I see Thorne shift in his chair out of the corner of my eye.

"She's an only child, right?"

The man beside me nods slowly. But there's more there that he's not divulging.

"Which means that whoever is threatening her intends to take over the Noire line of power by force. You know what that looks like as well as I do. They're not diverting to another blood heir; they're planning to get rid of the only living descendant, probably with the intention of inserting someone from outside the Noire line in Fox's place."

She's vulnerable, and we don't have time to fuck around coming up with a plan. The Serpentine moon is drawing closer, which means whoever is plotting something is going to be making their move any day.

"There hasn't been a Pledging ceremony for a long time," he mutters quietly.

Because the previous ones all turned into blood baths. Invariably, they were ceremonies used by the Anguis to pass power down a lineage, and at the last moment, there would be plots to assassinate the heir and insert someone else into the claim for power instead.

It's a tactic that has been used for hundreds, if not thousands, of years.

Only now, that threat is hovering over Fox's head, and our place in this was cemented the moment Thorne confirmed the Pledging ceremony with the Anguis.

While Ky and I both had our motives for fucking with the legacy of Noire House, the reason Thorne decided to commit to a Pledging when we could have easily murdered the girl and taken her power is something I can't get my head around.

He says that she's just a possession we own.

But my gut tells me there's something more insidious lying beneath the turbulent waters of Thorne Calliano.

"We take her to the fight." I keep my eyes on the girl in question. Her lilac hair is loose and wavy from swimming in the ocean. The freckles across her nose have darkened after a day spent in the sun. And she curls into Ky like the two of them are peas in a pod.

Thorne remains quiet for a while beside me.

I can still feel the heat and intensity of last night every time I close my eyes.

Things have changed between all of us; I can feel the difference. Something feels more settled and sure in my blood than ever before, yet, I'm also crawling out of my skin.

With want? Or something else.

Sharing Ky with others has never been an issue for me—or him. But now? A possessiveness over all of them is surging to the surface.

Like I'd carve out the hearts of anyone who dared lay a hand on any of these three.

Learning to trust doesn't come easily to the likes of me. But Thorne has proven time and time again that he'd lay down his life for both me and Ky.

Now, in the cruelest twist of fate imaginable, Foxglove Noire is included in that list.

CHAPTER 46
FOX

Ky holds up a gold vintage chain with three teardrop-shaped amethyst jewels hanging in the middle that match the color of my hair. The largest sits at the center, while two tiny ones sit on either side.

It's stunning.

Only, as he dangles it in front of my eyes, I notice there's no clasp to fasten it around my neck, just two small loops of fine gold thread that definitely don't link together.

"It doesn't go around your neck." Ky's loaded gaze drops from my eyes…down.

To the part of me this chain is designed to be attached to.

My nipples harden into diamonds as I realize where this jewelry is made to be worn.

"Does that go…" My mouth is dry as I swallow heavily.

"Indeed it does." He winks. "Underneath your dress."

I'm trying to get ready for tonight's event—a fight night organized at Noire House where the Gathered will mingle and bet on their chosen warriors and bay for blood.

We've been back from the island for less than a day, and I

can still hear the gentle lull of waves and taste the salt coating my skin.

But now we've returned to the mist-coated forest of Port Macabre.

My wolf is on the feature card for this evening's fights.

I know who my money would be on every time.

And even though they've barely filled me in on details for the occasion, instead of leaving me alone to do my hair and makeup, there's a very naughty boy taunting me with the promise of edging and pleasure while we're in attendance.

"We've also got another present for you." Ky's expression is pure, glimmering mischief as he hands me a velvet drawstring bag. "This one is also to be worn *underneath* your dress."

Sitting in my towel on the edge of the bed, butterflies take flight in my stomach as I take both *gifts* from him.

He bends down and captures my lips, stealing my breath and sucking on my tongue for a long moment, before pulling away.

"Hurry up and get yourself ready, baby girl."

Excuse me while I peel my sanity off the floor. He has no right waltzing in here with a mouth that tempting.

"Sadly, we don't have enough time for you to sit there drooling over my dick. You're the guest of honor, don't forget."

A petulant snort does nothing to disguise the fact I am, indeed, staring at his groin.

"Oh, really? How could I forget?" I roll my eyes.

"I'll meet you at the car." Ky whistles as he saunters out the door, hands shoved in his pockets, fine as ever.

An event at Noire House would be nothing without the heir being present. Even if I'm now fully complicit in *mostly* everything these men are doing to take my father's legacy apart. At least now, they seem to trust me enough to know that I am on their side in all of this.

I think.

Heading to my bathroom to finish getting dressed, I let the towel drop and then gasp a little when I catch my reflection.

Bite marks form constellations across my skin, all in various phases of healing. God, the sight of the teeth indents and mottled bruises makes me feel so goddamn powerful. Three murderous, dangerous men...who all took turns claiming me as their own in the most primal of ways.

Men who couldn't keep themselves off me.

As I twist and turn in order to fully look at myself in the mirror I pick up my phone. Quickly taking photos of my naked body, cataloging the marks they have coated me in. My breasts, thighs, ass—every soft part of me bears evidence of their ownership, and it makes my heart do a little double bounce. Scrolling through my camera roll showcases a record, a living proof of their desire for me.

While I'm certain to never experience love from these men, at least I'll have this reminder long after the marks currently embedded in my skin heal and fade.

There's a broad grin fighting to take over my face as I set my phone back down and swipe up the small bag. Pulling open the drawstrings, the contents are revealed and I can't help but bark out a laugh. Why am I not surprised? It's a small, black, conical-shaped device, one that I recognize is usually controlled with a remote—although that part of the toy is missing. It winks at me with a matching purple jewel on the flared end.

And it is most definitely meant to go in my ass.

A very, very naughty boy indeed.

I wonder if the others know about Ky's little plan for getting up to mischief tonight, and if they do, the bubble of a thought that they've all been talking about this among themselves makes my core flood with heat.

Well, I am certainly not one to back down from this challenge, and if multiple orgasms and having all of my men inside me is promised at the grand climax of this evening, then I'm going to be the Belle of this fucking ball.

TWO SETS of eyes devour me in the vehicle's rearview mirror, all the way to Noire House. It's late, the forest is blanketed by night. Raven left much earlier with the now-familiar rev of his bike to prepare for his bout. Thorne drives us through the darkened and deserted streets of Port Macabre, and Ky fills the front passenger seat.

I had to shoo him off when he tried to dazzle me with that charming smile and slip in the back alongside me. There was zero chance of arriving in any fit state to attend the evening if he came near with those wandering hands. Especially knowing the secrets going on beneath my dress, he'd have been trying to slip into more than just the backseat of this car.

When we pull up outside the mansion, Ky is quick to open my door and help me out. His tongue touches against his canine as he extends a hand in my direction. As I slide out, my dress' high slit opens to reveal my tattooed thigh, and I eat up every moment he appreciates what I'm wearing tonight.

I've worn a simple, silky black strapless gown that flows from my waist, with a padded corset top wrapping around my breasts. The chain I'm wearing is affixed by small loops clamped over my nipples. It hangs against my sternum, hidden beneath the firm material. No one can see that my breasts are swollen and the sensitive buds are hard and turned a deep shade of dusky rose, but I know—and these two men know—exactly what is happening beneath my beautiful gown. The added friction where the material rubs the tight peaks, combined with the pinching sensation from the weighted jewels every time I walk or shift my weight, has me squirming already. The amethyst gemstones look gorgeous set against the vintage gold chain, but they also amplify the tugging against my nipples, and I know it is going to take everything to not fall apart unbidden tonight.

Which is going to be much easier said than done, considering that my clit is already throbbing and demanding attention.

As I exit the car, Ky slides his hand down my lower back, and while we're still hidden from view, he explores lower. Finding the jewel nestled between my ass cheeks, he rubs his palm over the spot. Jostling it a little to make me gasp.

"Holy fuck. I've never wanted to leave one of these events faster." Ky groans in my ear and starts to push at my shoulders. "Lie down in the back seat right now so I can wrap your legs around my head." He demands.

"Ky." I hear Thorne's growl from where he stands on the driver's side. His scowl lands on the two of us, like we're a pair of deviants about to ditch school. This man knows exactly what is going through my troublemaker's mind.

"Behave, naughty boy." I pat his chest. "If you do, you can have my ass later."

He tilts his head back with a grumble. "This is torture for me, too, you know."

"Good." Since my tits, pussy, and ass are all humming with need, it seems only fitting.

"Wait til Ven sees you. He's going to lose it."

My greedy little heart preens with delight. I have to duck my head to not make a complete fool of myself. I'm painfully aware how my heart has leapt out the plane without a parachute since our time together in island paradise.

Do not, under any circumstances, blurt out something ridiculous simply because you're turned on as all hell.

As we round the front of the vehicle, Thorne offers me the

crook of his arm. Looking down at me with achingly beautiful blue eyes. I want to wrap myself up in this man and never let go.

Yup. My heart is plummeting in total freefall.

Splattering into oblivion as I hit concrete shall occur imminently.

"You look beautiful, as always, Foxglove."

I nibble my lip and flash him a small smile. Why does any little compliment from him always feel so wonderful?

"Thank you."

"You bring beauty into a world that for so long has been bleak. I hope you know that."

Surely those words did not just come from this solemn creature's mouth. I nearly fall over my own feet.

A nervous little laugh bubbles out of me. "Oh, no, it's nothing. Really." Trying to wave off him and his charm offensive while fighting the flush threatening to coat me from head to toe is a precarious feat.

"I'm serious. You are a wonderful artist, Foxglove. That much is evident in everything you do."

Oh, goddamn this infuriatingly captivating man.

But apparently he's not done melting my brain, yet.

"It takes a special person to bring art or beauty into the world...especially in the face of callousness or a grim reality. Don't forget that."

The unexpected hit of praise tugs like a hook in my stomach. So much so the force almost drags me toward him physically. I turn to walk away—or maybe float—glowing all over. But Thorne catches my elbow and drags me back against his broad frame.

He lowers his lips to brush the shell of my ear as we start making our way to the entrance. "Now, with all that said, I'm going to give you ten minutes before I need to inspect your present."

My thighs clench, and the sensation in my ass intensifies immediately. Thorne is never usually wicked like this. Whenever we attend these kinds of events, he's all stern, business-Daddy. And I'm caught off guard by the fact he wants to fool around.

There's officially no hope for me, being left in the tangled web of these two men tonight.

CHAPTER 47
FOX

My nipples are so sensitive I'm pulsating rather than walking, and my pussy grows slicker with every second spent making my way through the throngs of the Gathered at Noire House.

I'm also a little giddy with trying to count down the minutes left until Thorne makes good on his promise.

Making my way through into the enormous ballroom, memories of our last visit here—and what transpired immediately afterward between myself and Thorne—ensure they make themselves vividly present in my memory.

My men remain close tonight. In the past, when we arrived, they would usually disappear into the crowd to occupy their positions, watching the room. But now that there are unknown threats hanging over my head, they have taken it upon themselves to flank me, two burly sentinels guarding my every move.

I can't deny that it feels incredible to have them attending to me in such a public way.

Fighting has long since commenced, and judging by the thick cloud of blood-lust hanging over the Gathered—who are all seated at various tables arranged around in a horseshoe shape around the boxing ring—I'm assuming we've made it in time to watch Ven's bout since he is the final attraction for the evening.

The Anguis' murderous crown jewel.

An empty table lies up ahead, positioned with a full view of the room, though slightly elevated and at the back. The heir to Noire House is given prime placement, lording it over everyone else in attendance. I had been concerned I might be swarmed by the usual locusts being my late father's friends, but the sea of skull masks are all trained on the fight going on at present inside the ring.

As I walk past, various guests acknowledge my presence and greet me, as they would have done for my father, I imagine. But the closeness of Thorne and Ky behind me prevents the usual clamoring for my attention and unwanted, wandering hands.

To my relief, the creeps hiding within the Anguis who want to try and lay claim to me are staying away.

Ky's hand settles on my lower back as we reach the table. He leans in and speaks in my ear. "I'll be with Ven for the fight. Thorne will stay with you."

"Ok." I breathe.

He inhales deeply against my neck, making my knees give out a little. "Ven and I will be able to see everything from up there. Make sure to put on a good show for us." With that, he chuckles and strides away, while heat tingles in my cheeks. I don't know what he means by that, but I suspect it has something to do with Thorne.

My thighs clench, and warmth pools low in my belly.

Thorne pulls out a seat at the very back of the table. It's draped with thick black cloth that sweeps the floor, and there are bottles of champagne stacked on ice surrounding a centerpiece made of white roses.

He doesn't let me take my own chair, however. Instead, he lowers himself, then tugs me to fall into his lap. Cradling my back against his chest, he guides both my legs to fall over one of his broad thighs.

Holy shit.

The pressure of sitting down with the toy in my ass adds a fresh wave of fullness and pleasure straight down to my toes. This position settles it deeper, something I'm sure is in no way accidental. Not where this man is concerned.

"Ten minutes is up, Foxglove." His voice rumbles deep and desirous against my spine.

Oh, my god. He can't possibly intend to do whatever it is he has in mind right out here in the open. I was half expecting him to drag me off into a private room or a bathroom, at the very least. This is madness, and I don't know how I feel about messing around in front of a room full of people I despise.

"What are you doing?" I'm already breathless, and he hasn't even touched me. "We can't...not here."

"You're the heir to Noire House. You can do whatever you want." His hands roam over the silky material of my dress; the heat from his palms dragging across the thin fabric feels like it is scalding me.

From across the room, I hear a sickening thud as a bloodied fighter hits the canvas. He doesn't move. The room erupts in a feral chorus of cheers as his opponent hoists a gloved hand aloft and is pronounced the victor.

The tang of sweat and coppery wafts of fresh blood hit my nose.

"Lean forward."

My eyes fly up to stare at Thorne. Mouth hanging open a little at the sight waiting for me when I crane my neck to look at him. There's a sapphire pool of molten lust that traps me, forcing the breath to expel from my lungs in a rush.

Right now, I get the feeling this version of Thorne would

have absolutely no problem bending me over this table and fucking me in front of every single person present in this room.

"Don't you want to be a good girl for me?" He whispers into my neck.

I fold instantly.

God, I can't handle the way my heart is seemingly ready to lurch into his rough hands without question.

I'm almost certain it did the day he walked into my tattoo studio.

"Yes. I mean, I do," I reply, more than a little shakily.

"Then lean forward, Foxglove." Pure seductive power coats his voice.

Pushing my weight off his lap, I do as he says and lean my forearms on the table. My ass perches on the edge of the seat, nestled between his thighs. As I do so, the gemstones tug on the chain affixed to my nipples, and my eyes glaze over a little. In front of me, there's action and more noise, and I realize that my other two men are approaching the ring.

Raven is bare-chested, his tattooed torso glistens with sweat, and his sculpted abs descend in a v below the waistband of the fight shorts he's wearing. Wet hair hangs across his eyes as he bends and threads himself through the ropes bordering the ring.

He looks like a fallen angel.

Ky takes up a position in the corner closest to him, and I watch as they lower their heads together to talk. My wolf doesn't shake or bounce around like the guy who is waiting in the other corner. He's calm and focused.

Lethally so.

"He looks good, doesn't he." Thorne runs his hungry touch up the outside of my thighs, and as he goes, the material starts to bunch up around my waist. I suck in a ragged breath, eyes darting around the tables in front of us.

"What are you doing?"

"*Shh*, just be a good girl for me."

"Everyone will be able to see," I whine.

"Don't you think I would have already taken care of that... Don't you think I would take care of my girl?" Thorne's lips nibble at my ear.

God, I can barely contain the fluttering in my heart and my pussy hearing him like this.

"Do you trust me?"

"No." Yes. I'm unwilling to admit how much of a lie that might be.

Thorne grunts in amusement. I do my best to ignore how dangerous hearing him laugh might be for my health.

"You're a smart woman, Foxglove." The handsome devil himself is hot and sinful against my neck.

Oh, fuck. I think my soul might have just died from swooning too hard.

Swallowing heavily, my attention falls on our position overlooking the room. No one can glimpse what we're doing back here. I see it all clearly now. The tablecloth hangs right to the floor, and we're oriented so that all the guests in front of us are facing forward. To look in our direction, someone would have to get up and turn around, and even then, they'd only see me from the waist up.

Thorne is indulging in a very calculated game tonight.

Because now, I also see what Ky meant about putting on a good show for them. Where they both stand, elevated in the ring, they will be able to see my face.

They might not be able to see what Thorne does to my body, but they'll know every squirm and gasp and expression of pleasure. There's no hiding from their scrutiny.

"You like having him see you like this." It isn't really a question. Thorne already knows too many of my secrets. I only wish

I could say the same for the man currently edging me into slutty oblivion.

"You like watching him too." My voice is a throaty rasp. I know we're teetering on the edge of there being something more between Thorne and the other two men who have been in his life for a long time.

He fists my dress and shoves it over my hips. Exposing me fully to his inspection.

"Fucking hell." His heavy palms grab each of my bared ass cheeks and he clutches my soft flesh. Jostling the butt plug and making me scrunch the tablecloth beneath my fingers with a gasp.

"Perfection." The weight of his praise is almost too much. "You look incredible. Such a pretty and obedient girl for us, aren't you?"

"Thank you for my present, Daddy." I can barely get the words out.

Thorne grips one side tighter, his other hand slipping between me and where I'm perched with all my weight tipped forward. Roughly fondling my core he quickly discovers exactly how much of a mess I'm already in.

"Bare and dripping wet like a slut under that dress this whole time?"

I hum and nod my head. Shame flushes my chest and neck.

Movement drags my attention for a second, and I see the fighters shift toward the center of the canvas. An official stands between them, and that's when my wolf turns his head and looks me straight in the eyes. Thorne chooses that exact moment to strike, and pulls out from under me, reaching around to push his digits into my mouth.

"Show him how much you love tasting yourself on my fingers."

My pussy convulses, and I moan softly as the evidence of

my arousal bursts across my tastebuds. Thorne holds his fingers coated in my slickness in my mouth, pressing down on my tongue, and I'm caught by all three devils.

Raven's lips curl into a snarl.

My eyes flick over to Ky, and he's watching too.

Jesus.

And that's when the punches start flying.

I'M TRAPPED in Thorne's lap while watching Raven exchange blows with his opponent—a beefy man with a bald head and scarred jaw.

In the previous round, the fighters wore boxing gloves. This bout, however, is bare-knuckle rules and entirely brutal.

Each has landed sickening hits on the other. Ruby flecks of blood are everywhere I look, and the crowd screams with unrestrained thirst, longing to see more crimson spilled.

Ky might be yelling, but my two men in the ring are spending most of the time looking straight at me.

And Thorne is doing his best to make a complete mess of my body.

"He's going to get hurt," I moan as Thorne starts to fondle the jewel nestled between my ass cheeks. Shifting it so that it gently moves in and out.

"That's the idea."

"I don't understand..." What, or why this is happening is beyond me. I'm panting and squirming in Thorne's lap, and from the expressions both Ky and Raven wear, they can pinpoint every wave of pleasure passing over my face.

"Keep doing what I say."

"Thorne." I gasp, as he shifts my weight back into his lap, which in turn causes my nipples to be further tortured by the weight of the chain.

"You have to be very good and stay quiet for me."

My brain goes to ask why, but my body spasms as an unexpected vibration starts up inside my ass. Rippling waves of pleasure extend right through me from the butt plug. I bite down on my bottom lip to prevent the cry that threatens to escape.

I'm a live wire of throbbing need. Everything tingles and sparks beneath my skin, and as the building sensation rises from my toes, Thorne clicks off the vibrations leaving me nearly doubled over on the table, gasping for air.

"Fuck you." I stammer out. Thorne lets out a breathy laugh.

As I try to shift my position in his lap, I feel it. He's rock hard, and a tiny moan bursts out of me.

"My good girl. You're going to give me more." He clamps my hip to keep me in place, holding my body tight against his cock, and the vibrations start up again. They roll through my body with drawn-out, sparking intensity. He's getting off on the buzzing spreading through his lap, too. Thrusting upwards, slowly and seductively with languid rolls of his hips, it's enough to have my pulse roaring in my ears. Causing me to try and push back and arch in an effort to rub harder against him.

If he's going to edge me, then I want to drag him right alongside me to the gates of hell.

While I'm dry humping and grinding all over Thorne's lap, my Viking and my wolf's eyes remain glued to me, even though there's bare-knuckle fight-porn happening on the other side of the room.

At the point I'm certain I couldn't possibly take any more, Thorne shuts it off, and this time, he hauls me back against his chest. I sag into him, the cresting wave of my orgasm is right within reach, and I just want him to finger fuck me right here at this table.

Hell, I'm so drugged with pleasure, he could actually fuck my ass right here in a crowded room, and I'd say thank you.

"Please, Daddy," I say quietly as my heartbeat pulses in my swollen clit.

But he slips the remote in his pocket and softly strokes up and down my arms. Leaving me dangling right on the edge.

"You're doing so well for me."

"Don't stop." I'm certainly not above begging.

"Look at you, perfect and beautiful with your ass full and pussy throbbing."

He's such a gorgeous asshole.

I'm pretty sure I say something to that effect out loud. Thorne bites off a low chuckle.

"*Please.*"

"Such a sweet thing when you beg, Foxglove. But you're going to be a good girl for me, aren't you?" Seductive, gliding fingers keep moving up and down the length of my arms. I don't answer him, at least not out loud. Instead my mind is a swirling duality of sensation.

"Watch." He commands. Guiding my attention back in the direction of the fight going on. The backdrop to this man's devious game of edging me toward euphoria.

I want to tell him no. In fact, I'd rather straddle him and ride him and screw this stupid fight night and everyone in this room because they can all go jump off a cliff for all I care. But instead, I raise my eyes, and what I see is the moment a switch flips inside my wolf. It's as if, up until now, he's been humoring his opponent. As he looks over at me, limp and flushed against Thorne's chest, his upper lip forms a dangerous snarl.

One fist shoots out, connecting with the other man's jaw. The force sends the man's head snapping backward with a sickening crunch.

The guy crumples into a heap.

I have no idea if he's still alive.

Raven wins amid an eruption of noise and screaming adoration from the ocean of skull masks clamoring for a speck of his attention.

But his coal-black eyes are only on me.

CHAPTER 48

Ky

How the hell we made it back to the compound without pulling the car over and fucking on the side of the road, I have no idea.

Thorne wasn't taking any chances. Forcing me to drive and being a gorgeous, controlling asshole keeping Fox glued to his lap in the back seat.

But, no matter how much she begged, he refused to touch her. Just whispered filthy shit in her ear to keep her right on edge and looked at me in the rearview mirror the whole time.

Jesus, that man is on a different level when this kind of mood strikes.

My cock is leaking everywhere, and I'm coiled so tight by the time we get home I can't even think straight. Ven is already there, his bike parked up, and I can almost see the skidded tire marks.

He yanks open the door beside Thorne with a snarl and lifts Fox out. His face is cut to shit and bruised from the fight, and he really should be icing his fucking knuckles right now, but he'll be as wound up as I am.

The two of them put on a fucking show, alright.

Now we have to wait and see what that public performance might have done to bring more information to light about whoever is daring to threaten our girl.

"Your face..." Fox might be dangling on the precipice of coming after the way Thorne's been tormenting her all night, but she's looking at Ven with wide eyes. She cares, and fuck if that doesn't make me fall for this purple-haired beauty even more.

"Come on his tongue, and you'll make it all better, baby girl." I slide up behind them and throw Ven a grin. He's looked worse. The handsome asshole will live.

Fox clings to him, gazing up at the evidence of his victory. She raises a hand, but hovers over his skin, not wanting to touch him, but at the same time dying to do so. "I was so worried about you."

He makes a grunting noise, but keeps a tight hold of her hips.

"And you looked so fucking hot up there." Oh, the little minx. She's playing with fire now.

Ven growls and nips her lip between his teeth, tugging on it roughly. Fox simply dissolves.

I know the exact feeling.

"Get inside." Thorne slams the door shut and levels all of us with a look that says he's done playing around.

My stomach clenches.

I don't know how much longer I can keep pretending I don't want more with him.

Ven wraps Fox around his neck and waist, kissing her as they make their way into the house. Seeing him kiss is an unusual sight, and it's arousing as all hell. She's making all sorts of sweet little noises, moaning into his mouth, and Thorne's dark presence prowls behind me as we trail after them through the hallway.

"My room." He instructs Ven, and a fluttering riot of bats or some shit takes up residence in my gut. *This is happening.*

I've never been in Thorne's bed before. He's never been in mine. Holy fuck.

The four of us head through his doorway, with the huge glass panels covering one wall illuminating his perfectly made bed with a pale glow from the moon. It feels sensual and intimate, and the scent of him curls through my blood straight away.

"I get your ass tonight." Ven tosses her onto the bed with a bounce, and she's staring up at all of us with glazed eyes and puffy lips from biting them so hard.

"Am I your prize for winning?" Those thick eyelashes flutter, like she doesn't know exactly how precious she is.

Goddamn. This girl...

Ven falls on top of her, bracing his hands beside her head, and sliding a knee between her thighs. "More like a fucking punishment. Having to watch that slutty little show." He drags her bottom lip between his teeth again.

"I might like that better," Fox purrs against his mouth.

"We fucking our little plaything, or what?" I know that'll wind her up some more, and she makes a horny little noise. Ven's gonna be fucking toast the way she's panting and wriggling beneath him.

"Get her undressed. Leave the toy in." Thorne strips off as he issues his order, and I do the same.

Ven practically rips her dress off along with his pants and shirt. Fox gasps and flushes a little harder as she's laid out bare and dripping for us. The nipple chain worked perfectly while hidden away, turning her breasts a perfect swollen, deep shade of rose.

"That's the hottest fucking thing, sweetheart. I think I've found my new favorite game to play." Kneeling beside her to gently unclamp the loops, I ease them off her tortured nipples.

As soon as they're freed, I swoop in and cover one breast with my mouth. Softly drawing the swollen bud in with my tongue, and she nearly levitates off the bed.

"Oh, fuck. Oh, fuck." Her hands tangle in my hair, and she's trying to get away from me and hold onto me at the same time. "Just like that." Fox is writhing around so much Ven cups her pussy possessively and holds her down. Joining me on the opposite side, running his tongue to swirl around her other breast.

She starts babbling right away. *Please. Fuck. Oh, god. I need you. All of you. Please, fuck me.* Fox is a vision when she's begging, and with one hand, she starts tugging at Ven's hair trying to pull him closer.

He pops off her breast with a wet noise. "You need to sit on my face first."

Well, shit. This side of Ven is an unexpected surprise.

He moves up the bed, then flops on his back, and I have no idea what Thorne has been doing this whole time, but I'm really hoping it involves having his thick cock wrapped in one hand.

Fox scrambles up over Ven, with a perfect shade of pink dusting her cheeks. His tattooed hand taps her thigh and guides her to spin around so that she's facing us while straddling over him. For a moment, she hesitates, and he emits a growl from beneath her.

"When I tell you to sit, woman, you fucking sit."

Her blue eyes are lust-blown, and yet she looks at me and Thorne in question. As if we're going to tell her 'no' for some reason. Like hell we'd even consider putting a stop to this. She's going to ride Ven's face until she hopefully squirts everywhere, and then I'd quite happily pull her onto mine to do the same.

But I see her inner struggle and so I lean forward, kneeling between Ven's thighs to get close enough where I can lick at her kiss-bitten lips, thumbing one of her nipples as I do so. "If he dies, he dies, baby girl. I'm sure Ven would much prefer his final moment involved having his tongue shoved inside your pussy."

"Oh, my god." She shudders. "You're such a naughty fucking boy."

I nip her bottom lip. "Don't deny you love it. Now come all over his face. Soak him good."

The wash of pleasure looks stunning rolling over her as she lowers herself down. The sweet noise that escapes once his mouth sets to work is enough to have my balls tingling and my cock jerking in response.

When I drag my eyes off Fox, I can see that Ven is hard as stone. His fat cock bobs against his stomach, and there's a smear of pre-cum across his tattooed abs where he's leaking from the tip.

The bed dips on the other side of Ven's torso, and the magnetic presence of Thorne makes me lose my mind for a second.

He's fisting himself, and guides Fox to balance her weight against him.

"I've wanted those pouty fucking lips wrapped around my cock all night." She stares up at him with the sort of awestruck look I'm pretty sure is mirrored on my face. "You're such a good fucking girl for me."

"Mmhm, please, Daddy." She breathes, lips hanging open as Ven sucks and laps at her pussy.

Thorne guides her down to take him into her mouth, and I can taste him on my tongue as I watch on, transfixed. Fox is moaning and desperate, her saliva coating him as Ven keeps teasing and tempting her toward the edge.

"Jesus. Fuck." As she gets sloppier and sloppier, Thorne drags her off him and is breathing hard, watching her start to unravel. She's lost in the build-up to her climax, and that's when baby blue eyes flick to me.

"*Fffuck.* I'm so close." Her fingers dig into his abs as she whimpers.

God. I'm staring at his veined dick, and it's right fucking there. My throat works down a heavy swallow as I wrap my hand around my own length and start stroking. Right now, I don't care about the Anguis or anything outside these walls. They can go to hell. All I want is for us to have some little glimpse of pleasure and enjoy this moment.

If it takes blocking out whatever shit-storm is to come and hiding away in here for a little while, I'll gladly take that chance at grabbing hold of something good.

"Ky." Her throaty little rasp says my name, and I see that she's got her small fist wrapped around Thorne's cock, but she's so close to coming she's imploring me...begging me.

I lick my lips, and my gaze bounces up to check in with Thorne.

His eyes are hooded and dark, and all of a sudden, I'm more nervous than I think I've ever been in my life.

"Ky, please." I'm done for with that final plea. The way she's about two seconds from falling apart, while sitting on Ven's face, and is asking me to help suck Thorne's cock.

Taking him in hand right at the base, I lean forward and slide his crown through my parted lips. Above me, Thorne's breathing hitches, and beneath my touch his dick throbs, while I'm swept up in a weird storm of realization that I've wanted to do this for so much longer than I ever admitted to myself.

He tastes and feels unbelievable. Allowing him to glide in, heavy and commanding is a hit I'm going to forever be chasing. With Ven, we give and receive equally, but with Thorne, there's unspoken dominance in even the most subtle press of his hips.

I'm already fucking obsessed.

Relaxing my jaw, the musky scent of him and taste of his skin mixed with Fox's saliva makes my stomach clench. I close my lips around his velvety length for the first time, and the noise that comes out of him is nearly feral.

"*Oh, god.*" Fox whines.

"Get me nice and wet," Thorne rumbles. "Let me fuck that throat good and deep."

I make an entirely desperate noise as I invite him to pump his hips and press further to the back of my throat. He's so smooth and full in my mouth, and I can't believe this is finally happening.

"That's it. Let go." Above me, he's coaxing Fox through her orgasm, or maybe he's talking to me, fuck I don't even know. But I hear her come apart with a low moan. The warmth of her gaze is on me the whole time as I take Thorne deeper and deeper. My throat closes around his tip, and a shudder rolls through his muscles as he tries to hold back from choking me.

That's when I feel it. His strong hands sink into my hair just like they did that night in the backseat of the car, and his fingers flex against my scalp.

"Such a good fucking boy."

With each determined thrust, the wash of unspoken additional praise flows over me like syrup. I was already hooked on Thorne; now I think I'm gladly lost inside him.

I'm burning up beneath my skin when those strong hands tighten in my hair, dragging me off him. I swipe over my lips with my tongue, letting my eyes bounce between Ven and Fox for a moment as I try to catch my breath.

My heart is somewhere in my mouth.

Ven gives me a smug fucking expression, reclining against the pillows like some sort of tattooed beast surveying his kingdom. I'd look pretty fucking pleased with myself, too, if I just had our girl's thighs wrapped around my head and her cum all over my tongue.

Fox swoops in to grab my face in both palms and devours

my lips with horny little whimpers. I'm guessing she liked what she saw.

"You're so fucking beautiful." She croons at me, and my already thundering pulse climbs further up the peak. I'm at such a dizzying altitude I'm either going to pass out or need oxygen.

"Come here." Ven paws at her ass, shifting her around.

The gasp that comes out of Fox has her eyes rolling back as Ven sets to work on the toy nestled between her cheeks.

Well...Fuck me.

CHAPTER 49
Thorne

My dick is aching. I want to fuck my girl, and I want to fuck Ky, and I'll gladly fuck Ven, too, if I didn't think he'd break my arm for trying.

"Relax for me. You gotta breathe." Ven is working lube over her perfect ass while Ky helps shift her to the right position on her knees.

"*You* breathe." She's whining and worked up, and I don't blame her. I nearly burst down Ky's throat the moment he swallowed around my tip. Knowing she was watching us both and at the same time feeling his hot mouth close around me...this feels like a fever dream.

One that I don't want to wake up from.

I don't know how things have gotten here so quickly since we first brought this lilac-haired scrap of mayhem into our lives, but now I'm watching my friend about to fuck our girl's ass, while I maybe-most-definitely am about to fuck his boyfriend.

"Help her move." There's no disguising that Ven is nearly at his limit, baring his teeth at Ky.

Chuckling a little, he guides her to ease back. "Play nicely, baby." Ky and Ven exchange a look over the top of her head.

"But, I don't want *nice*." She grumbles.

I scrub my hand through my hair. This girl is going to be the death of us, I can tell.

"Jesus." Ven grunts and fists his cock, slowly working himself inside. "You keep pushing back on me like the desperate little slut you are."

All I know is she's flushed pink and eats up every filthy word from Ven like he's just called her his fairy princess.

"Ah, fffuck." He grits his teeth, and her body relaxes for him, and pretty soon, she's sinking against his chest and he's fully seated inside her.

"Holy shit." The sound of her porny little moan is what snaps me out of the trance I've been in. "You feel—So good."

Ven fights to keep his head. "Ky, get your dick over here. She's so fucking tight."

Foxglove Noire looks like perfection, with Ven filling her up, and her pussy spread wide and glistening with how soaked she is.

And then, there's Ky in front of me.

He's got his cock in one hand, with that mouthwatering fucking piercing winking in the moonlight, and our eyes lock. I reach over and grab the back of his neck, and we're breathing the same air. Both our chests rise and fall to match the frantic pace of our heartbeats.

"You want this?" I search his eyes.

Ky nods slowly. "I do."

My nostrils flare and I turn to check in with Ven. His gaze is dark and intense, and he's looking turned the fuck on. I know they share. But what I don't know is whether this is going to be a step too far for whatever their bond is.

"You gonna fuck our good boy, or what?" Ven's eyes challenge me in a way that tells me he knew this thing between us was inevitable. Like he's already seen this all play out, and I'm the idiot finally catching up with the game plan.

He tosses me the bottle of lube.

Our girl is biting her lip and making small noises of pleasure as Ven subtly shifts his hips below her.

"Looks like that pretty little cunt needs to be filled." I glance down at Ky's cock, and see it pulse at the thought of being buried inside her.

"Christ." He chokes.

"Got something you wanna say?" I tug on his hair and watch his eyes darken. "Then, move, and you might just earn my cock."

He's looking at me with an expression that says he doesn't know whether to hit me or kiss me, and I quickly decide I want to see him like this...a lot.

But he does as I say and positions himself in amongst the tangle of legs on the bed. The perfect fucking girl beneath him takes his cock like a dream. She's so wet and turned on that the moment he notches his pierced tip at her entrance, a flurry of frenzied noises burst out of her. Ky continues his favorite pastime of teasing her by running the piece of metal up and down and over her clit a few times first, casually ignoring her pleas.

Ven grunts and curses at him. "Hurry the fuck up. She's squeezing me so goddamn hard every time you do that."

"I love making you feel good, baby," Ky murmurs, and I'm guessing his words are for both of them, but obliges and sinks inside her. Leaving the three of them breathless amid little groans and moans of pleasure.

"We need you, Daddy." My girl's voice is like sin and temptation, because she's so damn smart, she knows. She knows I need that final push to cross this line with Ky. The person who I helped raise and who, for all intents and purposes, has been a brother to me for years.

But nothing about this feels wrong or confusing. It's just Ky, and I guess it's always been him.

"Thorne..." There's a hint of a whine in his voice as he says my name and it brings something roaring to life inside me.

"What? You think you get to demand something all of a sudden, hmm?"

Ky drops his head forward with a deep groan. "Fuck, you're gonna come in hot with that Daddy dom shit aren't you?"

"Look at the way your ass is already clenching for me." I run a knuckle along the seam between his cheeks, relishing every tiny flex in his taut muscles. Ky has always been fucking hot, but right now, he looks like *mine,* and that makes every tiny aspect of this moment somehow even more incandescent.

"Jesus. You're killing me here." He licks at Fox's neck and groans. They're all moving together each time he sinks deeper, waiting for me to join them.

"Let me hear you say it, *naughty boy.* Let me hear just how bad you want my cock." My voice comes out husky, throaty. This is turning me on as much as him, and the erotic noises coming out of Fox and Ven light up my body.

"Fuck...mmmfuck..." He slides out nearly to the tip, pressing back against my hand. "I want you. I want your cock."

"That's it. Dirty fucking boy. Let me hear all those sexy noises you make while I play with this tight little hole."

Ven grunts something that sounds an awful lot like *fuck you Thorne.* Fox whines, completely out of her head with pleasure and lust.

Lowering my mouth, there's bolts of lightning running through my veins. I spread him wide and swirl my tongue over the bundle of nerves, devouring every groan and low sound he's making.

He gasps as I press my tongue harder against him. "*Unnggghhhh.* Oh, shit. Thorne."

My senses are filled with his muskiness and the thick scent

of sex in the room. I'm working him relentlessly, drawing out and savoring each delicious shudder beneath me, with my dick rock hard in anticipation of feeling him wrapped around me for the first time.

"Please. *Please.*"

The sound of Ky begging for my cock is what finally breaks me. I pull back and drizzle a generous amount of lube over his firm ass and my length. Making quick work of pressing myself against him and the moment my tip slips inside, goddamn, I could almost spill right then and there.

"Christ. Fuck. Hold still for me." Words like *baby* are already on my tongue, and I nearly draw blood biting down.

"Oh, god, you feel so fucking good." Ky's opening for me and letting me slowly work my way deeper, and as I do so, we're all starting to move as my weight shifts.

It was so different when we were last all together like this on the island. That time felt like I could sit back and allow my voyeur out to play. But now, here, this is sucking me under, and I'm right there falling apart with all of them as our bodies move in time with one another.

"You good?" I grit my teeth. Not really sure who I'm talking to, but feeling the need to check in before I give everything over to the unrelenting impulse to start pounding into Ky.

"I swear, if you don't start fucking his ass properly..." Ven's face is a mask of pleasure laced with pain, and sweat lines his brow.

Our girl is off in subspace somewhere, and as I sink forward the last bit and fully seat myself inside Ky, I quickly grab her chin. Demanding her attention to come back to earth for a moment.

"Talk to me, Foxglove."

She shudders as I say her name. Her pretty blue eyes are hazy with pleasure and her mouth goes slack. I can't resist dragging her bottom lip down with my thumb.

"Yes."

"Proper words."

"Yes, Daddy. *Oh, god.*"

Well, fuck.

I slide back out nearly to the tip, and then glide forward. The force shifts all of us, and Ky's ass clenches around me, nearly making me black out. Shit, this isn't like anything I've ever experienced before, and I do it again.

All of us are barely hanging on.

"I'm so close." My girl—our girl is trembling.

"That's it. Come for me, baby girl." Ky is fucking her every time I thrust into him, and I know exactly what it's like to feel his pierced dick rubbing inside her walls. Ven might actually be dying from the way his teeth are clamped together, his eyes screwed shut.

We're all joined in the most carnal and primal of ways. Limbs and beating hearts and unrestrained cries of pleasure. The pressure builds and builds, and our perfect little thing is the one who finally breaks when Ven snakes his hand down to tease her clit, guiding her to shatter on the most beautiful trembling symphony of sweet noises.

"Oh-OH. I'm coming. I'm coming." Soft feminine moans fill my ears, and it's absolute perfection watching our girl come for us like a supernova.

Ven grunts and bites down on her neck. "*Fffffuck.* Just like that."

He jerks below all of us, and that's when Ky loses control. My cock hits his prostate and he makes a strangled noise.

"God. *Thorne.*" I pound into him again and again as the others are still rolling on waves of their orgasms, and he tenses beneath me.

"Come for me. Come for me like a good boy." I sink my fingers tight into his hips and soak up every moan when he does as I say.

"*Unggggh*. Yes. Yes." He's a mess as his cum floods our girl's pussy. She's sucking on his pulse point, and her fingernails dig into his shoulders, and the tension low in my stomach winds tighter.

Pulling out, I drag Ky back with me and flip him over. Pushing his knees up toward his chest, I sink back inside him. His dick is wet and slaps against our abs, leaving a sticky trail of their cum mixed together smeared all over us. My cock thickens, tingling intensifies low in my spine. He's staring straight into my soul with those gorgeous green eyes of his as my balls tighten and my hips falter.

I fucking need every part of him. The sensation of finally having this moment takes over and time stands still as I crash my mouth down on his. My tongue slips past the seam of his lips, and he melts into me, tasting like the most heady mix of all of us. Perfection and desire meld together on his plush lips as his beard rasps against my skin with a series of dizzying sparks. Grabbing his hands, I push them together over his head and momentarily slow the roll of my hips. Ky's face is glazed with delirious bliss and he looks so goddamn gorgeous like this, I could live right here forever.

"I just want to savor you. Learn every inch of you." Speaking against his lips, I drive into him with long, measured strokes. "But I've got no control whatsoever. You feel too fucking good."

Ky's fingers curl between mine. His muscles ripple and he freely gives me every inch of his attention. Even though the four of us are all here in this bed, in this room, in this pleasure, in this moment, there's enough space for the two of us to fit together on the deepest of levels.

To finally speak to one another's souls in the way we've always wanted to.

"Please." The forest green of his eyes swirls darker with lust. "Take it slow next time. Right now, I want you to fuck me the way I've always dreamt you would."

He lifts up to meet me, shoving his tongue into my mouth, and we're suddenly kissing like animals. Nipping and sucking and tugging on each other's lips as my hips begin to work and I pound into him. Over and over. Heat and sparks wrap tightly around our bodies, contentment flows from Ven and Fox as they watch us grinding and rocking together.

With every stroke of his tongue against mine, the walls I've had so carefully constructed around my heart when it comes to this man crumble like clay. Christ. Maybe I'll just explode from the sheer thrill of this moment, of this *thing* between us finally being laid bare.

I've always loved him. Rationally, I know that. Now I know exactly how deep that well of protection and emotion goes.

"Fill me up, Thorne. I want your cum inside me," Ky groans out a whisper against my mouth, and I'm done for. His hole squeezes the life out of my cock, tumbling me over into oblivion.

"Fuck. Fuck. Ky." I barely get the words out as my dick throbs and my release bursts out of me without warning. Spots flicker around in my vision, and my hips pump into him for what feels like forever. Filling his ass with my release, our chests damp with sweat, our fingers locked together above his head on the mattress.

I'm panting and can't even think. My balls are empty, and my brain is nothing more than a ragged mess of blissful emotions I don't have names for. All I can do is drop my forehead against his shoulder and lie there breathing heavily.

We all lie there. Soft hands stroke over me amid Fox's calming scent, mixed with the others. It's like time vacates and agrees to call a truce—standing still for all of us to soak in the waters of this precious moment we've been granted.

Ven shifts around, pressing a kiss to Ky's mouth before lifting our girl in his capable arms—taking her to get cleaned up. Leaving the two of us lying in my bed, surrounded by the thunder of our pulses still racing each other.

I don't know how to do this next part.

But I don't have to figure it out, because his fingers gingerly brush over my nape, then push my hair back off my forehead.

My eyes flutter closed.

God, I love having his hands on me.

And because it's Ky, and he makes it feel so easy, he lets out a small, hoarse-sounding laugh.

"I think we should go join them in there. Let's get cleaned up before Ven tries to start round three."

I pull back a little and silently hold his gaze.

His lips tip up into that cheeky smirk I want to kiss off his perfect face. But then his expression changes, and he looks a little sheepish. "Although...I'm pretty sure you just fucked all our brains out, so maybe our girl is safe for now."

My lips roll together and I gently ease out of him.

"You ok?" He's looking at me, and I want to dive into him again.

I nod and help him sit. We're definitely not just brothers anymore.

"That was..."

He smiles and takes my arm. "Yeah. That *was*..."

And we don't need to say anymore. We've known each other for so long; it's a whole language we don't need to exchange in order to know each other's thoughts.

"Come on."

Ky tugs me after him, and I follow.

Gladly.

CHAPTER 50
Fox

An unfamiliar noise startles me.

I've been curled up in one of the loungers beside the pool, sketching designs for the past few hours, and the alert on my phone that disrupts the quiet daydream I've been in sounds different from usual.

Technically, all my men are saved as contacts in my phone, and I do have Poe's number, but we haven't talked since the night when she sent me those cryptic messages about Thorne and my father. Aside from that, there's only one person I get texts from, and that is Ky.

A fluttering sensation occupies my chest.

Is it Thorne?

Or my wolf?

I've never felt confident enough to dare send a message to either of them, and they haven't bothered with contacting me unless it's face-to-face. Or, is that until now...

My eyes nearly pop out of my head. There's a message from Em on my screen, and her contact has been saved in my phone without me realizing.

It's happened, hasn't it?

I hurriedly tap my reply. There's no way I'm going to miss an opportunity to actually text my bestie. Whoever was pretending to be me has obviously felt like I can finally be trusted with being in contact. Mentally, I make a note that I really need to grill my men about this entire situation.

Acting nonchalant, like it has been me texting her this whole time...because, you know, ruses and lies and death threats and all.

What has?

I can see your eyelashes batting from here.

They are not.

You're blushing

Am not.

No idea what you're talking about.

She's smitten. Done.

Been hijacked by three men with presumably enormous dicks.

OMG.

Emerald.

What? Tell me I'm not wrong

A flashback moment swoops in, replaying the early, darkened hours of this morning. Waking up soaked and horny and feeling one of my men sliding into me from behind. Not knowing which one of them was pressing into my wet heat, and not caring either, because yes, I am a complete lost cause. Surrounded by Ky's wicked words against my ear as he stirred my sleeping body into a frenzy, pumping in and out of me with wickedly slow strokes.

"I know exactly how you like it, little Fox."

Hastily swallowing a gulp, my reply is as flimsy as my resolve around my men.

You're unbelievable

Not denying it.

Ding ding ding. Results are in.

I bet you don't even have to touch that cornucopia of toys of yours any more.

I will disown your pretty little ass.

You love me.

I do. I miss you so much.

What's new… Tell me everything.

Managed to get rid of your protection detail yet?

You can stop worrying about me. I'm a big girl.

Like I said… it wasn't what it looked like.

It looked like a straight-up kidnapping.

More like…professional misunderstanding?

You're gonna have to walk me through the details.

Because right now all I can think of is you in a ghastly tracksuit and with a fucking HOOD ON YOUR HEAD.

That tracksuit was hideous, wasn't it? Burned that motherfucker immediately.

Be real with me, Em.

Are you sure you're safe?

I see dots dance on the screen, then they disappear. Eventually, they stop altogether, and a sigh escapes me. Clearly today is not the day for getting a straight answer out of my friend.

Honestly, part of the reason I've avoided bringing the topic of Em up around any of my men is there's a tiny little part of me that still worries they might somehow use her against me.

Even though I've fallen in much too deep too fast with them for my own good, I'm still concerned, even if *they* don't pose a threat to her life anymore, would there be others within the Anguis who might choose to harm her if they discovered our connection?

Especially if there are unknown threats being made against me, might they go after someone important in my life?

Maybe I do need to woman-up and ask what the deal is with the security they've arranged for her. I don't doubt that Thorne will have put people he trusts in those roles, but after whatever was going on with the whole *hooded, cuffed, and gagged* routine, I'm still not sure what to think.

Even if Em seemed to be completely fine with it all.

Which still baffles me.

Just as I've given up on any hope of a reply, picking up my sketchbook and resuming sketching, my phone buzzes.

Anticipating some acerbic reply from Em's wicked tongue, I quickly close my notebook and pick up my phone. Except the notification on screen shows an unknown number, and when I open up the message, I can only stare open-mouthed at the words.

Something hot and sick curdles in my stomach.

My eyes can't make sense of what I'm reading.

UNKNOWN NUMBER

Your time under the protection of Thorne Calliano is up.

Will he be prepared to do the same for you, as he did for your mother, Giana?

As I read and re-read the two lines of text over and over, the phone in my hand buzzes again, and this time, I nearly drop it from my fingers.

What appears next isn't more words. It's an image. Grainy and in black and white, but the faces are clear.

The man in the photo is unmistakably Thorne—similar to the younger version of him I remember seeing all those years ago.

He has his hand pressed into the lower back of an elegant woman with blonde hair. One who I recognize immediately, even though I haven't seen her face in years.

My mother.

The trembling in my hands grows with each passing second I look at the image. I'm haunted by the despair at seeing the ghost of my own flesh and blood who was taken from me too soon, and the way my focus can't escape where his hand is on her body.

How close they're standing together.

Their apparent ease with one another.

The two of them are dressed in evening wear; this could have been taken at any one of the hundreds of events held at Noire House over the years. How many nights did they spend together like this?

Every inch of my skin shivers with goosebumps, and I let the phone fall from my grasp onto the padding of the seat as if it scalded me. There's a thudding rush of blood drowning my ears as I try to grasp at explanations for the image taunting me from the screen of my phone.

Who else has my number?

And why would they send me this?

Even worse, is the guilt and disgust I'm currently feeling. I don't know if it's more with myself or the people I'm seeing in this tiny image. He's never once mentioned knowing my mother.

Oh, my god. My hand flies up to my mouth as that curdling feeling intensifies.

I've been trapped in his sick maze, right from the beginning.

I'm on my feet with the phone clutched tight in one hand while I fly through the glassed-in corridors of the compound. Everything shrinks into a dark tunnel around my vision. I'm desperate for answers, and yet I don't want to hear them.

But there's one man who has lied to me, repeatedly.

Right now, I need to look into his ice-blue eyes and demand to hear every detail. To extract from his blackened heart what he knows about my family. The unknown secrets he's been hiding from me are pumping poison through my veins with each step.

I don't even stop as I reach his study, flinging open the door and bursting inside.

Thorne is seated at his computer, tapping something on his cell phone. I don't have a plan, but I spot his gun and holster laid out on the end of his desk.

Heat and rage pricks behind my eyes as I dive for it, wrestle the weapon free, then remove the safety. Fuck him. Fuck this place. Fuck Noire House and the endless secrets and lies and misery that has been my life.

This asshole threatened my mother's memory, and lied to me about knowing her.

My hands are unsteady as I blink back the tidal wave of emotion threatening to crush me. Meanwhile, I'm standing in bare feet and one of Ky's giant tees, and the man in front of me is the picture of calm.

He swivels to look at me, taking in my wild appearance, running his gaze the length of my figure before settling on the trembling gun I have aimed at his heart.

In true Thorne style, he slides his chair closer, readjusting the barrel of the gun to point upwards, pressing below his chin. "This is the angle you want. It'll do the most damage. From here, you'll easily blow right through the back of my skull."

My fingers flex around the trigger.

"Explain this." With my free hand I toss him my unlocked phone, still open on the unknown messages and photo.

I quickly wrap both hands around the gun, but it still shakes. Blood rushes through my body, sending chills right down my arms and legs, and I can feel my heart being torn in two before he even speaks.

He runs a thumb across his jaw, barely glancing at the phone, instead he keeps his gaze on mine. "Who sent these messages to you?"

"How the fuck am I supposed to know?" My lungs burn. "You control my phone. My life. Everything."

"That photo was taken a long time ago."

My nostrils flare with the intensity of my breathing.

"Don't you dare lie to me." I'm equally furious and terrified.

The man before me is like a lake, calm and smooth at the surface, and all I want to do is hurl my weight at the water to disturb that serene exterior.

"You don't want to know the real truth, Foxglove. It's better this way."

"That's all you ever say, and it's *bullshit*. You're a fucking coward." I shove the metal harder against his stubbled jaw.

Thorne's fingers dig tight into the fleshy part of my hips, holding me firmly in place as I stand between his knees.

"Ask anything of me, except this." There's a warning in his voice, and I'm intent on ignoring it. If he thinks he can own me, control me, manipulate me... and now keep secrets about my own family from me? He's going to live to regret the day he even tried.

"You knew my mother," I scream the words at him.

There's a long pause as my hysteria hangs in the air between us.

"I did," He says the words carefully.

Revulsion boils in my gut. I don't want to hear it, but at the same time, can't breathe without knowing this ugly, awful truth.

The grainy image and where his hand is caressing that intimate spot on her lower back is seared in my mind.

"What was she to you?" I don't know if I'll survive this. Is this why he was so reluctant to get close to me? Because my mother and him were...

As if he sees the dots connecting in my brain, he flexes his fingers. Applying more pressure to ground me back into this room and his presence as he shakes his head ever so slowly. "Not like that." Thorne's voice is low and even.

"Then tell me." My eyes brim with tears, and my hands holding the gun tight against his skin shake uncontrollably. But I'm stuck here until I reach the inevitable, awful conclusion.

"Be grateful you didn't know your parents, Foxglove."

"Don't patronize me."

Thorne's scent swirls around me and it digs a hole in my

chest. I want him so badly, and yet I'm trembling with what this is all going to mean.

"Be thankful they didn't spend time with you...that they left you to nannies and tutors and hidden away in boarding schools."

"I deserve a straight answer."

"And what if you deserve better than knowing their sordid truths?"

"You don't get to make that choice for me." I can barely feel my fingers.

He studies me. Scalds me with the kind of expression that makes me want to latch onto him and inhale deeply from the base of his neck. But I stand firm.

There's a moment when his jaw clenches tight, the fine lines around his eyes crease, and I know he's going to relent, no matter how awful and eviscerating to my sanity this might be.

"Your father would find the children." I'm trapped in his cool, blue gaze. "We were held in the far wing at the other end of the mansion. Just one small insignificant corner in amongst the hundreds of rooms."

Oh, god. I'm going to throw up. Breathing through my nose, I try to keep the dark spots on the edge of my vision at bay.

"She would come and inspect the boy's room at night. The place where we all slept together for the short time any of us were required to be held at Noire House." He's stroking one thumb over my hip, and all the blood drains from my face as he carries on. "Hawke and I had only been there a short while, and were expected to be trucked off somewhere else with the others the following day, but she stopped by our bed that night."

My mouth is open in a silent plea for him to stop. Piercing shards wrack my body as the heart inside my chest shatters for both him and his brother.

"Your mother liked us a little too much."

I let out a strangled noise.

"I'll spare you the details, but she kept us. That's how we ended up in this world. How we came to rise through the ranks." He senses me slumping, and gently wraps one hand around the barrel of the gun. But instead of shifting it away, he moves it down to his chest while my fingers go fully numb.

The weapon points at the spot where I know his tattoo lies—the very ink I've embedded in his skin. Where Thorne Calliano carries my markings and artwork and the tremor building along my nerves feels all too much to bear.

"She liked them young. We grew too old for her tastes, eventually. But you could say that it became my destiny to prevent other children from suffering the same fate."

"You're lying." Tears track a silent path down my face.

"In this case, I would never lie to you. Not about this."

Thorne studies me with a solemnity that I can't stand.

"Then why were you with her?" I'm suffocating beneath the crippling weight of what this man is telling me—and all that he's sparing me from hearing.

"In that photo?" He picks up the phone, glancing at it for barely a second, before sitting it on top of some papers on his desk. "I don't know. Maybe it's an angle chosen to make it look like there was something more between us. Back then, I would often be requested to provide VIP security, and it's likely your mother happened to be there."

"But—" My tears flow thick and fast.

"I never wanted you to find out this way." He swipes at the wetness with a thumb.

That's when I crumble. My bottom lip quivers, and I shove the metal barrel harder against his chest.

"You want to shoot me, baby? Go ahead. I won't stop you. I deserve a much more brutal death for all my sins, but I'd gladly give my heart over to you to end it all if that's what you want." With one hand, he presses down on the place where my tattoo lies beneath his shirt, and my fingers itch to tangle with his and rub that part of him. To caress those inked lines against smooth skin that I've stared at so many nights recently.

I want to bury my face in his neck, but I'm rooted to the spot, holding him at gunpoint while the world crashes around my ears. Sobs wrack my body as emotion pours out of me like a cataclysm. All the while, Thorne holds my stare and lets it consume me.

She was a monster, just like *him*.

The whole time, I thought that woman was my mother, when really she was a vile creature who preyed on children.

No wonder Thorne wanted me punished for what both of my parents did to him.

A sickening thought strikes me as swift and blindingly as lightning, and I rear back, my puffy red eyes blink at him several times, and the gun goes slack beneath my fingers.

"*Ky*?" I can hardly bring myself to say his name.

Thorne's warm hand reaches up to push away the fine hairs clinging to my damp cheeks. I don't know how he can even bear to touch me. Why doesn't this man want to take me to his warehouse of nightmares and make me suffer?

He shakes his head. "Hawke and I couldn't do much; we had to always be so careful not to reveal ourselves. But we were lucky enough to rescue Ky before anyone could touch him."

There's so much pain behind his eyes, it wrenches my heart into a thousand pieces.

"I only wish there were more we could have saved."

I can't see through the tears spilling out of me.

I'm going to be sick.

CHAPTER 51
FOX

I run.

It's cowardly, and pathetic, and I give into the impulse without a second thought.

Thorne was abused by my mother, and I want to claw my own eyeballs out. How can he not despise me for an eternity after everything he's been through? Doesn't the thought of me touching his skin—of me fucking him—make him want to be violently ill?

If I had dared to believe in a glimmer of hope that our future locked in this vengeful entanglement might evolve into something else, a version of a future where he perhaps one day cared for me...now I know for certain that will never be possible.

I'm going to forever be tortured by knowing that I am in love with Thorne Calliano, and he can't love me back.

There's too much agony that I represent.

I'm a living, breathing, flesh and blood memento of the predators who abused him and his brother. Seeing as they're dead, all that is left as a constant reminder of what the Callianos have endured, is me.

Hot tears blur my vision. I don't know where I'm going. My

bare feet carry me as far away from Thorne's office as fast as possible. Maybe I won't stop until I reach the ravine deep in this forest, and I'll hurl myself down there just to cure the pain ripping my men apart once and for all.

I'm blinded by the rage and shame and disgust crawling beneath my skin when I collide with an immovable force.

The scents of woodsmoke and the forest weave around me.

My wolf stares down at me, bracing my shoulders with firm hands.

His eyes narrow as he takes in my tear-stained appearance and shivering limbs.

"I can't be here." Please. Don't force me to stay. I need to be able to breathe, and *oh, so utterly selfishly* I want to be able to forget, and I can't do any of that with the walls currently closing in on me.

The living nightmare of my bloodline.

Raven glances in the direction I've just come from, but I can't bear to look back to see if Thorne has followed me. The expression on the face of the man before me doesn't change, he gives nothing away, simply turns and drags me along behind him.

His grip is rough and biting, circling my wrist tight.

We're out the front door and moving toward his bike before I know what is happening. The biting air nips at my bare legs, and the chill of the ground amplifies the numbness already filling every part of me.

But I don't care about my state of undress, or whether I'm going to freeze to death out here surrounded by banks of fog and the oppressively tall pine trees looming like silent giants overhead.

All I can think of is how useless and insignificant I am. My life is the byproduct of foul perversions, and knowing the truth of the lineage I was born into leaves my throat hot and prickly as I struggle to keep down the rising bile.

Tattooed hands shove a helmet onto me, adding to the sensory overload when I inhale an overdose of his masculine, woodsy scent. The forest in my line of vision sways, and through the visor, there's a glimpse of Raven swinging his leg over the seat as his dirt bike roars to life. I've never been on a motorbike before, but I scramble on behind him. Cold leather bites the backs of my thighs, and for a brief moment, I worry that my bare toes are going to get lacerated by the gleaming metal of the wheels.

Raven leans down and steadies my feet on the footholds before grabbing my arms and wrapping them tight around him. Does my presence feel cloying and foul? I'm assaulted by fears that he can't stand the thought of my touch either.

Not bothering with a helmet for himself, he simply revs the engine and guns the accelerator. We shoot off at a frightening speed. A terrifying slingshot into orbit. The forest rushes toward us, and I slam my eyes shut. Icy wind slices through to the marrow of my bones, and if we crash, I'll be mincemeat on the ground with only a flimsy cotton tee and my underwear to protect my fall.

Maybe that's what he wants.

He's made no effort to disguise the fact he is happy to see me bleed.

We don't follow the road down the peninsula; the bike tips to one side, and my eyes pop open as I shriek out loud. I'm certain the whole machine is going to slide out from under us, but my wolf is in complete control. We turn and head upward into the forest. It's a barely formed track, and the off-road bike makes easy work of the rough terrain.

We climb and weave our way deeper and deeper into the pines. It feels like forever; at times, we have to slow to barely a crawl as Raven guides us through impossibly difficult obstacles.

But then it's like we emerge into a different world.

The treeline stops abruptly, and we're on the top of a cliff, overlooking a wild, frothing, gunmetal sea. Wave after powerful wave seems intent on punishing the shoreline below.

I'm frozen. Every part of me numb and whipped raw by the wind. My limbs have stiffened in place, locked around his torso, still clinging to him perched on the back of his bike in an effort not to fall.

And I don't care.

Everything hurts, and I deserve to hurt.

Raven kicks down the stand and climbs off, flicking my hands away from his shirt. It takes effort to unclench my stinging fingers when I try to fumble with the helmet. I can't do it myself. As my hands drop back down to my sides, I notice he's only in a t-shirt and ripped black jeans.

If he feels the cold, he doesn't show it.

He digs his fingers through his hair while looking down at me. There's an expression on his face that is impossible to read, but his energy bristles with chaos.

It matches the frequency of the mayhem boiling inside me.

I want more than anything for him to give me the pain I'm craving right now. For him to sink his claws and teeth in and tear me to shreds—it's all I deserve.

The helmet I couldn't remove on my own is pulled off and I have to blink a couple of times to readjust to the rush of light and sound. Everything feels like the volume has been turned up. It's pure adrenaline. The ferocity of the ocean beats a relentless hollow thud at the base of the cliffs, so much so I'm certain the ground should be shaking. Howling wind bowls along the coastline, tossing the sea into a frenzy of white caps and tumbles the rolling mist through the treetops behind us.

"What do you need?" My wolf grabs my chin so tight it makes me wince. He looms over me while I still sit here straddling his bike. *Quaking.*

Raven understands.

He gets that right now I don't need to talk. I'm seeking an escape from this thing eating me alive.

This is a man who is an expert in taming his own monsters.

"I don't know." My lips feel blue.

"Oh, I think you do." He sneers at me.

Shame curls in my belly.

"I just—I don't want to think," I mumble as he pinches my chin with a punishing hold.

"That's because you're just a horny little slut who wants to be filled with cock."

My eyes drop to the side.

"Isn't that right? You're nothing but a dirty whore who will open her legs for anyone."

I nod. Still looking at the ground. *Wreck me, shatter me, destroy me.*

"Nothing more than a hole to fuck, who doesn't even deserve to get off."

Knots ball up in my stomach at the cruelness in his voice.

"Walking around begging for it all day from anyone with a dick who will bother to look at you. It's about time someone taught you a lesson."

Rough fingers spear into my hair, heaving me off the bike so that I'm standing. Then he shoves me forward to fold over the widest part of the seat. It forces my body into an awkward position, where my hips are so high that my toes barely brush the dirt and pine needles on the ground. My hands fly out to steady myself, and all I can feel is the heat of metal and sharp edges of the foot pedal.

"Please." I choke out. Not really sure what I'm asking him for because my body is a mess of emotions, and I want him to take control of everything for me.

Right now, I'm crawling my way to the safety of submission.

I hear the clank of his belt buckle, followed by the glide of leather. My core clenches as it becomes clear he's not unzipping his fly, but instead snaps the belt between both hands. He then runs the folded leather up the inside of one of my thighs until he reaches the hem of my t-shirt, lifting it.

This feels like the night in the kitchen all over again.

Me, bent over and at his mercy, once again wearing nothing but a baggy t-shirt and tiny panties.

Maybe I really am every inch the slut he likes to tell me I am.

I squeeze my eyes shut as he flips the edge of the shirt high above my ass, then strokes the belt back down the other thigh. As if he's mapping out the exact shape of his canvas to paint with reddened strokes.

Scents of salt spray mixed with high-octane fuel clog my nose as blood starts to pump harder in my ears. I'm suspended, waiting for that first strike to land on my exposed flesh, but instead, the cold metal of Raven's rings appears. As his fingers close around the waistband of my underwear, I flinch. He's so rough as they're tugged down my legs; the material burns my frozen skin, yanking them off me completely. That act leaves my ass and pussy completely bared to him and the elements. But that's the least of my concerns when I hear his footsteps crunch across the pine needles, crossing to the other side of the bike that I'm bent over.

I want to keep my eyes screwed shut; I really do. However, there's no knowing what is about to come, and as Raven draws close, I force myself to witness whatever my punishment is going to be. Crouched in front of me, the ripped fronts of his jeans and heavy boots fill my line of sight. As does the balled-up silk of my panties clenched in his tattooed fist. The black fabric is encased in the matching black of the ink covering his knuckles, and the image makes my clit throb. In his other hand, folded on itself and resting across one knee, is his belt.

He strikes as my mouth drops open. Stuffing my panties between my lips with a brutal shove. On reflex, a muffled protest tries to get past the intrusion, though I know it's to no avail.

Using the looped end of the belt, he tilts my chin to meet his blazing, dark eyes. "No one can hear you scream out here."

I whimper against the silk and scent of myself filling my mouth.

Then he's gone. Moving back around to stand behind me with ominous steps.

"Wider, slut." He kicks my ankles apart with one boot.

Anxiety and anticipation collide inside my chest.

The first smack comes straight away. Searing my ass cheek and I scream against my gag.

"One."

Oh, god. The welt feels like it pops up immediately. It stings and burns and he's going to count this out with a voice so low and dangerous it feels like I might be ripped in two. My heart is in the back of my throat, but this is exactly what I need because my mind has something else to cling onto like a liferaft in a storm.

Another crack across the same spot brings fresh tears to my eyes.

"Two."

He soothes the skin, gliding the flat of the leather in a circle.

Then follows it up with two quick smacks of my ass on the other side.

I'm clenching and writhing, while sobbing into the material stuffed in my mouth.

"That's four. I think a dirty girl like you deserves ten."

My head nods while my eyes scrunch closed. The pain is soaring through every part of me, and yet it gradually dissolves into a golden sensation. Humming a seductive tune below my skin.

And with every strike, my pussy grows slicker. I'm winding closer to a peak lingering beyond arm's reach.

The next four spanks are alternated on either side of my ass, and I can feel the wetness dripping between my thighs by the time we reach number eight.

Raven's voice is thick with desire as he grunts out the tally.

The final two he delivers as a stripe to each of the backs of my thighs. I'm hurtling toward oblivion as pleasure and pain intermingle in white-hot jolts thundering through me. My panties are soaked with drool, and my freezing nipples feel almost raw from rubbing against the t-shirt and seat beneath me.

I hear the belt drop to the ground with a metallic thud. The next moment, thick fingers drag through my swollen pussy. Fondling me harshly and discovering exactly how soaked and needy I am.

Muffled moans burst out of me at the unexpected contact. Although apparently every part of me is greedy for more and more of his coarseness. My clit pulses and I'm aching for him to fuck me into next week.

"Look at this cunt of yours. Dripping wet and begging to be filled even after having your ass striped red."

All my blood has rushed to my head now...am I going to pass out? The collision of sensations is so overwhelming, and my desire rages through my veins like a wildfire. Holy fuck, would he leave me hanging here like this without getting to come just as he threatened earlier?

Oh, god. He would. This man definitely would.

I start to plead nonsense into the sodden silk filling my mouth.

The world spins as I'm hauled up off the bike, and through my damp lashes, I see Raven. His pupils have bled fully black, and there's a snarl on his lips as he hitches my body against him.

We're moving and I'm beyond caring about being in an isolated forest with a murderer for hire. Desire has taken my rational brain hostage, leaving me liquified into wanton need, grinding my pussy against his abdomen. The noises coming out of me from behind the gag are desperate and high-pitched, which seems to match his energy. Because he effortlessly holds me up against him with one hand underneath my ass while I cling to his neck. With the other, he frees himself from his jeans, and in the next moment, my back hits a tree.

Raven shoves inside me.

We both groan at the same time.

His head drops forward for a second as my pussy stretches to accommodate his thickness. But the moment shifts and ignites the air between us, he begins to punch forward with his hips, deep and fast. One of his hands brackets my thigh with fingers digging so hard against me there will definitely be a handprint there tomorrow. With the other, he paws at my shirt.

Right now, he's treating me like I'm nothing more than a dirty fuck in the middle of the forest.

And I think I love him for this gift he's giving me.

The thin fabric gives way at the neck with a loud tear, exposing my breast on one side. My wolf takes a handful of the soft flesh, squeezing and kneading while his cock thrusts in and out. Hitting so deep I can feel him in the back of my throat.

"That's it, my pretty little cock whore."

He pinches and tugs on my hardened nipple while I moan against the wad of fabric. There's nothing I can do but hold on as he drives into me over and over and over. Somewhere in my brain, a voice demands oxygen. I try to remember to inhale through my nose, but it's a feeble effort in the face of how my body is being utterly used. My pussy walls flutter and clench around him, and after how close I was while bent over getting spanked, I'm easily dragged to the edge of my climax by force.

I come on a desperate sob and anguished cry, clamping down, squeezing his length buried inside me. Everything gets swept away with the force of how far I'm tugged underneath the surface, and all I can do is shut my eyes and hope never to come up for air again.

Strong hands grip me as his thrusts intensify, my walls still rippling around him as he jolts and unloads with a series of grunts and curses. His cum jets inside my pussy, and he keeps on slowly fucking me. Guiding me down from my orgasm. My eyes are shut, but his attention is laser focused on every muffled noise I make.

Grief bubbles out of me. Wetness clings to my eyelashes.

He rests his forehead against mine and doesn't say anything. But I can feel what he's not saying. My wolf is the eye of the storm, keeping me calm and grounded and holding me so tight I never want to escape his grasp.

His cock is still buried inside me, when I start to shiver. The cold creeps in to claim my bones as I begin to come down.

But I don't want this to be over. I don't want to have to return to reality just yet. Keep me here, hidden away, where I can wallow in the knowledge of how awful my bloodline truly is.

As if he hears my thoughts, Raven yanks the shredded shirt off me, then drags his own tee over his head in one movement. He carefully bunches it over my hair, then threads my arms through the sleeves, and try as I might I can't fucking help but melt even more wrapped in his arms. The soft fabric is warm and surrounds me with an addictive hit of his scent.

Keeping me braced against the tree, he uses one hand to brush my tangled hair off my tear-soaked face. Then he carefully takes my panties out of my mouth, swiping a thumb over my bottom lip before shoving them in his pocket.

"I don't have anything else to give you."

His voice is low and hoarse, and he's not referring solely to the shirt.

None of that matters. It's perfect. *He's perfect.*

I'm still cradled tight in my wolf's arms, clung around his

neck, feeling like a toddler, when he carries me a little deeper into the trees beyond the clifftop. To a small wooden hut hidden amongst the thick pines; even though I can barely raise my head off his shoulder, I can only assume *this* is where he comes when he disappears.

We enter the tiny wooden structure. It's dark and musty. There are no windows, and in one corner of the square room is a simple little firebox with a wooden sleeping platform along the far wall. I'm set down on the edge of the makeshift bed—if you could call it that—as Raven goes about lighting the fire for us. There's a gray wool blanket that looks like something from the army folded up on one end, which I wrap around my shivering limbs.

Readjusting myself on the unforgiving wooden surface, I can't help but wince. The welts on my ass and backs of my thighs pinch and sting when they come into contact with the wood.

"Turn over." Raven's command is gentle, but no less authoritative than usual. When I do so, he murmurs something to himself.

"What is it?" My voice is a hoarse whisper.

"When we get back, I'll give you something to put on that." He's not touching the hot, punished flesh, but I sense every lingering moment of his visual inspection all the same. "I didn't think I broke the skin, but it was worth checking, just in case."

I curl onto my side, instead of sitting, and Raven moves back over toward the fire.

More silence stretches between us as the small space begins to warm. It's not an uncomfortable quiet, though. More pensive than anything. Thoughtful even.

"You're not afraid of me." He doesn't look in my direction, so I take the opportunity to soak in the sight of his profile. Dark features and lines of ink illuminated by the flicker of orange light.

"Not exactly." I tuck the blanket a little tighter beneath my chin.

He grunts. "That's not an answer."

How do I explain it, when none of this even makes sense to me.

"No, I'm not afraid of you as such...but I am terrified of what you represent. I am terrified of the things inside me you call to, and I absolutely know that you might be dangerous to my health."

Raven continues to poke at the fire, absorbing my words. Or maybe he's ignoring me.

"But unfortunately, it would seem that I like whatever this strange kind of madness is that you draw out in me."

Kindling cracks and pops as it burns.

"Raven," I say his name a little hesitantly.

"Mmm?" He drags a hand through his hair, tousling it.

"Will you tell me something about yourself?" Anything. I don't care what it is, really. He could talk to me about oil filters or crushing windpipes. All I want is to hear his voice and be soothed by the sounds that will hopefully keep my mind at bay for a little longer.

"You don't want to know my shit."

Readjusting my position a little, I curl my fingers in the blanket. "Maybe I do."

"Nothing good comes from looking too hard. You're liable to get burned."

"I'm right here, aren't I? I'm willing to look." The slope of his strong nose and angle of his jaw seem so impenetrable. Honed by years of fighting men and monsters. "Besides, I've already stuck my hand in the flame more than once."

Larger pieces of wood begin to flare and crackle as the fire grows, and he's got his back turned to me, still crouched in front of the amber glow. In all honesty, it's impossible to tell if he'll concede to this. Would Raven be willing to share more than the fractured shards I've been permitted to glimpse so far.

This time when he starts to speak, his voice is low, almost as if he's talking to the fire rather than me.

"Cara developed faster than I did. Even though we were only a year apart in age, she looked older. I guess that's why your father chose her."

Oh, god. His sister.

"I was only a scrawny little kid, with a bad attitude, but they saw something in my scrappiness. The way I used to try to fight anyone and anything, no matter the size or age of my opponent. So, instead of keeping me at the mansion like they did with her, they sold me off. Separated us, and gave me to people who would teach me to become a weapon they could use for the Anguis. I don't even think I was still in the same country, but every day for years, I tried to figure out how to get back to her and rescue her."

One by one, he prods another stack of split kindling into the mouth of the firebox.

"I found out she was dead about a year after she hung herself. Thorne and Ky, well, we had just crossed paths for the first time within the Anguis...with his contacts, Thorne helped me track her down. Or at least, found out what had happened to her. I don't even know what they did with the body."

My knees are tucked against my chest as I rest my cheek on one hand and watch his silhouetted form. Witnessing this complex man dredge up terrible memories and speak them into the flames.

"You have every right to be disgusted with me." I can't stand me right now. Here I am, still living and breathing, and there are people like his sister who had their entire future ripped away by my parents.

He stands up and crosses the space to where I'm lying. In his expression I expect to find fury and hatred framed by a row of snarling teeth. But instead, his face is almost serene. There's a calmness flowing off him, and I can't even begin to imagine the torture he's put himself through for years knowing that he didn't manage to save her despite his best efforts.

"It hurts," I whisper.

"I know it does, beautiful." He stops just in front of me and reaches out to tuck a strand of hair behind my ear.

"How do you live with it...How do you cope with all this pain?"

His calloused palm slides along my jaw, pausing to cup my cheek as he stares down at me. "When I find out, I'll let you know."

I allow myself to soak up every second of his touch. It's so rare that he offers me this kind of intimate contact, and I'm struck by a tinge of fear that this might be the first and last time I'm ever permitted such closeness to him.

"Do you mind if we stay here a little while?" I ask. "I know this is your sacred space, and I've intruded..." My words falter off into nothing. For whatever reason, he brought me here, and without him, I have no way of leaving. Not with only a t-shirt and welted ass to show for myself.

He doesn't seem to be in a rush to toss me out of here, or at least, he surely wouldn't bother to light the fire if he intended on leaving straight away.

"Sure." He nods. And climbs onto the wooden boards behind me.

I turn in on myself, keeping my knees hugged to my chest. Even though we just fucked, I don't expect Raven's touch or for him to willingly get close in any way. Not after everything I've now learned and what he's shared about how my family destroyed his.

Dark thoughts consume me, so much so, that I startle when his strong arm wraps around my body from behind. He's careful not to scrape against my abused ass and thighs, but still tugs me against his solid chest. There's a little sting and burn as we fit together and at first, I'm stiff, but slowly, my body softens and molds against his. Against my back, Raven's steady heartbeat settles me with a peaceful rhythm. One that begins to tempt me toward sleep.

We lie there in silence for what feels like hours. The wind is an eerie groan and howl as it whips and swirls through the trees creaking overhead.

After a while, my body slackens as sleep begins to crawl through every limb. My eyelids are lead weights as I give up fighting and succumb to the way they insist on drifting shut.

All the while, listening to mother nature raging outside, and the wild creature steadily breathing at my back.

Just as that falling sensation hits, when my fingertips slip from where they've held me on the ledge, his fingers flex against my stomach. Holding on tight. As sleep demands that I surrender for a brief reprieve, Raven's lips brush my ear. "Anytime you need help with that pain, you know where to find me... I'll always help you."

CHAPTER 52
Ky

I don't know what went down between Ven and Fox yesterday, but the curious beast inside me cannot wait to press our girl for details until she squirms and submits.

That's why, for now, I'm sitting here trying not to laugh into my coffee as they fumble around the kitchen. Ven's doing his best to scowl in her direction, and Fox is hiding her blushes.

He's every bit as gone for her as I am.

My phone alarm goes off in my hand, dragging me away from my vantage point of soaking up their cute flustering around each other. The clock tells me it's time to leave, and not only that, but I'm going to have to figure out what the fuck is going on with Thorne while we're in the car together.

"Behave, you two." I hop up and drag Fox into a long fucking kiss, leaving her a little breathless, before giving Ven a wink. She's a little quieter than usual, with whatever has blossomed between them, and it takes everything in me not to blurt it all out right here and now.

The words I want to say to her.

Ones that I want to say to all of them.

But this morning isn't the time or place for heartfelt confessions, no matter how much it pains me to turn around and walk out that door. Fox doesn't need grand gestures or shit like that, but at the very least, she deserves my undivided attention.

Maybe I'll tell her just at the moment she shatters on my tongue.

For Christ's sake. Thinking about her sweet taste has got me halfway hard by the time I haul ass outside.

Thorne is already in the car with the engine running when I jog across from the front door. I honestly haven't seen him since the other night, and my nerves start making themselves known as I open the passenger's side door.

"Hey." I slide in, hoping I don't sound as anxious as I feel.

Thorne grunts, which is about normal for him. Nothing unusual there. I wasn't expecting a big romantic fucking moment or anything, but we've also got to figure out how things are going to stand between us now that we've crossed beyond the carefully constructed boundaries that used to separate us.

Used to.

He steers us away from the house, down the access road through the forest.

"You ok?" Fuck it. I'm not going to sit here in silence. Fox's sweetness lingers on my lips, and we've got to attend one of the council Gatherings of the Anguis downtown. We don't exactly have the luxury of time to sit around *not* talking to one another.

He shoots a look at me as we leave the compound. Those cerulean eyes are dulled by an emotion I don't know if I've ever seen in Thorne Calliano before.

Guilt.

"Thorne. It's ok." On instinct, or intuition, or whatever it damn well is, I lay a reassuring hand on his arm. "What happened the other night..."

But he cuts me off with a shake of his head.

"Ky, no, it's not that."

There's more than a little relief in the hasty breath I blow out. Ok. It's not about us fucking for the first time. I can handle whatever else this might be, I think.

"Fuck." He drags one hand through his air. "She found out the truth about her mother. It wasn't pretty."

"Shit." I don't need him to spell it out. There's not much imagination needed to figure out that Fox would be devastated, and not to mention, I know how hard Thorne has worked to keep that sickening truth hidden from her.

"I'm trying to give her some space."

"Ven's got her." I don't move my hand off his arm. "He'll make sure she's ok."

"I know, I just wish..."

Yeah. Don't we all. Wishing things were different to the way they've been, and knowing that you can't change a goddamn thing about all the sick shit we've been through.

Silence flows between us for a long while, as the forest starts to give way to the outskirts of Port Macabre. Both of us a little lost in imaginings of what our lives might have looked like had things turned out differently.

"How did she find out?"

There's a muscle ticking furiously in Thorne's jaw. "Our plan at the fight night worked a little too well. A message was sent directly to her phone. A photo of me and her mother from, I don't know, fucking years ago."

Everything in me stiffens. "They could get to her that easily?" I know it's only a text on a phone, but it sends a message that they can access her anytime and anywhere they like, and that makes me feel like I want to start blowing heads apart like watermelons with my shotgun.

"We can work on tracing the message and see if it turns up anything. But the damage is done. I don't know if she'll ever look at me again, now that she knows."

The rest of the drive passes mostly in silence, until we pull into the discreet basement parking. We're early, getting here well before the council arrives as always, so the lot is vacant.

Thorne looks like shit, and also a little too much like he'll murder anyone from the Anguis who even looks at him sideways today. Fuck. The last thing I need is for him to fall apart, not when we're so close to succeeding with this plan of his for the Pledging ceremony.

As he parks the vehicle and cuts the engine, usually, we would be on the move straight away, but this time, neither of us touches our door. The scent of leather and *him* is swirling and making it so damn hard not to want to turn us straight back around and get the hell out of here.

But we can't do that. He knows it. I know it.

"I fucked up. I should have done more to protect her. There's so much more I could have done." He rests his head back against the seat.

"Thorne, look at me." I twist my body so that I'm facing him as much as possible.

Muted blue eyes follow my movement.

"You put everyone and everything before yourself, and you've done all that was in your power, I know you have."

"What if I haven't?"

"I know you, Thorne Calliano."

"You'd all be better off without me."

"Fuck that." I shake my head. "Want to know something? You've never *just* been a brother to me; it's always been something more—at least on my part, it felt that way. Hawke is my sibling, but you were my protector, and the one who I always looked for in a room." I lean forward to rest my hand on his shoulder. "It was your sorry ass who I lost sleep worrying about whenever you didn't come back at night, because I knew the only reason you were putting yourself in danger was to keep me safe."

There's so much tension lining his face. All I want to do

right now is help, and it's always so fucking hard to get him to open up. There are glimpses and cracks that I slip into whenever they appear, like they did the other night, but it's so rare.

So maybe that's what pushes me at this moment. Seeing him suffer and torture himself over shit that wasn't his fault.

"None of this is your fault. You've always put yourself in harm's way…I don't even know if I ever thanked you properly in all those years…"

"I would have put a bullet in every last one of them if they'd ever touched you." He bites off my fumbled words, holding my eyes with such possessiveness I can't help but drown a little more in him.

"Of course you would. And you're doing the same for her. Fox knows you are." My fingers creep up to slide around the back of his neck, brushing over the short hairs there, his pulse ticking up in response.

"What can I give you?" I flex my fingers against his nape. There's no doubt that Thorne is coiled so tight right now; he's going to be a liability if we try to face down a room of the very people who fraternize with the ones he wants to see with their brains splattered all over the wall.

"Ky." His teeth grit, but I can see he's fighting the urge to admit what he wants.

"I know you, Thorne Calliano. You're a man who takes what he wants…and I'm offering."

His fist flies up to grab the front of my shirt, and we're hovering somewhere over the center console together. The dark concrete box of this underground car park is empty, and the silence feels deafening as the man in front of me wrestles with himself.

All while his captivating stare bounces between my eyes, and my mouth.

"You took care of me. You take care of everyone." I let my

own gaze fall to his lips. "So, give me the chance to do the same for you."

There's a tight noise that comes out of his throat.

"Why can't I say no to you?" He murmurs.

An answer—a very specific word—dangles tantalizingly out of reach, but it would be madness to say it right now. So instead, I drop my hand from his neck, letting him continue to hold me tight by the front of my button-down, and find the bulge in his pants.

"You sound just like Ven." I hum as my palm covers his erection, and I take the opportunity to rub him through the material.

A mess of emotions that have never fucking existed inside me before, all collide and wrestle for space. Wanting to help ease his burden, to show how much I've always cared for him, while at the same time as letting myself admit I'm in love with him, I'm falling in love with Fox and Ven a little bit more every day.

The way his throat works down a swallow and his eyes flutter closed is like a drug.

He lets me stroke him, and our foreheads drop together as both our breaths echo raggedly in the small space inside this car.

"What happened, that was not a one-time only thing, is that clear? I cannot and will not fuck you and not give you my heart at the same time, do you understand me?" Thorne hovers so close to my mouth. His proximity is exhilarating and sucks me deeper into the spiral of emotion I've been trapped in for so long when it comes to him.

The deepest, sexiest noise comes out of him when I cup and squeeze harder. "You know I've spent so much time in that house knowing you were just down the hall. Wondering what you'd taste like. Wondering how you'd feel coming apart underneath me."

God, my dick is fucking throbbing hearing him admit this hasn't been a one-sided thing.

"I've wanted you for so long. But I never knew..." I run my tongue over his bottom lip, while my palm keeps working over his length.

"Christ. *Ky*." There's pain in his voice as my name whispers through the air between us. Like he still feels so guilty for finding some little shred of enjoyment for himself—as if true pleasure is a luxury this man couldn't afford amongst the bloodshed and the trauma he's been through.

"I want this. Let me make you feel good before we have to go in there."

My fingers take over. I'm unbuckling his belt, and he's not stopping me. The weight of his stare is heavy on the place where his cock strains at the material, and he widens his stance so I can free his erection.

"Fffuuuck." Thorne grunts as my fingers wrap around his length. "If we're doing this, I'm gonna need you to take out that pretty boy cock of yours and show me."

Goosebumps run down my arms. I'm always caught off guard when he starts to dom me, and the hit is addictive.

So, of course, I do as he says.

My dick is aching; I should probably be embarrassed at how eager I am. It takes a mountain of effort to bite my tongue and not beg Thorne to shove my head into the leather and pound me right there in the backseat.

He lets go of my shirt, dropping his hand down to my groin and my leaking tip. With a smolder in his eyes, he thumbs my piercing, and I nearly fucking die.

"Do you like that, hmm?" Each time he slides the metal bar back and forth, I can't help but groan and shift my hips. He's only taunting me, not really touching or stroking. Still, the feeling of the softest brush of his fingers makes me twitch.

"I'm supposed to be taking care of *you*. Not the other way

around." My head spins. There's a thump in my balls as blood rushes to my dick.

"Maybe knowing that you're in there beside me...needy and hard and leaking cum every time I look at you...maybe that's exactly what I need?"

"Jesus." A choppy breath escapes past my gritted teeth. This man is way too good at fucking with my sanity.

I sit there helpless, letting him tease me for a few more minutes, my fingers digging tight into my thigh and the back of the driver's seat beside me while he wraps his own cock in his fist. But I'm begging pretty quickly. Turns out, that's what I do now for this man.

"Please. Please, just let me..." My words dissolve into a groan as he swipes his thumb over my tip and smears wetness around the head.

"You gonna swallow every drop like a good boy?"

I'm nodding and shifting my weight and Thorne allows me. Sitting back in his seat as I contort myself to get in a better position to take him into my mouth. But as I brace myself to lean over him, he grabs my collar for a second and halts my progress.

"Spit on it."

The growl in his voice sends heat pooling in my groin.

I lick my lips and take a shaky inhale through my nose. His thick cock is right in front of me, and I let a trail of saliva drop from my mouth, coating the head of him. As soon as my spit touches his skin, the length of him kicks before my eyes.

God, I love knowing something so small can have this effect on him.

Thorne's chest rumbles before hands slide up to dig in my hair. Thank fuck, because I'm panting and writhing here, and he knows how eager I am to please him.

That small shift gives me the permission to sink down, and I take him into my mouth. He's so velvety smooth and big, and I don't think I'll ever get over the taste of him or the fact that I'm finally allowed to have him like this.

My tongue swirls, and I bob up and down over him, and it's pure exhilaration how fast he's unraveling.

"That's it. Take every fucking inch."

His hips punch up, and the hold in my hair flexes and tightens. My throat closes around him, and there's a delicious shudder that races through his muscles as he tries to chase the way that feels.

"Put that pretty mouth of yours to work. Just like that." His husky voice melts all over me.

I'm drooling and moaning around him, sending vibrations through his dick that I know would have me losing control almost straight away if I was on the receiving end.

"Ky. Fuck. Holy fuck." Thorne's voice hitches, his cock throbs.

My balls are tingling with how recklessly hot this unexpected moment is.

"I'm gonna come," he warns, before spilling across my tongue.

And because I am every inch Thorne Calliano's good boy, I swallow him down and nearly fly out of my head with pleasure.

"Come here." I'm barely done cleaning him up when he drags me off his length, pulling my lips to his.

While we clutch at each other in the front seat of the car, not caring about the world outside for this small moment in time, he kisses me with the type of tenderness and reverence that has my stomach doing swan dives.

It's the type of kiss reserved for lovers, and my heart wants to leap out of my chest into his oh, so powerful arms.

"Feel any better?" I smile against his mouth, and he rests his forehead against mine. My dick is about to fall off, but I resist every temptation to stroke myself. If it guarantees I can expect a reward later on, I'll agree to Daddy dom's torture.

"You're fucking trouble." He holds me with our heads pressed together, and I can feel the black cloud has eased enough that I don't need to worry he's going to start bashing skulls in and send us all to hell.

"And you're the lucky bastard stuck with me. I hope you're pleased with yourself that I'm now going to have to have the world's biggest boner through this whole fucking meeting."

That drags a small huff of a laugh out of him.

"This was all your idea, *Harris*. So you'd better put that fancy cock away, we've got shit to do."

But his blue eyes crinkle at the edges with a small smile as he tucks himself back into his pants.

And all of a sudden, even though we have to descend into the snake pit with the scum of the earth, I know it'll be ok having him by my side.

Getting through this with *all* of them by my side.

CHAPTER 53
FOX

I'm walking into a sex club for the first time, and I am the absolute definition of not-chill.

My heart has been replaced by a racehorse, and my knees just about knock together.

Settle the fuck down.

In what world did I think this would be a good idea? I've got Raven and Ky with me, and yet I'm uneasy as anything because my third man has been MIA since I threatened him with his own gun and forced him to reveal his deepest, darkest trauma to me.

Now that I've had a couple of days to stew on that, I definitely feel like I owe Thorne an apology. I almost rang him. Then, instead, I composed the world's longest text message before deleting everything. And the more time that passes when I don't see him has me suffering the worst kind of dread, fearing that he might never touch me or hold me again. It wasn't my place to force him to tell me, but then again, none of this would have unfolded the way it did if he hadn't been keeping so many secrets.

Round and round I spin inside my mind, like a ballerina on crack, and I only end up making myself feel nauseous every damn time.

So, here I am, taking up Poe's invitation to come survey my inheritance...purely as a curious onlooker. She'd been blowing up my phone the past few days, and evidently Ky's also. He was the one who convinced me it would be ok to come tonight, but I suspect it was more about getting Poe off his back than anything.

I've chosen to wear a dress that looks like a mirror ball, with a low v-neck and long fitted sleeves. It shows off my sternum tattoo perfectly, and the silver fabric feels heaven-sent for my curves, stopping mid-calf to reveal my peep toe wedges.

Even if I might pass out from nerves, I look hot.

Poe made a convincing argument, telling me to join her in spending a night touring the club, and all I have to do is make an appearance. No partaking in sex club proclivities required.

There's no need for me to be this nervous, I can have a drink, be shown around—seeing as I am the heir to this entire establishment after all—and in doing so, I'll also show my face among the Anguis who frequent Noire House to chase their pleasure.

Embedded within their secretive world, there are those who deserve to be buried for their sins. The pure evil my men are hunting down and disposing of day by day. But Poe assures me that there are also many members loyal to the Household who have no idea of the foul truth of the hidden organization Andreas and Giana Noire used to operate.

From what I understand, Thorne and his brother have nearly achieved everything they set out to do. With a final trafficking ring they have yet to take apart, and the last step in claiming Noire House's power for themselves. Which is where my role in the Pledging ceremony comes in.

I'm still only a possession—a thing to be owned.

However, the way things have evolved between all of us, I don't exactly know that I'm worried about belonging to these men.

If we were free of the sickness infecting Noire House, and the threats now hanging over my head, would I even want to return to my old life? What would I do if given the choice to leave their side?

Barbed wire closes around my throat at the thought.

I've become the monster's pet, who will happily stay put, even if the door to her cage is left wide open.

"Fox, you are such a babe. I demand you come and hang out here every night." Poe wraps me up in a friendly hug the moment we reach the foyer to Noire House. "Having your fine ass on the floor would quadruple business overnight." She gives a little wave to my two men. Ky winks and Raven gives her a look that could turn mortals to stone.

They've been unusually somber during our ride in, even Ky. Tonight, the mansion reflects their energy, the place is much quieter than when we've been here before for the large events. It feels more intimate, with only low lighting and candles flickering inside lanterns lining the dark interior.

"I don't know if I'll ever get over coming back here. It's just..." I glance around at the onyx, marble, and gold finishes, at the wide formal staircase filling the foyer and sweeping up to the next level. This place is so vast that there were entire wings I never once set foot in. My apartment where I used to live was far removed from this area, and it feels like it could be a million miles away at times like this. I simultaneously know this entrance hall like the back of my hand, with all the hiding places and escape routes through long, hidden corridors—while also feeling like a stranger.

"Things have changed since you lived here, no doubt. Especially once the club opened formally, but that was after you left, wasn't it?" Poe grabs my hand and starts leading me up the stairs.

Raven and Ky follow after us. I glance over my shoulder and am met with reassuring green eyes and a smile telling me to keep going with her.

"You mean, escaped." I deadpan.

"Yeah. About that..." She giggles and rolls her eyes at the men behind us.

At least we can laugh about my being dragged back into this world by force. I'm beyond crying anymore. *I think.*

"Let me give you the grand tour. Will you boys allow me to steal Fox for a little bit?" We're moving through a set of ornate gold double doors, each with an ouroboros symbol on the paneling, and I can hear in the breezy tone of Poe's voice she's not actually asking for their permission.

She's going to do whatever she wants, and it's up to them to try and keep up.

"We'll be here waiting for you." Ky dips his chin, and Raven sort-of grunts, which I'm taking to mean he gives his approval.

That's when I catch him looking at my mouth. Blush creeps up from my chest as my body immediately reacts to the smallest of gestures from my wolf.

Ky quirks an eyebrow in faint amusement, threading his fingers with mine before bringing them up to his lips.

My knees nearly give out.

With my stomach a fluttering mess of confused feelings for these men, I'm being led away into the heart of the mansion's most exclusive and notorious business.

A sex club, where only those sworn to the Anguis can join. The world's most wealthy and powerful, who pay for their membership in secrets, and millions, at a time.

"This entire wing of the mansion has been converted. We

have several different levels, depending on your tastes and preferences." Poe gestures around the expansive room, which is lit by candles and firelight, with velvet and bronze touches and crystal glassware. There's a long bar and scattered seating. It almost looks like a luxury hotel lobby. Except for the fact there are people openly kissing and running their hands over each other. Some wear collars around their necks, others kneel with eyes kept firmly on the floor.

"It's gorgeous." It really is. Even if hot, prickling attention falls on me as we approach another set of stairs. These are covered in plush burgundy carpet.

"Up here is where things can progress a little further, if our clients desire." Poe leads me to the next floor, and I see what she means. The mood here is different. More visceral. There's a lot more than touching and kissing going on, with an ocean of bare flesh on display, artfully lit by the tasteful placement of low lights and chandeliers.

And the noise. The unmistakable chorus of moaned pleasure greets us the second we step onto this level.

"Holy shit." My eyes widen, as I see a woman spread out on a backless couch between two men. One is buried between her thighs, the other fills her mouth. My body heats at the thought of how I've been that woman. *I am that woman.*

"They're regulars. Always interested in new friends to play with, by the way." Poe chuckles, and we keep moving.

She's explaining their policies around drink limits, providing clear tests in order to remain a member and the types of events she organizes, like the fight night and auction. Her dark eyes sparkle when she makes mention of some haunted house annual open night, when there are a small number of highly sought after tickets made available to the general public.

All the while, we move toward a corridor at the back of the open-plan room.

"They're happy to allow non-members in?" Non-Anguis members I'm meaning.

Poe raises an eyebrow with a hint of amusement. "When it suits their games, yes. Once a year, this place becomes something of an initiatory experience. Let's just say there are people who pay to enter by choice, and then there are others who have been selected to attend without their knowledge." A ghost of something plays on her lips.

"Seems I've got some stories to pry out of you, Poe."

Twirling in place to continue on, I don't miss the exaggerated wink thrown my way.

"And over here, this is the start of our wing of private rooms."

"The start?" I glance back as I hear some particularly loud grunts. They're coming from a man getting pegged by a woman dressed in pale-pink latex. She's also got two men on leashes, each is knelt quietly alongside her impossibly high heels.

"On this floor are themed rooms, which can be booked by any of our members." We wander along the dimly lit space lined with doorways on either side. From what I can see, there must be at least twenty or so doors. Some have lights glowing gold above them, while others have no light at all. I'm guessing it indicates if they're currently occupied or not. "Impact play, sharing, cuffs, wax, bondage...we take requests and have the rooms prepared in advance."

"And there are more? Than just this, I mean?" The further we go, I see that some rooms have clear panels to allow anyone outside to look in. While in some cases the glass is frosted, but you can very clearly make out the dark shapes thrusting up against the opaque window.

My mind immediately flicks to the first night Thorne fucked me up against the vast wall of glass overlooking the forest.

God, I hate how much I'm craving him, and this place has

had my pussy wide awake ever since I saw that first couple kissing downstairs.

"Beyond here, we have rooms that are reserved by members exclusive to their use only. They are customized and equipped for their specific tastes and desires, supplied with their own key to come and go as they please." Poe points to a smaller, ornate spiral staircase that ascends up to the next floor above us.

"Those rooms also have a private exit elevator, taking guests out through the rear of the mansion... if they feel the need for a little more privacy...afterward."

My insides do a little flutter. Would my men ever be interested in having a room like that? I have to quickly side-step those thoughts because otherwise I'm liable to spiral rapidly into wondering about all the other times the three of them have frequented this place. A murderous, possessive heat starts to flare behind my ribs simply entertaining the idea.

"We can look through some of the suites if you want?" The voice beside me pulls my brain out of its imminent tailspin.

"Maybe next time, I—" Faltering, I twist my hands together.

"Of course, Fox...this is a lot to take in on your first visit." I'm so grateful that she gets it, and doesn't press the issue. "Come for a more in-depth tour anytime you want."

As relieved as I am feeling that we can continue this another day, I don't want her to think I'm not impressed. "It's...I honestly don't know what to say. You've created something incredible." I truly mean it. Beyond the fact that my father was a sick asshole, there is a world within the Anguis that this woman and Hawke Calliano are running in respectable standing.

The world will never be rid of power-hungry individuals who choose to pledge their lives to these sorts of organizations. And they are willing to work with that to create something better than existed while Andreas Noire was in control.

"You know, you really should come and enjoy an evening

here sometime." Poe bumps her shoulder against mine. My cheeks turn crimson.

"I don't—Umm—Maybe?" The words are tangled in my mouth like fishing line.

She laughs and encourages me to follow her the way we just came, checking an alert on her phone as we start heading back toward the main room.

"Don't have a heart attack on me. But keep it in mind."

"I definitely will." Although I really don't know what or when or how that would ever happen. If I'm truthful with myself, I don't want to come back here without my men. And I also don't know how any of them would feel about being here with me, especially since I know they've all previously taken part in the pleasures on offer here.

God. That sends the jealous bitch in my chest into a feral, screeching, clawing mess again.

But who am I to judge anything? I wasn't exactly some pristine Barbie doll left in her packaging and never played with before I met them. Add that to the fact that they're all older than I am, and I really cannot be feeling any particular way about their activities here in the past.

Even so...I hate it. Violently.

"Come on, let's get a drink and see where those bulldogs of yours have gone, hmm?" Poe taps out a message on her phone as we walk back down to the first floor, where there is decidedly *less* explicit fucking going on out in the open.

As we reach the bottom of the stairs, my heart rate triples. Heading toward us are the two men I should not be surprised to see here at all, but I'm still faltering a little anyway.

Thorne and Hawke Calliano.

It's easy to tell the difference between them tonight, even though it feels like forever since I last saw Thorne...while shoving a gun below his chin, no less. He's immaculate in a white dress shirt with collar buttons popped open, sleeves rolled up. Seeing him dressed like this reminds me of the man who asked me out on a date and was charming, but also a stand-offish prick, and my core clenches as he draws closer.

Thorne carries two glasses, one in each hand, which makes me suspect that Poe has masterminded this whole *chance* encounter judging by the way she's beaming from ear to ear. As I almost reach the last step, he's right in front of me. My tiny perch to stand on draws us eye level, despite him usually towering over me even when in heels.

There's no hatred or malice or disgust in his eyes, just a warmth and affection there that I don't deserve.

"Did you enjoy your look around?" His eyes drop appreciatively down my body. "More importantly, did Poe behave herself?" There's a crease at the corner of his eyes, and I know he's trying to tell me all is forgiven. He's not making this awful, or hard, or punishing me.

I want to kiss him senseless and rub all over him.

That kind of thing is probably encouraged here.

"I did. We did." Darting my tongue out to wet my lips, I manage to give him a small smile in return. This man makes me giddy in a way I've never experienced before. One glance is all it takes to reduce me to a blushing mess.

"Would you like a drink?" He offers me one of the glasses, which looks like whiskey, and I gladly take it. My fingers brush his as I reach for the beverage, and there's that same familiar spark that I always get jolted by when it comes to him.

"Come join us in a booth for a bit. You don't have to rush off or anything, right?" Poe is angling herself to herd me over to one of the luxury leather seats over at the far end of the room, where it's a little less crowded. "I'm sure even Thorne Calliano can have a little downtime every now and then."

I see Hawke giving him a look that must be brother-code for *listen to the woman.*

Taking a small sip from my glass, the burn of the whiskey

going down actually feels superb, especially considering my jangled nerves. That's when Thorne does the most surprising thing he could possibly do at this juncture, and wraps my hand in his. He intertwines our fingers, leading me behind him as we head over to the booth.

There's every chance I fell and hit my head on the way down the steps, because this cannot be real. He's surely not holding my hand like we're lovers, and this is what we do on a regular occasion.

My eyes fixate on the spot where our fingers link, and my brain ceases all functionality.

He flexes against my hand, and I nervously bring my gaze up to meet his. Resembling a gaping fish, I imagine. He sits and tugs me to follow, keeping me tucked close. It's like he doesn't want to stop touching me. Those sapphire eyes shimmer under the low lighting, pausing on my mouth, and I immediately transform into the horniest little bitch alive.

If my Viking and wolf don't get their asses here immediately and either take me to one of those rooms upstairs or fuck me in the giant car we drove here in, I will scream.

To try and keep my lusty brain in check, at least while we're in company, I gulp back some more of my drink. Then some more.

Thorne is here, and he's not mad at me, and I've never felt more at ease around him.

In fact, I feel fucking fantastic. More relaxed than ever.

Poe sits across the booth, talking animatedly with her hands, but I can't seem to make out what she's saying. Her features turn into a Monet painting and start swimming in front of my eyes.

"Fox?" I'm pretty sure Raven's voice says my name from somewhere far away.

My head is being turned to one side, and I clumsily try to swat at the fingers pinching my chin.

I'm fine.

A little tired.

I just need to go to the bathroom.

Swinging my legs out from the booth, I go to push past the bodies in my way.

That's when the floor rushes up to greet me, and I only hear the roar of endless blackness.

CHAPTER 54
Thorne

"She's lucky her head didn't hit the corner of the table, Calliano. At least this way we're only dealing with the after-effect of whatever was slipped in her drink, not a concussion."

I'm glaring down our man Doc as he stands over Foxglove Noire's limp body laid out on her bed.

"Do you know what it was? What caused this?"

I know. Of course I fucking know, but I can't reveal why, or how I do. There's murder roaming freely through my veins, knowing that my girl has been targeted like this. Out in the fucking open too.

What a way to send a message. That anywhere she goes, they can get to her.

Even if she's right under our protection.

Especially because she's ours.

I hate that they've been able to orchestrate this and I couldn't do anything to prevent it from happening. I couldn't stop it, or else it would crumble everything Hawke and I have been working toward for so long.

We're so close and it carves me wide open that Fox has

ended up in the crossfire. Especially since I'm the asshole who dragged her back into this world by force.

Doc's voice drags my attention back to the scene before me. "Hard to say without running full labs, but she's responsive, just out of it. She'll probably be high on whatever is in her system for a while."

My fists ball tighter.

Ven stalks the far side of her bedroom, wearing a hole in the floorboards.

Ky sits on the side of the bed, looking like he's about to lose his shit.

We all are really.

It's one a.m., and I'm itching to go line up those responsible and execute them one by one.

"She'll be fine, Calliano. I'd be worried if there was a head injury or broken bones to handle, but this will wear off. Her pupils are dilated and her pulse is up, but otherwise heartbeat is steady, and temperature is what I would expect."

"Will there be any after-effects?" Ky asks.

"My guess? She'll feel no different to a come down off a massive bender. It might be rough, but it's no worse than a brutal hangover."

"But you don't fucking know, do you?" Ven explodes from his lair in the shadows.

Doc looks at him and inclines his head. Giving him a respectful pause. "No, until I get a tox screen back, I won't know. But I'll be sure to give you the results as soon as they're ready."

"How long?" My instincts keep a close watch on Ven. The last thing I need is for him to put a bullet in the skull of the man who is about to go run emergency bloods for us at this time of the morning.

He checks his watch. "By the time I get back to Port Macabre...give me a couple of hours?"

"Fine."

Doc then crosses back over to the bed, and bends onto one knee. Taking one of her hands, he tests her pulse and seems satisfied. Then he flashes a torch in her eyes again. "Fox, honey, can you talk to me?"

I have trusted this man countless times, and he's one of our men within the ranks of the Anguis, but hearing him call my girl *honey* is setting him on thin fucking ice.

Especially when she stirs and makes a groaning noise, trying to shield her eyes from the light.

Should I be relieved?

Right now, I don't know what to feel.

"Easy, baby girl." Ky helps her adjust to a better position on the pillow.

Ven appears beside the bed, with arms crossed, hovering.

"How are you feeling?" Doc fishes some painkillers out of his bag and deposits them on the bedside table. I'll be swapping those with ones I know one hundred percent are safe, before she gets a chance to take them.

It's not that I don't trust Doc...but...

Soft, pained noises come from her direction, and then she shifts up onto her elbows, peering through groggy eyes at the man crouched beside her.

"Holy shit, you look just like that actor." Her slurred words are heavy on her tongue.

Doc chuckles.

"At least she can talk. That's a good sign, right?" Ky runs a hand through his loose hair.

"You know the guy...he's hot...older...everyone's dreammm Daddy." She croons.

My eyes flick over to Ky, and his eyebrows shoot up. She's high as a fucking kite.

"Is this how they pick you for your little club?" A loopy grin forms on her face. "You all gotta murder people and look like you could make ovaries explode with a single glance?"

Doc shakes his head. Yeah, he's a good-looking guy, even I can see that—older than me by at least five years, give or take.

What I do not like is that Foxglove has noticed him in *that* way. Absolutely fucking not.

"I guess I'll take the compliment." He straightens up, and she's making weird oohing and ahhing noises.

It's time for this guy to fucking go.

"My friend is single. Emerald. Emmmeraaaaald—her name is so pretty, isn't it?" Her head lolls back on the pillow. "But I already have a Daddy...and a naughty boy...and a filthy wolf." She dissolves into a fit of giggles.

There's a shit-eating grin on Doc's face, and I'm going to have to smack it off him if he ever dares bring this conversation up again.

"Bye, Fox." He raises an eyebrow at me as he heads out the door.

"Get those bloods done," I growl at him.

"Already on it."

"Please."

My girl is a whining, panting mess.

She's high, although coming down, but now that she's awake, her body is wanting us and there's only so many times you can hear a gorgeous girl beg for your cock before you give in.

"Jesus. Thorne, it's not a big deal." Ky is practically crawling out of his skin. He's lying with her cuddled naked against his chest, and she's grinding against his thigh.

The man is dying, just like Ven and I both are.

"She fucking likes it when you play with her while she's sleeping." Ky glares at me. "Don't you, baby girl?"

Her horny little whimpers get louder.

I'm feeling so fucking guilty, and the last thing it feels like any of us should be doing is messing around with her, especially if she's not completely lucid.

"Please. I want it. *Please.*"

"This is different." I pinch the bridge of my nose. The asshole, Doc, still hasn't sent through the labs, and I can't let this happen in good conscience without knowing for sure.

"Let me take the edge off for her." Ky's hands are already roaming freely, playing with her tits, and she's arching against him.

Ven looks like he wants to throw himself out the window. I don't even know if he's said a word other than briefly yelling at Doc earlier. He was the one that caught her as she collapsed at the club. If he hadn't been standing there, she definitely could have hit her head on something, and then we'd be in a completely different mess.

This one is horrific enough to witness as it is.

"Maybe I should ask the hot doctor to come back. He was good to me." She pouts and shoves against Ky.

That thought alone—that she would want to go seek out someone else—is what breaks my leash.

"Fuck it." I start yanking off my shirt.

"Hell, yes. Come here, beautiful." Relief flashes over Ky's face, and he dives against her mouth. Tangling his hands in those lilac curls.

"But only one of us at a time." I point a finger at him first, then at Ven. "And be fucking gentle." I hiss at him.

"Pretty sure it's up to Fox to decide if that's what she wants from me." Ven returns a dark glare my way.

Just as we stand there with nostrils flaring and drowning in the desperate little moans coming from our girl on the bed, my phone buzzes in my pocket. When I rip it out and check the incoming attachments from Doc, I already know what the results will show. But there's a part of me that had to hear from him directly. I needed that moment of reassurance to confirm she's going to be ok.

His message explains that she'll be fine, and other than feeling shitty and hungover in the morning, it'll be out of her system fairly quickly.

"Yes. Oh, god. *Ky*."

Jesus. I look up from my phone, and he's already pounding into her. He's got her hands pinned above her head and one leg thrown over his shoulder, and his determined thrusts make her breasts bounce with each snap forward.

My cock is hard as a rock, and I'm still caught in a minefield of remorse over tonight.

She trusted me.

I should have protected her.

Why couldn't I stop it?

"You feel so good when I fuck you raw, baby girl. You want to walk around all day full of my cum, don't you?" The way Ky's talking to her, I know she's going to fall apart fast, and he is, too.

I swallow hard. The sight of them both together is goddamn hot, and I've barely had a chance to get undressed before they're both coming.

"That's my girl. Taking my dick like you were made for me."

He quickens, thrusting into her with more force, slick sounds filling the quiet of the bedroom along with their heavy breathing.

"Fuck yes. Squeeze me tight. Give that orgasm to me." They're both falling apart as Ky talks her through her climax. His own follows fast behind as he grunts and jerks inside her.

Their lips seal together, and he keeps lazily punching deep as she rides the wave, moaning into his mouth.

Finally, he pulls back. Licking a wet trail down her neck before tugging one of her nipples between his teeth. "Baby, I think our girl needs your cock." He hits Ven with a salacious look.

He's already stripped down, all his tattoos on display, and shifts over the bed to take Ky's place. All I can do is stand here, feeling out of my body. I don't even deserve to be part of this, or to be anywhere near her right now. My hands tug at the hairs on the back of my head and I'm shifting my weight. Even though I'm beside the bed now only wearing my briefs, I'm still caught in a minefield of indecision, not really knowing what to do about any of this.

"*Thorne.*" My head snaps up and Ky is looking straight at me. "You gonna just lurk over there or what? Your girl needs you, so you better move your ass."

I mutter curses under my breath.

But I cross over to his side of the bed, sliding in beside him. He's half slumped against the headboard and looking extremely fucking pleased with himself. I can't help but notice his dick is halfway hard again, and we're both sitting watching as Ven flips our girl over and thrusts into her from behind.

She's whimpering and moaning low each time he drills into that deep spot she fucking loves. The one you can hit perfectly from that angle.

"My little cock slut, you like it just like that, don't you." Ven holds her hips and drives forward. "Such a filthy little thing who loves taking it like this. Already full of cum and ready for more."

The way she arches her back for him gives the perfect opportunity for Ven to grab her hair in his fist. Holding her tight like that, he fucks her from behind, and it's dirty and slick, with Ky's release already slipping out of her. My balls tingle, and my stomach muscles bunch up, knowing that by the time I'm pushing into her silky channel, her pussy will also be brimming with Ven's cum.

Holy shit. I slide my briefs down and fist my cock, having to pinch the head to settle myself down a little.

"*Fffffuck.* You two look so fucking good together, baby girl."

Ven keeps pounding into her, flesh slapping against flesh, and it's not much longer before she's crying out.

"I'm almost...Oh, god."

"Ky, play with her clit." Ven grits his teeth and drags her hips higher.

Of course, the man beside me needs no second invitation. He slides a hand between our girl and the mattress and starts murmuring all sorts of dirty shit, while rubbing over her sensitive bud.

She detonates. Convulsing on the most sensual, beautiful noise ever, and Ven chases straight after her with a few more thrusts until he's pumping inside her with a dark groan.

"Give us one more. You're taking us so well." Ky praises her and rolls her over, peppering kisses to her tits, as Ven collapses to the other side of him.

It feels like I'm watching from outside my body right now. My hands reach for her softness, taking this fragile, stunning girl out of Ky's arms, dragging her to me. I want her on top. I want her curled into my neck with her lips on my pulse point and moaning in my ear. I want every fucking bit of her to drip over me and wash away the sins I'm carrying around.

"Be a good girl and ride my cock." I guide her lax body to drape over mine. Between the drugs and the orgasms and the slick evidence of the others dripping out of her, there's not a lot I can do other than just manipulate her body and position myself to glide her over my length. Easily filling her to the hilt.

"Fuck." I groan. Her cunt is so slippery, my eyes roll back. Cum runs down my skin, coating my balls.

"Yeah, you try telling me to take it easy. Now you know how good that shit feels." Ven grumbles at me from somewhere over on the far side of the bed.

"Daddy. *Yes.* I missed you." Those soft lips I crave find their way to my collarbone, roaming hot and wet over my neck as I drive upwards.

As my cock hits home, I'm eating up every word, and hating myself for being so greedy.

I want to tell her I missed her too. How the past couple of days have been hell. But instead, all I've got to give this girl is an orgasm and to help her get through the comedown tomorrow. It feels like it's not enough; it'll never be enough. She deserves so much more than the ruination I've got to offer.

Pretty soon, my girl is whimpering into the crook of my shoulder. Her fingers tangle in my hair while I roll my thumb over her slippery clit until those rippling sensations turn into her pussy pulsing a sweet rhythm around my cock. Milking me and triggering my own release that I've been holding back.

"That's it, baby. Take it all. It all belongs to you." My hands roam up her sides and back down over her curves, holding her tight to me as my dick pulses and fills her cunt. We're a complete mess, and there's no way we're sleeping in this bed. Not in the defiled state it's in.

She slumps against me, and I'm trying to get my heart rate back under control when her fingers reach blindly for Ky and Ven. They're still right there beside us, and she makes a sweet little contented noise upon making contact with their arms.

"I think...I think I'm in love with you."

Those words, even though she's not herself right now—spoken while mumbled and groggy and directed not to any particular person, but all of us in the dim light of the room—rip my chest wide open.

Ky is quick to reply. Without hesitation, he lays his emotions out alongside hers. "Baby girl, I love you too. You've had my heart for a long time now." Tilting her sleepy face to meet him with a forefinger, he kisses her softly.

His soul is too fucking good for this world.

Ven grunts. But I know she wouldn't expect anything more, or less, from him.

And I wish I could find some sort of response, or find adequate words, or tell her how I feel.

But, like a coward, I can only press my lips to her damp forehead.

How can I tell her, when she may never forgive me for what I've done.

For what I'm going to do.

CHAPTER 55
Ven

I'm in the mood for a pre-dawn massacre.

Someone thinks they can threaten what belongs to me? They'd better be prepared for the river of blood that Port Macabre is about to be fed with.

As soon as it happened, I knew exactly where I intended to start. With the man cuffed to the chair in front of me, who is currently choking behind the thick layer of tape covering his mouth.

His greasy hair is already slick with blood from where I've carved her name in the side of his face. The white silk pajamas he's wearing are equally drenched where he's pissed himself, added to the crimson free-flowing down his neck. Reminders of the last time this piece of shit dared lay hands on Foxglove Noire are still present. Stitches run up the side of his jaw, and mottled bruising hasn't yet faded below his skin.

Massimo Ilone has been marked for death for a long time in my eyes. Looks like he's the lucky one who will get my undivided attention today, until he starts squealing.

I run my fingertips over the tools laid out on the dining table beside me. At times like this, I prefer to get creative.

Finding whatever I can use is all part of the process. Because there's nothing quite like watching the horror play out on their faces when realization dawns that you're about to saw off their hand with their own bread knife. In this case Massimo has quite the collection of helpful implements. A power drill. Hand saw. Kitchen blender. Any of those will do nicely.

His wild eyes follow every movement as I hover over the drill, tapping my rings against the long, thick metal attachment. It's designed for boring holes into wood, and I'm certain his skull will crack nicely with that churning against his temple.

Thorne shifts his weight, leaning against the table behind me. Watching on.

The fucker followed me when I left the compound under the cover of darkness, but didn't say a word.

In fact, he hasn't said much at all since last night, and while his quiet frequency matches my own most of the time, this feels different.

There are too many secrets, and right now I want to hack open as many chests as I possibly can until I get to the bottom of them.

Most interesting in this blood-soaked scene, is that he's not trying to stop me. But I suspect Thorne is here just in case he needs to save me from myself.

Not that I fucking care at this stage.

Seeing my girl collapse last night brought everything back. Knowing I couldn't do anything and that they had already gotten to her was my snapping point. The only thing preventing me from doing this earlier was the need to make sure of her safety first.

I want to tattoo her flawless fucking skin and leave the undeniable truth for all to see—that girl is *mine.*

We left Fox sleeping off the aftereffects of the drugs and the fucking.

Ky is with her. The toxins are purging from her system.

She's locked inside the safest place I know of, with the person I trust the most in this godforsaken world. So I can focus on this asshole, and even if he doesn't have any information that might be useful, I'll enjoy the satisfaction of knowing there's one less man like him left walking this earth.

Thorne remains on the other side of the table, with both palms braced flat against the glass surface. This place drips with gold finishings, white marble, and reeks of the sick empire he ran alongside Andreas Noire.

Picking up one of the short knives and the roll of tape, I cross to the man. He starts struggling and trying to scream behind the silvery gag covering his mouth. I tear off another strip and, this time, shove it over his nose.

Massimo writhes against his restraints. But his hands are cuffed behind his chair, and each leg is tied to the seat he's in. This fucker isn't going anywhere, and I don't care if he chokes on his own bile; I'm content to sit back and watch him suffer.

He thrashes.

Oxygen doesn't come.

Just as his pathetic noises reach their peak—when I know he'll run out of anything left in his lungs—I stab the knife in, slicing between his lips. Blood erupts where the blade gashes open his skin, but it creates enough of an opening that he sucks in desperate gasps and slumps forward as far as his restraints will allow him.

"You know who I am?"

He nods. A gurgling sound comes out of the hole I cut in the tape, followed by a trail of reddened saliva falling into his lap.

"Good. That means we don't have to dance around. We're going to agree to have a nice little conversation. One where you tell me everything you know about the plot against Foxglove Noire, and in return, I might let you leave here today with at least one-half of your face."

I'm not going to. But I like seeing that flicker of hope, right before I get to stomp it out for good.

"She's not the true heir." He splutters. Blood flies from his mouth.

"Then, kindly do tell us." My knife blade fits through the hole in the tape and I saw back and forth to widen it. There's blood running freely down his chin, and the man is sobbing as I don't give a fuck whether I'm cutting away chunks of flesh. "Go on then, don't go all shy now."

He shakes his head, which only does more damage as the adhesive tears at his skin.

"They don't tell me anything."

"But you know something."

Massimo winces and shrinks back in his chair as I run the knife down toward his chest. Then his lap.

"You can't stop them. They'll keep coming for her."

"Who?" I sink the tip of the blade into his groin.

As the knife breaks the surface of his skin, he starts howling with pain.

"I don't fucking know..." He chokes as I twist it and dig in harder. "None of us know. It's whoever put the hit on Andreas."

Tugging the knife out, I wipe the residue on his pants. "And who wanted him dead? Maybe it was you? So you could try and claim Noire House and his daughter?" My snarl echoes around the white marble surfaces.

"*No*. No, I promise."

"You dared to touch her. I should really have taken your hands for that."

"They had your sister." He blurts out. Snarling. Trying to go down swinging. "All I know is they were the ones who had her."

My blood turns to ice.

"What the fuck did you just say?" It's barely a whisper that comes out of me.

"She was one of their favorites." Massimo gulps as more red trickles and drips down his front. "I heard a rumor of plans to make her the heir years ago… before the cunt offed herself…" He's a mask of pain and spits in my direction.

I'm losing the battle with the violent thoughts consuming everything. My sister took her own life, and maybe what he's saying is a lie, but there's no benefit to him in dredging up Cara's memory.

Before I can react, a blur goes past me. Thorne is charging at the man and tackles the entire chair backward to the floor. He's got the drill in his hand and a knee on Massimo's chest.

"What did you call her?" Thorne presses the metal drill bit into the man's eye socket.

"She was a worthless cunt. Just like Foxglove Noire."

My ears are pounding, and I already know that if Thorne doesn't do it, I'll hack every single limb off while he's still conscious.

"I thought that's what you said." There's nothing but malice in Thorne's voice. And as he says the words, the drill starts up. Grotesque noises of flesh and bone giving way underneath the machine are mixed with terrified screams.

Thorne drives a hole through Massimo Ilone's skull, and when he draws back to survey the bloodied mess of pulp and brain matter, he spits on the man's mangled face.

His chest heaves, the drill clatters onto the floor as he tosses it aside.

"No one ever disrespects you or your sister. As long as I am still walking this godforsaken earth, I'll make sure of that. You hear me?"

I nod.

Stepping back, he kicks the corpse with a boot. "Carve him up good, then."

Dragging the switchblade out of my back pocket, I weigh it in my hand and survey the macabre scene he's created.

Thorne might have ended this man.

But this…this is mine to finish.

CHAPTER 56

Fox

Pooling, liquid heat fills my body.

I'm still halfway between sleep and dreaming, and here I am, already wound into a state of desire.

That's when I realize my body is exposed. I can feel the cool air brushing over my nakedness, but my skin feels tingly and warm all over. My head is pounding mind you, I'm sore in places I didn't know I could be, and a yucky metallic taste coats the back of my throat.

Oh, and there's a weight nestled between my thighs.

At first, I think it's Ky. My naughty boy who loves to tease my body while I'm still asleep, and regularly wakes me up on his tongue. Or by sliding his cock inside me after playing with my body until I'm right on the edge and dripping wet for him.

But as my fingers dive into his damp hair, I don't feel the familiar long, bleached strands.

There's a roughness against my skin, but it's not the prickle of his short beard.

Holy fuck.

Thorne.

A gasp rushes out of me as he shoves his tongue in my pussy.

My very wet, throbbing, over-sensitive pussy.

“Fuck, Ky was right; you make the sweetest little noises when you come in your sleep.” The voice between my thighs is low and husky.

Oh, my god.

He nibbles and licks and swirls his tongue, leaving me with no option but to try and hump his face because my entire body is on fire with a shimmering sensation rolling down to my toes.

“Soak my face. You’re such a good fucking girl.” His words ignite those sparks and another climax roars in at full throttle.

Now that I’m more awake, everything is raw and my nerve endings are a fuse ready to blow.

He hums against my pussy, sending delicious vibrations through me that leave me arching off the bed.

“Oh, fuck.” I whine and open wider for him.

“That’s it. Spread for me.” He bands an arm across my pelvis and holds me down. Even though I’m squirming, the weight and pressure forces me to submit to the way he’s playing my body and I think I’m going to explode.

He keeps going, massaging my clit with his tongue as my thighs shake and a potent wave begins rolling up through my muscles.

“God. Right there. Don’t stop.” My head sinks back into the pillow.

One of his hands runs through my wetness, coating his fingers and pumping into me just for a second, before slipping beneath me. He presses against my ass, rimming over the bundle of nerves while holding my pussy tight to his mouth.

His tongue pushes into me, and I nearly levitate off the bed. I think there are words coming out of my mouth, but I honestly don’t know what I’m saying.

Then he moves back up to flick over my clit, before swirling and sucking down.

And when he dips a finger inside my ass, I fall apart.

"*God*. I'm coming. I'm coming."

My body is clenching and jolting as I soar off into the sky.

Thorne massages my thighs with his calloused palms and continues to stroke me with his tongue as I somehow, after what feels like an age, make my way back into my body. I tug at his hair, demanding his affection, wanting him even closer. Thankfully he obliges, shifting his weight up and over my body, resting on his elbows beside my head.

There's triumph gleaming in his eyes.

"So damn pretty when you scream my name."

My toes curl as his deep, sexy voice washes over me. Everything in this man's expression radiates how pleased he is that I'm splayed out beneath him, boneless, and flushed with satiated bliss.

I'm so fucking hungry for him. He's freshly showered and it's all I can do not to clash our teeth together when I thread my fingers into his dark curls and pull him against my mouth. He's coated in the taste of me and it stirs up a new round of need, even though he's just got me off twice—that I know of.

"You've been learning some very dirty tricks off Ky." I suck on his bottom lip.

"Oh, believe me, I can be dirtier if you want." His gaze turns molten, hinting to me that I should be fucking worried about all the plans he has in store. Like he's been plotting all the things he wants to do to me.

Jesus. This side of Thorne only comes out every now and then, and I'm such a slut for him when he's playful like this.

I *definitely* want.

"Are you sore?" His brows pinch together.

"Achy? Not sore...as such." The pounding in my head resembles more of a dull thud now. But my pussy is definitely feeling a little tender, and that doesn't seem as though it has anything to do with Thorne teasing my body while I was still asleep.

Holy shit. Even thinking about that has my cheeks flushing with renewed lust.

"I didn't want to wake you up to take some painkillers. Figured a couple of orgasms would be just as helpful." His sapphire eyes hold mine, and I don't know what the expression is that he's giving me right now. Somehow, I sense there's a depth of unspoken emotion there, but it's being blown out by the desire running hot through his veins. Feeling how turned on he is—how much he clearly enjoyed playing with my body—holy hell that makes me want to push him to the mattress and ride that extremely hard cock of his currently jutting into my thigh through his sweats.

"Here." He rolls over to one side of me and encourages me to sit up. I'm handed a couple of small white pills and some water. But it's as I'm tossing them back that my post-orgasm brain recollects how to function.

"Why can't I remember last night?" I hand him back the glass, wiping my mouth with the back of my hand, but I'm busy searching through a haze of memories. What happened between the moment I sat down next to him in the booth at the club, and this moment right here when he woke me up by licking me to climax?

For a beat, I nearly say the words that pop into my mind. Wondering if it was my men who did this to me...again.

"You were drugged." Raven's voice appears from the other side of the room. "By someone who won't be breathing for much longer." As I blink at him, it dawns on me that we're in Thorne's bedroom. My wolf comes in looking every inch the Grim Reaper. There's blood up his neck, and even though he's shirtless, wearing only black pants and his heavy boots, I can smell the gasoline and ash and a very specific kind of metallic tang clinging to him.

My mouth drops open. Fuck.

Although, I hardly have a moment to process all the pieces of information I'm taking in, before he crosses the room.

"Here." He's holding something in his tattooed hand, and the silver of his rings flash against smears of red over inked knuckles when he pauses beside the bed, handing me a box.

On the top of the black lacquer is a gold stencil of the ouroboros. Judging by the size and weight of the item he's handing me, I already know what's inside.

I swallow hastily.

Oh, god, this is not what I expected to be presented with while I'm still recovering from Thorne's wicked ways this morning, nor while I'm currently still feeling needy as all hell.

With shaky fingers, I lift the lid. The pungent, coppery stench of blood is overpowering, and as I do so, the potent weight of both my men staring at me is unmissable.

In this world, what they've given me is a powerful offering indeed. To the Anguis it is symbolic of removing someone's power, or eliminating their presence. Turning them into nothing more than an empty carcass and reducing them to dirt.

Nestled inside the box is a bloodied lump of flesh.

A cut-out tongue.

While I'm possibly going to gag, there's an unexpected sensation that washes through me.

It's glowing and warm and sits somewhere high in my chest.

Not a normal reaction to being presented with a dismembered body part. But it would seem, I really am a creature forged by the Noire legacy. Whether I like it or not.

"Here I've been sleeping, and you've been busy." I look up at Raven's unruly hair and bloodstained face. "Thank you," I murmur softly.

His energy feels like a reckless storm. Entirely alluring, even though it should be a dire warning to seek shelter.

I don't know what these men have been up to while I was passed out, but obviously they've taken action in my name without waiting around. And this gooey feeling of being protected and cared for has no right to insistently weave through my veins. Yet, it does all the same.

"Come on, let's get you showered." Thorne shifts beside me, preparing to scoop me up against his chest. I gladly let him, because my legs are more than a little wobbly.

As I cling to his neck, he walks us toward his bathroom, and over the back of his shoulders my eyes lock with Raven.

"Will you come, too?" I have no idea where the boundaries lie between us. How much he's willing to listen to my wants, or whether he's only interested in taking what he needs from my body when he desires or demands it.

Whenever sleep comes to claim me, Ky will hold me trapped against his chest. If I wake during the night I always *feel* Thorne's eyes on me. I'm not entirely certain that he sleeps.

But Raven? He's an enigma. Sometimes, I don't know if he only stays because Ky is there, and at other times, it seems like he might steal me away and lock me in a tower. Like the day he took me to his secret hideaway in the forest.

Asking him this...right now...feels like the edge of something new between us, only I have no idea which way the blade is going to slice as it falls.

He imprisons me with pitch-black eyes for a breathless moment.

Then stalks toward us.

WARM WATER SLUICES over our bodies as I rinse away the blood coating my murderous man. I'm surrounded, with Raven at my front while Thorne presses against my back. Both of them are rock-hard. Their impressive cocks press against the softness of my belly and the curve of my spine.

As I trace my fingers all over his tattooed skin, it bubbles into my mind that this is the first time it has been just the three of us together like this.

"I need you inside me," I whisper up at my wolf, tentatively resting my hands over his tattooed chest.

Thorne brushes my hair over one shoulder and his sinful lips caress the sensitive, damp skin. Of course, I arch my neck on reflex to allow him more access, because I'm far too gone for this man. Too mesmerized for my own fucking good.

"Are you certain...you're not too sore?" I suspect he knows something I'm missing here, but my neediness wins out...and I like Raven's brand of pain mixed with my pleasure anyway.

"No. I want you both." There's a hunger prowling around inside me that won't seem to go away. Maybe it's the aftereffect of whatever drug I was slipped last night, but it feels like I can't ever get enough of them.

Why am I so turned on after they literally gave me someone's tongue in a box?

My wolf roughly shoves my legs apart with a knee. An ungodly moan escapes my lips.

"Always so desperate for cock." His crass words set my core alight. "What if I told you all you get is to grind that wet pussy on my thigh until you come? I bet you'd do it just to get yourself off."

He grips my chin between strong fingers, seizing so hard it stings, holding me captive, devouring me alive with hooded, spellbinding eyes.

I'm besotted with this deadly, tempting man.

"Please." The word is so soft it's almost drowned out by the shower.

"You're going to have to do better than that." He taunts.

Swallowing heavily, my tongue runs over my lips. This man knows exactly how to twist me and turn me inside out and leave me absolutely panting for more.

"Please, may I have your cock." Humiliation burns a trail up my chest and my clit throbs in time with the pounding water.

"Are you going to be a good girl and let us play with you?" Thorne's teeth scrape the skin of my shoulder.

Raven's ring and middle fingers fill my mouth like a brutish intrusion before I can answer, pressing down on my tongue. "Still not specific enough, little Fox. I could shove you on your knees, choke you on my cock, then give you over to Thorne to do the same."

Shame ignites my core, his crass words make me whimper around him, loving the way he's controlling my mouth.

Even so, I can't help but make a wanton noise of protest, my eyes watering a little as he forces my jaw to hang open and soaks up every flicker of emotion crossing my eyes.

"You want dick...then maybe after we've both fucked your pretty little throat, we'll come wherever we goddamn want, and make you clean it up."

Jesus.

This man has me just about dead and buried. My tongue tries to flick against his fingers, but it only spurs him to push further, deeper, causing a pool of spit to gather at the corners of my lips.

"You'd look so pretty on your hands and knees licking my cum off the floor."

Thorne groans behind me and sinks his teeth down into the back of my neck, seemingly at a loss for words while our wolf runs his mouth.

"Now's your only chance. Or else I'll decide for you."

He withdraws his fingers, allowing me to talk, all the while my heart shoots off like a rocket inside my chest.

"I want both of you to fuck me at the same time."

One arch of his dark eyebrow is enough to tell me that's not what he wants to hear.

"Please, fill my pussy with your big cock, Raven, while Thorne fucks my ass."

He tuts. "That's not what you call him when you're being a slut for his fat dick, is it?"

My stomach dips, the pulsing in my clit just soared in intensity.

Is the room spinning? Or is that just my lust spiraling me out of my head.

"Please, Daddy." Gulping, I look up at the man who makes me crave having him tattooed all over my skin. He surveys me with the signature cool, aloof disdain that for whatever fucked up reason feels like being kissed tenderly on the forehead.

But that seems to please him, for now.

"Such a dirty fucking girl." The words drip from his lips, raspy and heavy with his own desire. Honestly, he could ignore me and tell me to drop to my knees, and I'd still fucking do it.

Striking quickly, a shudder roams through me as Raven grips beneath my thighs, lifting me up. More water splashes over us as Thorne moves away for a second and my wolf uses the opportunity to spin around, bracing my back against the tiles. We both look down and are captured by the space between us where his cock is already poised at my core.

"Watch how your cunt knows exactly who it belongs to." The tip of him pushes forward, breaching my entrance...and holy shit, it's the filthiest sight.

"Fuck," I breathe. Obediently keeping my eyes fixed where he wants them, as he slowly presses forward. It's so different from how he usually is when we've fucked before now, and I whimper at the burn when his cock drags against my inner walls, stroking further inside.

He repeats the process. Pulling right out to the tip and I'm hypnotized by the sight of my pussy stretching around his thick length. "That's it. Swallow every fucking inch like you were made to take my cock."

"God," I whimper as my walls flutter around him.

There's a dark noise that leaves his chest when I do so.

"Come here." Thorne rejoins us, looking damn near feral. "Ven, turn our girl around."

The two of them work in tandem so that my wolf is now the one leaning against the tiles, with water continuing to flow over us in a steady stream, caressing our wildly overheated skin. Thorne begins to glide the familiar cool sensation of lube over my ass.

"You ready, mayhem?" Inky eyes drill into my very lungs. Thorne's fingers tease me from behind.

They're surrounding me, enthralling me, and I'm so ready to give myself over to both my men.

And yet I'm entirely unequipped at this moment for Raven's duality. To be presenting me with the most powerful symbol of the Anguis, while leaving me coated in hot shame at his obscene words. Not prepared for the way he's currently stretching me around his cock like I'm nothing more than a hole for him to use, then calling me by a pet name.

He's going to carve my heart right out of my chest at this rate.

"I need you both." My spine bows as Thorne guides his cock against the slickness he's worked all around my hole.

"Breathe for me. Bear down." His lips are at my ear as his tip nudges forward. "Good girl. Relax and let us take care of you."

Oh, god. The thickness of Thorne burns so fucking good as he presses the crown inside. But the sensation is only there momentarily, and in a divine way. There's a bit more sting as my body adapts to him, but he's so damn careful with each second he keeps working forward.

"Shit." Raven hisses as he feels it. The full length of him begins to press and rub through my inner walls. That's when he ducks his head and takes my mouth. It's more of a bite than a kiss, with my bottom lip pinched between his teeth, but it drives my pleasure into a rapid climb and I can't help but clench around them.

"Fuck. Ven. *Jesus*." Thorne pants behind me. "She's already so fucking tight; you're gonna kill me winding her up like that."

I swear, the flash of a devil's smile occupies his eyes.

"You keep asking if I'm ok, but do we need to worry about you being able to handle us, Daddy?" I tease, more than a little breathlessly. He pushes further inside, and I'm so fucking full I can't do anything but moan as his hips finally settle against mine.

"I should stripe your ass red again for being such a brat." Raven bites at my jaw.

The man behind me makes a raw noise.

"You'd love to see how wet she gets when you spank that sweet little ass, Thorne." A wicked expression curves his lips.

If the drugs last night didn't end me, these two are going to.

"Holy fuck, you're so fucking good." Thorne starts to shift his hips, thrusting into both of us. Raven holds me to him with bruising fingers, and we both lose ourselves in the sensations.

"Don't stop, Daddy. Oh, god."

My orgasm builds and rages toward me like a torrent. I'm begging and making all sorts of ungodly noises as Thorne dips his hand around the front of me, seeking out my clit. His fingers slide down the front of Raven's stomach, jammed tight between the joining of our wet skin. He barely needs to stroke circles through my wetness more than a few times before the wave crests and a thousand starbursts erupt behind my eyelids.

The only thing I can do is hang on as his pace picks up,

driving into Raven and me until the rippling feeling sweeps both of my men under, too. Their cock's throb and pulse inside me with their cum. Leaving me limp and floating somewhere high above us all on a fluffy cloud, shimmering from head to toe.

"That wasn't really what I meant when I said let's get you showered." Thorne's wet hair and forehead rests against my shoulder.

"I prefer this version. Highly recommend. Five stars." I smile into Raven's tattooed skin and hear a little rumble from deep inside his chest.

But true to form, as always, they ease out of me and take care to make sure I am actually cleaned up, while I do my best to do the same for them. Even though I think I spend more time ogling their muscles and patting them in my blissed-out state.

"Oh, for fuck's sake. You know I've been slaving away out there making breakfast, and you lot are in here fucking... without me?" Ky's voice cuts through my haze and the water spray.

I peer out from below the running water and steam, to see he's holding a fluffy towel spread wide for me.

"You could have joined us." I give him a stupidly wide grin that says I regret nothing.

He tuts and motions for me to get out of the shower. It's at that moment my stomach protests loud and long at the apparent lack of food situation.

"See? This girl can't survive on you filling her with cum alone." Ky gives the other two a scheming look and I swat at him.

"Ky." My scolding does nothing. He just wraps me up and pushes my wet hair back off my face. I'm circled in his arms and he's looking down at me with a sweetness that makes my heart do a double bounce.

But then I remember that there's a giant cavity where my

memory should be, and I haven't had a chance to see him since I woke up.

"So, I don't remember anything. Whatever I was drugged with fucked my memory up."

I see his brows furrow a little.

"Nothing at all?" His green eyes draw me in, so effortlessly.

"No..." It feels like I'm missing something important here, but nothing is clueing me into what that might be. "I'm sorry if I said, or did, anything weird." Going with an apology feels like my only option, until someone decides to fill in my blank spots.

He looks crestfallen for a split second, but seems to shake it off, and his grin bounces back. "Well, you did beg for my cock...*a lot*."

I stare at him. Stunned. Hell, no wonder I'm feeling deliciously sore today.

"No."

"Mmmhmmmm. Oh, yes."

"*NoNoNo*." Burying my face in my hands, I hope the floor will swallow me up.

He pries my fingers away from my face. Making sure to bend to my height and get right up and close with his green eyes. "A. Lot." He emphasizes each word with a waggle of his brows.

"Oh, my god. Your ego is big enough already." I wail.

"That's not the only big thing you like about me, baby girl."

"If I find out you're messing with me..." My protests only drag out more of a glint in his eyes.

"What? These assholes didn't tell you about that part before cornering you in a filthy little shower threesome?" He shakes his head with a rueful smile. "Horny Fox likes to demand all her men fill her up one after the other."

I twist to look at the other two in question with open-mouthed incredulity. Both are in the process of wrapping towels low on their hips and scrubbing at wet hair to dry off from the shower. They each look the picture of innocence and corruption rolled together into two muscular packages. Goddamn them, it is entirely unfair how gorgeous they all are.

"Ok, that's more than enough cock for you." Ky rolls his eyes and steers me away by the arm, not caring that I'm barely clinging to the towel tucked around me.

"Get your sweet little ass out here and eat something."

CHAPTER 57
Ky

"Baby, you want some coffee?" I stumble into the kitchen, finding Ven hunched over his laptop. He looks like crap, and I feel like shit.

Somewhere in all of this we need to actually sleep.

Not that I minded having to stay up and take care of Fox last night—and I'm never going to complain about hot as fuck midnight sex—but between things turning to hell at the club and worrying myself sick about her, there's going to inevitably be a moment when we all reach breaking point.

Ven is running on empty. He's flipped into that state where he's not quite himself, and I trust that he knows how to take care of his own needs, but it doesn't mean I can't keep an eye on him.

He was the one to catch her when she collapsed, and I don't think I've seen him look more murderous than when he realized that someone had fucked with our girl.

While he might have purged a little of the bloodlust from his veins this morning, there's going to be nothing that stands between him and putting a bullet in the skull of whoever did this to her.

And that's if he's being merciful.

It'll be more likely that he'll have them hacked apart and bleeding slowly to death over the course of a week, before he'd even consider ending their sorry existence.

"What the fuck?" He growls at the computer screen.

Hearing the tone in his voice that makes my heart pound with worry, I drop my fumbling attempts to coordinate the coffee and the filter, crossing over to whatever it is he's looking at.

"Where is she?" Ven's eyes are lumps of burning coal when he glances up at me.

My hand runs through my hair as I try to remember what Thorne told me before he left earlier. "Uh, they went back to the club. Fox wanted to see Poe and let her know she was ok, and Thorne was going to run through security footage with Hawke."

There's already a chill creeping down the back of my neck as I watch Ven click rapidly through screens of information and camera footage.

"Her phone is being blocked." He furiously scrolls through the logs and data. "It's like the spyware has been tampered with, but I can see there's activity happening. There's data incoming. Someone is trying to fuck with her."

Shit.

"What about her tracker?" I peer over his shoulder, but none of it makes any sense to me. I'm not good with tech stuff like Ven is, and right now, I feel useless.

"Fuck. FUCK." He digs one hand into his hair. "That's offline, too. What the hell is going on?"

Think. We need to goddamn think.

"Where's Thorne?" I dig out my phone and try dialing him, but his number goes straight to voicemail. Usually he turns it off while he's working with Hawke just in case someone tries to interfere—preventing anyone from listening in who shouldn't be.

"Check the club live feed," I grunt, fisting my phone tight. My heart feels like it's about to explode out of my chest. There's not only a fear for Fox in this, but it brings back all my nightmares from when I was younger that something would take Thorne away from me, too.

I can't lose either of them.

"I don't have access to recorded footage..." Ven's teeth are gritted tight. "I've told Thorne we need to get remote access to more than just the live cameras." He jabs at the keyboard and brings up panels showing different camera angles covering Noire House at the main entrance and the club levels.

"Their vehicle is there." I stab at the screen. Parked up outside is one of our vehicles, which sends a wash of relief through me that they've at least made it to the mansion.

"He shouldn't have taken her on his own." Ven is vibrating with barely leashed rage. I'm right there with him. He's right, we all should have gone, and the fact we didn't sits like a stone in my gut.

"There. Stop." On one of the camera feeds in the bottom corner of the screen, I see her. It's grainy and dark, and hard to make out exactly where she is—maybe one of the upper-level corridors? "What part of the mansion is that? The fuck is she doing there?"

But as I say those words, that's not what makes my blood start to boil over.

It's the sight of someone in the shadows beside her. They've got a hand wrapped around her upper arm. We both watch as she tries to wrench free of their grip, and fails. In her other hand, she's holding her phone, which makes me think she was either just reading whatever had been sent to her, or was trying to call one of us for help.

She's being forced—cornered in whatever darkened part of the club this is—against her will.

"Whoever that is. They're already dead." Ven is a coil of

fury. He goes to stand up, and I shove him back down in his seat by the shoulder.

"What are you gonna do, huh? Kill yourself in the process of driving there? By the time you reach Noire House, she might be long gone if whoever that is takes her."

"I don't fucking care," he snaps at me. "She's already been hurt, and that's one time too many."

I see all my own fears for our girl reflected in his troubled eyes.

"Thorne is in the building. He can get to her quicker than either of us can. We need to be fucking smart about this, and you can murder whoever you want later. Keep your eyes on Fox." I have to take a deep breath because my fingers are itching to hammer a hole through the skull of whoever this is, and it's taking every inch of my own self-control to keep Ven from racing over there and blowing up Noire House.

He shifts in his seat, but at least remains fixated on the silent images on screen.

"How much of a delay in the footage?" I try dialing Thorne again. Still nothing.

"A minute, tops." Ven keeps the sight of Fox in the main part of the laptop, but starts pulling up a few other browser windows. We can see Poe is on a different floor entirely, dealing with some clients in the main foyer. The rest of the club seems to be empty, considering the time of day. But as our eyes scan the footage for a possible sighting of Thorne, we both still.

The footage shows their bodies shift around in another tussle, and we finally catch a glimpse of a face emerging from the shadows beside Fox.

"That slimy prick."

"Motherfucker."

Miles Crane. He's unmistakable. The very same asshole who tried to openly paw her on the dance floor weeks ago at the Anguis ball right before Thorne stepped in and put a stop to it.

"Can't we get any goddamn audio? Anything?" My hand is wrapped so tight around my phone, I might shatter the screen. All I can focus on is the way his hand is bruising her upper arm and how he's getting right in her face. It's clear that he's threatening her in some way, and while Fox is trying to wrench free of his hold, she's not fighting him off either.

Ven curses, flying through multiple levels of data and coding and all kinds of shit I don't understand. It's a blur on the screen as he works, and finally, there's a crackle in the laptop speakers, and some audio bursts through.

It's from her phone. At least that part of the spyware must still be working.

"...A single word of this, and they're dead. You understand me?"

There's some rustling, and Fox makes a noise as she thrashes against him. "I said. Get the fuck off me."

My thumb punches Thorne's number again, and I swear under my breath as the phone jostles against my ear. But there's little chance the call will connect through to him, it seems that luck is refusing to join our side today. Sure enough, there's the infuriating beep of his voicemail to greet me on the end of the line once more.

"Thorne Calliano's little plan to get you under him at a Pledging ceremony is bullshit. There's no way he's high-ranking enough to have that kind of privilege. I've petitioned the council to throw it out."

"Fuck you."

I watch the man get right up close with a fat finger raised.

"I've already paid to buy you out of the ceremony; it's only a small formality of the council signing it off, and the deal will be done. Your father promised you to me before he died, and I'll be sure to break you in nice and good. Just how I always wanted."

"They'll kill you first." She spits at him.

All I want to do is scream at her to fight. To defend herself the way I've shown her how to do. But I also know that Fox is still coming down off whatever drugs have barely left her system. On a good day, I'd have full confidence in our girl, but at this moment, she's hardly in a fit state to fend off a man twice her size.

"Oh, the Anguis will make sure that doesn't happen. Especially when they find out what those bastards did to Massimo."

Fox doesn't miss a beat. "He deserved it. Anything they did to him, I'd have gladly done myself ten times over."

She might not be able to physically shove this prick off, but hearing how much she can't stand any of his circle of sick fucks is about the only thing keeping my sanity hanging on by a thread.

I've already held the phone up to my ear, again, pinching my brow. This time I'm calling Hawke, but his line is also dead.

"Fuck. This is goddamn bullshit." I growl.

Ven is deadly quiet, watching and listening to the whole altercation unfold in black and white on the laptop screen.

"Remember, you little bitch, if you dare breathe a word, those three men are going to be dead. But not before I've forced them to watch while I screw you until you bleed."

Fox recoils and swears at him. Her back is up against the wall, and I can't think straight. My palms sweat, and the room sways around me. If he dares do anything else...

But that's the moment he finally releases her.

My pulse is through the roof as I watch him lean forward, getting right in her space again. "I own you. That cunt is my property, and Noire House is my right. Andreas signed a contract with me. You'd better believe that the Pledging Ceremony is happening, and it's going to be me who claims what is rightfully mine."

With that, he disappears down the long corridor, leaving Fox slumped against the wall.

Ven quickly brings up more footage to track the man's

movements through the building while I'm consumed by the need to keep eyes on my girl. She doesn't move. Just looks down at her phone for a long moment, then wipes at her eyes with the heel of her palm.

Christ. I want to tear my hair out.

"He's already pig food. We'll make sure of it." My voice comes out hoarse. "I don't care what we have to do to make it happen. But he isn't going anywhere near her."

We watch as the dead man walking leaves the mansion, and the camera feed covering the gravel car park shows him getting in his car and driving off.

Meanwhile, Fox has slowly made her way back downstairs. She's alone, and I don't fucking like it one bit. But as we keep tracking our girl, she heads out to our vehicle and proceeds to shut herself inside. At least she had enough sense to get herself somewhere secure.

Ven clenches and unclenches his fists before pushing up away from the laptop. He crosses to the far side of the kitchen and leans on the edge of the sink, with his head sunk down between his shoulders.

The room hangs silent between us.

"You know what I'm here wondering?" His voice is way too fucking calm for what we just witnessed. "How the fuck Thorne made this arrangement anyway, when he's not a council member? The Pledging ceremony. All of it."

My jaw tightens.

Ven resembles a building tempest. "Something feels off."

There's a tightness in my chest as he puts a voice to some of the thoughts that have strayed across my mind in quiet moments. I can't say I disagree, but we don't have time to be trying to figure out the details of the Calliano's plans that they've kept close to their chest. He and Hawke have been working toward taking down Andreas Noire's estate for years.

In spite of that, I know how he feels about Fox, I see it

written all over his face. He couldn't truly hurt her, of that much, I'm certain.

"Thorne will take care of it." My finger presses the call button again, and as I raise it to my ear, Ven turns to face me with violence oozing out of him.

"If he doesn't, I'll put a bullet in his chest myself."

CHAPTER 58
Thorne

My girl is already in the car waiting for me when I walk out the front doors to Noire House.

In the time we've been here, it allowed me to run through everything with Hawke. The plans we set in place years ago are finally within reaching distance, and there's every chance we might fail...but if we succeed? That's going to make all of this hell and all of the torture so many of us have been through worth it.

There are too many years of pain and suffering, none of which can possibly be erased, but we are within reaching distance of finally eliminating the last vestiges of poison infiltrating Noire House.

We're going right for the snake at the top this time, and we'll finally assume control over this place once and for all.

None of us can change how embedded in society the Anguis are. They hold the seats of power on a global scale. But at least, in this small part, we can make the biggest difference of all.

Getting rid of the final trafficking ring that has been a plague on Port Macabre.

If that's our legacy, then Hawke and I will gladly see it through. Even if it means sacrificing ourselves in the process.

Fucked if I'm going to let any more children be abused and sold and forced into a life of hell.

Now, we have to make it to the Pledging Ceremony. The Serpentine Moon is drawing ever closer, and we've got one more week to ensure everything is ready.

One final week before all of this will be over, one way or another.

I don't want to think about what might wait for us on the other side. There's a part of me that is terrified I might just make it through this alive, but at what cost?

My shoes crunch on the gravel as I approach the car, and those baby blues follow me from behind the window as I round the hood. The door locks pop open, allowing me to slide into the driver's side, and I drop my jacket in the backseat.

"Do you feel tired?" I lean over and tuck a curl of lilac hair behind her ear. There's a small nod my way and a tight smile. Foxglove Noire is many things, and undoubtedly strong, but I suspect the events of the past twenty-four hours have caught up with her.

My throat tightens. I can't think about last night too much, or I'm going to lose my shit.

Keep it together for one more week.

Putting the car into gear, we follow the long driveway and wind our way out of the estate. Heading through the mist-covered rolling hills, the world outside feels heavy. The sky paints itself in thick brushstrokes of charcoal as evening steals in.

What I really want right now is to have her on my lap. So instead, I settle for reaching across and laying my hand on her thigh. She's wearing a short, flowy black dress and chunky heeled boots. The tattoo of peonies and her namesake flowers on her upper thigh peeks below the hem, and she feels so fucking soft. The contrast between my calloused, blood-stained palms against her smooth skin only tightens the grip around my throat. I can't help but hold her tight, toying with the edge of the soft fabric between my thumb and forefinger as we drive in silence.

I wonder if she knows exactly how much I need her—them all—to keep grounding me in amongst this madness.

That makes my brow furrow for a moment, wondering why I haven't had a check-in from Ky. Usually, I have a landslide of messages to contend with, but I haven't switched my phone back on yet after meeting with Hawke.

Fuck. "Can you get my phone from my jacket and turn it on for me, Foxglove?"

I'm not moving my hand.

She looks at me a little cautiously, then swivels to reach into the backseat. When she twists back around with my phone and presses down on the button, the screen lights up. It's barely a second before it explodes with numerous buzzing notifications, all arriving at once.

Before I can say a word, it starts ringing. Ky's name flashes up immediately.

"Put it on speaker." My stomach twists as she taps the screen.

"Jesus, Thorne. Where the fuck have you been?" Ky's yelling before the call even connects, and his voice blasts through the previously quiet space like a shotgun.

Every muscle in my body clenches as I listen to Ky unleash over speakerphone. It's like watching a car crash in slow motion. He explains the events from inside the club, the ones Foxglove had been threatened to conceal under some flimsy excuse of protecting us.

Motherfucking rat.

As he rants into the phone, my pulse ratchets into a frenzy. I'm a cobra with dripping fangs.

They saw everything that man tried to do to our girl.

They heard nearly everything, too.

Miles Crane has just ensured his head is going to be ripped from his shoulders and tossed on a bonfire.

I've got one hand gripped around her thigh so hard this girl will be wearing my fingerprints for a month.

"We're on our way back to the compound." I bark over the speaker, and the line goes dead, Foxglove's trembling hand still clutches my phone.

"Thorne." She hardly breathes as my name echoes into the charged silence.

"Were you going to tell me?" My teeth clench together in an attempt to keep my voice calm.

She works down a lump in her throat.

"You put a tracker in me?" Her refusal to answer my question makes my molars grind to dust.

"This is how I take care of my property."

"Without my permission..."

Slamming on the brakes, I pull the car over onto the side of this deserted stretch of road. Tall trees surround us in heavy shadows.

My snarl is a low vibration right through my abdomen. "Goddamn it, Foxglove, you belong to us. How else do you think we would find you if someone else tried to take you?"

Her eyes widen at me, pink lips hang open.

"Would you rather end up bleeding and broken, all because someone like that man thought he could dare take you from us when we weren't looking?"

"He wouldn't succeed."

"There are a hundred more like him where he came from who want to take you from me." And a hundred more after that who want to do foul things to her.

"You know I'm yours." Brushing her fingertips over the back of my hand in a gentle caress, my chest aches in response. I don't miss the way she winces as my fingers dig in tighter to her pliable, soft flesh.

"How the fuck am I supposed to protect you in all of this?" Somehow, I'm holding myself back from exploding, but only just.

The thing is, I've known right from the start that I'd ruin this girl if I got too close to her, and yet here I am. She's next to me, pressed back in her seat with pupils dilated, pouty goddamn lips parted, and pink spots high on her cheeks.

The longer I've tried to resist her, stay away from her, the further my obsession has tunneled down and festered away deep inside.

"You are protecting me."

"Don't fucking look at me like that," I snap.

"Like what?" Her chest rises and falls and the tiny breathy way she says those words has my pulse kicking up a thousand notches.

"Like you want—no, like you're going to beg me to devour you alive."

My girl makes a barely there noise filled with need. And it's the final tether that breaks. I'm fucking done for.

Leaning close so I can inhale every delicate note of pear blossom and jasmine and that hint of coconut—the one that immediately reminds me of holding her while tucked away in our island escape—my nostrils flare. "Sweetheart, if I wasn't one second from losing my goddamn mind I would drag you out of that seat, bend you over the hood, and show you exactly how much I own you. I would sink my cock inside you on the side of this road, mark you the fuck up, and leave you under no illusion that I absolutely *will* eat your entire fucking soul... whether you want me to, or not."

"Thorne..." She's panting, writhing on the leather.

"Fuck, I love it when you moan my name. Such a horny little thing, aren't you?"

"You're all insane." There's not one hint of fight in her voice right now. Only desire echoing the raging need I'm battling to stake my claim on her body.

I hum and finally release her thigh, using that hand to brush my thumb over the column of her neck, tracing the spot where her pulse thunders in response to my touch.

That draws a satisfied grunt out of me.

"I'm insane for you, Foxglove."

Her eyes go glassy as I purr her name.

Goddamn, I could get drunk on this girl's gift of submission alone.

"Slide those panties off." My order comes out raspy and low.

Whimpering softly, she does so. Her hands are shaking like a leaf and it stirs my need for her into a frenetic thing inside my blood. But ever the good girl for me, she hands them over straight away. Instinctively she knows what my next command would be, and fuck if that doesn't feel like the sweetest taste of something good I don't deserve. Soft black lace glides through my fingers as I squeeze them in my fist, feeling the dampness of her arousal coating the fabric.

"Back against the door. Show me how wet that pretty pussy is." I hook her panties over the gear stick, hanging the evidence on display to remind her just how much she craves the kind of shit I do too.

She's not getting them back, either.

"I'm so wet." It's hardly a whisper, but the admission out loud makes her cheeks pinken. "I'm always wet for you, Daddy." Lust flashes in her eyes, and those thick lashes flutter as she repositions herself. Curling her fingers below the material, she drags the hem over her soft thighs, revealing her glistening cunt.

Leaning across the center console, I fix her with a steely expression. Closing the space between us. "Give me your fingers." My voice is harsh, but it's driving her wild. Her teeth trap her bottom lip, and she obediently raises one hand to press two fingers against my mouth before sliding them past the seam. I run my tongue over them, sucking hard, drawing a shudder out of her.

"Good girl. Now spread yourself and finger *my* pussy."

"Oh my god." She whines, slipping her hand between her legs. Tilting her head back to hit me with the sexiest glimpse of bedroom eyes through thick lashes.

"Wider." My eyes fixate on the flush of darkened pink, the sheen of wetness coating her fingers, the way her thighs quiver.

My cock is a steel bar inside my pants, but I don't give a fuck. My entire focus is on the girl in the seat beside me, gulping down every hitched breath, and horny little noise she makes as she does what I tell her to do. Heat flashes at the base of my spine as the filthy sounds of her wetness and her fingers dipping in and out of herself fill the car.

"Christ, you're a vision." She blushes perfectly under my praise.

"I need you...so bad." Her admission stokes the raging fire building in my core. Fucking hell, as her tongue slides across her bottom lip, it's taking every ounce of willpower I have not to blurt out something irrevocably stupid.

The kind of revelation that would likely destroy our world entirely.

I'm so sick of the secrets and the shit that I've had to endure over and over for the Anguis, to get close enough to this final move of the chessboard.

It's killing me, but her hatred might be the knife that finally ends it all.

So for now, stealing every drop of goodness she brings to my life will have to do.

"Come here, Foxglove." My hands work quickly to unfasten my pants and free my painfully hard dick. Moving the seat back, I help guide her to climb over onto my lap.

As she positions herself with one hand against my shoulder, I snatch up her wrist, trapping her wet fingers in my own. Lifting that hand to my mouth, I close my lips over them, and my eyes hold her bright blue orbs as I let my tongue roam freely. Lapping up every goddamn drop of her sweetness as she squirms above me.

"You have no idea how much I always want you." *Always.* I guide that hand up to support her weight against my chest, and really wish this was somewhere I could take my time. All the things I'd want to do to my girl. But here and now, I'll take this moment, and if it means fucking her until she forgets her own name and filling her with my cum in the front seat of my car... well, so be it.

"Please...I need you inside me." Foxglove begs so prettily, surrounded in these close confines by the scent of her pussy and fragrance, it's a headrush.

Fisting my cock that juts up between us, I tap it against her clit. Her teeth sink into her bottom lip, and her face slackens with pleasure. Again and again, I smack against the bundle of nerves and rub against the spot that melts the girl perched on my lap.

She looks fucking delicious.

"That's my good girl, take my dick, I want you coming apart while I'm deep inside you."

Her tiny little cries and sweetly desperate noises come faster as she lifts up and then slides down over my cock. Already dripping wet and easily taking the full extent of me in one glide, impaling herself like a damn dream.

We both let out a groan.

"Holy shit." She starts to move, and both of us are going to collide into our climaxes hard and fast.

"You gonna come for me, baby?" My lips find the hollow of her throat, as the softness of her hips feels like an invitation to knead and squeeze and worship this woman. Already, my balls are drawing up, and the way her pussy grips around me has my vision hazing.

"Yes...yes, I'm close." The begging in her voice matches the way she fucks down on me harder. Rubbing her clit against my pelvis each time I drive my hips up to meet hers.

We're both panting, her fingers fist my shirt, and I suck down hard on her neck, hoping to mark my girl there just as deeply as my cock wants to stay buried inside her. Leaving something to witness this intimate moment long after we tumble through this orgasm together.

"I want you to come the fuck all over my cock. Right fucking now." At the same time as nipping the skin at her throat, I glide my thumb over her clit, and she cries out.

God. I'm coming. There. Don't stop. Yes. Right there.

Give me every single one of those noises on repeat forever.

"Fuck yes. Jesus. Soak me, I fucking love how you shatter for me." Her cunt grips me so unbelievably tight as she falls apart and slumps forward against my torso. I'm rocking up into her with my mouth pressed tight against her collarbone as I shudder and groan and lose track of all sorts of words that fall from my lips. Telling her how beautiful she is and calling her baby, and feeling like I could float out of my mind on the way she moans my name over and over.

My cock throbs and jerks and I spill long and hard deep inside her pussy.

God-fucking-damn, I don't deserve her.

I don't deserve Ky...or Ven.

I don't deserve even the briefest taste of feeling like *this.*

Wrapping my arms around her, I hold her softness against my chest as the waves continue to wash over the both of us, and we float on the aftermath of our intense orgasms.

Our hearts thunder wildly alongside each other, echoing around the small space, where it would be all too easy to hide away and forget the outside world even exists.

The worst part of me still isn't satisfied, however. That fucked up black-hearted core that wants to own and claim and make sure no one dares come near what belongs to me. To the three of us.

Shifting my hips a little, the welling of slippery wetness forms where we're joined at the base of my cock. Swiping my hand down to where she's still stretched around my length, I gather up as much as I can, then wipe my cum across the tops of her thighs, over the creases at her hips, across the short triangle of hair covering her pussy. My girl doesn't react, but watches on with a small gasp, captivated by the sight of me smearing the evidence of who fucking well owns her into her skin.

I do it again. And again. Covering the softness of her stomach beneath her rucked-up dress and then, lastly, running my fingers over her lips.

Meeting her wide, blue eyes, I push my fingers into her mouth so she can suck down and taste the mixture of the two of us. "That's who you fucking belong to, and I will end anyone who dares to think they could take you from me."

Humming around my fingers, she nods slowly, running her tongue along the pads to the knuckles. When I finally withdraw from her mouth, we've both managed to come down off the powerful high we've been floating on.

"Thorne, I—" Her voice cracks.

"It's ok, sweetheart. I'm right here. I'm not going anywhere."

She's so fucking perfect and the most precious thing I should never be trusted with.

I swallow deeply. My heart aching with the need to keep her wrapped around me and constantly by my side. Ideally forever, if that's even possible for an asshole like me. Maybe we don't get shots at happiness, but I'll try and thieve away as much as I can, stealing straight out of the jaws of destiny.

"Baby, there's something I've been wanting—needing to tell you." My fingers stroke her hair, pushing it back off her face slightly. I trace the curve of her jaw with a thumb.

"What is it?" She barely whispers.

There's nothing but her sparkling blues drowning me.

Words evade me, taunting my brain that is entirely captivated by the girl in my lap. Who has nestled herself squarely in my heart.

It should be simple...elegant. Something like this is supposed to be as easy as opening my eyes to find her on the pillow next to mine, isn't it?

I love you, Foxglove.

I understand if you refuse to ever return those feelings.

Please don't leave me. Us.

Especially once you find out the truth.

"Are you ok?" She toys with the collar of my shirt.

No. Yes. When she holds me, time stops, and for the slenderest of moments, I think there's a chance I might be.

"I need you to know that I—"

My confession is abruptly cut off as my phone vibrates loudly against the dash. I already know it's Hawke. We both flinch at the sudden intrusion.

Fuck. *Fuck.*

"We need to go, Thorne." She kisses me so tenderly on the crease of my brow it rips my heart straight from my chest. My fingers flex against her spine, hugging her tight to me and taking a deep inhale of her subtle fragrance where my nose grazes her collarbone.

I hate that she's right.

After I help her clean up, and we pull back onto the road, continuing toward the safety of the compound, I interlink our fingers over my lap. Hoping I can convey with that small touch a fraction of the depth to my feelings for this girl.

About all of us, together.

CHAPTER 59
FOX

Is this what being a trapeze artist walking a highwire feels like? The knowledge that putting one foot wrong could leave me plummeting hundreds of feet to my death?

Following Thorne inside the house once we arrive is terrifying. I have no idea what to expect on the other side of this threshold. I can see the other vehicles are here, including my wolf's motorbike.

What lies in wait for me behind this door is potentially going to be much, much worse than being trapped in a car with a furious Thorne gripping hold of my leg and fucking me senseless.

Ky is the one who rushes me as soon as I set foot inside. He bands me tight against his warm chest and strokes my hair.

But it's the scuffle behind me that has my pulse skyrocketing.

"Don't even fucking think about it."

When I twist my body inside Ky's hold, I see Thorne using his bulk to shield me.

"Get the fuck out of my way, Calliano." Raven's voice is pure ice, leaving a chill running down my spine.

Ky is holding me tight, not only because he wants to...but possibly to protect me.

"Stay right here, ok." His lips press against my hair, while his strong arms cinch me tighter, and I'm feeling like if someone was to strike a match this entire room might combust.

"I'm not asking." Raven's black eyes are on me, and I can't look away. He's pure malice and hatred and agony all churned into a frenzy.

"Ven." Thorne barks at him. "You want her to see you like this?" He advances on him, still keeping his body between the two of us.

There's a tremor running through me. I don't know if I fully processed what that man did or said back at the club, but now, in the afterglow of that orgasm, shock starts to wind a sickly path through my veins.

"Is that what you really want? To hurt her? To fuck her up so badly she'll never be able to look at you again?" Thorne keeps pushing him backward, and Raven shifts to keep a distance between the two of them. All the while, his eyes drill holes into me, sucking every ounce of oxygen out of the room.

"He wouldn't hurt me," I whisper against Ky's chest, and I hear a rumble of agitation come out of him.

Ky knows this man the best out of all of us, and yet, even he's concerned for my safety at present.

"Fuck off." Raven spits the words out. He's backed up against the glass overlooking the courtyard. Thorne stands his ground, even in the face of the wild creature who looks like he'd gladly tear his throat out. The two of them are one wrong move away from descending into a punch-up. Or worse.

None of them have confirmed what Raven does for the Anguis, but I'm smart enough to know that this man probably kills people with his bare hands. I'm terrified for both of them, and don't want either to get hurt. Not like this. Not at the hands of one another.

Especially not over something that isn't Thorne's fault. I was the one who went to explore the club on my own while Poe was busy with clients. But all they've seen is footage of a man cornering me, threatening me, and have latched on to the fact I wasn't being protected by Thorne.

He's already being eaten up inside by that notion, but the wild, chaotic rage swirling around Raven isn't about to listen to reason.

That much, I can tell.

"It's not his fault." My voice comes out unsteady. I don't even know if it's loud enough for the other two to hear me from all the way across the room.

There's an immovable wall holding me tight. Ky doesn't want to let me go near the two of them, and I'm shaking uncontrollably. If they start brawling, I think I'll lose my mind.

"Ky, let me go." I press my hands against his chest. Trying to get free, all the while keeping my eyes glued on the two men staring each other down.

Their energy is feral.

I know exactly how tightly wound Thorne was in the car, and I can only imagine that Raven is a thousand times worse.

He'll want to murder someone, and right now, Thorne is standing right in the line of fire.

"Ven." My Viking is pleading with him. There's worry in his voice, and I know he'll be just as concerned for the safety of the man he cares about—and who is currently putting himself in the way—as deeply as I do.

All I can feel is my pulse in my throat and a tightness in my chest that has nothing to do with the man clutching me against his body.

"Keep standing in my way, and it might be the last thing you ever fucking do."

Oh, god. I can't let this happen. I can't.

"He needs to feel me." I struggle against Ky's punishing

grip. "You and Thorne have both had a chance to touch me." My body keeps pushing to be freed, until I hear Ky curse under his breath and his hold relents.

As soon as he lets me go, I rush to Thorne's side. I see my wolf's chest rising and falling, and the tumult of emotions swirls off him like a shimmer of heat radiating off a desert. It's primal and threatens to scald me with a single touch.

My fingers wrap Thorne's forearm to let him know I'm there, and I inch forward. Raven's eyes consume me, with blown-out pupils as I approach just a little nearer.

I'm not afraid of him, as such.

But I am more scared than anything I've ever experienced to think of the worst happening between these two men.

"Hey." I breathe. Keeping my fingers lightly against Thorne's arm as I search Raven's face.

This feels like one of those moments I'm sure I've heard survivalists talk about, where you simply make yourself small and non-threatening and allow the wild beast to scent you.

Either that, or you get torn to pieces by savage jaws tearing straight through flesh.

I'm hoping to God it's the first option.

"Are you in on it?" He vibrates with rage. Hurling the words at the man beside me.

Thorne clenches both fists.

"You left her unguarded and alone. Are Hawke and the rest of them in on it, too?"

"Ven, of course not." I hear Ky from closer behind me, where he's followed.

Thorne makes a menacing noise beside me.

"It was all on me." My words tumble out quickly. "I'm the one who wandered off when I shouldn't have. If you want to be angry with anyone, take it out on me."

His furious eyes narrow. As if he's calculating every way he'd like to punish me, but doesn't know where to begin.

I shudder, but decide to take that moment to step closer still.

"Nothing happened to me. It was nothing more than words. He didn't hurt me; he didn't touch me."

"He had his hands on you," Raven snaps. Both fists are clenched so hard his tattooed knuckles are blanched white.

"And do you want to know what I was thinking the whole time?" I insert myself fully between him and Thorne now. Keeping my hands by my side, I tilt my chin up, keeping eye contact as his nostrils flare, and a tic madly pulses in his jaw. "All I thought of was how I knew, I knew with absolute certainty, that this man would have those hands taken from him. How he'd not only be reduced to nothing more than tiny pieces, but that you'd make him pay for even looking at me."

My tongue darts out to wet my lips, and I cautiously reach for one of his wrists.

When my fingers brush up against his skin, he jolts.

Fury tightens each line on his face, gauging them into even deeper crevasses.

"It's ok." Circling my fingers around his wrist, I lift it toward me just a fraction. His limb feels like a lead weight with how tightly his muscles are locked up.

Raven doesn't need an invitation to touch me, but I can tell he's trapped in a battle inside his mind, where he doesn't know which way to swing first. And right now, I need this man to focus all of that murderous, vengeful energy on me.

As soon as I tug gently on his arm, he strikes.

The hand I'm carefully touching shoots out—all lethal reflexes being the born fighter he is—fisting the shoulder of my dress. The room blurs. I'm spun around, my back colliding with the glass wall overlooking the courtyard. With a single motion, my wolf shoves his hand between my thighs. Cupping my bare pussy through the thin layer of material, digging in with such force, I'm lifted onto my toes.

Thorne and Ky both make a noise of protest, but I shake my head, quickly meeting both of their eyes. "I'm fine."

"Ven." Both of them speak his name at the same time, with warning and grave concern.

I brace myself against his biceps. Jesus, it stings and pinches, but I don't want him to stop if this is what it takes to bring him back from the edge.

"You always know how to take care of me. You told me you'd always help with my pain." His fingers tighten against the softness of my pussy. There's no attempt to bring me pleasure in this; it's solely his need to stake a claim over my body.

In the same way I'm still coated in the dried evidence of Thorne's need to possess me in the most primal of ways.

"If that's what you need...I can give it to you, but, I'm sore." I wince a little as he goes to prove my point and tightens the point of contact against my pussy.

That hint of weakness captures Raven's attention, and he slams the other palm against the window beside my head.

"You're too fucking easy to break." He sneers at me.

I nod, holding his gaze. But he's talking to me, and that surely has to be a good sign. One that confirms I've maybe succeeded in reaching through the churning inferno to reach out a hand toward the version of him who takes care of me.

Even if it is in our own fucked up way.

"Feel that?" I squeeze his forearm, reaching down between my thighs. "I belong to you. This is yours, Raven. There's no one else outside of this room that can touch me."

His eyes flare, followed by a warning growl.

"Ven," Thorne repeats his name. But I don't dare break eye contact with the man consuming my vision and pinning me to the wall.

Ky comes around beside him. Sensing the tiny shift and grabbing hold of the opportunity. "You want to keep holding her, baby? That's fine. She can stay by your side all night long."

Miracle man that he is, somehow Ky keeps his voice steady, but I know how challenging it must be to sound this calm. "I think what our girl needs right now is to sleep. Hell, we all fucking do after today."

Ky's the only one of us who can steer us away from disaster right now and defuse this bomb about to go off. Even though I'm sure he's as exhausted as I am.

"Can you do that for me? Keep hold of me? Please." I bring my hands up to lightly rest over Raven's shoulders.

When what I really want to say is, *don't let me go.*

None of them have mentioned what happens on the other side of this Pledging ceremony. Once Thorne's plan has been completed. The unknown of how life will look and feel after I've served my purpose is like a bell tolling in the far distance.

They say I'm their property—that they own me and intend to keep me. They're ruthlessly possessive and willing to murder for me. But once they take control of Noire House will that still ring true, or will the rules shift with a new playing field.

It feels as though that inescapable horizon is approaching far too fast.

The storm keeps on brewing and manifesting, and I know it's only a matter of time before we're consumed by the force of it. But for now, that's a concern I keep to myself.

I have to focus on surviving one day at a time.

"Come on." Ky is the first to make a move. Giving our wild wolf a kiss on the shoulder before tugging on Thorne's arm. "And please, please, can someone make it a priority to organize getting a big enough bed to fit all four of us."

CHAPTER 60
Ky

I blink a few times. Pre-dawn murkiness still clouds my sight as I roll over. Every limb feels languid with the pull of sleep, and all I want to do is curl around my girl. Leave me to lie here for an eternity, please and thank you, with my little Fox's sweetness to act as a balm to my sins.

My arm stretches toward the place where I'm expecting to find feminine curves and softness, but my fingers only glide over cool sheets. At first I wonder if one of the others has stolen her to their side during the night. When we all collapsed into Thorne's massive bed together, Ven had her tucked tight against his chest. But only after first stealing her away to spend hours in the bath together, just the two of them.

At least we survived without losing Ven to his darkness entirely. Sweet Fox has no idea the power she truly holds over that man. When they finally emerged, she pulled him into the bed to join us. Truth be told, I was more than happy to wriggle in on the other side with Thorne's steady presence at my back and heavy arm draped over my waist.

Although, now, when I pop my head up off the pillow to sit up a little, all I see is Ven's shaggy mess of dark hair as he lies sprawled out and face-down. To my other side is Thorne's face, softened with sleep.

I don't want to panic or disturb either of them, but after the shit that has been going on lately, they won't hesitate to kill me if I don't wake them up.

There's no telling how paranoid we need to be, with threats seemingly popping up every direction we turn.

I reach across Ven's back in order to grab my phone off the nightstand. Quickly opening the tracking to look for her location. The fucking thing is still offline, and now my heart really starts to pound.

It doesn't matter that I was asleep barely a minute ago; adrenaline rushes in like a stampede, and now my feet are moving of their own accord. Both Thorne and Ven stir as I hurl myself out of the bed.

She could be in the bathroom. Or the kitchen.

Or not.

Fuck.

Dragging a pair of sweats on that lie crumpled on the floor, I couldn't give a shit if they're mine or not, and I'm halfway to the kitchen when I hear the others hard on my heels.

"Tracking is still off," I inform them.

Ven curses. His throat thick with sleep.

There's only silence rippling off Thorne, his worry is instantaneous.

My phone is at my ear as I dial her number, and that's when I stop dead. A dull vibration rebounds off the top of the kitchen island, only a few paces in front of me.

And the room is sickeningly empty.

"Shit. *Shit. Shit.*" Dread cements itself in the pit of my stomach. Everything feels like it's spiraling out of control, and this girl—this fucking lilac-haired wonder that I've fallen so hard and so fast for—is at risk no matter what any of us seem to do.

There's no time to fuck around with questions about why

the tracking device isn't functioning. I don't have answers to half the crap that seems to be happening. She's not here, and the worst part is, I've already halfway convinced myself that she's left us.

That she's finally woken up after all these weeks and decided to run.

If we go after Fox, we might successfully get her back in physical form, but mentally? Would forcing her to return if she's chosen to escape finally be the thing that tips her over the edge into a place where she hates us so deeply we can never come back from it?

"She's not inside the compound anywhere." Ven has his phone out, with the motion detectors pulled up.

"Goddammit." Thorne is looking back at me, and his blue eyes are haunted.

He's mirroring the feeling currently sewing my gut into sickening knots.

"Do you think..." I can't even put words to the thought. It sticks in my throat like a knife. Did our girl leave, or was she taken?

"Get dressed." Ven issues us all with his order. "We need to search the forest."

CHAPTER 61
FOX

There's nothing but mist clutching at my skin with damp tendrils. My hair plasters against the side of my face, and my cheeks sting with cold.

It's eerily quiet out here.

As the murky gloom began to give way to a blue-ish haze this morning, I carried on walking. Not really knowing where I was headed, or what I hoped to find. But I needed to clear my head.

My men were all still sleeping when I snuck out in the dark. The turmoil of yesterday had taken a heavy toll on all of us, and I wanted them to snatch as much sleep as possible while they could. There's no telling what today and the repercussions of my run-in with Miles Crane might bring. And as I'd laid there listening to their quiet snores, I felt my heart crush itself in a tortured vise.

I'm in love with all of them. In their own ways, and with all their own intricacies.

Never in my wildest imaginings did I think I'd find my heart's home in three such different men. And the way they make each other happy? That brings me a deeper sense of contentment than I could ever have hoped for in life.

Is there such a thing as being at peace from seeing others find their own happiness? From seeing the way other people you love, in turn, love one another? From being overjoyed when someone you care about is able to reconcile their own feelings for someone else and start to bloom because of it?

If that's at all possible...then unfathomably, I think I've discovered that here, with them.

Which is why I'm out here at an ungodly hour of the morning, standing amongst the damp, gloomy bank of misted pines overlooking the valley below.

It might seem like a dumb decision on any other day, to leave the house without at least informing them of where I've wandered to, but I felt like I was suffocating inside those walls. And anyway, there's the whole reality that I have a fucking tracker in my neck, so it's not like I can go anywhere without them knowing where I am.

God. How did I go a whole life without love, only to slam into it with such immense and exquisite force. *Threefold.*

There's no way any of them could ever love me back. Ky, maybe, in amongst his love for both Ven and Thorne. But the other two won't ever be able to offer that part of themselves—I don't think there's anything left in there for either of them to be able to give, even if they wanted to.

My family destroyed them, leaving a legacy where I would end up tortured with longing for the part of them stolen while they were still only children themselves.

What a fucking way to ruin me even further. My parents seem to endlessly be able to reach out from beyond the grave and twist a rusty knife even deeper into the wounds they inflicted while they were still breathing.

I draw the blanket tighter around my shoulders. My skin is

numb, face raw thanks to the icy wind sweeping up from the ravine down below.

Coming out here in nothing but some thin leggings and an oversized hoodie wasn't exactly dressing for the elements. But in my defense, I wasn't thinking of anything but the need for open space and a reprieve from this insanity.

Sucking in a deep lungful of the brisk, damp air, at least one thing I can know for certain is that I'm alive. My heart is still beating, and I'm still here after everything I've been through.

If only my lungs didn't burn and my wretched heart didn't ache with every thump inside my chest.

The events of the past day flash through my mind like a whirlpool.

Along with the revelation they put a tracker in me, I also have it confirmed for me in black and fucking white that my phone is bugged. Oh, and both of the grotesquely invasive aspects of my life appear to have been interfered with by outside, unknown sources.

Apparently, being tracked and monitored without consent is the least of my concerns.

I'm still spiraling after the altercation with Miles Crane and his horrific threats to buy my body. Somehow, the knowledge that these men put a chip in me without my permission or knowledge feels like child's play in amongst the pile of awful promises and threats looming over my head.

Of course, I had my suspicions these men might have done something to me along those lines. That's the way the Anguis tend to do things...I'm no naive little girl, after all.

These three are monsters, even if they are *my* monsters.

The words from Ky barely registered when he was shouting down the phone yesterday. All I could do was look at the spot where Thorne held on to me so tight, it was like he thought I might vanish out of the car right out from under his nose.

While terror is still an ever-present queasiness in my

stomach after what Miles Crane said he was going to do, I'm not angry or upset with Thorne or my other two men for what they did.

The truth is, that even though it's an unforgivably invasive gesture, it is the kindest thing anyone has ever done for me. Going to those sorts of lengths to make sure I don't end up taken by the worst breeds of disgusting men lurking within my father's shadows.

Or, at least, if the unthinkable happened—that I was ever ripped away from them—at least they could find me.

Although now that my men have discovered someone is tampering with that, too, I can only imagine the fury that knowledge might unleash.

Since reaching this particular spot in the forest, there's a rock I've been holding onto. It's jagged-edged and looks like slate. The entire time I've been standing here, trying to wrap my head around my life and what might come once this Pledging ceremony has been completed, and my use has run its natural course, I have had it clutched tight inside my palm.

The sharpest side, has indented into the fleshy part of my hand, which is now mottled and pale with the cold.

It's just a rock. Just like I'm only a girl. Neither of us matter in this bigger scheme of things, and what use am I beyond being the payment owed in exchange for my parents' crimes?

Raising my arm, I hurl it over the edge and watch it spin through the mist, until it disappears from view. As quickly as I throw it, the stone is gone. I don't even hear it clatter on the way down.

I'm guessing my life won't matter beyond all of this.

Did it ever matter?

I turn back toward the direction of the house and nearly shriek out loud.

All three of my monstrous protectors are watching me from the depths of the trees with ferocity in their eyes. They look pissed as all hell, and I don't know how long they've been standing there.

"Are you alright?" Ky is the only one to stride over to me. The angular lines of his face are strained.

"Honestly?"

"I wouldn't want anything else from you, baby girl."

"I don't know."

The way he's looking at me—god, it's like he would destroy anyone and anything and scorch the very earth we stand on to prevent them from hurting me again. I fight the urge to look away, because it feels like it's all too much. I don't deserve someone, anyone, who would fight for me like that.

Ky pulls me into his warmth: sodden hair, damp clothes, and all. The glide of his big hands up and down my back feels like he can take all the stress knotted and embedded in my bones and melt it away with ease.

"Please don't disappear like that again. My heart can't fucking take it." His soft lips and rasp of his beard meets my forehead, and I can't help but want to curl into him on reflex. "*Please*."

A lump forms in my throat, and my bottom lip wobbles. I'm so pathetic. Why am I defenseless against his charm and his charisma, and his damn brutality? At times like this, I could so easily drown in the fantasy of these men returning my feelings for them. But I know that I have to chisel that anemic piece of my heart off and toss her into the raging ocean, leaving her to drown if I'm going to survive any of this intact.

He murmurs against my forehead. "Good thing we didn't have to go too far to find you. These two assholes were going to burn the entire peninsula to the ground if we didn't find any signs of where you'd gone."

Crap, I didn't even think about how long I'd been out here. Somewhere in my attempt to clear my head, it didn't cross my mind that they might wake up before I returned to the house.

"I'm sorry...I wasn't thinking...I—"

My weak attempt at an apology is interrupted when a loud incoming message tone blares through the trees. Three phones explode at the same time with a notification. It's so unexpected, I jolt with fright.

Ky rubs my back and continues to hold me to him, not bothering to reach for his phone that went off in his pocket. Instead, Thorne is the one to check the message. One that I can only assume is the same for all of them.

Beside him and a little further back, stands Raven. He seems only marginally less lethal than last night. *Marginally.* I'm guessing that waking up to find me missing hasn't gone down too well with my wolf. His arms are folded across his broad chest, and his hooded eyes scan the length of my body as if he's assessing me for damage.

I wonder if he can see all the broken pieces embedded in my veins. The shards hidden beneath my skin.

My stupid heart pitter-patters at the memory of being held by him in the bath last night without a single word. Just listening to the reassuring thud of his heartbeat while burrowed against his warm chest for what felt like hours.

Thorne quickly types something on his phone, and when he looks up, his eyes are a searing brand across my flesh.

"What is it?" Ky asks over the top of my head.

A flicker of something unreadable passes through his expression, followed by a grimace, and his next words are spoken through a tight jaw.

"We've been summoned. The Anguis have instructed us to bring in Foxglove Noire."

Ky shifts a little. I hear him swear through his teeth.

Fuck. Whatever this is, it can't be good.

Thorne continues to hold my gaze, and it feels like ice trickles straight down my spine. "Preparations for the Pledging ceremony have been moved to today."

CHAPTER 62
Thorne

The elevator doors seal us in with smooth efficiency, commencing our descent.

Beside me stands the last person I ever wanted to bring to this hellhole. Foxglove stands in the middle of us, with tense shoulders, braced for whatever might face us once we emerge into the council chambers of the Anguis. I doubt her life growing up in the world of Noire House has prepared her for this moment.

Even I'm not entirely certain of what is to come.

That's what has all of us on edge.

This summons from the Anguis was unexpected, to say the least. Perhaps more so because of the specific mention of her name. It left no uncertainty that we were required to present her this evening, and that has my pulse racing.

This is not part of the plan.

There is always a preparation before a Pledging ceremony, but this kind of urgent and unannounced ritual is stomach-churning, to say the least.

Dread eats its way through me and reaches sharpened claws for my throat.

Claiming her power and taking control of Noire House has been the intention right from the start. Only, now I'm finding myself tormented with the knowledge she might loathe me forever after this is all over.

If all I can do is keep her alive, that will have to be enough.

Do men like me deserve forgiveness after our souls have been irrevocably stained?

Right now, I'm not so sure.

The metal surface reflects back the warped image of the four of us, all dressed in black and wearing our skeletal masks. It's a familiar sight, yet the fourth skull, flanked by the rest of us, shouldn't be here. She should really be a million miles from the vile creatures concealed within this place.

The elevator slows before coming to a gliding halt. When the doors whoosh open, the long corridor stretches ahead of us in the usual darkened manner.

Down here, there's no daylight, only small alcoves lit by wall sconces, and there's always a lingering odor of ceremonial smoke and pungent incense.

I want to take her by the hand, but there are ways and customs that the Anguis demand. For us to remain hidden amongst them, we have to go through the motions today.

No matter how painful that might be.

So we file along the corridor, me at the front followed by our girl, while Ven and Ky are shoulder to shoulder behind her.

The four of us enter the chamber, the space already filled with a handful of council members—far fewer than I expected to be here—who are seated behind their long tables around the hexagonal-shaped room. Most of the time, when Ky and I are present for their gatherings, we have our stations where we watch over proceedings from the perimeter. However, today for the first time, we will be at the heart of events as they unfold.

Each of them wears a skull mask and blood-red, floor-length robes. Without looking closely, it is hard to distinguish one from another, particularly in the low lights scattered on the walls.

The air in the chamber is thick and oppressive.

There's an onyx stone altar in the center of the room. One that I've witnessed in countless rituals and ceremonies and power-hungry dealings held here. Usually, it is adorned with a golden cloth and ritualistic ornaments. However, it has been cleared of the usual book of the Anguis and ceremonial tools that occupy the stone top.

Instead, it sits empty and polished, and the sight of the bare surface reminds me of exactly what act that ancient altar is used for during a Pledging ceremony.

"Foxglove Noire, the pleasure is all ours to have you join us today." From among the seated members a man stands and crosses over to us.

As he draws near, my jaw clenches like a steel trap.

It's the asshole who tried to bid against me at the auction. The entitled prick who wanted my girl.

"My name is Ivan Victore. I shall be inspecting you on behalf of the council of the Anguis." He extends a slender hand through the draped fabric of his robe. "If you'll kindly step this way."

She doesn't immediately go with him, and while that should make me relieved to see her hesitation, it also has me fearful of any repercussions that might come of being seen as uncooperative during her inspection.

"Miss Noire." He repeats her name with a clipped tone that makes me want to shatter his jaw against the corner of that stone altar. "This is not *optional*."

Ven's darkness threatens to spill out of him as he sucks in a breath through gritted teeth. Ky isn't faring much better.

"Fine." Her tone is distant.

He leads her over to the polished slab of stone and guides her to sit on the edge. Foxglove is wearing a long-sleeved black dress that wraps around her and ties at the waist. Her hair is braided over one shoulder, and her bright blue eyes seem to glow behind the skull mask covering the upper half of her face. As her body turns to face us, I catch her gaze, willing her with every silent force I can muster to keep her focus on me.

Please.

Please don't let this be the beginning of the end.

"We'll begin with you lying back." Ivan stands over her, and the claws in my throat start to shred my skin.

"While this might be a tradition overlooked by time, the *inspection* prior to a Pledging ceremony has been resurrected just for you, Miss Noire." His eyes wander all over her body as she is laid out atop the altar.

My stomach curdles immediately seeing her there.

"A long time ago, this was a process intended to confirm chastity on the part of the heir to be offered up in a Pledging, and to guarantee that a lineage was being safely guarded by the Households. But now it serves more of a ceremonial nature."

Ivan adjusts the front of his robes, like this is some fucking privileged position he's been given by whoever on the council is overseeing this bullshit.

"The Anguis uphold our rites and customs with pride, as you know." He continues. "And one can only assume you are no pure, unsullied virgin considering your recent choices...shall we say."

Ky lets out a rough noise.

My own breathing grows more unsteady the longer this man hovers over her like a predator about to swoop on his prey from a great height.

I don't know what an inspection prior to a Pledging ceremony entails, but seeing this man again after the way he wanted her the night of the auction—knowing *who* he is connected to—alarms ring a shrill warning in my mind.

"The heir to Noire House..." he runs a finger to lift her braid, and that tiny point of contact is almost enough to have me launching across the room. "Who would have known you would grow up to be such a prized possession."

His hand begins to wander further down her shoulder, and then it happens, he tugs at the bow, tying her dress in place.

The three of us move in unison. I've already got my gun out and trained on the man's torso, and Ky is reaching for his. Meanwhile, Ven hasn't bothered with a weapon. I'm pretty sure he plans on punching straight through this man's chest with his bare fists.

"I wouldn't step any closer if I were you, Calliano." Ivan surveys me with disdain. "Keep your dogs on a leash, lest we have to put the lot of you down."

"Don't fucking lay a finger on her." Ky growls.

Ivan gives us a perverse smile. "Your bravado is rather touching, but perhaps you have forgotten that we are the ones who oversee all the necessary requirements of a Pledging ceremony. And the inspection of Miss Noire must be completed before we can allow you to secure a transfer of her inheritance."

"This is complete bullshit." Ky continues to reach for his weapon, and I haven't lowered mine.

My eyes flick down to meet hers. I can see where her lips have turned pale.

"You forget your place," he snaps. "This girl is the direct descendant of Andreas Noire, and an unclaimed heir. In the eyes of the Anguis, her body belongs to us until the Pledging ceremony."

This man is already dead. If I don't see to it, Ven will most likely carve him to pieces in his sleep. But we're trapped until the final piece moves on the chessboard.

"Right now, you gentlemen have no recourse here. The handover of power in the eyes of the Anguis is yet to come. This is not some silly little auction where you can buy your way to success, and until the Pledging ceremony, may I remind you that threatening a council member can be very hazardous for your health indeed."

As he speaks, he continues to unwrap the material of her dress until she's laid out and exposed atop the stone altar, except for her bra and underwear. The fabric falls open on either side of her chest and stomach.

I lower my gun and stare, helpless, at our girl being subjected to this lewd and archaic ritual.

"It's ok." There's a softness in her voice as she keeps her eyes trained on me.

Ivan moves around to stand beside her head, and runs a finger from her sternum tattoo right up to her throat. "So obedient. So pliant."

My stomach flips at the sight of his hand daring to make contact with her bare skin. "While the designated power of the Noire lineage is not yours, *yet*, I can see that she will be the perfect subordinate for you, Calliano. You've chosen well."

I'm imagining every way possible to hack his arms off. Then I'll feed them to him as strips of flesh.

But his filthy fingers keep wandering along the length of her exposed figure.

All we can do is stand there, frozen and tortured, when he runs two fingers across the tops of her breasts and begins to murmur phrases in an old language as he drags over her skin. Maybe he's speaking Latin, maybe it's the devil's fucking tongue itself, but either way, I don't care. Sweat beads on my forehead, and I'm about two seconds from giving into the rage consuming me.

She belongs to me. Foxglove Noire is ours.

Only the three of us get to touch her.

"Keep your eyes on me." My words feel like gravel and chipped stone between my teeth. I'm begging her with my stare locked onto hers to *just hold on*. To know we will get through this monster's twisted gamesmanship.

Out of the corner of my eye, Ivan watches me the whole time. Guzzling down every flicker of reaction that I fail to conceal behind my mask.

I know this is his way of getting me back for the night of the auction. The night he desired her and lost.

This explains the urgency of this meeting today. It also explains why there are so few of the council present. No doubt, these are all his personal friends from within the ranks of the Anguis.

This isn't part of the plan, and yet, there is nothing I can do because he's connected to the very scum we are about to destroy.

If I give into the emotion I'm raging with, everything we've suffered will have been for nothing.

Each of us is an inch from losing it as we endure witnessing his actions. Acid rises in my throat as I tighten my grip around the base of my lowered gun.

He wanted his chance to publicly humiliate me. To lay hands on our girl right in front of us, in the very place where he knew there was nothing we could do without guaranteeing a death sentence should we dare retaliate.

I see her grimace as his fingers carve a sickening path down the softness of her stomach, still pressing and touching her in the most harrowing display possible. She flinches as he reaches her lower stomach, and I'm so fucking sorry for all of it. For everything. Regret drowns me as Ivan continues his vile progress.

The moment he lays a hand over her covered sex, Ky has to grab hold of Ven. Frenetic violence threatens to erupt out of all of us, laying waste to this entire chamber. There's a dull roar in my ears as I struggle to remain standing.

Baby blue eyes hold my own, and even behind her mask, I can see her agony at the way he's defiling her right out in the open. Just like her father had always threatened.

She's so fucking strong, and this is all my doing.

My heart is trying to crawl out of my chest and get to her. What if he goes further? What if he violates her even more than this? Can I live with myself weighed down by guilt that I let that kind of thing happen to my girl?

As I'm about to lose my goddamn mind, he stops. But not before giving me a look that tells me he's enjoying every second of this fucked up power-play.

A look that says he's done me some kind of favor by not molesting her with his repulsive fingers.

"Wonderful. Thank you, Miss Noire." Ivan says the words like she's pleased him somehow, and it makes me want to be sick. All the memories of my own past are floating close to the surface after witnessing his inspection. Unwanted soft caresses and squeezed flesh. Perfume suffocating me as I was held down, unable to speak or move.

He adjusts his robes and stands beside the altar, seemingly content that he's torn all of our chests open with his disgusting excuse for a ritual. "You may cover yourself now."

This chamber reeks. All I can smell is death and the rotting corpses this place has been founded on. Foxglove sits up, trembling, and wraps her dress hastily around her. Folding in on herself as she fumbles with the ties. I'm right there beside her now, taking over to secure it for her as her hands drop into her lap.

My only care is how to remove her from this shithole as fast as possible and scrub every last hateful vestige of this place from her perfect skin.

"I'm going to get you out of here." The words taste poisonous on my tongue. Right now, I'm trapped in a world where I've set fire to everything around me, and the house of cards I've built with my brother is an inferno raging around my ears.

"We have one final matter, before you are free to leave...the council has an issue to attend to." Ivan gestures in the direction of the doorway we entered through.

Behind us, there's a shuffling noise, and two men dressed in crimson robes with skulls covering their faces enter the room. Despite having their identities partially concealed, I don't recognize either, and they lead in a third figure who has a black hood covering their face.

"Is this a fucking joke to you?" Ky spits. He's still got one hand planted in the center of Ven's chest and gun trained on Ivan gripped in the other.

I help Foxglove down off the altar. Not wanting her to be up there any longer than absolutely necessary, and drag her against my side. There's a stabbing pain in my chest at how cold her skin feels; the way she's numb beneath my arm. She's locked away inside her own mind and doesn't respond to my touch.

It's exactly what I used to do in order to cope, too.

"The Anguis are aware of this man's undue threats against Miss Noire." Ivan pulls off the black hood, to reveal Miles Crane. His nose has been busted, and there's dried blood coming from the corner of his purple lips. A rope gag is tied around his mouth. He stinks of methylated spirits and vomit.

"We do not take kindly to those who attempt to interfere in a Pledging ceremony for their own gain." Ivan kicks out the man's knees, and he slumps to the ground. His eyes are glazed over, and it's obvious he's only loosely aware of his surroundings. "We offer our humble apologies, Miss Noire, that this man threatened your life and those you are Pledged to."

How dare this motherfucker try and manipulate this situation for his own gain. To act as if what he did two minutes ago wasn't a gross violation in its own right? Crane absolutely deserves to be eliminated for what he did, but I'm seething with rage that Ivan is attempting to claim this as something the Anguis have done for her out of kindness.

They don't give a shit. These people are only out for one thing, and that is power.

"Flannaghty." He snaps his fingers in the direction of Ven, and my jaw is clenched so tight I hear a pop. "If you would be so kind."

Fuck. *Fuck*. FUCK.

This is what he wants. To use Ven in the worst way. Abusing him a little more, because the Anguis trained him to be the one who bloodied his hands on their behalf over and over.

Like some sort of robot, he steps past Ky, tearing the gun from his hands as he does so, and advances on the man knelt in front of the stone altar.

Raising the gun, he aims the barrel at the man's forehead. There's nothing but ice in his expression, as he stands there without saying a word.

Jesus Christ. I've got my girl damn near catatonic beneath my arm, and Ven in what looks to be a similar state. Ky is about to explode where he stands just off to my left, and I can't even tell which way is up.

He lets the gun hang there in the air. Allowing the bruised and battered figure of Miles Crane time to slowly focus on the scene in front of him. Ven is giving him a moment to come to terms with the finality of these seconds. Before the gavel falls and justice is delivered when his skull is blown to pieces.

Ven casts a glance over to one side. Ghosting a look in our direction.

And that's when I see it. I see it in every strained muscle in his neck and jaw, that he doesn't want to be their monster-for-hire paraded on display. Obeying orders on command like the mindless servant they want him to be reduced to in her eyes.

Ven has been the executioner for the Anguis longer than any of us can remember, and this...this matters to him.

She matters to him.

It's killing him to have her witness this stain forever

marking his blood. The heart he lost a lifetime ago has found a way to struggle back to life, against all odds, and I know with every second his finger flexes against that trigger...he's churning on the inside.

Because it's exactly how I feel, too. Wondering if there's any hope left for her to do anything except push both of us away once she catches a glimpse of what our blackened and bloody souls are truly capable of.

The gritty reality is that we've been raised by the foulest of the foul, and our insides are rotten. I can't stop and think too long about what this girl might see whenever she looks at us. Is it three flawed men who have been bound up in circumstances beyond their control, or three beasts with nothing but bloodlust pumping hot and thick through their veins?

Ven doesn't draw it out.

The moment is over in an instant. The double pop ripples around the room, and Miles Crane slumps to the floor. That shithead deserved to die, but not like this. Not when it's under the command of Ivan Victore and the Anguis. It should have been the three of us hunting him down and taking our revenge in her name.

A swathe of ruby-red blood spills across the polished stone from the hole in his head, and I don't hesitate a second longer.

I get my girl out of there.

All while praying that she'll maybe one day look at me with anything but hatred in those blue eyes.

CHAPTER 63

Ky

"That rat bastard. I'll bury a hatchet in his chest and feed him to the pigs myself."

I slam the door and pull Fox onto my lap so she can straddle me. There's no way I'm going to survive this drive back to the safety of our home without having her this close.

Our girl is hardly with us as it is.

She's ice cold to the touch as I wrench the skull masks off both of us and toss them into the empty backseat beside me. Stroking her face, I try to draw her eyes to mine. Right now, they're way too glazed over for my liking. But if that's what she had to do to cope with what she just went through, then we'll have to deal with it.

"I'm here. I'm right fucking here, baby girl. You come back to me whenever you're ready."

Fox blinks a couple of times before burying her face in the crook of my neck.

As I run long strokes up and down her back, my eyes meet Thorne's in the rearview mirror from his position in the driver's seat. He looks fucking wrecked. Ven is a black hole in the passenger seat next to him. The chunky silver rings on his fingers gleam as he drums furiously on the car door.

"I should have slaughtered the lot of them." He barks out after we've been driving for a good fifteen minutes in stony silence.

My chest aches for him, knowing what he had to do in there like some sort of lap dog. The way that asshole clicked his fingers and demanded his services was the worst kind of penance. Forcing him to be their death dealer, when I know how much it would have devastated him to show Fox that side.

"You'll get your chance." Thorne's voice is steady, but I see the remorse pouring off him. This goddamn plan of his was all well and good when Fox was just a name and a vengeance we were due to collect on paper...but now...

Jesus, now, she's part of us. We're all embedded in each other's DNA, and hers binds us all together in a way none of us ever anticipated.

Tentative fingers play with my hair at the nape of my neck, and at least I know she's in there. Even if it's somewhere far away for the time being.

We make it back to the compound, and follow each other inside. I don't know where we go from here, but this needs to be dealt with right now. And I'm not letting anyone leave this room until we figure out which fucking way is up.

"Both of you. In the lounge." I point at Ven and Thorne, as I guide Fox to walk in front of me. When we reach the first of the large couches, I settle her down and crouch in front of her.

"Fox, you gotta talk to me. Tell me what we can do." I cup the side of her face.

Her gaze lands on me with a fire raging deep within. She glances over at Thorne, who hovers by the big windows, and Ven, who leans on both hands against the back of the couch.

"Whatever it is, you name it. Rake those claws of yours down all our faces and make us fucking bleed if you want." I don't care if that's what this girl needs to do. "Baby girl, I'll gladly shed blood for you. It can't make up for what happened in there, but if it can do something—anything—to fix this, then I'll willingly slice open my veins if that's what you want."

For an agonizingly long moment, Fox looks at me, then shakes her head. "I thought about it. I honestly did. But no, I don't need that from you."

"Anything. Just talk to us."

She takes a deep inhale through her nose.

"You know what I thought about in there? Was how you were right. You were right about everything. That man was exactly the kind of evil who would have eventually laid a claim, if you hadn't come for me." She covers my hand with her own, and my heart beats a harried rhythm. Fox isn't screaming or trying to murder any of us with her bare hands. Even though she'd have every right to, the energy coming off her now is calmer than any of us deserve.

"And to make it worse, if it wasn't him, it would have been a man like Miles Crane. And if it wasn't that slimy asshole, it would have been Massimo Ilone."

Thorne crosses over and crouches down beside me. Resting a forehead on her knee and gripping tight to her hip. "I didn't know what it would entail—" He murmurs against her skin.

Fox runs her fingers through his hair. "I know you didn't."

"How do I fix this, when I didn't properly protect you?" His voice is layered with guilt.

"I'm yours...and that's what I need."

I tilt my head up to look at her and make sure of what she's saying.

"Gonna need you to be really specific for us right now."

"Being in there, it confirmed for me what I already knew. I don't want to be owned by anyone but you."

Thorne lets out a shuddering breath, and he presses a kiss to her thigh. Ven's fingers tighten against the chair. He's still bristling with so much violence, I don't know if he's going to be able to give Fox what she needs, or if he's going to collide into her with a cataclysmic force demanding release.

She senses that he can't, or won't, move—deciding to close the gap between them like she always fucking instinctively knows how to do. Fox gives Thorne and I both a quick brush across the sides of our faces and then gets to her feet.

Fox tugs on the tie of her dress, wrenching at it until the entire thing comes free, and she balls it up in her hand. Standing before Ven, she holds the scrunched-up material out. Our girl is so fucking perfect, all of her curves and tattoos and strength on show as she finds a way to bring us to our knees for her.

"You see this? I want to burn it. I don't want a single memory left of being touched by anyone except you. Make me yours, however you need to do that. If you need to piss all over me, I'll kneel right here and let you."

Holy shit. The room around us crackles with the conviction of her words.

"Take away the feeling of that asshole still crawling all over my skin. *Please* do this for me."

CHAPTER 64
Fox

Ven's face contorts as I toss the dress so that it slides across the floor. Give me a lighter and I'd gladly set it aflame right here. That is one piece of clothing I never want to come near my skin ever again in my life.

Standing before him in only my heels and underwear, I keep my face turned to his.

My deity. My god. My fucking salvation in all of this.

They all are.

"Use me." I bring both my wrists together and offer them up to my murderous prince of night. "Make me forget everything that cunt did."

Raven's eyes are two furious voids as he stares down at me. But he can't scare me off. I've looked into the eyes of a real monster tonight, and if this man needs to cut out my heart to prove it only beats for the three of them, so be it.

"Why should we even bother?" He looks ready to spit on my face.

Maybe I'd like that.

"Please. I need—" My eyes drop to the side. Heat flushes

across my chest as the words tingle on the very tip of my tongue.

"You think we give a shit." He swirls with fury, and right then, I know I can trust them all with this. They won't judge me for it or question why. My three beasts are the only people in the world I could ever dare admit this to.

"Fuck me like you hate me. Use me. I don't care, do whatever you want to me." My heart thuds manically against its cage behind my ribs.

The room turns electric.

His upper lip curls, and dark hair falls across his eyes in a way that leaves my knees weak.

Raven is sin, and I'm running as fast as I can away from salvation, heading straight into the deadly sharp jaws of these men.

I push my wrists up higher, confirming my offering.

"It's either your belt, or mine, Ven." Thorne is on his feet now, his voice has an edge to it that makes my thighs clench together. Ky moves to the other side of me and slides his fingers into my hair. He yanks the tie out of the end, before tugging and working my braid loose, freeing my curls to fall over one shoulder.

My eyes stay locked on the man in front of me. I keep my hands together and dutifully wait.

"I just killed a man, and you're begging me to fuck you." Raven snarls.

"Yes."

"What does that say about you, that your pussy gets wet for cold-blooded murderers."

He's right. I don't know what that says about me and how I'm just as fucked up as anyone else in this room. But there's no denying that I crave the nectar of their darkness.

"Please."

There's a cold laugh that bursts out of him.

"I've already killed for you."

My pulse kicks up.

"And I will fucking destroy anyone who dares touch what is mine."

I'm trembling, but not out of fear.

"Let's see how breakable you really are. Since you're offering yourself up like a willing little sacrifice." His tattooed hands reach over his head, and he drags his shirt off in one smooth motion. The silver of his chain and rings catch the light, drawing my eyes down his planes of muscles and ink.

A throb pulses in my clit when I see his fingers work at his belt. Remembering when he last used it on me in the forest. Holy fuck, what would it be like to have him do that in front of both Ky and Thorne.

I can feel the flood of wetness in my pussy just thinking about them all seeing exactly how drenched I get being spanked.

He slips the leather through the loops of his waistband, then expertly binds my wrists together in front of me. As he cinches it tight, I notice how the notches go all the way to the end—my mouth goes dry, that detail hadn't registered the day I was bent over his bike.

Does he use this same belt—the one that has brought me pain intertwined with pleasure—on his victims before they meet their death?

I don't have time to focus on that, with his next actions coming fast and aggressive. The beast writhing inside him acts, first yanking the front of my bra down to expose my breasts. My nipples pebble with the rush of cool air, and he pinches one of them so hard I gasp.

Beside me, Ky has moved over to join Thorne. They're both standing in my line of vision, allowing themselves a front-on view of me. And when I see my Viking's strong hands working to undress them both, I have to bite my lip. God, I love seeing them together, and it only ratchets up my need for all of them.

"Jesus. One look at the two of you and her cunt is already dripping." My wolf slides his tattooed hand up over my collarbone, wrapping the front of my throat and squeezing. I'm so close to whimpering, my teeth dig harder into the swell of my bottom lip as I give him the attention he's demanding from me with unrelenting pressure around the column of my neck.

"We're gonna make a mess of you, baby girl." Ky's lips are on Thorne's neck as he speaks, and my core tightens with pure, greed-soaked lust.

Raven flexes his fingers. "I might just chain you to my bed and keep you there like a filthy little fuckhole to use." He bears down with increased pressure, slowly restricting my breathing as his incendiary stare devours me alive. "Maybe I'll put a collar on this fragile little neck."

Bonfire sparks fly through my veins where blood used to be.

That image, of myself naked and collared and curled up beside his heavy boots is what finally drags a whimper out of me. The one I've been battling to contain.

"What do you say, Thorne? You want to see our pretty little slut on her knees in nothing but a collar?" Ky watches me with the devil in his eyes.

Thorne's jaw pulses. His azure eyes follow the spot where Raven's hand firmly grips my throat, and the sight causes his pupils to blow out.

Holy shit. *Holy shit.* He likes that idea as much as I do and I think my brain might have broken more than a little.

"This cunt is ours to use whenever and however we want."

I nod.

Raven's upper lip curls. "Say it."

"Yours." My throat works a swallow underneath his palm. "Yours to use."

He lets go of my neck, and slaps the side of my tit. Then he's on me, his hot mouth closes over my flesh as teeth bite down on the side of my breast, leaving bruising marks, before he shifts across and does the same to the other.

Right now, I wish my hands weren't bound because as much as I want to shove him off and punch him in retaliation for the pain searing beneath my skin, I also want to sink my fingers into his dark hair and hold him there.

Having his mouth on me feels like a dream scenario. But the brute senses me attempting to chase after his path of punishment. Pulling back, he withdraws faster than I can catch my breath.

"So damn easy to bruise." He taunts.

My stomach caves. I'm entranced with the idea of waking up tomorrow painted by their marks.

"Bend her over, Ky." Thorne's rough command sends my pulse fluttering. Fuck. He nudges my Viking toward me, and the wicked expression right there on his face—as he obeys the man we both happily would do anything for—tells me everything I need to know about what is coming next.

"Look at these perfect tits. Begging for attention, just like your pussy is." Ky's green eyes bounce between the reddened welts left by Raven's teeth, and back up to my mouth. I know exactly what he's doing. He's calculating how far he can bend the rules, while still technically following Thorne's instruction.

His tongue touches against his front teeth for a moment, before he chooses to pounce. Fisting his hand in my hair, he shoves me sideways in the direction of the armrest along the L-shaped couch. The force tips me over, and with my wrists bound together, I have no way to prevent myself from falling face-first into the cushions.

Leaving my ass high in the air, exposed to all three of them.

Ky makes a filthy noise and shoves my head harder, instructing me to stay exactly where I am. "Before we came along, you had to have a drawer full of rubber dicks just to keep yourself satisfied. A horny little bitch who wanted someone to pin you down and rail you whenever and wherever."

Oh, god. Every raw nerve ending pulses with desire when Ky starts running his mouth. My pussy is a mess, clenching and already aching in response to his crass words. Fingernails scrape and scratch against the cushion beneath me. This angle is humiliating, and yet knowing that all three of them are looking at me bent over for their use sends heat pooling in my core.

Ky slides a finger beneath the side of my panties and tugs backward, wedging the material between my pussy lips. "Did you fuck yourself with those toys every night, praying for us? I bet you got on your knees and rode your fake cocks and still never got off the way you do when we use your body." The lace is pulled tight against my clit, and he uses it to create rough friction against the part of me that screams for their touch.

"Oh, fuck. Ky. *Please.*" I arch my back and try to push against the movement of his hand. If I can tempt him to slide his thick fingers through my slit and plunge inside me...

"That's enough," Thorne growls, taking back control. Probably sensing that Ky has about as little restraint as I do right now. "You want to be truly owned by us? You're going to take two of us at once."

My eyes nearly drop out of my head. God, yes, please.

"Little whores like you love being stuffed full, since one is never enough." My wolf's voice is mocking. Filled with disdain. He's playing this part to perfection, and it sends shame burning hot and bright through my chest.

The cool of his rings makes me flinch when his palm glides over my hip. Then he fists the side of the fabric and yanks it down. He leaves the soaked evidence of my arousal on display, stretched tight, halfway down my thighs.

Humiliation swirls in my stomach and I try to adjust my

weight, but I'm trapped with my heels tipping me forward over the armrest.

"Jesus. She's so fucking wet just hearing that. It gets you off, doesn't it? A little cum slut like you will crawl around with her ass in the air all day long if you think there's a chance of someone filling you up."

My mouth sinks into the cushion. There's hot, burning embarrassment in my throat. Because he's right, and it's snaking me into a spiral of pathetic lust.

"*Christ.*" I hear Ky's voice. He sounds like he's as wound up as I'm feeling, and while I can't tell for certain, movement indicates he's sunk down on his knees behind me. "Please, Thorne." He's begging, and I'm whimpering with the anticipation of finally being given some small amount of relief.

"What do you want, hmm?" Thorne's dark voice looms closer, and I know he's not talking to me. I can only hear the rasp of material and slick noises of wet flesh. It sends my horny brain wailing that maybe Ky is eye level with my pussy, while on his knees worshiping their cocks. "Has our good boy earned the right to lick her pussy?" He gruffly asks Raven.

I'm so fucking wet, it should be shameful.

That's when the cold of my wolf's rings presses down on both sides of my ass, sending a shudder straight up my spine. He spreads my cheeks, and something wet drips down over my exposed hole. God, I know straight away it isn't lube. It's definitely saliva.

"Make her shake. Don't let her come."

Ky is feral as his mouth closes over me from behind. The scrape of his beard sends flashes and sparks down to my fingers and toes. He's so fucking wicked with his tongue. I'm addicted to the way this man uses his mouth on me and worships my pussy. With each swirl and flattened drag through my slit, I'm making desperate noises muffled against the cushions.

Spearing into me, he uses both hands to spread me as wide

as possible for him while my panties dig into my thighs. The sensitive buds of my nipples rub against the couch. Heat surges through me, and my clit begs for more as full body quivers take hold.

"Enough."

Blood pounds like a drum in my ears, but there's no mistaking how rough Thorne's voice comes out as Ky is dragged off me.

Both of us are panting.

Maybe all of us fucking are.

The muscles in my calves strain as my toes dig into the front of my heels. I'm left trembling on the precipice of my climax that has been ruthlessly denied. Damp coats my brow, and the edge of Raven's belt twists and digs into my wrists.

Cold metal slides between my shoulders and my bra straps, followed by the feel of them drawing tight, before being sliced straight through. The same happens on the other side, then the clasp at the back is either torn apart or cut open, I'm not sure. Right now my blood is spinning and I don't know which way is up.

My head gets yanked back, and I yelp at the sting against my scalp when I'm pulled upright by my hair. My wolf's heat and muscled frame presses the length of my spine. Along with his rock-hard cock digging into me from behind.

"Such a dirty girl, dripping all over his face." He bites at my ear lobe.

Right now, too many sensations are flying through my body, but I'm vaguely aware that I've got my panties bunched around my thighs and my sliced up bra falls away from my body. They really are using me, exactly like I asked, and even though I'm a shaking mess, I can't help but succumb to the way my heart grows about ten sizes bigger in my chest.

This is their version of worship, and I feel nothing but treasured.

"Get over there and ride his cock like a good fucking girl." Thorne instructs me, then adds, "Leave the heels on."

Holy fuck. I'm an absolute slut for filthy Thorne when he comes out to play.

Raven grunts in my ear, "What do you say?"

"Thank you, Daddy."

As I wet my lips, my wolf seizes the opportunity to bite down on the fleshy part at the top of my shoulder. Reminding me with that sharp, stinging pain; even though he hasn't touched me yet, he's still owning my body just like I begged him to. The marks he's leaving patterned all over my body are going to be embedded in the fabric of my being.

"Ky's going to stretch you out and fill you up. We need that greedy cunt of yours nice and loose to take both of us."

I gulp and nod. Not entirely sure that I'll make it to where my Viking is positioning himself on the couch without falling over.

"Lose the panties, baby girl, and bring that pussy over here."

He's got his cock fisted in one hand, stroking himself as his green gaze rakes down my body. Goosebumps coat my skin, and I awkwardly manage to slide my underwear off. I'm still tied up in my wolf's belt, so I have to use my knees to cross the couch and straddle him, then pause, waiting for his approval.

"Always such a good girl." The way his voice rasps over me is way too fucking dangerous for my health.

The metal of his piercing juts up between us, and my mouth waters as he uses one hand to stroke through my slickness. Coating his length, all the while his hungry eyes stay fixed on me.

Make that three sets of hungry eyes on me. I know there are two more watching the show I'm about to put on with Ky.

"Oh, fuck." Mouth hanging open, he slides the tip over my clit, rubbing the silver bar against my swollen bundle of nerves.

I'm so close from when he was eating me out just before that my orgasm comes racing back in hard and fast. "Fuck. Don't stop. Please, don't stop." Shackled hands shoot out to brace against his chest as I beg relentlessly. I'm rolling my hips to chase how good it feels, my stomach tightening and tingles spread through to my toes.

Thorne grabs my jaw and forces me to meet his piercing blue eyes. "Come for us." With his other hand he reaches down and shoves his thumb against my clit. "Now."

I do.

I fall apart on a whimpering moan. My body hunches over with the force of sensation crashing over me.

That's when Ky lifts my hips, and shoves inside. Sinking me down over his length to take him all the way in one movement. My pussy is still clenching, and he hisses out a dark curse.

"Jesus. Fuck. She's so fucking wet."

"Good. Fill her up and get her messy. She needs to come again." Thorne forces his thumb past my lips, making me suck on it and taste myself.

My eyelids flutter closed. I'm glowing. Heat thunders around my body as Ky fucks up into me, making my breasts bounce with each thrust. He's stretching me with each pump of his hips, and the feel of his piercing against the perfect spot inside my pussy is like heaven.

"You're gonna have to spin around, Ky."

He doesn't ask questions, simply does as instructed. Moving us both so that he's still lying on his back and now both our heads are facing toward the edge of the couch. It tips me forward and that's when I understand exactly why he's shifted us to this position.

"Our slut gets extra wet when she's got a dick in her mouth. Let's see how well she handles two at once." Raven slaps the side of my face with his hard cock. Making my insides squirm with how degrading it feels to have him use me like this.

My other two men stand before me shoulder to shoulder, each stroking their thick, veined lengths, and I let out a needy whimper.

Well, shit.

This is really fucking happening.

I'm getting railed from underneath by Ky, and these two gods fist their cocks so that I can try and suck both of them at the same time. It's not elegant or skilled; I'm really nothing more than a sloppy mess of saliva as they take turns pushing past my lips. Feeding me their lengths and sliding across my tongue while I try my best to relax and let my jaw hang open as wide as possible.

"That's it. Gag on both of us." My wolf grips my hair as I press both their cocks together with my wrists still bound, and fit both their heads in my mouth.

It feels awkward and filthy, and I'm out of my head with pleasure.

Spit collects at the corner of my lips and runs down my chin. My eyes are watering as I hum around their velvety lengths. They both feel so fucking good and their musky scent is coaxing my next climax closer and closer.

"Fuck. She's squeezing my cock like a fist." Ky's fingers dig into my hips as he holds me in place and punches into me from below. "I'm gonna fill you up, baby girl. That's it. Take all of me just like that."

His filthy words tease the crest of my orgasm, beckoning it ever nearer.

"Fuck. Your mouth is too fucking good." Thorne pulls back, and so does Raven.

Have these two ever shared anything this intimate before? I don't know and right now I can't stop to try and work out how much they might be enjoying rubbing their cocks together because I'm being dragged over the edge of my next orgasm.

Ky slips his hand between our bodies and rubs my clit.

It only takes a few firm circles of his thumb for me to shatter.

He's grunting and cursing as his hips punch up, shooting hot cum inside me. I'm floating off somewhere up in the night sky. My body is limp and overwhelmed with pleasure and I don't know how I'm going to take any more.

"Sit her up. She needs her legs under her."

At this point, I'm their plaything to use. I don't even know if I'm capable of thinking straight. What I do know is that this feels an awful lot like worship and nothing like them hating me.

I'm so fucking in love with them, it crushes my lungs.

I don't feel hollow, or desperate, or ashamed at the way they're using me. Instead, it feels like I'm torched alive with a fire lit beneath my skin. Everything melts away into oblivion and it's just them.

Protecting me.

Taking care of me.

I've never had this sensation before, the sense of being desired. It's a heady, delirious feeling. One that makes me want to blurt everything out to them while floating on this unbelievably soft bed of serenity and rose petals.

Firm hands move me off Ky, and guide me backward. "That's it, beautiful. You take my cock so well."

Oh, god. It's Raven. And he's got that same tone in his voice when he took care of me at his cabin. Hearing his praise has me flown out of my head.

I don't know what flipped in him between when we started this, and now, but I'm not equipped to handle caring from my wolf.

My moan is needy and full of overstimulated pleasure as I sink over him. My back leans against his chest, and someone has guided my feet under me, opening me up wide.

Raven's fingers tease the spot where he's buried deep, and there's the welling of my cum mixed with Ky's. He presses at my entrance, working a finger in beside his cock as I stretch to fit both.

Then he gently eases out, bringing that hand up to my mouth and presses his digit on my tongue. "See how good you both taste. Show me how much you love us all being mixed together like this." My lips close over his knuckle, and the tangy burst of flavor coats my tongue. I do love it. I love *them*.

He fucks my mouth with his finger for a moment, then draws out with a wet noise, finding the place where we're joined once more. Stretching me a little further.

"Foxglove, you need to relax for me." Thorne has shifted over the top of us both. Bracing himself on his hands, he runs a tongue over my sensitive nipples and sucks one into his hot mouth. Ky fastens over my other breast, and he lets out a gravelly noise against my blazing hot skin.

My back curves giving them greater access. Begging, incoherent strings of words tumble out.

"Daddy. Please. I need you." *Please.* I hook my bound wrists over his head and gaze at him from beneath a layer of heavy lashes.

"Christ." Thorne swoops in and takes my mouth. As he kisses me, Raven's cock twitches, and his lips work the sensitive skin above my pulse point.

I moan against Thorne's mouth as his fingers mingle with Raven's, both of them press at my entrance. Swiping through the cum gathered at the base of my wolf's fat cock, Thorne uses it to stroke over himself.

"She's fucking dripping," Raven murmurs against the side of my throat.

He hums his approval. "Good girl. Breathe. Focus on how good you feel. Stay nice and loose for us, baby."

My mouth hangs open as he talks me through it. My wolf's hand drops away, chased by Thorne pressing the head of his cock against my entrance. Fitting himself to slip just inside.

I gasp as the tip of him breaches my entrance and he holds there. Letting me adjust to the fullness for a second.

Raven wraps his fingers around the front of my neck to collar me. Not squeezing, but he's holding me up as I melt beneath the sensation of them both.

Thorne strains for control, and a grunt reverberates through my body as he shifts forward and keeps working himself deeper inside my pussy. The stretch verges on painful, but my body is so lax and boneless, it melts quickly into the most divine sensation.

"Ffffuck."

"You're doing so good, baby girl." Ky is somewhere close, but I'm so overwhelmed by the fullness I squeeze my eyes shut and dissolve. Lost to the intensity and divinity of this moment.

Their cocks are both inside me, and Thorne sinks forward some more. We're all joined together as my walls stretch, and the feeling of having both my men like this—at the same time—is turning my entire world on its head.

I want more of this. I want more of them.

Need bubbles up, and I'm moaning and whimpering with the rush of pleasure gripping hold of me.

"You good?" I hear Thorne's voice and he's placing the softest kisses against my mouth, the kind that makes me fall even harder, like the lovesick fool I am.

"Thorne." My wolf's voice is raspy. "Jesus. You need to start moving."

"God. You feel..." Even in my blanked-out state, I know Thorne's throaty voice isn't really talking to me. He's just as lost in this, and from the way Raven is panting behind me, he's rapidly falling apart, too.

"I'm nearly there." Fingers dig tighter in my throat as the man behind me tenses up.

"We're going to fill you, baby." Thorne's mouth hovers over mine. Then he glides slow and deep, fucking all of us, and goes in for the killer blow. "Fill her right up, Ky. Stuff her pretty little mouth with your dick and show her what a good girl she is."

I'm done. Expired. Gone and flown off somewhere amongst the stars.

My head is guided to the side, and that sinful pierced tip pushes into my mouth as I whimper and flutter around both their lengths, filling me to the point that I'm spun out of my head.

"Clean him up, and say thank you for letting you have that pretty boy cock."

Thorne's dirty talk does us all in as he thrusts his hips, sliding their dicks together inside me. I fall apart, moaning sloppy, incoherent sounds around Ky's length. My pussy clamps down on both of them as my inner walls squeeze in a rhythm, and I explode into a million pinpricks of white light. I'm riding a bright, streaking trail through outer space as both my men grunt and lose it. Ky pulls out, but the weight of his praise washes over me more than I hear the words specifically. I'm pretty sure all I can hear is my thundering pulse. Thorne fucks us through our climaxes, rocking our bodies together in unison as their cum fills me and floods my pussy.

We're nothing but racing hearts and murmured words, and therc's the feeling of hands caressing every part of me.

And as they treat me more gently and carefully than I could ever hope for, I curl into the warmth of their touches and kisses and whispers.

These men who claimed me, held me captive, and stole me, have done exactly that. Only the victim here isn't my heart; she has willingly flown to them without a backward glance.

I don't know if I'll ever want to escape.

CHAPTER 65
Ky

"How does Thorne Calliano have access to a private island?"

Fox twists around in the passenger seat so she can sort of face in my direction while we're driving. Fuck, me. This girl is even more stunning than ever. Wearing her hair in two loose braids, ripped black jeans that worship her ass, and an off-the-shoulder sweater.

"Access?" I laugh, bringing her fingers locked in mine up to my mouth. I've got one hand on the steering wheel, fucked if I'm not going to hold tight to the gorgeous creature next to me the whole way to Noire House. "Baby girl, we own it."

I press my mouth to her knuckles and soak up every wide-eyed moment as the wheels spin behind that hypnotic blue stare. Ven is away preparing for a fight this evening, and Thorne has been with Hawke all day in the aftermath of our summons to the Anguis council.

But the man we'd both gladly crawl for texted me about an hour ago asking if I could bring Fox and meet him at Noire House.

Right now, it feels like we're in a bubble, where this is a

tempting glimpse at what life might be like in a future where she's safe, and we've eliminated the last threats from within the Anguis. Maybe I could drive her into Port Macabre and take her out to dinner somewhere. My mind is already starting to race ahead of itself, imagining having her curled up on my lap while we watch the lights dance over the water from a fancy restaurant or some shit.

Her favorite is sushi. When we get to Noire House I'm one hundred percent searching up the best place to go in Port. Preferably one where I can hire out a private balcony overlooking the water and finger fuck our girl under the table while hand feeding her.

"Are you for real? So...we could go there anytime?" Fox interrupts my date night plotting and scheming by toying with the cuff on my shirt, peeking at me through her long lashes, and it's like I'm living in a goddam fairytale.

One where I get to have the girl of my dreams, and the two men who have had my heart for as long as I've known how to give it to someone, and I'm fighting the urge to pull the car over and sink against her mouth.

"Sounds to me like you might quite fancy us after all."

Fox ducks her head, but I see the pink tinging her cheeks all the same.

"I liked it there. The company was ok, I guess."

Shaking my head, I nip at her fingertips. "You're asking for a spanking with cheek like that."

She lets out a small squeal of laughter and tries to tug her hand away, but there's no way in hell I'm going to release her fingers. Instead, I drop our hands down to rest over the center console.

"Of course, we can. Technically, we co-own it with Hawke and his partners, too."

"What? Like some sort of murderer's time-share situation?"

Fox is still sniggering as she traces the veins on the back of my hand with her free one.

I could fucking soak in a bath of all her small touches and never get sick of having her softness wrapped around me.

"More like an insurance policy. Somewhere any of us could go if we ever needed to lay low for a while."

Fox keeps stroking my hand, but I spot the way she twists her lips.

"Which is why you took me there after the threats started coming."

"Something like that."

God, I wish we could be there right now. "Maybe after this is all over, we can go. Stay there a while, even."

Her face brightens at my words. Leaving me far too hungry for more of that exact expression.

"Would the others come, do you think?"

I love how she still tries to pretend they're not obsessed and entirely captivated by her. Or like they're not so completely wrapped around her little finger that they would follow her through the pits of hell if she so much as batted an eyelash at those two broody fucks.

"Can I tell you something?" I rub my thumb over her soft palm, keeping our fingers loosely intertwined.

Fox looks at me a little suspiciously. "Only if it's something good."

"Trust me. It's more than good." I wet my lips for a second. "You said you don't remember anything from the night you were drugged at the club...the night we got to meet your horny little alter-ego."

She turns about five different shades of crimson and makes a strangled noise.

"Please don't torture me with that. I can't even face what I might have said or done. It's so embarrassing."

"There was definitely nothing to be embarrassed about...I'll play with your dirty little demon side anytime you want."

"Ugh. Is there a point to this? Or are you every bit an asshole enjoying watching me squirm?"

"Maybe both." I chuckle. "But in all seriousness, that night, there were some things that became pretty damn clear to me."

She's still looking suspicious.

"First, was that if anyone so much as touches a hair on your head, you would have the three of us ready to tear the entire world apart, just for you."

"Oh." Fox shifts in her seat, looking a little hesitant. Like she doesn't fully believe me that we would do that for her. This girl has had a lifetime feeling like no one, or nothing cared for her. And that shit is over.

"Then the second, was that you gave me—all of us—something that night, but you don't remember. Although I'm pretty sure it was the truth hidden away and so tightly guarded you never want anyone to know it exists."

There's a softness in her face as I glance out of the corner of my eye.

I want to tell her.

I don't think I can keep on acting like she didn't say those words, and I didn't say them back to her that night without a second's hesitation. Because I meant every single one of them, and she deserves to have that certainty as we get through this Pledging and then figure out whatever the fuck we're doing with our lives.

Whatever life looks like on the other side of Thorne Calliano's plan. I sure as shit know that my version, and theirs, too, has her firmly involved in it. Not as a payment or a debt, but as someone endlessly important.

Fox is someone I can't breathe without.

"There's a moment before the sun breaks over the horizon, when you know it's coming, the sky has brightened, and the whole world is starting to morph into color for the first time. That tiny point in time when you grasp that it's no longer gray and darkness swirling around you, but you can distinguish the greens of the forest from the amber tinges to the long grass, and the clouds take on that ethereal kind of pink glow you only see in paintings."

Fox is staring back at me as I talk, and I don't know where the words are coming from. She pulls them out of me in a way that feels so natural—like they've been sitting waiting for her. Locked away for this very moment between the two of us.

"It's my favorite time of day. When everything is still, and the forest is first starting to come to life, and there's so much promise of what might lie ahead after dawn breaks over that horizon."

I swallow heavily. Fuck it. In our world, you don't get down on one knee; you don't define your life by one person and one person only. But Fox is one of my *persons*. She completes the part of me that has always needed her, in addition to Ven and Thorne.

"I love that time of day." She breathes. Looking at me with glittering eyes and her plump bottom lip trapped by her teeth. The mad hammering in my chest has me feeling like I could float on out of this car as I sink into the surety of how much I love this girl.

"Ven is my midnight hour. He's alluring and mysterious and makes me want to play in the shadows. Thorne is like my goddamn sun, and I'll follow him wherever he goes. You...you are my dawn. My hope for something fucking good. A glimpse of the world when everything is possible."

Bringing her soft fingertips back up to my mouth, I place a kiss there, while I collect myself. My throat bobs with a heavy swallow.

"That night, you said something to all of us, and it has eaten away at me ever since that you didn't remember my answer. I wanted you to know—"

"*Ky.*"

Fox's face is the flicker of warning, before it happens.

Her eyes grow wide, and there's a silent alarm hanging on her lips as her mouth drops open. But the fraction of a second in which I see it written all over her face, followed by a blunt force slamming into us. It leaves no time to react.

A shockwave and giant grill of a semi-truck plows into the rear door just behind me at high speed.

Glass shatters everywhere. A violent tearing of metal follows. We spin end over end over end. All I hear is Fox's screams before she goes silent, and it's a roar of static and smoke and fumes that clogs my senses.

Something warm slides down the side of my face.

That's what wakes me up.

How long have I been blacked out for?

The car is a wreckage, and I'm slumped forward, close to the steering wheel. There's something tightly banded across my ribs, and I can sense movement and noise beside me, but turning in the direction I want to, is proving impossible.

Liquid pain sears all down my right arm, side, and back.

I need to see my girl.

Have to check if she is ok.

But the effort it takes to form words is too much.

Blackness clouds my vision and swirls across my mind, robbing me of the understanding of how or where or when we are.

And as hands grab me, dragging me from the vehicle, I see the worst thing possible in the seat beside me.

It's empty.

Fox is gone.

CHAPTER 66

Ven

One text.

One motherfucking text is all it took to turn my life on its head.

They've been taken.

Thorne doesn't need to say who.

The worst fears I've ever allowed to fester inside my chest gut me from the inside, leaving nothing but a hollow shell. Sick and contorted with the knowledge that someone dared to take the two of them.

He sends me a photo of the wreckage. There's nothing to indicate what caused it, but judging by how fucked up the car looks, another vehicle took them out at high speed.

I'm still coated in blood and flying on the adrenaline of the fight I just won coursing through my veins.

My heart is pumping somewhere outside my body as I hit the call button.

Thorne answers, but he's yelling at people in the background. "...Fucking move. You've got the location coordinates." There's the sound of boots and the revving of engines as our security team loads up to head to whatever this is that awaits us.

We've been readying ourselves for years, and this is a goddamn war.

"Why were they there?" I shout into the phone. This can't be fucking happening.

"I asked them to meet me at Noire House. When they didn't show up, I was able to briefly get a lock on her tracker before it dropped out again."

My mind is screaming at me. There's too many goddamn pieces not adding up.

"Do we know if Ky is still with her?"

"No. Both phones were found in the wreckage. Whoever took them knew to leave them behind in case they could be traced."

"Fuck." I run bloodstained and bruised knuckles through my wet hair.

"We'll target the location where her tracker last showed as active. If she's already been moved, we'll have to put out further recon."

My teeth grind. This is hell, I'm certain of it. "They could have her out of the damn country by now."

I can't even begin to think about what might have happened to Ky. If I let myself go there for even one second, I'm going to spiral into a pit of self-destruction.

"Don't you think I fucking know that?" Thorne's got that tone about him that I recognize in myself on the worst of the worst days.

The one where you've reached the point of no return. Where

you've given up clinging to what might be considered normality and no longer care how tarnished your own soul is going to become. Accepting the inevitable...that you'll be leaving a trail of carnage burning in your wake.

"Send me the coordinates. I'll meet you there." Trapping the phone between my ear and my shoulder, I shove a new magazine into my gun.

"I've got half a dozen of our guys with me. More on the way with Hawke."

There's a vibration as the message with the details comes through.

"Whoever has done this, they're not going to get the courtesy of death at my hands. They're going to be chained up and ripped apart piece by piece. I'll keep a son of a bitch barely alive on machinery if I have to." I tell him.

Checking the pin dropped on screen, there's a curdling in my blood.

This place isn't familiar to me. There aren't any particular Anguis associations or dealings with this location that I can think of. But there's the familiar scent of bullshit that tells me I know who is behind all this.

Even if Thorne is refusing to share what he knows.

Because he *does* know.

I've been doing my own research since the first threats started popping up against Fox. And if what I've discovered is correct, this is going to be more than a war. It's going to be an extermination.

Before I hang up, I take one last look at the red dot telling me the last known location of Foxglove Noire. It's going to take me the better part of an hour to get there, whereas the man on the other end of the phone is much closer. The site is showing in the warehouse district of Port Macabre, and he will be there way ahead of me.

"And Thorne..." Gripping my phone tight against my

mouth, the engine rumbles to life beneath me. "Just so we're real crystal fucking clear...I can promise you that I will stop at nothing to get them back. I don't care *who* I have to slaughter to do so."

CHAPTER 67
Fox

"I'm capable of walking and feeding myself, you know." I playfully slap at Ky's shoulder, who ignores my protest and hoists me—fluffy towel and all—onto the kitchen island.

"Keep that sweet ass right there. Don't even think about moving." He points at me, green eyes glowing in the diffused light streaming through from the courtyard.

"Yes. Sir." Clutching the front of my towel in one hand, my other gives him a mock salute.

"And to think...here I was slaving away, making you special pancakes, and you're busy getting railed, my dirty little thing." Ky slides a mouthwatering-looking plate in my direction and hands me a fork. "All 'Fox approved' ingredients." He adds, catching my momentary hesitation.

My throat tightens a little. This man is mystifying. Infuriatingly cheeky and endlessly naughty, while at the same time, his heart is so big it can wrap around all of us without a second thought, it seems.

Thorne and Raven join us in the kitchen, just as I'm scooping a mouthful of pancakes and fresh fruit into my mouth—still with wet hair and wearing nothing but sweats after our impromptu shower-threesome.

Holy fuck. Even though I'm busy being distracted by their nakedness...these pancakes...might officially be the best thing I've ever eaten.

Judging by the way they both clear their throats, I probably just emitted an obscene noise.

Who would have guessed, my Viking whips up a damn good breakfast. Or lunch? Or whatever the hell time of day this is. And here I thought my wolf was the only one with talents in the kitchen.

More stacks are plated up as they join me at the central counter. Coffee is produced from somewhere and Raven places a steaming mug beside my hip, before handing one to Thorne, too.

"Look at that smile. Maybe I need to start bringing you body parts if that's what it's going to take to get you beaming like that all the time."

"God, please don't. I'm trying to eat here." I groan.

"Fuck, baby girl, if I'd known that was what it took...I'll give you a whole goddamn freezer full of limbs. I'll chop up any and every asshole who ever dared lay a finger on you and put them all on ice."

Ky ignores my protests and helps himself off my plate with his fingers. Still giving me a shit-eating grin as he chews and allows his eyes to rake up and down my bare legs.

Now, the super-sized helping that is far too much for me alone to eat makes sense.

"That reminds me..." I wave my fork with a strawberry stabbed on the prongs in his direction. Doing my best to divert attention away from the revelation that I spent last night out of my head after being drugged, apparently begging for their cocks. Or the fact that being presented with a tongue possibly did things for me. "Where is all your food? There's nothing but the things I asked for in the fridge these days, or in the cupboards either, for that matter. Do none of you eat anything while you're here anymore?" It's been bugging the hell out of me ever since that little detail first caught my attention.

Thorne studies his mug. Raven is hunched over his plate of food, guarding it with one arm as always.

I cock my head to one side, waiting on Ky to give me a straight answer.

He steps closer, lifting the coffee he has wrapped in one hand to his lips, and watches me over the rim. After swallowing a mouthful, he sets it down beside me on the counter and proceeds to wedge himself between my thighs. The smug ass nips his teeth at me playfully, stealing the plump strawberry off the end of my fork while he's there for good measure.

Shaking my head, I let out a little puff of frustration, watching him chew the fruit, then gulp it down.

"The reason we only have things here that you can eat or drink," he crooks a finger under my chin, tilting my face to meet his, "Is so we can do this *anytime we like."*

Ky's lips seal over mine. He tastes like berry sweetness, the caramelized sugar of the pancakes he carefully made for me, and the earthy aroma of coffee with almond milk.

He doesn't take almond milk in his coffee...does he?

"I don't want any single thing coming between me and you, baby girl. Certainly nothing that is going to prevent me from kissing you whenever I damn well want to." Speaking against my lips, he sends my heart into a fluttering mess of emotions.

These three murderous men, all changed their diet.

For me.

FILTHY ROPE CHAFES the corners of my mouth, reeking of petrol and filling my senses with the taste of dirt. Not strawberries. Not sweet Ky. Only a rank, greasy film coats my taste buds.

That's the first thing that consumes my awareness as my eyelids fail to open. I'm groggy as fuck and feel like my head has been caved in. The mossy green of Ky's eyes after the memory of how he kissed me and stole a little more of my heart in the kitchen that day swims around my addled brain.

Am I lying on my side? The hard surface below me feels cold and unforgiving. A dank, mildewy sensation. Concrete slab against bruised cheek.

I want to push myself upright, but my hands are twisted behind my back. When I unclench my fingers and try to pull my wrists apart, there's a familiar metallic bite against my skin.

Handcuffs.

Handcuffs and a gag.

My head throbs like a bitch, and it's only as I blink a few times that I grasp at a few scraps of memory.

Oh, god. *Ky.*

The horrific sight of the silver grill of that truck speeding toward us flashes in front of my eyes. I only saw it coming from over his shoulder at the moment it was already too late. Even if I'd been able to warn him, there was no way we could have evaded the collision.

No. Not a collision. Not a crash.

It was a calculated ambush.

One that was entirely premeditated. Designed to take us out and then capture us. Or maybe just me.

My stomach plummets through the concrete floor below me. What if Ky didn't survive? What if he did, and whoever has taken me killed him anyway?

Or an even worse possibility...that he might still be alive, but wishes he wasn't because of what has been done to him.

Wave after wave of pain assaults me as my mind tries not to fall apart. I can't lose him. He can't be dead.

He was about to tell me...

A sob from the depths of my soul gurgles around the rope gagging my mouth.

I bend double as my body convulses, curling me into a ball on this cruel concrete floor.

The muscle of my heart aches like it's been pierced by a thousand blades.

I can see his smirk and hear his laugh.

Kyron Harris called me his dawn, and in that moment, it's like his warm palms are cupping my cheeks, telling me to fight.

He taught me how to fight.

This isn't the time to give up.

Streaming tears free-flow down my face, as the rawest form of emotion swirls through my blood. I love him. All his faults and quirks and ridiculous shit that makes me want to roll my eyes at him every single day. Even though our circumstances for finding each other in this life have been fucked up, to say the least, he's *my* little slice of fucked up heaven, and I refuse to believe the worst.

He would be raising an eyebrow, flashing me that dimple below his beard, and dragging a thumb along his jaw. *Are you really going to just lie down and give up, little Fox? I thought you had teeth and claws?*

With a slow, and extremely stiff struggle, I manage to roll into a sitting position.

The act of being upright nearly makes me pass out.

I have to breathe slowly and deeply through my nose to prevent the black spots from claiming me. As I do so, I'm pretty sure my ribs must be broken, because the searing heat radiating through my torso is damn near blinding.

How long have I been here? There's no telling. It could be hours. I don't think I've been drugged on top of being knocked out by the force of the vehicle hitting us, but it's hard to tell.

While I'm struggling to get my breathing back under control, I hear something. Voices outside draw nearer, talking low. I can't make out any specific words or details, but there's a thudding as heavy footsteps approach. My blurry vision can make out the rectangular outline of a door—light filters in from the other side, faintly illuminating the dark space I'm being held captive in.

The lock jiggles, and my pulse ratchets up. There's nothing I can do to defend myself against whoever is about to come through that door.

Helpless, again. Always so fucking helpless.

A metallic screech makes me wince, fluorescent light floods through from outside, and a single light bulb flickers and hums to life overhead.

I start sobbing with relief at the sight that greets me.

Thorne.

He storms in wearing a skull mask and black combat-looking gear. Heavy boots. A bulletproof vest. To my relief he has a gun in one hand.

He found me.

He came for me.

I can only hope he's managed to find and rescue Ky, too.

Oh, my god. I'm a fucking mess.

Muffled noises tumble out of me as he walks over, with the gun still gripped tight in one hand. Through my wet lashes, I watch as he stoops beside me, wrapping a hand around my arm, lifting me onto my unsteady legs.

With my hands locked behind my back, I can't do anything but sag against his hold. I want to hug him and cry into his broad chest, relief inundates every bruised muscle.

But he's not speaking to me.

And his grip hasn't relented. It's silent and bruising where his fingers dig into my upper arm and instead of finding comfort in his touch, a chill races up from the soles of my feet.

Someone else is here. Another person follows him into the room.

A sight that has my knees nearly giving out from beneath me.

I blink several times.

There's a woman standing in front of me, a little taller than I am, but she always was. Especially when she wore heels. Where she used to have long, curled blonde hair, it's now cut short into a sleek bob and has been colored dark brown. Or maybe that was always her natural hair color all along.

"You really have grown up, haven't you."

I'm staring at a ghost.

My mother.

CHAPTER 68
FOX

"Put her over there for me, darling." She gestures behind Thorne, and I'm tugged backward. No care. No familiarity. At this moment, he's a soldier of doom, and I'm a captive foolish enough to think this man was...God, I can't even finish that thought.

My numb feet drag over the floor, and everything around me spins. More metallic screeching noises claw at my brain as I'm dropped into a chair. The handcuffs clank against the hard back and dig into the bone of my wrists.

"Take her gag out, too." On command, his fingers dig at the rope, loosening it enough that he can drag it down over my chin, leaving it to rest like a noose around my neck.

His scent washes over me, and I have to fight back the urge to break down right then and there.

This is too fucking cruel.

Everything I thought I knew about this man was a lie.

Thorne goes to stand beside my mother as she drags out a chair for herself and folds neatly into it. His piercing blue eyes are on me, but there's no comfort or softness or *anything* there.

He's a heartless sentry, standing with legs splayed and gun still held in one hand, while he grips his wrist with the other.

Ready to shoot me the moment he receives the order to do so.

I'm certain I might swallow my own tongue.

"You look so different. Your hair." She's appraising me with a thin-lipped smile, like I'm somehow meant to be anything but devastated. "I mean, I've seen the photos of you, of course, but they don't do you justice in the flesh."

"Tell me what is happening." I croak out. This isn't some fucking family reunion, and I don't care about what she has to say right now. "*Thorne*. Where is Ky?" My eyes drill into the man I stupidly fell in love with, and he doesn't even show a flicker of emotion. Thorne Calliano is every inch the heartless bastard he appeared to be when I first met him.

"Call me sentimental, but I just had to come and see you one last time, before Thorne here does what he's so good at and disposes of you."

"Where. Is. Ky?" My lungs feel full of glass, and the stabbing pain in my ribs is the only thing preventing me from screaming.

"Oh, Fox, sweetie, I know it must all be confusing. But this has been the plan all along." She crosses her legs, wearing some sort of wide-legged pantsuit. This woman looks like she should be in a boardroom, not some warehouse like the foul mistress of abuse and rabid child molester that she is.

"You died."

My mother lets out a small laugh. "To the outside world, yes."

"What the fuck is going on? What plan? Where is Ky?" I don't know where to look. Seeing her in front of me is leaving a retching feeling rising in my stomach, and the thought of Thorne taking up his spot at her side so obediently is sawing my fucking heart in half with a rusty knife.

"Thorne has earned this."

"Earned?" My temples feel like they're on fire. "Why will no one tell me where Ky is?" The tears are back and flow down my cheeks in quiet rivers of anguish.

"For a long time now, he has been proving himself worthy of this task. More recently, his loyalty has been truly admirable." The face I thought I'd never see again looks like a death mask. Skin oozing with the terrible deeds she has perpetrated for so long.

"Why do this...why am I here?"

"You always were the favorite with Andreas. Your father made no secret of the fact he intended to make you his heir. Such a pretty little thing, with so many suitors interested in claiming your virginity, and the power of the Noire name."

There's no stopping the shiver that travels down my back, hearing her talk about my life with such indifference. There's nothing but disdain as she watches me.

"But you...you helped me escape." My mouth is so fucking dry, and my head is hammering; it's a struggle to get the words out.

The woman in front of me purses her lips and studies me for a long second.

"Perhaps you saw it that way. But, what I needed was for you to be *gone*. You saw it as escaping, whereas I saw it as a means to remove you from the picture until I could make other plans fall into place to rid Noire House of Andreas. My supposed death had two major benefits, as it turned out."

She gets up and crosses to me, brushing a manicured nail across my cheek. I don't want her hands on me. This woman is a stranger. A vile monster.

"There's a reason your father ended up chopped to pieces in his sleep. I needed to get rid of the head of the Noire lineage, and then I would be free to remove the other irritating obstacle in my way."

There's nothing about this woman that connects her to the

few memories I have. Between the nannies and the household staff who raised me, I'd see her and my father periodically, but it was all a charade. A lie, while she spent her time abusing children and trading in flesh.

My eyes shift to Thorne. He hasn't moved from his position, and I get slapped with the sickening realization that maybe he's always been hers. Just like I accused him of, but at the time, he denied it to my face. Maybe she didn't tire of him when he and his brother were young after all, but instead, this has been their joint plan to take over Noire House, together.

"But...you let me go."

"You thought I helped you get away from your father? Of course, I did. But only because I knew he would sell you off to one of his friends. He was making plans with Miles Crane and I couldn't have that. Having you still in the picture? Well, all of the Noire House inheritance would eventually flow your way. What I needed was a means to continue my stay in the shadows, while also finally getting to take what should have been mine all along."

My stomach is turning inside out as the point of her fingernail digs in deeper below my chin.

"Who wants to wait around for fate to be decided for them? I made my own plans, you see. I sold you to Thorne Calliano a very long time ago as a way to ensure your power and Noire House control would be given over to me. Now that the council has witnessed your inspection at the hands of Ivan, we have everything we need from you."

Sold.

This bitch sold me to Thorne.

My voice is a hollow echo on concrete. "You sold your own daughter."

"Yes. I sold you to him." She repeats with a huff. As if I need things spelled out for me like a child.

There was never going to be a future for me beyond any of this, after all.

"The Pledging ceremony..."

A dismissive flick of her fingers cuts me off. "In the eyes of the Anguis, you have already ceded your power and all rights to the Noire legacy. The Pledging was never going to happen. All that was needed was for Ivan to complete the formal ritual in front of enough witnesses."

She turns, crossing to Thorne. My she-devil of a mother dares to rub a hand up his arm.

My nostrils flare witnessing that point of contact between them. He tilts his head to look down at her, and it's as if I'm not even in the room.

There's a savage urge building inside me that wants to howl and fling myself at him. I want to sink my fingers into his eye sockets with the force of every woman in this world who has ever been screwed over by a man.

"I know how hard it's been, and you've done so well to set all this in motion for me, darling." Her nails drag along the collar of his shirt beneath the Kevlar vest he's wearing. "All the tests were worth it, you see? I had to know for certain where your loyalty lay, and now I have my answer."

Every part of my foggy brain tells me to look away. Not to see the evidence that she's touching him. I could close my eyes, but instead, I torture myself with every second she continues to have her hand on him.

"Why didn't you just kill me?" My skin feels like it's burning beneath my torn sweater and bloodstained jeans. "You wanted me out of the way so you could inherit the Noire estate instead? You should have simply put a bullet in me years ago."

The woman I don't even recognize anymore cocks her head to one side. Looking at me as if I'm some lost little lamb. "Oh, trust me. I thought about it, sweetie. But it's much easier for my business to run from the shadows. Being a dead woman makes things much simpler to keep operating smoothly. With your power and father's legacy passing to Thorne, he'll be the perfect face of Noire House for me."

That familiar need to vomit seizes me every time she keeps mentioning her and Thorne being so intimately connected.

I'm ready to finally break apart when a chilling voice cuts through the room.

"Not if you're a fucking dead man, Calliano."

At the sound, my head snaps in the direction to see a man standing there, with crimson staining his hands, and his gun aimed directly at Thorne.

A man painted in fury and deadly precision, armed with a weapon he could use in his sleep.

My wolf.

CHAPTER 69
Fox

"You know, something wasn't adding up." Raven holds the gun steady. Looking straight down the barrel at Thorne.

"How those threatening texts got through to the very phone that *you* gave to Fox. The whole Pledging ceremony itself. Then her drink got drugged at the club, when *you* were the one who handed it to her." Raven is preternaturally calm. The lethal energy rolling off him is terrifying to witness.

I'm choking on the relief that he's here, but scared of what this might mean for the man my foolish, broken heart loves. The one currently in the line of a lethal bullet at close range from a man trained to end lives.

"And then the way her tracker suddenly stopped working... yet, you miraculously knew where she was tonight."

Thorne shifts his weight so that his bulk shields the woman who I want to see dead and buried.

I don't give a fuck that she is my flesh and blood.

That person is a sick and twisted excuse for a human being.

"Well, aren't you a fucking genius, Ven," Thorne growls at

him. I see his hands flex around his own gun, but he keeps the muzzle pointed at the concrete beneath his feet.

I'm watching the standoff between two of my men while Ky could be dead for all I know, and this feels like the moment I finally crumble into dust.

The tortured winds of the Anguis can sweep through and carry me off into whatever miserable grave I'm destined for, because if I have to witness Raven murder Thorne, I don't know that either of us will survive that kind of devastation.

"This thought kept nagging at me, so I went back through the historical logs and security files from Noire House. And do you know what I found?"

He doesn't look at me, but I know my wolf is saying this for my benefit. Or maybe he's just choosing to fuck me over with the same ruthless savagery that Thorne Calliano has already done.

"When he was still coming up through the ranks, Thorne here was always posted to a particular part of the mansion. Year after fucking year, his security files show he was always stationed either directly outside, or close to a particular part of the wing."

My throat closes over.

"That wing belonged to the Noire family. In particular, the rooms belonging to a young girl named Foxglove Noire."

Tears well, and roll down my face in silent tracks.

"You've been Giana's obedient little bitch for years now, haven't you?" My wolf snarls and points the gun between Thorne and my mother, half-hidden behind him.

"And what of it, Ven?"

"Shoot him already, Thorne." The shrill voice of my mother is pathetic. She thinks this is going to end with either of them getting out of here alive? Raven is the murderer the Anguis themselves trained to eliminate targets as and when they so please.

Neither of them stand a chance against him.

"I thought Fox might want to know." My wolf narrows his eyes. "Just how many years her own mother had planned to screw her over for."

Giana hisses.

Raven's dark eyes narrow. "I couldn't work out why you were always stationed outside her rooms. Then it dawned on me...was Thorne Calliano protecting what was his? *His* child perhaps?"

The urge to be sick races up the back of my throat, blood drains from my face, and I have to bite down on my tongue to stop myself from screaming. Searching Thorne's stony profile in desperation for the faintest flicker that he might refute the most awful possibility.

It couldn't be that. Thorne wouldn't do...*that.*

Nonono. My face contorts as I look back at Raven, and he carries on speaking in low, measured tones.

"But just when I thought you might have been the foulest asshole I'd ever had the misfortune to meet, I found out something else...you and Hawke were both posted elsewhere by the Anguis for over a year around the time Giana became pregnant. So that led me on even more of a curious path. To figure out why the fuck all those years later, you would choose to be involved with the child of the woman who had been your abuser for too long."

I don't know if it's the sickening sense of relief washing through me, or adrenaline, but I'm trembling from head to toe.

"What could possibly have made you her obedient little puppy? The great and mighty Thorne Calliano, all this time, still loyal to the psychotic kiddy fiddler hiding in the shadows."

"Fuck you." Thorne spits out and raises his weapon, but barely lifts his arm, before two sharp pops ring out. Bullets rip from the gun aimed at him.

A keening scream slashes through my lungs as I collapse

forward. Doubling over with blinding agony as I watch Thorne —my Thorne—crumple to the floor, twisted away from me and with blood pouring from his shoulder. I can't see the second location he's been hit, but my gut tells me it's somewhere fatal.

Raven Flannaghty doesn't miss.

My haunting noises are nothing more than violent sobs, as my chest heaves. I'm thrashing against my restraints, and I don't know if the pain slicing my body in two is coming from my broken ribs or the shattered heart exploding inside my rib cage.

I can't even see through the lashings of hot tears. Sharp nails dig into my skull, and there's barely a second's reprieve before I'm being dragged to my feet by my hair.

"Don't. Or I'll end her right here, right now." The mother I thought I knew all those years ago, has a gun pressed beneath my ribs. Driving the metal against the broken and bruised remains of my body.

All I can see through the blur of tears is a dark outline where Thorne's body lies. He's unmoving on the concrete. Blood pools below his shoulder.

My wolf has his weapon directed at me now.

And his sights are fixed on the woman using my body as a shield.

His dark gaze consumes me. There's no remorse there for what he's done. Only pure vengeance and hatred eating him alive.

"That gets rid of your *chosen heir*, Giana. You don't want to go harming the only chance you have left of stealing power now, do you?"

"You don't know what you're playing with, boy." She sharply yanks my head again. My eyes can hardly focus on anything. I just want someone to bury me and end this nightmare.

"Fox is your only chance to steal the Noire lineage, isn't she? She's not Andreas' child."

I blink, certain I've misheard him.

Behind me, there's an unhinged peal of laughter. "God, you really should have had a bullet put through your skull as a child. Would have saved me a lot of fucking hassle, Flannaghty. No, Andreas and his rotten dick was never the father. Noire House was easy enough to find a no-body who thought they might get a chance at falling in my favor if they got me pregnant. Whoever it was served his purpose and was disposed of a long time ago."

Oh my god.

There's every possibility I'm going to collapse. With each hateful moment this insanity drags on, the blood seeping from Thorne's body continues to pool on the concrete.

"Andreas knew, didn't he." Raven keeps the gun pointed straight at us.

Spiders crawl across my skin.

"That asshole threatened to have me killed more times than I could count. I did what needed to be done. I organized my own death before his slimy hands had the chance, then got my own sweet comeback just at the right moment, once everything was finally in place."

"Only now, you haven't got your pathetic dog to control anymore, so the ruse is up Giana. You kill Fox and it all ends. You'll never so much as sniff a single scrap of the Noire House legacy."

We're locked in a standoff that I know can only end with bodies littering this warehouse floor.

"You know, I've hunted you for a long time, Giana." Raven's face is death incarnate. Retribution and reckoning. "Although, it wasn't until recently that I discovered it was you I was hunting."

This is the version of him who is nothing more than a soul

collector, and I cannot fault him for losing his humanity in all of this. How could I, when he has been tortured by the Anguis for so long?

"Get that gun out of my face, or I'll shoot her." The metal digs harder against my ribs, and another crack sounds as more shattered bone gives way. I can't help but wince and let out a cry of pain.

Raven circles closer, which causes my mother to shift to keep the distance between us. Continuing to hold me in front of her.

"My sister was who you originally wanted to replace Fox with as heir, wasn't she? Before you came up with your plan to use Thorne."

The woman at my back lets out a cold laugh.

"Ah, of course. How poetic. Cara Flannaghty's brother comes to avenge his dead whore of a sister."

Raven lets out a violent curse. But his hands remain steady, the gun trained on both of us.

I'm floating out of my body. It's like I'm no longer here, and this is a hellscape I'm drifting over, watching it all unfold from somewhere near the ceiling. Thorne is bleeding out and probably already dead on the floor. My mother is inching us backward toward the only door in this dank room inside some empty warehouse.

All the while, I'm losing my grasp on reality.

Perhaps I've already lost it, and this entire situation is just a twisted conjuring of my imagination.

But then the gun up against my busted ribs is shoved into me again, and I clench up with agony. The pain sucks me down into my body while tears continue to track a silent funeral procession down my cheeks.

"She suffered because of you. And I've been waiting a long time to look the person responsible in the eyes." Raven is coiled tight and ready to strike.

"It was such a waste. She would have been the perfect fit to take over Noire House. Better than my own pathetic scum." Her voice slithers at my ear. "Sorry, sweetie, but Cara was a promising and ambitious thing I had collected. Such a shame she didn't turn out to see things the same way, so I had to get rid of her somehow."

Even though he's the picture of deathly calm on the surface, I see it. There's so much pain in my wolf's eyes. He's suffered through years of not knowing what happened to his sister. And the woman whose blood I carry in my veins was not only her abuser, but her murderer.

He deserves his vengeance.

"Just end it," I whisper.

"He won't dare hurt you." She sounds so certain, but I know Raven.

He's already shot Thorne. This man should reap the satisfaction of avenging his dead sister. He's waited years for this.

"It's ok." I swallow. "If this is the only thing I can give you, Raven, let me make up for what they did to you and your sister."

His upper lip curls, tattooed fingers readjust their grip on the gun.

There's no way to shoot my mother without putting a bullet in me.

"*Please.* End this for all of us." Please. Take away all this pain. I'm willing him with my eyes to do the thing he promised he would always do for me if I asked.

I know he sees it.

There's a tic in his jaw as he draws the gun level with his line of sight.

"She's dead, Flannaghty. I'll put a bullet in this bitch. I'll—"

A blinding flash and intense pain explodes past my ear. There's nothing but heat and immobilizing agony that takes over one whole side of my body. My knees collide against the concrete with the force from behind. There's a dead weight taking me down as my mother's body slumps over mine.

My head slams into the concrete floor as both our bodies collapse together. A river of hot, thick blood splatter oozes across the side of my face and all down my neck. It feels like my whole left side has gone numb. I'm expecting the final gasping breath to leave my lungs any time now.

This must surely be when it happens. That moment when life officially leaves you a split second after you take the hit.

I'm waiting and waiting for that moment. The time that I'll float off on a cold wind, and all this mortal pain will be left behind.

My body is jostled. Hands grab at me, dragging my limp form across the floor out from underneath the dead woman with blood pouring from the bullet hole in the back of her skull.

The back of her skull.

She was shot from behind.

Metal clatters onto the concrete behind me as my wrists are freed, then wrapped in a warm caress, and somewhere far away, I hear an echo of my name.

Ringing fills my ears. A face swims before me as I see a mouth moving. It's a man's face. He's repeating my name, but I can't focus. I just want to sleep. Heaviness tugs my eyelids and tries to suck me under.

Words flood into my awareness like a dull roar of the ocean. "Beautiful, look at me." There's a warm touch pushing blood-soaked hair away from my face. Is it my blood?

"It's over. You're safe...I've got you."

The man holding me and cradling me looks exactly like Thorne.

But I know it's not him.

My heart is lying dead on the floor with him in the corner of this miserable warehouse.

"Foxglove. Baby, talk to me."

I reach a shaky hand up, touching his face. Searching for the tiny scar beside his eye that I know is going to be there. I know exactly what I'll find beneath my fingers when I touch his brother's identical face.

Pressing against the skin, I try to smooth the spot where I know that small imperfection must be. Although all I find is the familiar creases lining those azure blue eyes I could drown in.

"I'm here. I'm here, baby. It's me."

My head lolls to one side to look over at the body lying on the floor, and I see my wolf hunched over. It looks like he's administering first aid, but it must be my muddled brain causing my eyes to see things.

Raven wouldn't waste his time on a corpse.

"You're dead." My lips feel cracked. Every layer of my bones ache. The shattered remnants of my heart are blown apart like the bodies all around me.

The man holding me makes a rumbly noise that I know so well. It seems so unfair that even in this state, that soft laugh is what I remember. How he'd make that sound but would hide the smile like a secret, barely allowing it to touch his lips. It's so vivid; the sensation spreads through into my body with a gentle vibration of warmth as he holds me tight to his chest.

"Not today." I hear that deep voice that sounds exactly like him.

All of it is too much.

"We need Doc, *now*." There's shouting and movement, although I can't focus on any of it.

My body succumbs to the shock, and one too many knocks to my head, and as I slide into that bleak cavern of nothingness, where I don't know what reality is anymore. I'm praying that there's some version of this tormented scene where my three men have survived.

Because if that's not the case, I don't want to wake up at all.

CHAPTER 70
Fox

When I come to—in bed, alone—my initial fear is of still being trapped in that warehouse. The smell of blood and mildew and death clings to my nose.

Opening my eyes, however, the first thing I find is the imposing figure of Raven guarding me.

My protector sits right beside me in a chair, keeping watch from behind sunken eyes.

He doesn't say anything, but helps me out of bed after seeing that I'm awake. Carefully and diligently, he examines my bandaged ribs, then gives me painkillers with a glass of water. Someone had already dressed me in one of their t-shirts and some sleep shorts while I was passed out. My skin seems cleaned up, no longer a bloodstained mess.

I suspect that has also been my wolf's doing.

Now, he's got my hand wrapped tight, enclosed beneath his palm and inked fingers, leading me to the large deck area overlooking the forest. Silently understanding that I need to see with my own eyes whatever cruelty this day has chosen to deliver.

I pad on bare feet through the house, allowing him to guide

me and potentially shield me from whatever grotesque reality might await.

Everything is quiet, but I've been aware of a constant shuffle of comings and goings since last night. Voices and murmurings at my bedside as I drifted in and out of fitful nightmares.

Once the cool morning air hits my face, I immediately burst into tears.

My Viking is sitting out here surrounded by the gray mist of pre-dawn. He's battered as all hell, with his right arm in a sling and a swathe of purple bruising, cuts, and swelling down the side of his face and bare chest. The side that took the brunt of the impact from when we were run off the road.

"Oh, god. Oh, god, you're alive." There's nothing that can stop me from going to him. And Raven lets me, allowing my fingers to slip through his.

"Go easy on me, baby girl." He winces through a smile. There's a split on his lip, and I can tell he's hazy with pain. "I've never been happier to see your beautiful face."

All I want to do is throw myself at him, but I have to be content with stroking his forehead, and I place a soft kiss against his jaw, finding a spot that looks free of damage.

"Are you ok?" I pull back, and my brows crease as the state of him becomes more apparent up close.

"Thanks to these two assholes, I'm fucking fantastic." He uses the hand not currently immobilized to brush a thumb over my lips. My eyelids flutter closed at how divine that minuscule point of contact feels. There's heaven wrapped in the glide of the pad of his thumb over my mouth. I could reach out and touch the sky itself, feeling him warm and safe before me.

"I'm so sorry." That's all I can fathom to say. It's such a pathetically small word in the face of all this. Everything they've been through is because of me. Because of my family.

"Foxglove, you have nothing to be sorry for." Warm palms

glide up my arms, and I shiver a little, feeling Thorne's presence at my back.

It wasn't a dream.

Thorne. *He's alive.*

Straightening up, I turn and drink in the sight of him. He's wearing one of those soft long-sleeve t-shirts and sweats, and as my gaze tilts up to meet his blue eyes. Immediately, my bottom lip trembles.

"Hey...shh...it's ok." His strong arms pull me against his chest, making sure to carefully avoid my ribs, surrounding me with his scent and strength and steady thud of his heart.

"You were dead. Am I going insane? Nothing makes sense." I speak into his chest.

The way he's rubbing slow glides up and down my spine is drugging. My fingers cling to the soft cotton of his top.

"It's complicated to explain. Are you sure you want to go into all of that right now?"

I nod against his shirt, taking a deep lungful of the scent of *him*. The warmth of him feeling like a miracle I thought I was forever going to be left struggling to live without.

"Please. Tell me everything. No more secrets."

He makes a noise and tenses a little.

"It's fine, Thorne. It's time you told the whole thing." Ky's voice drifts over from where he's still seated.

He takes a steadying breath.

"The plan had always been to work toward a way to get Giana's confessions recorded. She wanted the Noire inheritance and to seize control more than anything. Hawke and I needed the footage to be able to show the council of the Anguis. It was the only way they could finally see what has been going on under their noses for years.

"The Anguis have turned a blind eye for too long, and we needed the evidence of not only the fact Giana was still alive, but that she'd been orchestrating shit for years out of the shadows. But it took the allure of capturing *you* for her to finally come out of hiding long enough that we could strike."

"Me?" My hazy brain is slow to absorb his words.

"She's been violently jealous of you for years, and seeing you paraded around as the Noire House heir, and with us, was what finally made her snap. If it wasn't for you, we never would have been able to secure the footage we needed."

Thorne draws back slightly and cups my cheeks in both hands. Studying me.

"The ambush?" My eyes flick to my battered Viking. God, we both could have been killed.

Ky winces and leans his head back. "Yeah, I could have really done without Giana being a psychopath and going all out on the near-murder plot."

"There were a lot of things outside of my control. I could only do so much to try and orchestrate events from the inside... regrettably there were a lot of things I had no way to know would unfold as they did. No one was more terrified than me when I discovered that she was planning to ambush both you and Ky like that. I knew she needed to keep you alive..." His voice cracks and I hear every layered meaning behind those unfinished words. Thorne genuinely didn't know if he'd lost Ky forever last night.

"Did you know about the drugging? The threats sent to my phone?" My body starts to sway a little.

"Yes." He clears his throat. "Those were tests of loyalty from Giana. She endlessly wanted proof that I was trustworthy enough."

Guilt rolls off him in waves as he cradles my body so reverently it makes my bruised and battered heart ache.

"Asking for your forgiveness feels too much, Foxglove. It's more than I could ever expect to ask you to forgive me for the things I had to do—the things I had to stand by and allow Giana to manipulate and dictate and instruct me to do to you, just so I could stay close enough to her for the moment we could end it all."

I look back at him, seeing the torment creasing the corners of his eyes. He's holding me so carefully, and all I can think of is what Raven was saying last night.

"Were you working for her? All those years?"

There's a tic in the corner of his strong jaw. He considers his words for a long moment, and I don't know if I can handle more secrets being dragged out and laid bare in this misty light.

But I have to know.

"When I was about fifteen and first moving up through the ranks of the Anguis security teams, I found out that the monster—the person who had nearly destroyed Hawke and I—had a daughter. Her very own child was living at the mansion, hidden away. You had just had your fifth birthday, and were reaching the age of so many other victims Giana and your father had chosen."

His brow creases, a pained expression clouds his eyes.

"I'll admit, at first, I requested those stations in order to watch you out of spite. I was young and fucked up after everything that had happened...I'm not proud of it, but I was so angry at everyone and everything and determined to burn Noire House down to the ground. I didn't care if I took your entire family with it."

Ky shifts in the seat he's occupying, and sees the struggle Thorne is having to get his words to come out right. "He couldn't let her do to you what she'd done to so many others before." My Viking supplies.

Thorne's face softens as he looks over at the man he's loved and protected for so long also, then focuses back on me. "That's why I stayed as close as possible. That's why I asked to be stationed outside your rooms. I did everything I could to make sure you could stay safe, even after you were grown up and escaped. Even if I couldn't be in the city myself, I made sure you were watched over by my security teams as you started your new life. Giana stalked you and obsessed over ways to manipulate you for years. Some of the awful things I had to do once we took you were her insane tests of loyalty—I needed to go along with in order to draw her out of hiding, and I can't even tell you the guilt at having to go through with any of it. But you have to know, it was never for her; everything was for you, Foxglove. It has *all* been for you."

There's a strangled noise that comes out of me. Tears well and drip down my cheeks, and Thorne uses his thumbs to swipe at the wetness with more tenderness than I could ever imagine possible.

"I'll always watch over you, Foxglove Noire. You've been in my blood longer than I can remember. Even when I tried to tell myself it wasn't true...even when I tried to convince myself I didn't care for you." His blue eyes hold mine in a trance, and there's a knot in my throat that has lodged itself there.

His jaw works as he keeps me steady. My fingers grip tight to the fabric of his shirt to hold my sanity in place. "There's not much I'm proud of in this life, but knowing I was able to protect you, and save Ky from the worst possible fate, that has been my mission for longer than I can remember." It's the only moment his gaze leaves mine, as those blue eyes flick up and over to where Ky is sitting for a split second, and then they are back on me.

"You were always there," I murmur. Feeling lightheaded.

"An idiot keeping endless secrets, hidden in the shadows." His brow lines as a darkness washes over him for a moment.

The part of his shirt I'm clinging to covers the tattoo I gave him. Where this man let me be forever imprinted upon his skin.

"I wanted better for you...better than anything I could give you at any rate. Maybe, originally, I wanted you to hate me. So much of my past was fucked up beyond all measure. But then... once you were finally here with us... God, how many ways can I tell you I was wrong? I'm sorry I'm not a better man for you, Foxglove. It's impossible to change who I am, or the past that made me, but I am always going to try to do the best I can...for all of us."

I'm so in love with him. Everything aches at the heartfelt way he holds me secure with his words and gaze.

"None of it brings Cara back, and it doesn't change what happened to my brother and me, but...but it's something."

Oh, god. His brother.

"Hawke...Is he..." I hardly dare breathe the words.

"He's going to be ok. The asshole is never going to let me live it down that he took two bullets for me, mind you."

"I thought he was you." Tightness constricts my chest. "He smelled like you...I was so certain..." Emotion grips me in a vise as the memories of last night feel like they're going to clamber all over me and threaten to drag me to the ground.

"He had my clothes on; we didn't want to take any risks."

My eyes fall shut. "I truly thought you were gone." My fists clench tighter.

"Giana always struggled to tell the difference between the two of us. When she decided to finally go after you last night, it was easy to have Hawke step in and pretend to be me."

"But...why?" It's bad enough being concussed, but with all these revelations, my bruised brain is fighting to comprehend it all.

"That was Ven's call. Once he figured out what was really happening before any of us reached the warehouse, he nearly damn shot both of us on sight before we got to you and Ky."

My eyelids pop open as I look over at my wolf, who stands with arms folded, silently listening on.

His jaw flexes. "I needed a clean target. By using Hawke in the room with you, I knew I could hit the right spot to injure, but not kill him."

"Oh, my god. So you knew the whole time?"

Ky pipes up from behind me. "Baby, just admit it, you couldn't have shot Thorne. But knowing it was Hawke—"

"Don't go reading anything into it." He growls, cutting him off.

There's a chuckle and then coughing from Ky as he groans with pain.

"What happens now?" This surely can't be it. The world of the Anguis is still a twisted mess, and we're forever tangled in the spiderweb of belonging to this madness.

Thorne clears his throat. "Hawke and I will take the evidence to the council of the trafficking rings Giana was orchestrating, her confessions of trying to kill her own daughter, plus the links to the death of Cara Flannaghty. There's too much we have at our fingertips for the Anguis to ignore, especially if we guarantee to expose what has been happening in Port Macabre for decades."

Around us, the mist coats the forest, and the dawn chorus of birdlife drifts through the air. There's a potent silence that hangs between the four of us.

Because they all know what I meant.

What I was truly asking.

What happens now...for us?

Thorne's big palms skate down over my shoulders, and Raven's energy bristles close by. Ky appears on my other side, with a limp and his sling holding his arm tight against his chest.

I immediately search Thorne's eyes, while my pulse begins to race.

"Noire House, the lineage, the inheritance of the Household—it all belongs to you. Full authority remains with you to do with it as you like and how you see fit. But this world isn't good enough for you; it's raw and bloodthirsty, and even though we've eliminated the worst, the Anguis will always be the way they are. They're all power-hungry, and that eventually manipulates everything."

Thorne pauses, swallows, and then I see his expression tighten.

"We've organized the jet, and you have a new apartment waiting for you, along with a full security team that will guard you twenty-four hours a day. You can oversee Noire House from afar, or choose to have nothing to do with it at all and we'll take care of the Anguis for you."

My breath hitches in my throat. What is he saying?

Thorne drops his forehead against mine with a heavy exhale. "We used you. I'm a piece of shit who started this whole course of events only thinking of a way to exact revenge on Giana. But I never wanted to see you get hurt. A part of me fell for you a very long time ago. I don't exactly know when it happened, but one day, I realized the woman I had been guarding in secret was embedded so deep in my bones, it physically destroyed me to think of being apart from you. I've been cursed to love you from afar; maybe that's all I'm worthy of because I certainly don't deserve someone as kind and generous and loving as you, Foxglove."

I'm outright sobbing. There's a desperate noise coming out of me, even though all of this has left me speechless. This impassioned, poetic version of Thorne Calliano has swept me out to sea and left me struggling to keep my head above water.

He loves me.

He loves me.

And yet, this stupid, wonderful man is telling me he's willing to let me go.

I turn my head toward Ky, who watches me with sorrowful eyes. The deepest glades of the forest greet me when I meet his gaze.

"You would let me go?" I sniffle.

Ky closes the distance between us, wrapping his hand

around the back of my neck. "Baby girl, all I want is for you to be happy, and love isn't about being selfish. Asking that of me? To let you go? It would damn near kill me, but if it's what you need..."

His voice trails off. I see him chew on his lip for a moment, and his fingers flex against my nape.

"Fuck it, I was telling you this, just before everything went to shit last night. Fox, you're my goddamn dawn. You're that daybreak about to make its way above the horizon over there." He nods toward the forest beyond the end of the wooden decking.

"I don't care what label you want to put on it, or whether you want none at all...but the only fucking thing that matters is that each day starts with you in my arms and that at night, I know you're curled up by my side."

He glances at Thorne and over to Raven, then back down at me. "Loving you is the most natural thing I've ever done, baby girl. And somehow, in amongst this insanity, I've been blessed to love these two assholes as well."

I choke out a sob and a small laugh at the same time.

"I love you with everything I can give. But if that means loving you enough to let you find happiness, no matter what that looks like, I have to respect your decision." Ky presses a featherlight kiss to my temple, and I fight back a soft whimper as his warm lips press against my skin.

Raw emotion inundates me; hearing those words of love from him is the healing balm to my fractured soul.

Turning away from Ky, I look over at my wolf. Who, through all of this, has stood by, quietly observing. Walls guard every part of his expression like a damn fortress. All while I'm a complete and utter emotional disaster ready to collapse in a shaking heap.

"What about you, wolf boy?" My lips twist, and through

blinking lashes, I peer his way, puffy-eyed from all the tears I can't seem to stop shedding.

Raven narrows his attention on me, flicking his stare up and down my body, leaving goosebumps tracking over my skin. His teeth clench, and the silver of his rings reflects the mist clinging to the tall trees surrounding us.

"You'd be happy with that? You'd let me go?" I ask.

He launches at me and grabs my chin with a snarl. "You get on that jet or leave this place, and know this...I'll fucking haunt you for the rest of your days."

I shudder at the possessiveness of his words. Drowning more and more in the well of love for him than I could ever have thought possible.

"I. Will. Fucking. Haunt. You." He looms over me. Impossibly dark eyes swirl with the severity of that threat. *A deadly promise.*

My eyes bounce between the three powerful figures, all holding onto me.

I'm standing at the crossroads of my life, stripped bare and flayed raw with how deeply I've opened my heart to these men.

My monsters.

This is the point where I could easily walk away from them, and the Anguis, and the fucked up world of my bloodline. I could start over, now that the threats to my life have been eliminated for good.

I lick my lips. Trying to scoop up the words that keep trickling through my fingers like sand.

On a shaky breath, I meet Thorne's steely gaze first.

"You're saying that you just want me to be happy, and that you want me to make a decision that will benefit *me*, but have you actually stopped to think about what might make me happy?"

Turning my chin, my eyes seek out Ky, who hovers close, with an expression I can't read.

"Maybe what will bring me happiness is standing right in front of me...My choice comes into this and know it might sound completely fucked up, but I have never been happier than with you all...I've never had a family. I've never had anyone care for me." My words tumble out in a rush. "And while I understand that you're giving me the opportunity to walk away—I value that, honestly and truthfully, I really do—what you don't realize is how my life would be a complete and utter misery if that was the direction my head chose to take me in."

With butterflies in my stomach, I shift now to look at Raven.

"Because my heart already knows what decision it wants to make."

Nibbling on my bottom lip, I'm grateful they give me space to carry on speaking.

"It scares me to death how I feel about all of you. Never did it cross my mind I'd find anyone to openly love and give pieces of my fractured heart to, yet you stole three pieces and didn't judge me for the battered condition you found those fragments in. You crept in and claimed the broken thing beating in my chest and now it finally has a home where those shards have started to weave their way back together.

"But even though it frightens me, I'm not scared of loving *you*, that part comes easily. What terrifies me is the thought of something happening to any of you. That's the part I'm going to have to learn how to live with if you'll show me how. If you'll hold me on the days I'm not strong and put up with me in the moments I feel like I'm falling apart. I promise to always do the same for all of you."

Ky swipes a thumb across my cheeks, collecting the tears that have welled and spilled over. Thorne holds my palm against his heart, studying me with yearning and a mirror of my own all-consuming trepidation. The enormity of how this moment and how it is finally unfolding.

"I'm yours. As much as you are all each other's. And making each other happy is the greatest gift I could ever ask for; it's terrifying and vast and feels overwhelming, but I couldn't breathe leaving you."

Looking between all of them, I reach my free hand for my wolf and hook my little finger with his. Wanting to touch him in some tiny way and hoping with a frantic beat of my heart that he's not going to run away from this confession I can't seem to stop from pouring out.

"Then don't...don't ever fucking leave." Raven holds my eyes, and it's like staring into a bottomless ravine.

My teeth bite into my bottom lip as my happy tears hitch in my throat and a soft noise bubbles up. I'm nodding and being enveloped by the three of them as much as we can, thanks to the injuries both Ky and I are nursing.

"Fuck, I've wanted to say this for so long. I love the cute way you all make each other coffee, and how you cook scrambled eggs in the morning. I love that you don't have a single television in this place. I love how fiercely you care for each other, and I want—no, I *need* you to understand that seeing you make each other happy makes my heart want to float out of my chest."

Pressing my lips to Ky's palm, I blink up at him through my watery lashes. "I love your stupid handsome face and ridiculous texts. I promise I'll never leave you on read, if you'll promise to keep making me laugh every day."

"Anything, baby girl. You've got my heart, and every goddamn piece of my soul is yours." He presses his lips against mine, and the butterflies swirl and float higher at his touch. "I love you. So fucking much." His whisper against my mouth is the most divine thing.

"And my love for you, that includes your love for Thorne and Raven. You never need to doubt that for a second."

He brushes my lips again with his and nods. "Likewise, little Fox."

Deep inside me, the pieces of my heart sigh with contentment. Turning back toward my wolf, I risk threading our fingers fully, and he lets me. My shaky inhale draws a small rumbling noise from him as he stares back at me.

"You don't have to—" He starts to speak, but fuck no. I'm not letting him away with glances and looks and unspoken emotions. Not today. Not after everything we've been through.

"Nope." I give my head a small shake. "You've busted the dam wide open, so you get to hear it too. I love that you terrify me, because when I'm with you there's no way I can feel anything but alive. You've addicted me, and if you think I can even consider walking away from you, then I'm sorry, but you're stuck with my bullshit. Good luck getting rid of my clingy ass, because I'll be wanting to sit up at midnight and clean your cuts for you, and I'll be worried about you anytime you're not here, whether you like it or not."

His lips twitch, and creases line the corner of his eyes. They glitter at me like blackened diamonds as he leans closer until we're breathing the same air.

"I don't know how to do any of this...with any of you. But give me time to learn." He says honestly, and I melt at the depth of caring behind his words. "And for what it's worth, this fucked up mess you've left inside my chest? That's yours. This right here, is yours." He nips my bottom lip as he slides my hand over the spot above his heart and squeezes my hand in time with the thudding rhythm.

A wobbly exhale gusts from my lips as I know what comes next. The person I haven't been able to look at for the duration of this whole blubbering confessional I've been busy sharing.

Tilting my gaze up, Thorne is there. Strong and solid and resilient.

My safe place to land, even when I had no idea he was there.

"Thorne—" I hesitate. Tears start to gather again, only they're pure happiness and a thousand sparkling emotions I can't put names to.

"Baby, I know." His voice resonates through me. "If you'll give me all the future days together when we can find ways to tell each other, to *show* each other love, then that's all I care about."

"But I want to tell you." I sniff.

He chuckles and lifts my chin, dipping his head down to meet mine, he hovers over my lips. "Then tell me."

As he says those words, he presses his mouth to mine, and I *feel* all those years of love flow out of him. It's hypnotic and spellbinding and utterly captivating.

So much so that I'm sure I have stars swirling in the place where my eyes should be when he draws back.

"I love you, Thorne. I love how big your heart is, and I can't wait to spend a life loving all of you."

He gives me the most boyish grin in return, and my knees nearly give out.

"A life loving you is more than I ever hoped for. But I'm an asshole, and I'll take it. You're mine, and ours, Foxglove, and I love you endlessly."

As I drink in my three men, one thing I know for certain is that they each represent my home—my men who, individually and together, mean more to me than any location or place ever could.

Wrapped up in that moment, I settle into the easiest decision I've ever had to make. One that glows warm and bright inside my chest with all the possibilities for the future.

I don't want to be a Noire anymore.

I choose to be theirs.

EPILOGUE

FOX

MENACE

What are you wearing, baby girl?

We're on our way back.

The scan on my shoulder came back fine. According to Doc I've healed perfectly.

Told him *of course* I have. Got this sexy as hell nurse, named Fox *wink*

I know I could wait and tell you face to face, but you said you wanted to know the results straight away…

My eyes are a little bleary as I open up the flurry of texts arriving from Ky.

As I read through his stream of updates, a damn furnace blankets me from behind. Weighing my body down against the mattress is the heavy presence of Thorne's arm draped over my waist.

He's still sleeping, holding me tight with my back against his chest. Reassuring, steady breaths whisper at my ear.

One thing about spending time in tropical paradise, as I've

discovered in the couple of months we've been here, is that three giant men who all want to cuddle results in overwhelmingly hot nights while attempting to sleep.

Thank fuck for ceiling fans and a cooling ocean breeze. Otherwise, I think I'd have abandoned the lot of them and chosen to sleep out in the hammock or on the sand from day one.

Before we left Port Macabre, Thorne and Raven had one final stop to make. Let's just say I received *another* tongue in a box, after my two men gladly carried out orders on behalf of the Anguis—ensuring Ivan Victore wouldn't be continuing the trafficking trade he had been involved in with my mother.

Ky won't stop teasing me that I've got a kink for receiving dismembered body parts. Especially after I may have been particularly enthusiastic to show them my thanks afterwards.

Weighing up my options on how best to play my naughty boy's game this morning, I tilt the phone, being careful not to wake Thorne, and take a photo. White linen sheets have been knocked down to rumple and pool below my thighs...this angle reveals *everything.*

Especially the bruises from Ky's fingerprints close to my hips, which is why I'm being an absolute menace and a dirty tease by showing them off.

(Image Attached)

Biting my lip as I send the image to our group chat, I count the seconds until I know my phone is going to start blowing up.

Ky and Raven had both gone over to the mainland twenty-four hours ago, primarily to get the final scan done on his shoulder now that we're both fully healed after the crash. My ribs have mended themselves, along with my concussion. Getting to laze around beside the ocean has been the perfect setting for our recovery.

After their meeting with the Anguis, Hawke and Thorne were able to coordinate things within their security teams, which meant we could spend several months here as we wait for the dust to settle.

While my other two men have briefly visited civilization, getting Ky checked out, they've also been put in charge of restocking supplies for us here on the island to bring back with them.

Which left me and Thorne, alone.

Annnnnd we might have ended up spending the entire time in bed.

Tropical paradise served with a side of veritable god who wants to fuck all day? *Yes, please.*

The biggest grin splits my face as the phone vibrates, once–twice, but I don't even get a chance to open the chat. A big hand lifts off my waist and steals it from between my fingers, tucking it somewhere over behind him on the other side of the bed.

"Mmm, I had this filthy dream that my girl woke up wet and needy." His deep voice is thick with sleep, and *holy fucking Christ,* my body ignites as he opens his mouth. That velvety rumble coats me from head to toe, leaving tingling sparks of arousal in its wake.

I don't even bother protesting about my phone. Not when there are promises of morning orgasms at the hands of the man right behind me.

It's not like Ky will care if I don't reply straight away; he would have seen Thorne's arm in the photo and knows there's every chance of me getting easily...distracted.

Besides, he had our wolf all to himself last night. Knowing those two, they would have one hundred percent fucked on every surface of the hotel they stayed in.

Wiggling backward, the long, hard length of his erection digs into my thigh.

"I think you want to make sure I can't walk." I tease.

But even if there's a little lingering soreness after our marathon sex-fest, I most definitely am soaked.

"Shhh," he rumbles against my ear, adjusting my leg so he can easily slip into me from behind. "Go back to sleep if you want."

"Oh, god," I moan quietly, turning my head into the pillow. "Why does that turn me on so much?" My pussy clenches and my clit aches, and no matter how much time we spend together —knowing that one of the men I love is right here with me, and my Viking and my wolf are on their way back to me, I can't get enough of *this.*

Of finally being wrapped tight by pure happiness.

"I want to fuck you nice and slow, sweetheart." Thorne's mouth explores the side of my neck, and he finds my clit with his thick finger. Then he pushes inside.

This goddamn man plays my body with complete precision.

I'm begging all too soon.

"How is it possible..." I whine. "That you're gonna make me come already." Liquid heat pools in my core. This man knows every cue and signal. He knows how to drag an orgasm out of me almost just by glancing in my direction.

He rocks into me with a steady, maddening pace. Matching that with the expert way he's playing with my clit.

"Because I know your body, and I know exactly what your pretty little pussy loves the most." He sucks down on the side of my neck. "How you moan louder when I rub like this." As he sucks down on my earlobe, his middle finger increases the pressure over my sensitive bundle of nerves.

My pussy tightens as his cock hits the perfect spot, and he rubs over and over.

"And because I love you."

The sensations intertwined with his words drag me over the edge. I fall apart, quivering and moaning how much I love him, too.

Thorne follows right behind me.

We keep rocking together through the gentle waves of pleasure as my climax sweeps on and on.

He strokes over my skin with featherlight touches, staying buried inside me as we lie there together. It's like I'm floating on those tropical waves right outside our little island hideaway.

"Lie still, and you can have this back." Thorne brings my phone across, handing it over to me, but doesn't make any move to pull out.

My pussy ripples around his length. Oh my god, this man is making it his mission to kill me with every new kink he unlocks.

I can see a pile of notifications waiting for me from the group chat.

MENACE

You're playing with fire, baby girl.

I know those marks are mine, but what about those fresh ones I can see all over your tits?

Not replying.

Wonder why.

Goddamn.

All I can think of is Thorne fucking you right now.

It's driving me out of my head that I wasn't there to see you shatter like our perfect little slut.

Thorne silently reads the messages over my shoulder before swiping the phone out of my hands. He brings up the camera and takes a photo of the two of us, just as he shoves deeper. Impaling me on his rapidly hardening cock, driving against the spot that has me seeing stars.

The look on my face is...well...freshly fucked and out of my head with pleasure, to say the least.

Rather than giving me back my phone, he sends the photo and quickly taps out a couple of messages.

(Image Attached)

What did you expect?

I take care of what belongs to me.

Ky's responses come thick and fast.

MENACE

Oh, you want to play dirty, Daddy?

Stay right the fuck there.

Do not move.

I'll be giving you a proper good morning kiss.

Raven replies.

For the first time ever.

MY WOLF

Be naked and on all fours when I get back. That pussy is mine.

Holy shit.

MENACE

Baby girl, I hope you realize what you've just done.

You've got Ven texting and FLYING all because you're out here driving us crazy.

My heartbeat whips into a furious rhythm all of a sudden. I don't want them getting into an accident because of me.

"It's ok. *Listen.*" Thorne must feel me tense up because he refuses to give me the phone back. This time, he really does toss it somewhere out of reach.

When I pause and do as he says, I hear the familiar buzzing drone of their helicopter coming in to land.

"How about I warm this pussy up for them, hmm?" Thorne starts moving inside me again as he teases my nipples, and my brain decides to vacate the premises.

"Daddy, *please.*" I'm pretty much begging for anything really at this stage. My body is a live wire of need and desire and anticipation.

The sound of the rotors whirring peaks outside, and then begins to recede as the engines cut. At least I know they've landed safely.

"Better be a good girl for Ven." The man behind me finally decides to slip out. "On your knees. Ass facing the door."

"Oh, god." A whimper tumbles out as my entire body clenches. This is so filthy. Embarrassment flushes up from my chest.

Thorne stretches out with one arm propped behind his head on the pillow, lying next to me as I reposition myself on all fours. He's got a prime view of not only my heavy tits hanging down, but the open doors leading out onto our private beachfront.

"Just look at you. A dripping wet cunt on display for your

men when they walk in." His wickedness knows no bounds, it would seem.

Heavy footsteps draw closer, thudding along the wooden decking outside, and my stomach swoops.

"Fuck yes. That's my girl." Ky's groan sends a shudder down my spine.

I can *feel* Raven's energy the moment he enters the room. Goosebumps pebble my arms and I have to bite down on my bottom lip to stop myself from making all sorts of desperate noises.

The bed dips behind me, and my heart leaps into my throat. It's so exposing being like this, but thrilling all the same. Knowing how much it will please my wolf to see me like this, well, I'm only ever going to try and find new ways to do exactly as he commands.

"Already leaking cum? What a dirty thing." Raven's fingers glide through the mess between my pussy lips, where the evidence of Thorne has gathered at my entrance and started to coat my inner thighs. Then he roughly shoves two digits inside right up to the knuckle.

"Goddamn." Ky blows out a low whistle. "Now that's the best kind of slutty little present to come home to. We missed you too, Daddy."

The man lying beside me chuckles darkly.

"Well, what are you waiting for? We already know Ven's going to stuff her cunt full. Put that pretty boy cock to use and let us watch you fuck our girl's throat."

"*Please*. Oh, god. I missed you." I'm a whining mess as their heated gazes covet my bare skin, plotting all the ways to use my body. Knowing exactly what we'll all enjoy. Meanwhile, Raven's fingers pump in and out of my pussy with a filthy wet noise.

Fuck, I love them so much.

"Open up, baby girl." Green eyes glow with pure mischief as

Ky kneels in front of me. But not before he leans over and gives Thorne a searing kiss.

He's already gloriously naked. Island life suits both of us in that regard. The two of us have probably spent more time *without* clothes than wearing any since we've been here.

"Look at how greedy you are. Trying to suck my fingers deeper." Raven's voice is gravel and sinfully sexy right behind me, moving to position himself at my entrance. Dragging his fingers out of me, he replaces them with the smooth crown of his dick.

My two men must give each other some kind of silent message over my head, because they both slide inside me at the same time. Ky fists his cock with one hand, my hair with the other, and pushes past my lips. While behind me, Raven's fat cock pushes in as he lets out a dark groan of pleasure.

Any little sound out of him always makes me feel treasured and adored. Right now, I'm soaring.

They take their pleasure and wind mine higher, while every second that Thorne watches on with a scalding gaze draws our climaxes nearer and nearer.

"Ffffuck. Mmmmfuck." Ky breaks first. "I'm gonna come, baby girl. Don't swallow."

Jesus. That command triggers me to fly headlong toward the edge of my own release.

Raven's hand snakes around and he finds my clit. "That's it. Shatter for me. Come all over my cock, you fucking beautiful thing."

My muffled cries around Ky come at the same time as his release floods my mouth. Behind me, my wolf tumbles into his own climax and his hips slap against my ass.

"Give me that mouth." My Viking swoops in and kisses me, collecting up his cum as he does so, then swipes over my lips with his thumb. I'm bleary-eyed with lust and orgasmic bliss as I peer up at him and see a devilish glint on his handsome face.

Raven pulls out of me with a grunt, but doesn't release the brutal hold he's got on my hips. Keeping my ass in the air, even though I'm boneless and ready to slump in a heap on the mattress.

That's when a second dip of the bed moves behind me, followed by the immediately recognizable sensation of Ky's mouth covering my pussy. His beard scrapes my sensitive skin, and oh my fucking god, his tongue pushes into me. Swirling his cum in with the evidence of my other two men.

"*ShitohfuckKyohmygod.*" I'm so overstimulated and wrung out, my forehead hits the sheets, and I'm a whining, shaking mess.

Then strong hands turn me over. Bodies all pile in as Ky drags us into a tangle of panting limbs, each of us lax and heavy with satiated desire.

"I fucking love you, baby girl." Ky finds my lips, licking and kissing me and letting me taste all of us. "I love you to the goddamn ends of the earth and back." He moves over and takes Thorne's mouth. "And I'm a fucking fool for you, always. I love you." Leaning over now to where Raven has fallen on the other side of me, he kisses him and shares *us* as their tongues collide.

I'm trapped between my wolf, halfway beneath Ky, and with Thorne on the other side of me.

"I love you. So damn much." I don't care how blissed out and besotted I sound. But I chase after him. Dragging Ky back against my lips, sliding our tongues together, and soaking up more of the way we all taste when combined like this. "And even though I'm sure I already told you a hundred times this morning, I love you." I turn my head to one side, seeking Thorne's sapphire eyes.

"I love you." He gives me a soft smile, then brushes his lips against mine. "And I love you two idiots. But Ky, don't crush our girl." Nudging his nose against Ky's, he lets out a rumbling laugh and drags him back to tuck our naughty boy against his chest.

"*Fox*." The voice to the other side of me is a quiet whisper at my ear, and I wriggle around so I can stare back into the shimmering, dark depths. "I don't know how to do any of this...but give me the opportunity to learn how you want to be loved, and give me the grace to make mistakes as I learn. That's all I ask."

Cupping my hand over Raven's jaw, I touch my lips against his. "And let me learn all the ways you want to be loved, too... I'm so fucking in love with you, my wolf. I don't think you even know." Speaking against his skin feels like utter bliss.

Surrounded by all of them, is the greatest gift I could ever have hoped for in this lifetime.

He nudges our noses together, and his eyes draw me in, dizzyingly deep.

"I love you, little Fox."

A tiny gasp pops out of me. I can't fucking help it.

He's never actually said...

Is this really happening...

Oh my god, I'm swimming in the waters of him.

Hearing those words from Raven for the first time sends my heart into a fluttering mess.

He squeezes my hip, then dives back in for the kind of slow and sensual kiss that leaves me completely melted against his warmth, drowning in his divine scent.

Hands trace over my back and thigh. Every little touch conveying just how much we all mean to each other.

My three men.

My heart's home.

THANK YOU FOR READING

I fell in love with these four *so hard* during the writing of Vengeful Gods, I just wasn't ready to let them go. Want to stick around and see a little more of our naughty foursome? (Including what the boys have in store for Fox's birthday?)

https://www.elliottroseauthor.com/bonuses

Have you been picking up those little moments between Thorne and Ven and are now dying to know how things might play out between our two favorite broody grumps? Don't feel like you want to say goodbye to Fox and her boys yet?

Me either...I've got schemes going on (*Ky would be so proud*) so make sure to come and join my reader group - this is where all the announcements and first peeks will be happening on future bonus content for Fox and her men:

https://www.facebook.com/groups/thecauldronelliottrose

INSTAGRAM | TIKTOK | FACEBOOK

ACKNOWLEDGEMENTS

This book and these characters (and the pigs!) owe a debt of thanks to my love of movies like Snatch, Lock Stock and Two Smoking Barrels, and honorable mention goes to the one and only Tommy Shelby. While other girls might have been falling in love with Taylor Swift and Twilight as teenagers, I was busy falling for tortured bare-knuckle boxing champs, British gangstas, and scrunching my nose up at awful characters who love to chop their enemies into six pieces and, *'feed 'em to the pigs, Errol.'*

Anyway, years later...here we are. Fox and her men have made their first appearance on page, and I'm so thankful for you picking up their story.

To my wonderful Mr Rose, who supports my disappearing off and being lost to the Words—I love you with all my heart.

Lazz, you are my champion, listener, alpha reader, support Queen extraordinaire... the Elliott Rose - verse would cease to function without you and your magic. ILY.

Sandra, you absolutely slayed the game with the covers for these books. I swoon so hard for all your magical creations. *Another*!

Heather, I'm forever grateful for your hype, your notes, your love of these worlds and characters. THANK YOU.

To my incredible supporters on Ream, thank you for taking a chance on an indie author and hanging out in my world month to month! Kari C and Rory ... you Goddesses, you... from my smutty little heart I send the biggest hugs. You have no idea how much it all means, and I adore the lot of you!

Of course, bringing a book like this to life takes a village behind the scenes. To my alpha, beta, and early readers, you are absolute magic and thank you for pouring so much love over our foursome. Thank you for being accomplices in my mischief, the chaos of chapter drops, and my endless questions.

My Street Team, you are EVERYTHING, my ARC team a thousand red-flag bouquets are coming your way, and to everyone who has shared about this book, you are just so damn wonderful.

To every single person who has helped promote Vengeful Gods, I am besotted with you, and swoon with heart eyes every time I get to see your creativity and excitement for an Elliott Rose character or story.

From the bottom of my heart, and from Fox, Daddy Thorne, Ky, and Ven... we send you all our love.

xo

LEAVE A REVIEW

If you enjoyed this book, please consider taking a quick moment to leave a review. Even a couple of words are incredibly helpful and is what us Indie Romance Authors thrive on.

(*Well, that and coffee*)

ALSO BY ELLIOTT ROSE

Port Macabre Standalones

Curious to know more about Poe, Hawke, Grey, and Angel?

Noire Moon - *Novella* - September 2024

Macabre Gods - October 2024

Also...Emerald's story will be told. (Date TBC)

Crimson Ridge

Chasing The Wild - June 2024

Nocturnal Hearts

Sweet Inferno

In Darkness Waits Desire

The Queen's Temptation

Vicious Cravings

Brutal Birthright

ABOUT THE AUTHOR

Elliott Rose is an indie author of romance on the deliciously dark side. She lives in a teeny tiny beachside community in the south of Aotearoa, New Zealand with her partner and three rescue dogs. Find her with a witchy brew in hand, a notebook overflowing with book ideas, or wandering along the beach.

- Join her reader group *The Cauldron* for exclusive giveaways, BTS details, first looks at character art/inspo, and intimate chats about new and ongoing projects.
- Join her Newsletter for all the goodies and major news direct to your email inbox.

Made in the USA
Las Vegas, NV
04 December 2024